P9-CAB-729

PENGUIN BOOKS

# LEGS

William Kennedy is a lifetime resident of Albany, New York, where Jack Diamond was finally murdered and whose legend persisted there through Mr. Kennedy's early career as a newspaperman. He currently teaches writing at the State University of New York, Albany. His next two novels in the cycle of novels set in Albany, *Billy Phelan's Greatest Game* and *Ironweed*, are published, respectively, in paperback by Penguin Books and in hardcover by The Viking Press.

# LEGS

## WILLIAM KENNEDY

PENGUIN BOOKS

Penguin Books Ltd, Harmondsworth,
Middlesex, England
Penguin Books, 40 West 23rd Street,
New York, New York 10010, U.S.A.
Penguin Books Australia Ltd, Ringwood,
Victoria, Australia
Penguin Books Canada Limited, 2801 John Street,
Markham, Ontario, Canada L3R 1B4
Penguin Books (N.Z.) Ltd, 182–190 Wairau Road,
Auckland 10, New Zealand

First published in the United States of America by
Coward, McCann & Geoghegan, Inc., 1975
First published in Canada by
Longman Canada Limited 1975
First published in Great Britain by
Jonathan Cape Ltd 1976
Published in Penguin Books in Great Britain 1978
Published in Penguin Books in the United States of America 1983
Reprinted 1983 (three times), 1984 (five times), 1985 (four times)

Copyright © William Kennedy, 1975
All rights reserved

LIBRARY OF CONGRESS CATALOGING IN PUBLICATION DATA
Kennedy, William, 1928–
    Legs.
    1. Diamond, Legs, 1895 or 6–1931—Fiction.
I. Title.
PS3561.E428L4    1983        813'.54        82-13285
ISBN 0 14 00.6484 2

Printed in the United States of America by
R. R. Donnelley & Sons Company, Harrisonburg, Virginia
Set in Times Roman

"My Mother's Rosary" copyright 1915 by Mills Music, Inc., copyright
renewed 1942. "Arrah-Go-On, I'm Gonna Go Back to Oregon,"
copyright 1916 by Mills Music, Inc., copyright renewed 1943. Used
by permission. All rights reserved.

Except in the United States of America,
this book is sold subject to the condition
that it shall not, by way of trade or otherwise,
be lent, re-sold, hired out, or otherwise circulated
without the publisher's prior consent in any form of
binding or cover other than that in which it is
published and without a similar condition
including this condition being imposed
on the subsequent purchaser

*This is for Pete McDonald, a first-rate relative,*
*and for all the archetypes lurking in*
*Ruth Tarson's lake house*

*People like killers. And if one feels sympathy for the victims it's by way of thanking them for letting themselves be killed.*
—EUGENE IONESCO

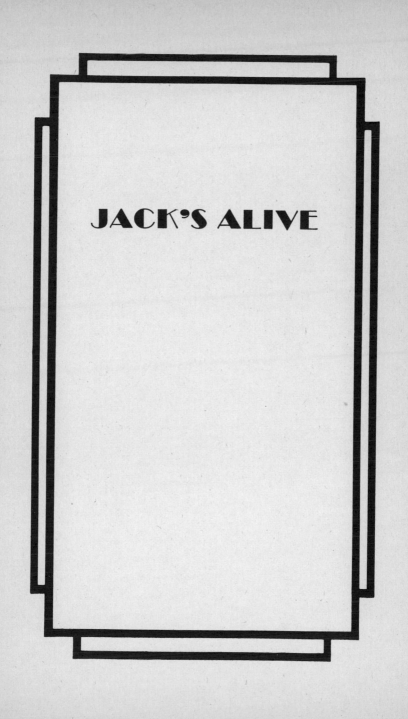

# JACK'S ALIVE

"I really don't think he's dead," I said to my three very old friends.

"You what?" said Packy Delaney, dropsical now, and with only four teeth left. Elephantiasis had taken over his legs and now one thigh was the size of two. Ah time.

"He don't mean it," Flossie said, dragging on and then stubbing out another in her chain of smokes, washing the fumes down with muscatel, and never mind trying to list *her* ailments. ("Roaches in your liver," Flossie's doc had told her. "Go on home and die at your own speed.")

Tipper Kelley eyed me and knew I was serious.

"He means it, all right," said Tipper, still the dap newsman, but in a 1948 double-breasted. "But of course he's full of what they call the old bully-bull-bullshit because I was there. You *know* I was there, Delaney."

"Don't I know it," said the Pack.

"Me and Bones McDowell," said the Tip. "Bones sat on his chest."

"We know the rest," said Packy.

"It's not respectful to Bones' memory to say he sat on the man's chest of his own accord," Tipper said. "Bones was the finest reporter I ever worked with. No. Bones wouldn't of done that to any man, drunk or sober, him or Jack the corpse, God rest his soul. Both their souls, if Jack had a soul."

"He had a soul all right," said Flossie. "I saw that and everything else he had too."

"We'll hear about that another time," said Tipper, "I'm now talking about Bones, who with myself was the first up

the stairs before the cops, and Jack's wife there in the
hallway, crying the buckets. The door was open, so Bones
pushed it the rest of the way open and in he snuck and no
light in the room but what was coming in the window. The
cops pulled up then and we heard their car door slam and
Bones says to me, 'Come inside and we'll get a look before
they kick us the hell out,' and he took a step and tripped,
the simple bastard, and sprawled backward over the bed,
right on top of poor Jack in his underwear, who of course
didn't feel a thing. Bones got blood all over the seat of his
pants.''

"Tipper," said Packy, "that's a goddamn pack of lies
and you know it. You haven't got the truth in you, and
neither did Bones McDowell.''

"So in comes big Barney Duffy with his flashlight and
shines it on Bones sitting on poor Jack's chest. 'Sweet
mother of mine,' says Barney and he grabbed Bones by the
collar and elbow and lifted him off poor Jack like a dirty
sock. 'Haven'tcha no manners atall?' Barney says to him.
'I meant no harm,' says Bones. 'It's a nasty thing you've
done,' says Barney, 'sittin' on a dead man's chest.' 'On the
grave of me mother I tripped and fell,' says Bones. 'Don't
be swearing on your mother at a filthy time like this,' says
Barney, 'you ought to be ashamed.' 'Oh I am,' says Bones,
'on the grave of me mother I am.' And then Barney threw
us both out, and I said to Bones on the way down the stairs,
'I didn't know your mother was in the grave,' and he says
to me, 'Well, she's not, the old fart-in-the-bottle, but she
oughta be.' ''

"You never got a good look at the corpse," Packy said to
Tip, "and don't tell me you did. But you know damn well
that I did. I saw what they did to him when he was over at
Keenan the undertaker's for the autopsy. Thirty-nine
bullets. They walked in there while he was sleeping and
shot him thirty-nine times. I counted the bullet holes. You
know what that means? They had seven pistols between the
pair of them.''

"Say what you will," I told them, savoring Packy's
senile memory, remembering that autopsy myself, remem-

bering Jack's face intact but the back of his head blown away by not thirty-nine but only three soft-nosed .38-caliber bullets: one through his right jaw, tearing the neck muscle, cutting the spinal cord, and coming out through the neck and falling on the bed; another entering his skull near the right ear and moving upward through his brain, fracturing his skull, and remaining in the fracture; and the third, entering the left temple, taking a straight course across the brain and stopping just above the right ear.

"I still don't think he's dead."

I had come to see Jack as not merely the dude of all gangsters, the most active brain in the New York underworld, but as one of the truly new American Irishmen of his day; Horatio Alger out of Finn McCool and Jesse James, shaping the dream that you could grow up in America and shoot your way to glory and riches. I've said it again and again to my friends who question the ethics of this somewhat unorthodox memoir: "If you liked Carnegie and Custer, you'll love Diamond." He was almost as famous as Lindbergh while his light burned. "The Most Picturesque Racketeer in the Underworld," the New York *American* called him; "Most Publicized of Public Enemies," said the *Post;* "Most Shot-At Man in America," said the *Mirror.*

Does anyone think these superlatives were casually earned? Why he was a pioneer, the founder of the first truly modern gang, the dauphin of the town for years. He filled the tabloids—never easy. He advanced the cause of joyful corruption and vice. He put the drop of the creature on the parched tongues of millions. He filled the pipes that pacify the troubled, loaded the needles that puncture anxiety bubbles. He helped the world kick the gong around, Jack did. And was he thanked for this benevolence? Hardly. The final historical image that endures is that corpse clad in underwear, flat-assed out in bed, broke and alone.

That's what finally caught me, I think: the vision of Jack Diamond alone, rare sight, anomalous event, pungent irony. Consider the slightly deaf sage of Pompeii, his fly open, feet apart, hand at crotch, wetting surreptitiously against the garden wall when the lava hits the house. Why he never even heard the rumbles. Who among the archeologists could know what glories that man created on earth, what truths he represented, what love and wisdom he propagated before the deluge of lava eternalized him as The Pisser? And so it is with Jack Diamond's last image. It wouldn't matter if he'd sold toilet paper or milk bottles for a living, but he was an original man and he needs an original epitaph, even if it does come four and a half decades late. I say to you, my reader, that here was a singular being in a singular land, a fusion of the individual life flux with the clear and violent light of American reality, with the fundamental Columbian brilliance that illuminates this bloody republic. Jack was a confusion to me. I relished his company, he made me laugh. Yet wasn't I fearful in the presence of this man for whom violence and death were well-oiled tools of the trade? Yes, ah yes. The answer is yes. But fear is a cheap emotion, however full of wisdom. And, emotionally speaking, I've always thought of myself as a man of expensive taste.

I chose the Kenmore to talk to Packy, Tipper, and Flossie because if Jack's ghost walked anywhere, it was in that bar, that old shut-down Rain-Bo room with its peeling paint and its glory unimaginable now beneath all that emptiness. In the 1920's and 1930's the Kenmore was the Number One nightclub between New York and the Canadian border. Even during the Depression you needed a reservation on weekends to dance in evening clothes to the most popular bands in the country: Rudy Vallee and Ben Bernie and Red Nichols and Russ Morgan and Hal Kemp and the Dorsey Brothers and all the rest who came before and after them. Naturally, limelighter that he was, Jack lived there. And so why wouldn't I choose the place to talk to three old friends, savor their memories and ring them in on my story?

I called Flossie first, for we'd had a thing of sorts between us, and I'll get to that. She was pretty back in those days, like a canary, all yellow-haired and soft and with the innocence of a birdsong, even though she was one of the loveliest whores north of Yonkers: The Queen of Stars, she called herself then. Packy's Parody Club had burned years before and he was now tending bar at the Kenmore, and so I said can we meet there and can you get hold of Tipper? And she said Tipper had quit the newspaper business finally but would be on tap, and he was. And so there we were at the Kenmore bar, me looking up at the smoky old pair of David Lithgow murals, showing the hunt, you know. Eight pink-coated huntsmen on horseback were riding out from the mansion in the first mural, at least forty-five hounds at their heels, heading into the woods. They were back indoors in the second painting, toasting and laughing by the fire while one of their number held the dead fox up by the tail. Dead fox.

"I was sitting where you're sitting," Packy said to me, "and saw a barman work up an order for Jack's table, four rum Cokes. All he poured was one shot of rum, split it over the top of the four and didn't stir them, so the suckers could taste the fruit of his heavy hand. 'I saw that,' I told him after the waiter picked the order up, 'and I want you to know Jack Diamond is a friend of mine.' The thieving bastard turned green and I didn't pay for another drink in this joint till Jack died."

"His name had power," Tipper said.

"It still does," I said. "Didn't he bring us together here?"

And I told them I was writing about him then, and they told me some of their truths, and secret lies, just as Jack had, and his wife Alice and his lovely light o' love, Kiki, had years ago. I liked all their lies best, for I think they are the brightest part of anybody's history.

I began by recalling that my life changed on a summer day in 1930 when I was sitting in the second-floor library of the Knights of Columbus, overlooking Clinton Square and two blocks up from the Kenmore bar. I was killing time until the pinochle crowd turned up, or a pool partner, and I was reading Rabelais, my gift to the library. It was the only book on The Index in the library and the only one I ever looked at.

That empty afternoon, and that book, gave me the insight that my life was a stupendous bore, and that it could use a little Gargantuan dimension. And so I said yes, I would take Jack Diamond up on his telephone invitation of that morning to come down to his place for Sunday dinner, three days hence. It was the Sunday I was to speak at the police communion breakfast, for I was one of Albany's noted communion breakfast intellectuals in those days. I would speak, all right, and then I would walk down to Union Station and take the west shore train to Catskill to listen to whatever that strange and vicious charmer had to say to an Albany barrister.

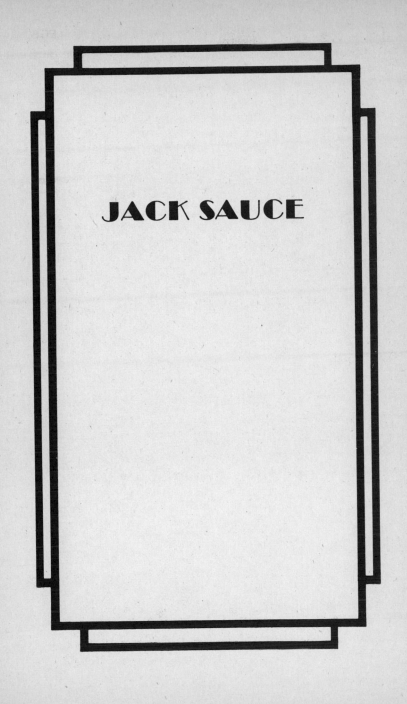

# JACK SAUCE

I met Jack in 1925 when he and his brother Eddie were personally running booze down from Canada. Jack stopped at the Kenmore even then, and he and Eddie and some more of their crew were at the table next to me, talking about Al Jolson. From what he said, Jack was clearly a Jolson fan, and so was I, and I listened to him express amazement that anybody could be as good at anything as Jolson was, but that he was also the most conceited son of a bitch in shoe leather. I broke into the conversation and said something windy, like: "He sings, whistles, dances, gives out the jokes and patter and it's all emotion, all a revelation of who he is. I don't care how much he's rehearsed, it's still rare because it's pure. He's so at home in himself he can't make a false gesture. Everything he does is more of that self that's made a million, ten, twenty million, whatever it is. People find this very special and they'll pay to see it. Even his trouble is important because it gives him diversity, pathos, and those qualities turn up in his voice. Everything he does funnels in and out of him through his talent. Sure he's conceited, but that's only a cover-up for his fear that he'll be exposed as the desolated, impoverished, scrawny, fearful hyena that he probably thinks is his true image, but that he can't admit to anybody without destroying his soul."

It all stunned Jack, who was a sucker for slick talk, and he bought me drinks for an hour. The next day he called to say he was sending me six quarts of Scotch and could I get him a pistol permit from Albany County? I liked the Scotch so I got him the permit.

I didn't have anything to do with him after that until 1929

when I represented Joe Vignola in the Hotsy Totsy case.
And a story, which I pieced together very painfully from
Joe, Jack, and half a dozen others, goes with that. It begins
the night Benny Shapiro knocked out Kid Murphy in eight
rounds at the Garden in '29. Jack, a serious fan of Benny's,
won two grand that night taking the short end of seven to
five.

"Stop by the club later," Benny remembered Jack telling
him in the dressing room after the fight. "We'll have a little
celebration."

"I got to meet a guy, Jack," Benny said.

"Bring her along."

"I'll try to make it, but I might be late."

"We'll wait," said Jack.


Herman Zuckman came hustling toward the bar as Jack
walked into the Hotsy Totsy Club with Elaine Walsh, a
singer and his special friend of the moment, on his arm. Fat
Herman had been sole owner of the Hotsy until Jack
Diamond decided to join him as a fifty-fifty partner. The
club was on Broadway, near Fifty-fourth, top of the
second-floor stairs, music by a six-piece jazz band, and
tonight Joe Vignola, the singing waiter, doubling on violin.

All thirty tables in the bar area were full, despite Mayor
Walker's nightlife curfew to keep decent people away from
racketeers, bad beer, and worse liquor. Wood alcohol.
Rubbing alcohol. The finest. Imported by Jack from the
cellars of Newark and Brooklyn. Drink me. The bartenders
were working hard, but there was too much work for the
pair, Walter Rudolph, old rum-runner with a bad liver, and
Lukas, a new man. Jack took off his coat, a Palm Beach,
and his hat, a white sailor straw, and rolled up his sleeves to
help the barmen. Elaine Walsh sat at the end of the bar and
listened to the music. "I'm just a vagabond lover," Joe
Vignola was singing. Joe Vignola, a merger of John Gilbert
and Oliver Hardy, fiddled a chorus, then went back to
delivering drinks.

Saul Baker, silent doorman, sat by the door with two
pistols in his pockets, one on his hip, another inside his

coat, and smiled at arriving customers. Just out of Sing Sing, a holdup man in need, pudgy Saul had found a survival point in the spiritual soup kitchen of Jack Diamond. Let no hungry thief pass my door. Don't try to tell Saul Baker Jack Diamond is a heartless man.

Charlie Filetti sat at the end of the bar. Filetti, it would soon be disclosed, had recently banked twenty-five thousand dollars in one day, a fragment of profit from his partnership with Jack Diamond in the shakedown of bucket-shop proprietors, shady dealers in the stock market.

"Who won the fight, Jack?" Filetti asked.

"Benny. KO in eight. He ruined the bum."

"I lose three hundred."

"You bet against Benny?" Jack stopped working.

"You got more confidence in him than I got. A lot of people don't like him ducking Corrigan."

"Ducking? Did you say ducking?"

"I'm saying what's being said. I like Benny good enough."

"Benny ducks nobody."

"Okay, Jack, but I'm telling you what talk's around town. They say you can make Benny lose, but you can't make him win."

"It was on the level tonight. You think I'd back a mug who runs? You should've seen him take Murphy apart. Murphy's a lunk. Hits like half a pound of sausage. Benny ate him up."

"I like Benny," Filetti said. "Don't get me wrong. I just like what Murphy did in his last fight. Murphy looked good that night I saw him."

"You don't know, Charlie. You shouldn't bet on fights. You just don't know. Ain't that right, Walter? He don't know?"

"I don't follow the fights, Jack," Walter Rudolph said. "I got out of the habit in stir. Last fight I saw was in '23. Benny Leonard whippin' a guy I don't even remember."

"How about you, pal?" Jack asked Lukas, the new bar-man. "You follow the fights? You know Benny Shapiro?"

"I see his name in the papers, that's all. To tell you the truth, Mr. Diamond, I watch baseball."

"Nobody knows," Jack said. He looked at Elaine. "But Elaine knows, don't you, baby? Tell them what you said tonight at the fight."

"I don't want to say, Jack." She smiled.

"Go ahead."

"It makes me blush."

"Never mind that, just tell them what you said."

"All right. I said Benny fights as good as Jack Diamond makes love."

Everybody at the bar laughed, after Jack laughed.

"That means he's a cinch to be champ," Jack said.

The mood of the club was on the rise and midnight seemed only a beginning. But forty minutes behind the bar was enough for Jack. Jack, though he had tended bar in his time, was not required to do manual labor. He was a club owner. But it's a kick to do what you don't have to do, right? Jack put on his coat and sat alongside Elaine. He put his hand under her loose blond hair, held her neck, kissed her once as everyone looked in other directions. Nobody looked when Jack kissed his ladies in public.

"Jack is back," he said.

"I'm glad to see him," Elaine said.

Benny Shapiro walked through the door and Jack leaped off his chair and hugged him with one arm, walked him to a bar stool.

"I'm a little late," Benny said.

"Where's the girl?"

"No girl, Jack. I told you it was a man. I owed some insurance."

"Insurance? You win a fight, break a man's nose, and then go out and pay your insurance?"

"For my father. I already stalled the guy two weeks. He was waiting. Woulda canceled the old man out in the morning. I figure, pay the bill before I blow the dough."

"Why don't you tell somebody these things? Who is this prick insurance man?"

"It's okay, Jack, it's all over."

"Imagine a guy like this?" Jack said to everybody.

"I told you I always liked Benny," Filetti said.

"Get us a table, Herman," Jack said. "Benny's here."

Herman Zuckman, counting money behind the bar, turned to Jack with an amazed look.

"I'm busy here, Jack."

"Just get us a table, Herman."

"The tables are all full, Jack. You can see that. We already turned away three dozen people. Maybe more."

"Herman, here beside me is the next welterweight champion of the world who's come to see us, and all you're doing is standing there making the wrong kind of noise."

Herman put the money in a strongbox under the bar, then moved two couples away from a table. He gave them seats at the bar and bought them a bottle of champagne.

"You feeling all right?" Jack asked Benny when they all sat down. "No damage?"

"No damage, just a little headache."

"Too much worrying about insurance. Don't worry anymore about shit like that."

"Maybe he's got a headache because he got hit in the head," Charlie Filetti said.

"He didn't get hit in the head," Jack said. "Murphy couldn't find Benny's head. Murphy couldn't find his own ass with a compass. But Benny found Murphy's head. And his nose."

"How does it feel to break a man's nose?" Elaine asked.

"That's a funny question," Benny said. "But to tell the truth you don't even know you're doing it. It's just another punch. Maybe it feels solid, maybe it don't."

"You don't feel the crunch, what the hell good is it?" Jack said.

Filetti laughed. "Jack likes to feel it happen when the noses break, right Jack?"

Jack mock-backhanded Filetti, who told him. "Don't get *your* nose out of joint, partner"—and he laughed some more. "I remember the night that big Texas oil bozo gave Jack lip. He's about six eight and Jack breaks a bottle

across his face at the table, and then *you* couldn't stop
laughing, Jack. The son of a bitch didn't know what hit him.
Just sat there moppin' up his blood. Next day I go around to
tell him what it costs to give lip to Jack and he says he
wants to apologize. Gives me a grand to make Jack feel
good. Remember that, Jack?''

Jack grinned.

The Reagans, Billy and Tim, came into the club and
everybody knew it. They were brawny boys from the
Lower West Side, dockworkers as soon as they knew they
were men, that God had put muscles in their backs to alert
them to that fact. Behind his back people called Billy The
Omadhaun, a name he'd earned at seventeen when in a
drunken rage he threw repeated football blocks at the
crumbling brick tenement he lived in. Apart from the
bleeding scrapes and gouges all over his body, an
examination disclosed he had also broken both shoulders.
His brother Tim, a man of somewhat larger wit, discovered
upon his return from the Army in 1919 that beer-loading
was no more strenuous than ship-loading, and far more
lucrative. Proprietorship of a small speakeasy followed, as
Tim pursued a prevailing dictum that to establish a
speakeasy what you needed was one room, one bottle of
whiskey, and one customer.

"That's a noisy bunch," Elaine said when they came in.

"It's the Reagans," said Filetti. "Bad news."

"They're tough monkeys," Jack said, "but they're
pretty good boys."

"The big one's got a fist like a watermelon," Benny said.

"That's Billy," Jack said. "He's tough as he is thick."

Jack waved to the Reagans, and Tim Reagan waved and
said, "Hello, Jack, howsa boy?"

"How's the gin in this joint?" Billy asked Joe Vignola in
a voice that carried around the room. Herman Zuckman
looked up. Customers eyed the Reagans.

"The best English gin is all we serve," Vignola told him.
"Right off the boat for fancy drinkers like yourselves."

"Right out of Jack's dirty bathtub," Billy said.

"No homemade merchandise here," Vignola said. "Our customers get only the real stuff."

"If he didn't make it then he stole it," Billy said. He looked over at Jack Diamond. "Ain't that so, Jack?"

"If you say so, Billy," Jack said.

"Hey, he can get in trouble with that kind of talk," Filetti said.

"Forget it," Jack said. "Who listens to a drunk donkey Irishman?"

"Three of the good gins," Billy told Vignola. "Right away."

"Comin' up," said Vignola, and he rolled his eyes, dropped the serving tray he carried under his arm, but caught it just before it hit the floor, then lofted it and caught it again, well over his head, and spun it on the index finger of his left hand: a juggler's routine. Others laughed. The Reagans did not.

"Get the goddamn gin and never mind the clown act," Billy Reagan said. "You hear me, you waiter baloney? Get the gin."

Jack immediately went to the Reagan table and stood over big-fisted Billy. He poked Billy's shoulder with one finger. "You got no patience. Make noise in your own joint, but have a little patience when you're in somebody else's."

"I keep telling him he's ignorant," Tim Reagan said. "Sit down, Jack, don't mind him. Have a drink. Meet Teddy Carson from Philly. We been tellin' him about you, how you come a long way from Philadelphia."

"How you makin' out, Jack?" Teddy Carson said, another big fist. He shook Jack's hand, cracking knuckles. "Some boys I know in Philly talk about you a lot. Duke Gleason, Wiggles Mason. Wiggles said he knew you as a kid."

"He knocked a tooth out on me. I never got even."

"That's what he told me."

"You tell him I said hello."

"He'll be glad to hear that."

"Pull up a chair, Jack," Tim said.

"I got a party over there."

"Bring 'em over. Make the party bigger."

Saul Baker left his post by the door when Jack went back to his own table. "That's a bunch of shitheads, Jack. You want 'em thrown out?"

"It's all right, Saul." Pudgy little Saul Baker, chastising three elephants.

"I hate a big mouth."

"Don't get excited."

Jack said he wanted to have a drink with the Reagans. "We'll all go over," he said to Filetti, Elaine, and Benny.

"What the hell for?" said Filetti.

"It'll keep 'em quiet. They're noisy, but I like them. And there's a guy from Philly knows friends of mine."

Jack signaled Herman to move the table as Joe Vignola finally brought drinks to the Reagans.

"You call this gin?" Billy said to Vignola, holding up a glass of whiskey. "Are you tryna be a funny guy? Are you lookin' for a fight?"

"Gin's gone," Vignola said.

"I think you're lookin' for a fight," Billy said.

"No, I was looking for the gin," Vignola said, laughing, moving away.

"This is some dump you got here, Jack," Billy called out.

Herman and a waiter moved Jack's table next to the Reagans, but Jack did not sit down.

"Let me tell you something, Billy," Jack said, looking down at him. "I think your mouth is too big. I said it before. Do I make myself clear?"

"I told you to shut your goddamn trap," Tim told Billy, and when Billy nodded and drank his whiskey, Jack let everybody sit down and be introduced. Charlie Filetti sat in a quiet pout. Elaine had swallowed enough whiskey so that it made no difference where she sat, as long as it was next to Jack. Jack talked about Philadelphia to Teddy Carson, but then he saw nobody was talking to Benny.

"Listen," Jack said, "I want to raise a toast to Benny here, a man who just won a battle, man headed for the welterweight crown."

"Benny?" said Billy Reagan. "Benny who?"

"Benny Shapiro, you lug," Tim Reagan said. "Right here. The fighter. Jack just introduced you."

"Benny Shapiro," Billy said. He pondered it. "That's a yid name." He pondered it further. "What I think is yids make lousy fighters."

Everybody looked at Billy, then at Benny.

"The yid runs, is how I see it," Billy said. "Now take Benny there and the way he runs out on Corrigan. Wouldn't meet an Irishman."

"Are you gonna shut up, Billy?" Tim Reagan said.

"What do you call Murphy?" Benny said to Billy. "Last time I saw him tonight he's got rosin all over his back."

"I seen you box, yid. You stink."

"You dumb fucking donkey," Jack said. "Shut your stupid mouth."

"You wanna shut my mouth, Jack? Where I come from, the middle name is fight. That's how you shut the mouth."

Billy pushed his chair away from the table, straddling it, ready to move. As he did, Jack tossed his drink at Billy and lunged at his face with the empty glass. But Billy only blinked and grabbed Jack's hand in flight, held it like a toy.

Saul Baker snatched a gun from his coat at Jack's curse and looked for a clear shot at Billy. Then Tim Reagan grabbed Saul's arm and wrestled for the gun. Women shrieked and ran at the sight of pistols, and men turned over tables to hide. Herman Zuckman yelled for the band to play louder, and customers scrambled for cover to the insanely loud strains of the "Jazz Me Blues." Elaine Walsh backed into a checkroom, Benny Shapiro, Joe Vignola, and four others there ahead of her. The bartenders ducked below bar level as Billy knocked Jack backward over chairs.

"Yes, sir," Billy said, "the middle name is fight."

Tim Reagan twisted the pistol out of Saul Baker's grip as Teddy Carson fired the first shot. It hit Saul just above the right eye as he was reaching for his second pistol, on his hip.

The second shot was Charlie Filetti's. It grazed Billy's skull, knocking him down. Filetti fired again, hitting Carson, who fell and slithered behind a table.

Jack Diamond, rising slowly with his pistol in his hand,

looked at the only standing enemy, Tim Reagan, who was holding Saul's pistol. Jack shot Tim in the stomach. As Tim fell, he shot a hole in the ceiling. Standing then, Jack fired into Tim's forehead. The head gave a sudden twist and Jack fired two more bullets into it. He fired his last two shots into Tim's groin, pulling the trigger three times on empty chambers. Then he stood looking down at Tim Reagan.

Billy opened his eyes to see his bleeding brother beside him on the floor. Billy shook Tim's arm and grunted "Timbo," but his brother stayed limp. Jack cracked Billy on the head with the butt of his empty pistol and Billy went flat.

"Let's go, Jack, let's move," Charlie Filetti said.

Jack looked up and saw Elaine's terrified face peering at him from the checkroom. The bartenders' faces were as white as their aprons. All faces looked at Jack as Filetti grabbed his arm and pulled. Jack tossed his pistol onto Billy's chest and it bounced off onto the floor.

# JACK,
# OUT OF DOORS

Jack lived the fugitive life after the Hotsy, the most hunted man in America, and eventually he wound up in the Catskills. I don't think I'd have ever seen him again if the 1925 meeting in the Kenmore had been our only encounter. But I know my involvement in the Hotsy case brought me back to his mind, even though we never met face to face during it. And when the heat was off in midsummer of 1930, when the Hotsy was merely history, Jack picked me out of whatever odd pigeonhole he'd put me in, called me up and asked me to Sunday dinner.

"I'm sorry," he said when he called, "but I haven't seen you since that night we talked in the Kenmore. That's been quite a while and I can't remember what you look like. I'll send a driver to pick you up, but how will he recognize you?"

"I look like St. Thomas Aquinas," I said, "and I wear a white Panama hat with a black band. Rather beat up, that hat. You couldn't miss it in a million."

"Come early," he said. "I got something I'd like to show you."

Joe (Speed) Fogarty picked me up at the Catskill railroad station, and when I saw him I said, "Eddie Diamond, right?"

"No," he said. "Eddie died in January. Fogarty's the name."

"You look like his twin."

"So I'm told."

"You're Mr. Diamond's driver—or is he called Legs?"

"Nobody who knows him calls him anything but Jack. And I do what he asks me to do."

"Very loyal of you."

"That's the right word. Jack likes loyalty. He talks about it."

"What does he say?"

"He says, 'Pal, I'd like you to be loyal. Or else I'll break your fucking neck.' "

"The direct approach."

We got into Jack's custom, two-tone (green and gray) Cadillac sedan with whitewalls and bulletproof glass, armor panels, and the hidden pistol and rifle racks. The latter were features I didn't know existed until the following year when Jack had the occasion to open the pistol rack one fateful night. Now what I noticed were the black leather seats and the wooden dashboard with more gauges than any car seemed to need.

"How far is it to Jack's house?" I asked.

"We're not going to Jack's house. He's waiting for you over at the Biondo farm."

"That wouldn't be Jimmy Biondo, would it?"

"You know Jimmy?"

"I met him once."

"Just once? Lucky you. The bum is a throwback. Belongs in a tree."

"I'd tend to sympathize with that view. I met him during the Hotsy Totsy business. We swapped views one day about a client of mine, Joe Vignola."

"Joe. Poor Joe"—and Fogarty gave a sad little chuckle. "Some guys'd be unlucky even if they were born with rabbits' feet instead of thumbs."

"Then you knew Joe."

"I used to go to the Hotsy when I was in New York even before I knew Jack. It was quite a place before the big blowup. Plenty of action, plenty of gash. I met my wife there, Miss Miserable of 1929."

"So you're married."

"Was. It broke up in four months. That dame would break up a high mass."

It was Sunday morning, not quite noon, when Fogarty left the station in Catskill and headed west toward East Durham, where Jimmy Biondo lived. My head was full of Catskill images, old Rip Van Winkle who probably would have been hustling applejack instead of sleeping it off if he'd been alive now, and those old Dutchmen with their magical ninepins that lulled you into oblivion and the headless horseman riding like a spook through Sleepy Hollow and throwing his head at the trembling Ichabod. The Catskills were magical for me because of their stories, as well as their beauty, and I was full of both, despite the little crater of acid in the pit of my stomach. After all, I was actually going to Sunday dinner with one of the most notorious men in America. Me. From Albany.

"You know, two and a half hours ago I was talking to a whole roomful of cops."

"Cops? I didn't know cops worked in Albany on Sunday."

"Communion breakfast. I was the speaker and I told them a few stories and then looked out over their scrubbed faces and their shiny buttons and explained that they were our most important weapon in saving the nation from the worst scourge in its history."

"What scourge?"

"Gangsterism."

Fogarty didn't laugh. It was one of his rare humor failures.

Fogarty was the only man I ever met through Jack who wasn't afraid to tell me what was really on his mind. There was an innocence about him that survived all the horror, all the fear, all the crooked action, and it survived because Jack allowed it to survive. Until he didn't allow it anymore.

Fogarty told me he was eleven when he understood his own weak spot. It was his nose. When tapped on the nose in a fight, he bled, and the sight and feel of the blood made him vomit. While he vomited, the other guy punched him senseless. Fogarty avoided fistfights, but when they were unavoidable he packed his nose with the cotton he always carried. He usually lost his fights, but after he understood his nose, he never again bled to the vomit point.

He was thirty-five when I got to know him, pretty well recovered from a case of TB he'd picked up during his last year of college. He had a Fordham stringency that had gone sour on religion, but he still read books, liked O'Neill, and could talk a little Hamlet, because he'd played Laertes once in school. Jack used him as a driver but also trusted him with money and let him keep the books on beer distribution. But his main role was as Jack's sidekick. He looked like Eddie. And Eddie had died of TB.

Fogarty was working as a bartender for Charlie Northrup when he first met Jack. He talked flatteringly about Jack's history when they sat across from each other at Northrup's roadhouse bar. Jack was new in the mountains and he quizzed Fogarty on the scene. What about the sheriff and the judges? Were they womanizers? Gamblers? Queers? Drunks? Merely greedy? Who ran beer in the mountains besides Northrup and the Clemente brothers?

Fogarty gave Jack the answers, and Jack hired him away from Northrup and gave him the pearl-handled .32 Eddie Diamond once owned. Fogarty carried it without loading it, giving it the equivalent menace of a one-pound rock. "You boys don't know it, but I've got you all covered with a one-pound rock."

"I don't want to get into any heavy stuff" is what he explained to Jack when he took the pistol.

And Jack told him: "I know you better than that, Speed. I don't ask my tailor to fix my teeth."

This arrangement suited Fogarty down to his socks. He could move among the big fellows, the tough fellows, without danger to himself. If he did not fight, he would not bleed.

Fogarty turned onto a winding narrow dirt road that climbed a few minor hills and then flattened out on a plateau surrounded by trees. Jimmy Biondo's place was an old white farmhouse with green shutters and green shingled roof. It sat at the end of the drive, and behind it stood a large unpainted barn as dilapidated as the house was elegant. Three moving shapes sat on the long front porch, rocking in green wicker rockers, their faces hidden from me by the newspapers they were all reading. The faces opened themselves to us when Fogarty stopped on the grass beside the house, and Jack, the first to stand, threw down the paper and bounded down the stairs to greet me. The woman, Alice, held the paper in her lap and looked at me with a smile. The second man was Jimmy Biondo, who owned the place but no longer used it, and rented it to Jack. He detached himself from Andy Gump to give me a look.

"Welcome to God's country, Marcus," Jack said. He was in white ducks, brown and white wing tips, and a yellow silk sport shirt. A tan blazer hung on the back of his rocker.

"God's country?" I said. "Fogarty told me Jimmy Biondo owned this place."

Jack laughed and Jimmy actually smiled. A smile from Jimmy lit up the world like a three-watt bulb.

"Look at this guy," Jack said to his wife and Jimmy, "a lawyer with a sense of humor. Didn't I tell you he was beautiful?"

"I only let my mother call me beautiful," I said.

What can I say? Jack laughed again. He liked my lines. Maybe it was my delivery or my funny old hat. Fogarty recognized me from the hat as soon as he saw me. It was all discolored at the front from where I touched it, crown and brim; the brim was split on the side and the black band raveling a little. It happened to be my favorite hat. People don't understand that some men need tradition as much as others need innovation. I doffed the hat when Alice came down the steps and characteristically asked me after our handshake, "Are you hungry? Have you had breakfast?"

"Catholic eggs and Irish bacon. That's extra greasy. About three hours ago at a communion breakfast."

"We just came from church, too," Alice said.

Oh? But I didn't say oh. I just repeated the story about

my speech on the scourge of gangsterism. Jack listened with straight face, and I thought, Oh Christ, another humor failure.

"I know what you mean," he said. "Some of my best friends have been taken by that scourge." Then he smiled, a very small smile, a smile you might call wry, or knowing, or ironic, or possibly ominous, which is how I looked at it and was why I laughed my courtroom laugh. That laugh, as they used to say in the Albany papers, is booming and infectious, and it had the effect of making Jack's line seem like the joke of the year.

Jack responded by standing up and jiggling, a moving glob of electricity, a live wire snaking its way around the porch. I knew then that this man was alive in a way I was not. I saw the vital principle of his elbow, the cut of his smile, the twist of his pronged fingers. Whatever you looked at was in odd motion. He hit you, slapped you with his palm, punched you with a light fist, clapped you on the shoulder, ridding himself of electricity to avoid exploding. He was conveying it to you, generating himself into yourself whether you wanted to receive him or not. You felt something had descended upon him, tongues of fire maybe or his phlogiston itself, burning its way into your own spirit.

I liked it.

It was an improvement on pinochle.

I mounted the steps and shook hands with Biondo and told him how overjoyed I was to see him again. He gave me a nod and an individualized twitch of each nostril, which I considered high graciousness. I would describe Jimmy as a giant maggot, an abominable toad with twelve-ounce eyelids and an emancipated nose that had nothing to do with the rest of his face. He was a globular figure of uncertain substance. Maybe all hotdog meat, goat's ears and pig's noses inside that salmony, shantung sportshirt. You said killer as soon as you looked at him, but he was not a killer. He was more complex than that.

"How's your buddy Joe Vignola?" he asked me. And he grunted a laugh, which went like this: "Hug, hug, hug."

"Joe is recovering nicely," I said, an exaggeration. Joe was in awful shape. But I should give Jimmy Biondo satisfaction?

"Dumb," said Jimmy. "Dumb, dumb, dumb."

"He never hurt anybody," I said.

"Dumb," said Jimmy, shaking his head, drawing out the sound like a short siren. "Dumb waiter," he said, and he laughed like a sneeze.

"I felt so sorry for his family," Alice said.

"Feel sorry for your own family," Jack said. "The son of a bitch was a stool pigeon."

"I'll feel sorry for anybody I feel like feeling sorry for," Alice said in modified spitfire manner, a trait I somehow didn't expect from the wife of Jack Diamond. Did I think he'd marry a placid cow? No. I thought he'd dominate any woman he chose to live with. We know from the movies, don't we, that one well-placed grapefruit in the kisser and the women learn who's boss? *Public Enemy*, the Cagney movie with that famed grapefruit scene, was touted as the real story of Jack Diamond when it played Albany. The advertising linked it unmistakably to his current escapades: "You read about him on yesterday's front pages in this newspaper. Now see the story behind the headlines," etc. But like everything else that ever had anything to do with Jack in the movies, it never had anything to do with Jack.

Well, we got past Joe Vignola as a topic, and then after a few anxious grunts from Jimmy ("Guh, guh, guh,"), he got up and announced his departure. Fogarty would take him to Hudson, across the river, and he'd take a train to Manhattan. His and Jack's presence on this front porch was not explained to me, but I didn't pry. I didn't know until much later that they were partners of a kind. His departure improved the conversation, and Alice said she and Jack had been to mass over at Sacred Heart in Cairo where she, and once in a while he, went on Sunday, and that Jack had given money for the new church organ and that she brought up Texas Guinan one summer to raise money at a church lawn party and Jack was going to bring Al Jolson up and so on. Revelatory.

An old colored man came to the foot of the front steps and said to Jack, "The tahger's ready, Mist' Jack." Tahger? Tiger? Could he be keeping a tiger? Was that what he wanted to show me?

"Okay, Jess," Jack said. "And will you bring out two quarts of rye and two quarts of champagne and leave 'em here on the porch?"

Jesse nodded and moved off slowly, a man who looked far older than his years, actually a stoop-backed fifty, a Georgia cotton chopper most of his days and then a stable hand. Jack met him in '29 through a Georgia horse breeder who had brought him to Churchill Downs as a stable boy. Jack heard Jesse had made moonshine back home and hired him on the spot at a hundred a week, a pay raise of about eight hundred percent, to come north with his two teen-aged sons and no wife and be plumber for an applejack still Jack and Biondo owned jointly, and which, since that time, had functioned night and day in a desolated patch of woods a quarter of a mile from the patch of porch on which I was rocking.

So the old man went for the rye and champagne, and I mentally alerted my whistle to coming attractions. Then Alice looked at Jack and Jack looked at me and I looked at both of them, wondering what all the silent looking was for. And then Jack asked me a question: "Ever fire a machine gun, Marcus?"

We walked to the garage-cooler, which is what it turned out to be, as luxuriously appointed a tumbledown barn as you'd be likely to find anywhere in America, with a beer refrigeration unit; a storage room for wine and champagne, paneled in knotty pine; a large area where three trucks could comfortably park; and a total absence of hay, hornets, barnsmell, cowflop, or chickenshit.

"No," I had told Jack, in answer to his question, "I am a machine-gun virgin."

"Time you shot the wad," Jack said, and he went dancing down the stairs and around the corner toward the barn, obviously leading both me and Alice, before we were out of our chairs.

"He's a nut on machine guns," Alice said. "He's been waiting till you got here to try it out. You don't have to do it, you know, just because he suggests it."

I nodded my head yes, shook it no, shrugged, and, I suppose, looked generally baffled and stupid. Alice and I walked across the side lawn to the barn where Jack had already pried up a floorboard and was lifting out a Thompson submachine gun, plus half a dozen boxes of bullets.

"Brand-new yesterday from Philadelphia," he said. "I been anxious to test it." He dislodged the magazine, loaded it, replaced it with what, despite my amateurism in the matter, I would call know-how. "I heard about a guy could change one of these drums in four seconds," he said. "That's handy in a tight spot."

He stood up and pointed it at the far end of the barn where a target was tacked on a windowless wall. The target was a crudely drawn face with the name Dutch Schultz lettered beneath.

"I had a couple of hundred of these printed up a few years ago," he said, "when Schultz and me weren't getting along. He looks just like that, the greedy prick. I drew it myself."

"You get along all right now with him?"

"Sure. We're pals again," Jack said and he let go with a long blast that nicked the Schultz forehead in two or three places.

"A little off," Jack observed, "but he'd have noticed."

"Let me try," Alice said. She took the gun from Jack, who parted with it reluctantly, then fired a long burst which roamed the wall without touching the target. With a second burst she hit the paper's edge, but not Schultz.

"I'm better with a rifle."

"You're better with a frying pan," Jack said. "Let Marcus try it."

"It's really out of my line," I said.

"Go on," Jack said. "You may never get another chance, unless you come to work for me."

"I've got nothing against Mr. Schultz."

"He wouldn't mind. Lotsa people shoot at him."

Jack put the gun in my hands, and I held it like a watermelon. Ridiculous. I put my right hand on the pistol grip, grabbed the other handgrip with the left, and raised the stock into my armpit. Absurd. Uncomfortable.

"Up a little," Jack said. "Against the shoulder."

I touched the trigger, raised the gun. Why? It was wobbly, cold. I pointed it at Schultz. Sunday morning. Body of Christ still undigested in some internal region, memory of prayer and holy bacon grease on my tongue. I touched the trigger seriously, pulled the gun tighter to my shoulder. Old feeling. Comfortable with a weapon against the pectoral. Like Army days, days in the woods as a kid. Put it down, fool.

"For chrissake, Marcus, give it a blast," Jack said.

Really childish not to. Raising the flag of morality. Powerful Irish Catholic magic at work that prohibits shooting effigies on the side of a barn. Bless me Father for I have sinned. I shot at Mr. Schultz's picture. And did you hit it, son? No, Father, I missed. For your penance say two rosaries and try again for the son of a bitch.

"Honest, Marcus," Alice said, "it won't bite."

Ladies' Auxiliary heard from. Altar Rosary Society Member attends machine-gun outing after mass, prods lawyer to take part. What a long distance between Marcus and Jack Diamond. Millenniums of psychology, civilization, experience, turpitude. Man also develops milquetoasts by natural selection. Would I defend him if some shooters walked through the barn door? What difference from defending him in court? And what of Jack's right to justice, freedom, life? Is the form of defense the only differentiating factor? What a morally confounded fellow Marcus is, perplexed by Mr. Thompson's invention.

I pressed the trigger. Bullets exploded in my ears, my hands, my shoulders, my blood, my brain. The spew of death was a personal tremor that even jogged my scrotum.

"Close, off the right ear," Jack said. "Try again."

I let go with another burst, feeling confident. No pain. It's easy. I leveled the weapon, squeezed off another.

"Got him. Eyeball high. No more Maggie's Drawers for Marcus. You want a job riding shotgun?"

Jack reached for the gun, but I held onto it, facing the ease with which I had become new. Do something new and you are new. How boring it is not to fire machine guns. I fired again and eliminated the Schultz mouth.

"Jesus, look at that," Jack said.

I gave him the gun and he looked at me. Me. Sandlot kid hits grand slam off thirty-game winner, first time at bat.

"How the hell did you do that?" Jack asked me.

"It's all a matter of the eyeball," I said. "I also shoot a pretty fair game of pool."

"I'm impressed," Jack said. He gave me another amazed look and put the weapon to his shoulder. But then he decided the shooting was over. What if he missed the target now? Bum of bums.

"Let's have lunch and toast your sharpshooting," he said.

"Oh nonsense," Alice said, "let's toast something important, like the beautiful day and the beautiful summer and having friends to dinner. Are you our friend, Marcus?"

I smiled at Alice to imply I was her friend, and Jack's, too. And I was then, yes I was. I was intuitively in sympathy with this man and woman who had just introduced me to the rattling, stammering splatter of violent death. Gee, ain't it swell?

We walked back to the porch where Fogarty was reading Krazy Kat.

"I heard the shooting," Fogarty said, "who won?"

"Marcus won," Alice said.

"I wiped out Mr. Schultz's mouth, if that's a win."

"Just what he deserves. The prick killed a kid cousin of mine last week in Jersey."

And so I had moral support for my little moral collapse—which sent a thrill through me, made me comfortable again on this glorious Sunday in the mountains.

We got into the car and left the Biondo place, Alice and I in the back seat, Jack up front with Fogarty. Alice previewed our Sunday dinner for me: roast beef and baked potatoes, and did I like my beef rare the way Jack liked it, and asparagus from their own garden, which Tamu, their Japanese gardener, had raised, and apple pie by their colored maid, Cordelia.

Alice bulged out of her pink summer cotton in various places, and my feeling was that she was ready instantly to let it all flop out whenever Jack gave the signal. All love, all ampleness, all ripeness, would fall upon the bed, or the ground, or on him, and be his for the romping. Appleness, leaves, blue sky, white sheets, erect, red nipples, full buttocks, superb moistness at the intersection, warm wet lips, hair flying, craziness of joy, pleasure, wonder, mountains climbable with a stride after such sex.

I like her.

Oxie was asleep on the enclosed porch when we arrived, more formally known as Mendel (The Ox) Feinstein, one of the permanent cadre. Oxie was a bull-necked weightlifter with no back teeth, who'd done a four-year stretch for armed robbery of a shoe store. The judge specified he do the full four because, when he held up the lady shoe clerk, he also took the shoes she was wearing. Justice puts its foot down on Oxie.

He got up immediately when the key turned in the front door. We all watched as Alice stopped to coo at two canaries in a silver cage on the porch. When she went on to the kitchen, Fogarty sat down on the sofa with Oxie, who made a surreptitious gesture to Jack.

"Marion called about a half hour ago," he whispered.

"Here?"

Oxie nodded and Jack made facial note of a transgression by Marion.

"She wants you to see her this afternoon. Important, she said."

"Goddamn it," Jack said, and he went into the living room and up the stairs two at a time, leaving me on the porch with the boys. Fogarty solved my curiosity, whispering: "Marion's his friend. Those two canaries there—he calls one Alice, one Marion." Oxie thought that was the funniest thing he'd heard all week, and while he and Fogarty enjoyed the secret, I went into the living room, which was furnished to Alice's taste: overstuffed mohair chairs and sofa; walnut coffee table; matching end tables and table lamps, their shades wrapped in cellophane; double-thick Persian rug, probably worth a fortune if Jack hadn't lifted it. My guess was he'd bought it hot; for while he loved the splendid things of life, he had no inclination to pay for them. He did let Alice pick out the furniture, for the hot items he kept bringing home clashed with her plans, such as they were. She'd lined the walls with framed calendar art and holy pictures—a sepia print of the Madonna returning from Calvary and an incendiary, bleeding sacred heart with a cross blooming atop the bloody fire. One wall was hung with a magnificent blue silk tapestry, a souvenir from Jack's days as a silk thief. Three items caught my eye on a small bookshelf otherwise full of Zane Grey and James Oliver Curwood items: a copy of Rabelais, an encyclopedia of Freemasonry, and the Douay Bible sandwiched between them.

When he came down, I asked about the books. The Freemasonry? Yeah, he was a Mason. "Good for business," he said. "Every place you go in this country, the Protestant sons of bitches got the money locked up." And Rabelais? Jack picked up the book, fondled it.

"A lawyer gave it to me when I had my accident in 1927." (He meant when he was shot three times by the Lepke mob when they ambushed and killed Little Augie Orgen.) "Terrific book. You ever read it? Some screwball that Rab-a-lee."

I said I knew the book but avoided mentioning the coincidence of Rabelais being here and also in the K. of C. library, where I made my decision to come here, and in the additional fact that a lawyer had given the book to Jack. I would let it all settle, let the headiness go out of it. Otherwise, it would sound like some kind of weird, fawning lie.

Alice heard us talking and came into the living room in her apron. "Those damn Masons," she said. "I can't get him away from that nonsense." To rile her, Jack kept a picture of an all-seeing eye inside a triangle, a weird

God-figure in the Masonic symbology, on the wall in the upstairs bathroom. Alice raised this issue, obviously a recurring one.

"It sees you, Alice," Jack told her, "even when you pee."

"My God doesn't watch me when I pee," Alice said. "My God is a gentleman."

"As I get it," Jack said, "your God is two gentlemen and a bird."

He opened the Rabelais to a page and began reading, walking to the kitchen doorway to serenade Alice with the flow. He read of Gargantua's arrival in Paris, his swiping of the Notre Dame Cathedral bells for his giant horse, and then his perching on the cathedral roof to rest while mobs of tiny Parisians stared up at him. And so he decided to give them wine.

"'He undid his magnificent codpiece'"—Jack read with mock robustness; his voice was not robust but of a moderately high pitch, excitable, capable of tremolos—"'and bringing out his john-thomas, pissed on them so fiercely that he drowned two hundred and sixty thousand, four hundred and eighteen persons, not counting the women and small children.'"

"My God, John," Alice said, "do you have to read *that?*"

"Piss on 'em," Jack said. "I always felt that way." And holding the book and talking again to me, he said, "You know what my full name is? John Thomas Diamond." And he laughed even harder.

Jack threw the book on the sofa and went quickly out to the porch, then to the car, and came back with a bottle of champagne in each hand. He put both bottles on the coffee table, got four glasses from the china closet.

"Alice, Speed, you want champagne?" They both said no and he didn't ask Oxie. Why waste champagne on a fellow who'd rather drink feet juice? He poured our champagne, the real goods.

"Here's to a fruitful legal relationship," Jack said, rather elegantly, I patronizingly thought. I sipped and he gulped and poured himself another. That disappeared and another followed that, two and a half glasses in one minute.

"Thirsty," he explained, "and that's prime stuff." But he was getting outside his skin. He finished what was in his glass and then stared at me while I drank and told him my experiences with bad champagne. He interrupted me, perfectly, at a pause, with obvious intentions of letting me continue, and said: "I don't want to interrupt your story, but how about a walk? It's a great day and I want to show you a piece of land."

He led the way out the back door and along a stream that ran parallel to the highway, and at a narrow point we leaped across the stream and into the woods, all soft with pine needles, quiet and cool, a young forest with the old granddaddy trees felled long ago by loggers, and the new trees— pines, white birches, maples, ash—tall but small of girth, reaching up for sunlight. A cat named Pistol followed at Jack's heel like an obedience-trained dog. He was an outdoor cat and had picked us up as we left the back steps, where he'd been sitting, gnawing gently on a squirrel that wasn't quite dead and that still had the good sense to run away whenever Pistol relaxed his teeth. But that old squirrel never got far from the next pounce.

Jack walked rapidly, stepping over the carcasses of old trees, almost running, moving uphill, slipping but never falling, surefooted as the cat. He turned around to check me out and at each turn motioned to me with his right hand, backs of fingers upright toward me, bending them toward himself in a come-on gesture. He said nothing, but even today I can remember that gesture and the anxious look on his face. He was not mindful of anything else except me and his destination and whatever obstacle he and the cat might have to dodge or leap over: an old log, jutting rocks, half-exposed boulders, fallen limbs, entire dead trees, the residual corpses of the forest. Then I saw a clearing and Jack stopped at its edge to wait for me. He pointed across a meadow, a golden oval that rolled upward, a lone, dead apple tree in the center like the stem and root of a vast yellow mushroom turned upside down. Beyond the tree an old house stood on the meadow's crest and Jack said that was where we were going.

He walked with me now, calmed, it seemed, by the meadow or perhaps the sight of the house, all that speed from the forest faded now into a relaxed smile, which I noticed just about the time he asked me: "Why'd you come down here today, Marcus?"

"I was invited. And I was curious. I'm still curious."

"I thought maybe I could talk you into going to work for me."

"As a lawyer or riding shotgun?"

"I was thinking maybe you'd set up a branch of your office in Catskill."

That was funny and I laughed. Without even telling me what he wanted of me, he was moving me into his backyard.

"That doesn't make much sense," I said. "My practice is in Albany and so is my future."

"What's in the future?"

"Politics. Maybe Congress, if the slot opens up. Not very complicated really. It's all done with machinery."

"Rothstein had two district attorneys on his payroll."

"Rothstein?"

"Arnold Rothstein. I used to work with him. And he had a platoon of judges. Why did you get me a pistol permit?"

"I don't really have a reason."

"You knew I was no altar boy."

"It cost me nothing. I remember we had a good conversation at the Kenmore. Then you sent me the Scotch."

He clapped me on the shoulder. Electric gesture.

"I think you're a thief in your heart, Marcus."

"No, stealing's not my line. But I admit to a corrupt nature. Profligacy, sloth, licentiousness, gluttony, pride. Proud of it all. That's closer to my center."

"I'll give you five hundred a month."

"To do what?"

"Be available. Be around when I need a lawyer. Fix my

traffic tickets. Get my boys out of jail when they get drunk
or go wild."

"How many boys?"

"Five, six. Maybe two dozen sometimes."

"Is that all? Doesn't seem like a full-time job."

"You do more, I pay you more."

"What more might I do?"

"Maybe you could move some money for me. I want to
start some accounts in other banks up this way, and I don't
want to be connected to them."

"So you want a lawyer on the payroll."

"Rothstein had Bill Fallon. Paid him a weekly salary.
You know who Fallon was?"

"Every lawyer in the U. S. knows who Fallon was."

"He defended me and Eddie when we got mixed up in a
couple of scrapes. He wound up a drunk. You a drunk?"

"Not yet."

"Drunks are worthless."

We were almost at the old house, a paintless structure
with all its windows and doors boarded up and behind it a
small barn, or maybe it was a stable, with its eyes gouged
out and holes in its roof. The panorama from this point was
incredible, a one-hundred-and-eighty-degree vision of natural grandeur. I could see why Jack liked the spot.

"I know the old man who owns this," he said. "He owns
the whole field, but the son of a bitch won't sell. He owns
half the mountainside. A stubborn old Dutchman, and he
won't sell. I want you to work on him. I don't care what the
price is."

"You want the house? The field? What?"

"I want all you can get, the whole hill and the forest. I
want this yellow field. Everything between here and my
place. Things are going good now and they can only get
better. I want to build up here. A big place. A place to live
good. I saw one in Westchester, a great place I liked.
Roomy. A millionaire owned it. Used to work for Woodrow
Wilson. Had a big fireplace. Look at this rock."

He picked up a purple stone lying at our feet.

"Plenty of this around," he said. "Have the fireplace

made out of it. Maybe face part of the house with it. You ever see a house faced with purple rock?''

"Never.''

"Me either. That's why I want it.''

"You're settling in here in the Catskills then, permanent-ly?''

"Right. I'm settling in. Plenty of work around here.'' He gave me a conspiratorial smile. "Lots of apple trees. Lots of thirsty people.'' He looked over at the house. "Van Wie is his name. He's about seventy now. He used to farm a little up here a few years ago.'' Jack walked over to the shed and looked inside. Grass was growing inside it, and hornets, birds, and spiders were living in the eaves. Birdshit and cobwebs were everywhere.

"Eddie and me did the old man a favor in here one day,'' Jack said, reminding me and himself, and, in his way, reminding me to remind the old man too that when Jack Diamond did you a favor, you didn't turn your back on him. He turned suddenly to me, not at all relaxed now, but with that anxious face I saw as he was moving through the forest.

"Are you with me?''

"I could use the money,'' I said. "I usually lose at pinochle.''

I can recall now the quality of the light at that moment when I went to work for Jack. The sun was dappling his shoulders as he peered into the shadows of the empty stable with its random birdshit, with his faithful cat Pistol (Marion later had a poodle named Machine Gun), rubbing its sides against Jack's pants legs, his head against Jack's shoe, the sun also dappling the black and white of Pistol's tiger tom fur as it sent its electricity into Jack the way Jack sent his own vital current into others. I mentioned to Jack that he looked like a man remembering something a man doesn't want to remember and he said yes, that was a thousand percent, and he told me the two interlocking memories he was resisting.

One was of another summer day in 1927 when old man
Van Wie came down the meadow past the apple tree, which
was not dead then, and into the forest where Jack and
Eddie Diamond were firing pistols at a target nailed to a
dead, fallen tree, recreation therapy for Eddie, for whom
the house, which would later be described as Jack's
fortress, had been purchased: mountain retreat for
tubercular brother.

The gunfire brought the old man, who might have
guessed the occupation of his neighbors but not their
identities; for Jack and Eddie were the Schaefer brothers
back then, a pseudonym lifted from Jack's in-laws; and
Jack was not yet as famous a face as he would be later in
that same year when Lepke bullets would not quite kill him.
The farmer did not speak until both Jack and Eddie had
given him their full attention. He then said simply, "There
is a mad cat. Will you shoot it before it bites on my cow? It
already bit on my wife." Then the old man waited for a
reply, staring past his flat nose and drooping mustache,
which, like his hair, he had dyed black, giving him the
comic look of a Keystone Kop; which was perhaps why
Jack said to him, "Why don't you call the troopers? Or the
sheriff. Have them do it."

"They'd be all week," said the old man. "Might be it's
got the rabies."

"How'll we find him?" Jack asked.

"I chased him with the pitchfork and he ran in the barn. I
locked him in."

"Is the cow in there?"

"No. Cow's out in the field."

"Then he can't get at the cow. You got him trapped."

"He might get out. That's a right old barn."

Jack turned to Eddie, and they smiled at the prospect of
making a mad cat hunt together, the way they had once
hunted rats and woodchucks in the Philadelphia dumps.
But Eddie could not walk all the way to the farmer's house,
and so they went back and got Jack's car, and with old man
Van Wie they drove to the barn which had not yet had its

eyes gouged out or holes made in its roof. And with guns drawn and the farmer behind them with his pitchfork, they entered the barn.

"What's going to stop him from biting hell out of us?" Jack said.

"I expect you'll shoot him 'fore he gets a chance at that," the old man said.

Jack saw the cat first, yellowish orange and brown and curled up on some hay, and quiet. It looked at them and didn't move, but then it opened its mouth and hissed without sound.

"That don't look like a mad cat to me," Jack said.

"You didn't see it bite on my wife or leap on the lampshade and then try to run up the curtain. Maybe it's quiet 'cause I whacked it with the fork. Maybe I knocked it lame."

"It looks like Sugarpuss," Eddie said.

"I know," Jack said. "I'm not going to kill it."

The mad cat looked at the men, orange and silent and no longer disturbed by their intrusion or fearful of their menace.

"You shoot it if you want," Jack said.

"I don't want to shoot it," Eddie said.

"Look out," old man Van Wie said, pushing past the brothers and sticking his pitchfork through the cat, which squealed and wriggled and tried to leap off the fork. But it was impaled and the farmer held it out to the brothers, an offering.

"Now shoot it," the old man said.

Jack kept his arm at his side, pistol down, watching the cat squeal and squirm upside down on the fork. Eddie put three bullets in its head, and the old man, saying only "Obliged" and grabbing a shovel off a nail, carried the carcass out to the yard to bury what remained of madness. And Jack then was triggered into his second cat memory of eighteen years before, when he was twelve, when he said to Eddie that he wanted to furnish the warehouse and Eddie did not understand. The warehouse was enormous, longer than some city blocks, empty for as long as they had been alive. It was made of corrugated metal and wooden beams and had scores of windows that could be broken but not shattered. Jack discovered it, and with Eddie, they imagined its vast empty floor space full of automobiles and machinery and great crated mysteries. At one end an office looked down on the emptiness from second-story level. There was no staircase to it, but Jack found a way. He rigged a climbing rope, stolen from a livery stable, over a wooden crossbeam, the stairway's one remnant. He worked two hours to maneuver a loop upward that would secure the rope, then shinnied up. It was 1909 and his mother had been dead two months. His brother was eight and spent two days learning how to shinny up to the office.

The brothers looked out the office windows at a fragment of Philadelphia's freight yards, at lines of empty boxcars, stacks of crossties, piles of telegraph poles covered with creosote. They watched trains arrive and then leave for places they knew only from the names painted on the cars—Baltimore and Ohio, New York Central, Susquehanna, Lackawanna, Erie, Delaware and Hudson, Boston and Albany—and they imagined themselves in these places, on these rivers. From the windows they saw a hobo open a freight-car door from inside, and they assumed he'd just awakened from a night's sleep. They saw him jump down and saw that a bull saw, too, and was chasing him. The hobo had only one shoe, the other foot wrapped in newspaper and tied with string. The bull outran him and beat him with a club, and when the hobo went down, he stayed down. The bull left him where he fell.

"The bastard," Jack said. "He'd do the same to us."

But the Diamond brothers always outran the bulls, outscrambled them beneath the cars.

Jack brought a chair to the office and a jug of water with a cork in it, candles, matches, a slingshot with a supply of stones, half a dozen pulp novels of the wild West, a cushion, and, when he could steal it from his father's jug, some dago red. He kept the hobo's hat, which was worn through at the crown from being fingered and had spots of blood on the brim. Jack took it off the hobo after he and

Eddie went down to help him and found he was dead. The
hobo was a young man, which shocked the brothers. Jack
hung the hat on a nail in the office and let no one wear it.

The brothers were asleep in the office the day the orange
cat came in. It had climbed one of the wooden pillars and
found its way along a crossbeam. A dog was after it,
barking at the foot of the pillar. Jack gave it water in the
candle dish, petted it, and called it Sugarpuss. The dog kept
barking and Jack fired stones at it with his slingshot. When
it wouldn't leave, Jack shinnied down, clubbed it with a
two-by-four, cut its throat, and threw it out by the
crossties.

Sugarpuss remained the mascot of the brothers and the
select group of friends they allowed up the rope. It lived in
the warehouse, and all the gang brought it food. During the
winter Jack found Sugarpuss outside, frozen in the ice, its
head almost eaten off where another animal had gotten it.
He insisted it be given a decent burial and immediately got
another cat to replace it. But the second cat ran away, an
early lesson in subtraction for Jack.

We came out of the woods onto the highway and walked
back toward Jack's house. A car passed us, and a
middle-aged man and woman waved and tooted at Jack,
who explained they were neighbors and that he'd had an
ambulance take their kid to Albany Hospital, some thirty
miles away, about six months back when the local
sawbones didn't know what ailed the boy. Jack footed the
bill for examinations and a week's stay in the hospital, and
the kid came out in good shape. An old woman down the
road had a problem with her cow after her shed collapsed,
and so Jack paid for a new shed. People in Acra and
Catskill told these stories when the papers said Jack was a
heartless killer.

Jack's Uncle Tim was working on the rosebushes when
we reached the house. The lawn had been freshly cut, some
grass raked into piles on the front walk. Tamu was watering
the flower beds of large and small marigolds, dahlias,
snapdragons, on the sunny side of the brown shingled
house. The flowers reached up toward a second-story

window where, it was authoritatively reported in the press
at a later date, Jack had his machine guns mounted. The
fortress notion was comic but not entirely without
foundation, for Jack did have floodlights on the house to
illuminate all approaches, and the maple trees on the lawn
were painted white to a point higher than a man, so anyone
crossing in front of one was an instant target. Jack installed
the lights back in 1928 when he was feuding with Schultz
and Rothstein, right after a trio of hirelings tried to kill
Eddie in Denver. Eddie went to Denver because the
Catskills hadn't solved his lung problems, and Denver must
have helped, for when they shot at him he leaped out of his
car and outran the killers. One killer, when he saw Eddie'd
gotten away, grabbed a bull terrier pup in front of
somebody's house and shot off one of its paws, an odd
substitute for murder. But then I guess in any realm of life
you solve your needs any way you can.

   Jack and I stood on the lawn and watched the grooming
of the landscape. Domestic felicity. Back to the soil.
Country squirearch. It didn't conform to my preconcep-
tions of Jack, but standing alongside him, I had to admit it
didn't sit so badly on him either.

   "Pretty good life you've got here," I told him. He
wanted to hear that.

   "Beats hell out of being at the bottom of the river," he
said.

   "A striking truth."

   "But this is nothing, Marcus, nothing. Give me a year,
maybe even six months, you'll see something really
special."

   "The house, you mean, the purple house?"

   "The house, the grounds, this whole goddamn county."

   He squinted at me then and I waited for clarification.

   "It's a big place, Marcus, and they pack in the tourists all
summer long. You know how many speakeasies in this one
county? Two hundred and thirty. I don't even know how
many hotels yet, but I'm finding out. And every goddamn
one of them can handle beer. Will handle beer."

   "Who's servicing them now?"

   "What's the difference?"

"I don't know what the difference is, except competition."

"We'll solve that," Jack said. "Come on, let's have some champagne."

Pistol, who had followed us out of the woods and along the road, pounced on a mole that made the mistake of coming out of his tunnel. The cat took him to the back steps and played with him alongside the carcass of the squirrel, who had died of wounds. Or perhaps Pistol had finished him off when he decided to take a walk with us. He let the mole run away a little, just as he'd let the squirrel, then he pounced.

We were hardly inside the house when Alice called out to Jack, "Will you come here please?" She was on the front porch, with Oxie and Fogarty still on the sofa. They were not moving, not speaking, not looking at Alice or at Jack or at me either when we got there. They both stared out toward the road.

Alice opened the canary cage and said to Jack, "Which one do you call Marion?"

Jack quickly turned to Fogarty and Oxie.

"Don't look at them, they didn't tell me," Alice said. "I just heard them talking. Is it the one with the black spot on its head?"

Jack didn't answer, didn't move. Alice grabbed the bird with the black spot and held it in her fist.

"You don't have to tell me—the black spot's for her black hair. Isn't it? Isn't it?"

When Jack said nothing, Alice wrung the bird's neck and threw it back in the cage. "That's how much I love you," she said and started past Jack, toward the living room, but he grabbed her and pulled her back. He reached for the second bird and squeezed it to death with one hand, then shoved the twitching, eyebleeding corpse down the crevice of Alice's breasts. "I love you too," he said.

That solved everything for the canaries.

We left the house immediately, with a "Come on, Marcus" the only words Jack said. Fogarty followed him wordlessly, like Pistol. "Haines Falls," Jack said in a flat, hostile voice.

Fogarty leaned over the seat to tell Jack, "We didn't know she was listening or we . . ."

"Shut your fucking mouth."

We drove a few miles in silence, and then Jack said in a tone that eliminated the canary episode from history, "I'm going to Europe. Ever been to Europe?"

"I was there with the AEF," I said. "But it was a Cook's Tour. I was in a headquarters company in Paris. Army law clerk."

"I was in Paris. I went AWOL to see it."

"Smart move."

"When they caught up with me, they sent me back to the States. But that was a long time ago. I mean lately. You been to Europe lately?"

"No, that was the one and only."

"Fantastic place, Europe. Fantastic. I'd go all the time if I could. I like Heidelberg. If you go to Heidelberg, you got to eat at the castle. I like London, too. A polite town. Got class. You want to go to Europe with me, Marcus?"

"Me go to Europe? When? For how long?"

"What the hell's the difference? Those are old lady questions. We go and we come back when we feel like it. I do a little business and we have ourselves some fun. Paris is big fun, I mean big fun."

"What about your business here? All those hotels. All those speakeasies."

"Yeah, well, somebody'll look after it. And it won't be all that long of a trip. Goddamn it, a man needs change. We get old fast. I'm an old son of a bitch, I feel old, I could die any time. I almost died twice already, really close. So goddamn stupid to die when there's so many other things to do. Jesus, I learned that a long time ago; I learned it in Paris from an old crone—old Algerian chambermaid with her fingers all turned into claws and her back crooked and every goddamn step she took full of needles. Pain. Pain she wanted to scream about but didn't. Tough old baby. I think she was a whore when she was young, and me and Buster

Deegan from Cleveland, we went AWOL together to see
Paris before they shot us in some muddy fucking trench,
and we wind up talking every morning to this old dame who
spoke a little English. She wore a terrycloth robe—maybe
she didn't even own a dress—and a rag on her head and
house slippers because her feet couldn't stand shoes. We
double-tipped her every day and she smiled at us, and one
day she says to me, 'M'sieur, do you have fun in Paris?' I
said I was having a pretty good time. 'You must, M'sieur,'
she said to me. 'It is necessary.' Then she give me a very
serious look, like a teacher giving you the word, and she
smiled. And I knew she was saying to me, yeah, man, I got
pain now, but I had my day long, long ago, and I still
remember that, I remember it all the time.''

I'd been watching Jack have fun all day, first with his
machine gun and then his champagne and his Rabelais and
his dream of a purple mansion; but his fun was nervous, a
frenetic motion game that seemed less like fun than like a
release of energy that would explode his inner organs if he
held it in.

We were climbing a mountain by this time, along a
two-lane road that wound upward and seemed really about
as wide as a footpath when it snaked along the edges of
some very deep and sudden drops. I saw a creek at one
point, visible at the bottom of a gorge. When you looked
up, you saw mountains to the left, and you climbed and
climbed and climbed and then made a hairpin turn and saw
a waterfall cascading down the side of a great cliff.

"Get a look at that," Jack said, pointing. "Is that some
sight?"

And at another sharp turn he told Fogarty to stop, and we
both got out and looked back down the mountain to see
how far and how steeply we had climbed; and then he
pointed upward where you could see more mountains
beyond mountains. The stop was clearly a ritual for Jack,
as was pointing out the waterfall. It was his mountain range
somehow, and he had a proprietor's interest in it. We made
a cigarette stop as we entered Haines Falls, a store where
Jack knew they carried Rameses, his exotic, Pharaonic

brand, and he dragged me to the souvenir counter and urged me to buy something.

"Buy your wife a balsam pillow or an Indian head scarf."

"My wife and I split up two years ago."

"Then you got no reason not to go to Europe. How about a cigarette box for yourself or a pinetree ashtray?"

I thought he was kidding, but he was insisting; a souvenir to seal our bargain, a trinket to affirm the working relationship. He fingered the dishes and glassware with their gaudy Catskill vistas, the thermometers framed in pine, toothbrush holders, inkstands, lampstands, photo albums, all with souvenir inscriptions burned into them, commemorating vacation time spent in this never-never land in the clouds. I finally agreed on a glass paperweight with an Indian chief in full war bonnet inside it, and Jack bought it. Forty-nine cents. The action was outrageously sentimental, the equivalent of his attitude toward that Algerian crone or the deceased brother, from whom, I would later come to know, Jack felt all his good luck had come. "All my troubles happened after Eddie died," Jack told me in the final summer of his life when he was learning how to die. Thus his replacement of the brother with Fogarty had a talismanic element to it. Talismanic paperweight, talismanic brother-substitute, talismanic memory of the Arthritic Witch of Fun. And here we were in old talismanic Haines Falls, the highest town in the Catskills, Jack said, and of course, of course, the proper place for him to stash the queenly consort of his fantasy life, the most beautiful girl I've ever known.

Jack said he once saw Charlie Northrup belly-bump a man with such force that the man did a back-flip over a table. Charlie was physical power, about six four and two forty. He had a wide, teeth-ridden smile and blond hair the color and straightness of straw, combed sideways like a well-groomed hick in a tintype. He was the first thing we saw when we entered Mike Brady's Top o' the Mountain House at Haines Falls. He was at the middle of the bar,

standing in brogans with his ankles crossed, his sportshirt
stained with sweat from armpit to armpit, drinking beer,
talking with the bartender, and smiling. Charlie's smile
went away when he met Jack eyeball to eyeball.

"Missed you the other night, Charlie," Jack said.

"Yeah. I think you're gonna keep missing me, Jack."

"That's a wrong attitude."

"May be. But I'm stuck with it."

"Don't be stupid, Charlie. You're not stupid."

"That's right, Jack. I'm not stupid."

Jack's face had all the expression of an ice cube,
Charlie's full of overheated juices. He was telling Jack now
about something I had no clue to; but from their tone there
were confidences between them. It turned out Charlie was
responsible for Jack being in the Masons. They had been
young thieves together on Manhattan's West Side in 1914,
running with The Gophers, a gang Owney Madden led until
he went to jail for murder. They both wound up in the
Bronx about 1925, with Charlie gone semi-straight as a
numbers writer and Jack a feared figure in the New York
underworld because of his insane gang tactics and his
association with the powerful Arnold Rothstein. Jack had
also opened a place he called The Bronx Theatrical Club,
whose main theatrical element was Jack's presence as a
performing psychopath. I say performing because I don't
think Jack was psychopathic in its extreme sense. He was
aberrated, yes, eccentric, but his deeds were willful and
logical, part of a career pattern, even those that seemed
most spontaneous and most horrendous. He was rising in
the world, a celebrated hijacker, and Charlie was a working
stiff with money problems. Charlie married Jimmy Biondo's sister and they vacationed in the Catskills. When times
got very rough in New York, Charlie and some two-bit
Jersey thieves bought a defunct brewery in Kingston and
went into shoestring bootlegging. In the years after, Charlie
opened his roadhouse and also became the biggest beer
distributor in Greene and Ulster counties. He was tough,
with a reputation for muscle if you didn't pay promptly for
your goods. But he was different from Jack. Just a
bootlegger. Just a businessman.

"I'm having a little meeting tomorrow night," Jack told him, "for those who couldn't make it to the last one."

"I'm booked up."

"Unbook, Charlie. It's at the Aratoga. Eight o'clock. And I'm all business, Charlie. All business."

"I never knew you to be anything else, Jack."

"Charlie, old brother, don't have me send for you."

Jack left it there, turned his back on Charlie and walked down the bar and into the table area where only one table was occupied: by that beauty in a white linen suit and white pumps; and at the table with her a five-foot-five, one-eyed, waterheaded gnome. This was Murray (The Goose) Pucinski who'd worked for Jack for the past five years.

"Oh, God, Jack, oh, God where've you been?" was Kiki's greeting. She stood to hug him.

Jack squeezed her and gave her a quick kiss, then sat alongside her.

"She behaving herself, Goose?" Jack asked the waterhead.

Goose nodded.

"How could anybody misbehave up here?" Kiki said, looking me over. I was struck by the idea of misbehaving with her. That was the first logical thing to consider when you looked at Kiki. The second was the flawless quality of her face, even underneath all that professionally applied makeup; a dense rather than a delicate beauty, large, dark eyes, a mouth of soft, round promise, and an abundance of hair, not black as Alice had said, but auburn, a glorious Titian mop. Her expression, as we visually introduced ourselves, was one of anxious innocence. I use the phrase to describe a moral condition in fragments, anxious to be gone, but with a large segment still intact. The condition was visible in the eyes, which for all their sexual innuendo and expertise, for all their knowledge of how beauty rises in the world, were in awe, I suspect, of her rarefied situation: its prisonerlike quality, its dangers, its potential cruelties, and its exhilarating glimpses of evil. By eye contact alone, and this done in a few seconds, she conveyed to me precisely how uneasy she was with The Goose as her chaperon. A quick glance at him, then at me, then a lift of

the eyebrows and twist of the pursed lips, was my clue that
The Goose was a guardian of negative entertainment value.

"I wanna dance," she said to Jack. "Jackie, I'm dying to
dance. Speed, play us something so we can dance."

"It's too early to dance," Jack said.

"No, it isn't"—and her entire body did a shimmy in
anticipation. "Come on, Joey, come on, puh-leeeze."

"My fingers don't wake up till nine o'clock at night,"
Fogarty said. "Or after six beers."

"Aw, Joey."

Fogarty hadn't sat down yet. He looked at Jack who
smiled and shrugged, and so Fogarty went to the piano on
the elevated bandstand and, with what I'd call a semipro's
know-how, snapped out a peppy version of "Twelfth Street
Rag." Kiki was up with the first four bars, pulling Jack to
his feet. Jack reluctantly took an armful of Kiki, then
whisked her around in a very respectable foxtrot, dancing
on the balls of his feet with sureness and lightness. Fogarty
segued into the "Charleston" and then the "Black
Bottom," and Kiki split from Jack and broke into bouncily
professional arm maneuvers and kicks, showing a bit of
garter.

Interested as I was in Kiki's star and garter performance,
it was Jack who took my attention. Was Legs Diamond
really about to perform in public? He stood still when Kiki
broke away, watched her for a step or two, then assessed
his audience, especially the bar where Charlie Northrup
and the barkeep were giving Jack full eyeball.

"C'mon, Jackie," said Kiki, her breasts in fascinating
upheaval. Jack looked at her and his feet began to move,
left out, right kick, right back, left back, basic, guarded,
small-dimensioned movements, and then "C'mon, dance,"
Kiki urged, and he gave up his consciousness of the crowd
and then left out, right kick, right back, left back expanded,
vitalized, and he was dancing, arms swinging, dancing,
Jack Diamond, who seemed to do everything well, was
dancing the Charleston and Black Bottom, dancing them
perfectly, the way all America had always wanted to be
able to dance them—energetically, controlled, as profes-

sionally graceful as his partner who had danced these
dances for money in Broadway shows, who had danced
them for Ziegfeld; and now she was dancing on the
mountaintop with the king of the mountain, and they were
king and queen of motion together, fluid with Fogarty's
melody and beat.

And then above the music, above the pounding of
Fogarty's foot, above the heavy breathing and shuffling of
Jack and Kiki and above the concentration that we of the
small audience were fixing on the performance, there came
the laughter. You resisted acknowledging that it was
laughter, for there was nothing funny going on in the room
and so it must be something else, you said to yourself. But
it grew in strength and strangeness, for once you did
acknowledge that yes, that's laughter all right, and you
said, somebody's laughing at them, and you remembered
where you were and who you were with, you turned (and
we all turned) and saw Charlie Northrup at the end of the
bar, pounding the bar with the open palm of his right hand,
laughing too hard. The bartender told him a joke, was my
thought, but then Charlie lifted the palm and pointed to
Jack and Kiki and spluttered to the barman and we all
heard, because Fogarty had heard the laughing and stopped
playing and so there was no music when Charlie said,
"Dancin' . . . the big man's dancin' . . . dancin' the
Charleston on Sunday afternoon . . ." and then Jack
stopped. And Kiki stopped six beats after the music had
and said, "What happened?"

Jack led her to the table and said, "We're going to have a
drink," and moved her arm and made sure she sat down
before he walked to the bar and spoke to Charlie Northrup
in such a low voice that we couldn't hear. Charlie had
stopped laughing by then and had taken a mouthful of beer
while he listened to whatever it was Jack said. Then he
swallowed the beer, and with a mirthless smile he retorted
to Jack, who did not wait for the retort but was already
walking back toward us.

"I'm trembling, brother," Charlie called to him. "Trembling." He took another mouthful of beer, swished it

around in his mouth, and spat it in a long arc after Jack. Not hitting him, or meaning to, but spitting as a child spits when he can think of no words as venomous as his saliva. Then he turned away from the direction of his spit, swallowed the last of his beer, and walked his great hulk out of the bar.

Holy Flying Christ, I said to myself when I understood Charlie's laughter and saw the arc of beer, for I understood much more than what we were all seeing. I was remembering what Jack's stylized terror could do to a man, remembering Joe Vignola, my client in the Hotsy Totsy case, a man visited not by Jack's vengeance but merely by the specter of it. I was remembering Joe on his cot in the Tombs, tracing with his eye a maze a prisoner before him had drawn on the wall, losing the way, tracing with his finger, but the finger too big, then finding a broom straw and tracing with that. And scratching his message above the maze with a spoon: *Joe Vignola never hurt nobody, but they put him in jail anyway.* Joe was dreaming of smuggling a gun in via his wife's brassiere, but he couldn't conceive of how to ask her to do such an embarrassing thing. And the district attorney was explaining almost daily to him, it's just routine, Joe, we hold 'em all the time in cases like this, an outrage, as you know, what happened, and we must have witnesses, must have them. Also a precautionary measure, as I'm sure you're aware, Joe, you're safer here. But I want to go home, Joe said, and the DA said, well, if you insist, but that's twenty thousand. Twenty thou? Twenty thou. I'm not guilty, you've got the wrong man. Oh no, said the DA, you're the right man. You're the one who saw Legs Diamond and his friends being naughty at the Hotsy Totsy. I'm not the only one, Joe said. Right, Joe, you are not the only one. We have other witnesses. We have the bartender. We have Billy Reagan, too, who is coming along nicely. An open-and-shut case, as they say.

Joe Vignola was in jail eight days when his wife got a phone call. Somebody, no name, told her: Look on such and such a page of the *Daily News* about what happened to Walter Rudolph. Walter Rudolph was the DA's corroborating witness, and two kids had found him lying off the

Bordentown Turnpike near South Amboy, wearing his blue
serge suit, his straw hat alongside him, eleven machine-gun
slugs in him.

I was called into the case at this point. Vignola's lawyer
was suddenly inaccessible to Vignola's wife, and an old
show business friend of mine, Lew Miller, who produced
Broadway shows and had patronized the Hotsy and gotten
to know Joe Vignola well enough to go to bat for him, called
me up and asked me to see what I could do for the poor
bird.

Memory of my first interrogation of Joe:

Why did you tell the cops what you saw? Why did you
identify photos of Jack Diamond and Charlie Filetti for the
grand jury?

Because I wanted people to know I had nothing to do
with it. Because I didn't want them to put me in jail for
withholding evidence. And a cop slapped me twice.

But why, really, Joe? Did you want your name in the
papers, too?

No, because Billy Reagan had talked and would be the
main witness and because the cops had at least twenty-five
other witnesses who were in the club, and they told the
same story I did, the DA said.

But, Joe, knowing what we know about Jack Diamond
and people like him, how could you do it? Was it time to
die?

Not at all. Basically, I don't approve of murder, or Jack
Diamond or Charlie Filetti either. I was brought up a
Catholic and I know the value of honesty. I know what a
citizen has to do in cases like this. Don't I hear it in church
and on the radio and in the papers about being a good
citizen? We can't let these bums take over America. If I
don't stand up and fight, how can I expect the next guy to
stand up? How could I look myself in the mirror?

But why, Joe? Lay off the bullshit and tell me for
chrissake, why?

Why? Because it takes big balls. Because Jack Diamond
was always cracking wise about the guineas and nobody is
going to say that Joe Vignola is a yellow-bellied guinea. Joe
Vignola is an Italian-descent American with big balls.

Big balls, Joe? Was that really it?
Right.
You dumb bastard.

I got in touch with the lawyer for Charlie Filetti, who
they caught in Chicago and hit with murder one. They
hadn't picked up Jack. I told the lawyer poor Joe was of no
use to the prosecution because he would not be able to
remember anything at the time, and that I wanted to be in
touch with somebody in the Diamond gang who I could
relay this message to at first hand so that Jack would also
know what Joe was up to, which was not much. The lawyer
put me on to Jimmy Biondo, who met me at the Silver
Slipper on Forty-eighth Street one night. We talked briefly,
as follows:

"You guarantee he's no pigeon?"

"I guarantee," I said.

"How?"

"Every way but in writing."

"The bum. The fuckin' bum."

"He's all right. He won't talk. Lay off the telephone
threats. He's got three kids and a nice wife. He's a nice
Italian boy like yourself. He doesn't want to hurt anybody.
He's an altar boy."

"Funeral for altar boys," said eloquent Jimmy.

"I guarantee you. What do you want from me? I'm his
lawyer. He can't fire me. He hasn't even paid me yet."

"Fuckin' . . ." said Jimmy.

"Easy does it. He won't talk."

"Fuck . . ."

"I guarantee."

"You guarantee?"

"I guarantee."

"You better fuckin' guarantee."

"I said I guarantee, and when I say I guarantee, I
guarantee."

"Fuckin' well better . . ."

"Right, Jimmy. You got my word. Joe won't talk."

"Fuck."

◆      ◆      ◆      ◆

Joe told me Jack Diamond, disguised as a Boy Scout, came through the bars of his cell one night and stood alongside Joe's bunk as he slept. "It's time to have your ears pierced," Jack said to Joe, and he shoved the blade of his Scout knife into Joe's left ear. Joe's brain leaked out through the hole.

"Help me," Joe yelled. "My ear is leaking." From the next cell somebody yelled, "Shut up, you looney son of a bitch."

But Joe didn't feel he was looney. He told the Bellevue alienist how it was when they wanted to know why he hid food under the bedclothes.

"That was for Legs Diamond. If he wants a bite to eat and I got nothing, that's trouble."

"Did it occur to you that the food would rot and give off a stench?"

"Rotten, it doesn't really matter. It's the offer that counts."

"Why did you cover your head with the blanket?"

"I wanted to be alone."

"But you were alone."

"I didn't want visitors."

"The blanket kept them away?"

"No, I could see them through the blanket. But it was better than nothing."

"Why did you hide the spoon?"

"So my visitors would have something to eat with."

"Then why did you scratch at the concrete floor with it?"

"I wanted to dig a place to hide so the visitors couldn't find me."

"How did you tear up your fingers?"

"When they took my spoon away."

"You dug at the concrete with your fingers?"

"I knew it'd take a long time; the nails'd have to grow back before I could dig again."

"Who visited you?"

"Diamond came every night. Herman Zuckman came, cut up the middle and half a dozen iron bars inside him, and wire wrapped around his stomach to keep the bars from falling out. He dripped muck and seaweed all over. 'What did you do wrong, Herman?' I said to him.

" 'Jew people have a tough life,' " he said.

"And I told him, 'You think it's easy being Italian?' "

"Any other visitors?"

"Walter Rudolph came in to cheer me up and I saw daylight through his bullet holes."

The night the dead fish leaped out of Herman's tuxedo Joe finally won his straitjacket.

The judge ordered the acquittal of Filetti after four days of trial, saying that the state had utterly failed to prove its case. Jack, still a fugitive, was never mentioned during the trial. Of the fifteen witnesses who testified, not one claimed to have seen Filetti actually shoot anybody. Joe Vignola, who was described as the state's most important witness, said he was dozing in another room when the shooting broke out and he saw nothing. His speech was incoherent most of the time.

Billy Reagan testified he was too drunk after drinking twenty shots of gin to remember what happened. Also, Tim Reagan's last words, originally said to have incriminated Diamond and Filetti, were not about them at all, a detective testified, but rather a violent string of curses.

Jack was a fugitive for eight months, and most of his gang, which was an amalgam of old-timers and remnants of Little Augie Orgen's Lower East Side Jews, drifted into other allegiances. The bond had not been strong to begin with. Jack took the gang over after he and Augie were both shot in a labor racketeering feud. Augie died, but you can't kill Legs Diamond.

Eddie Diamond died in January, 1930. Jack was still a fugitive when he met Kiki Roberts in April at the Club Abbey, and he immediately dropped Elaine Walsh. Half a dozen gangland murders were credited to his feud with Dutch Schultz during these months.

He saw the Jack Sharkey-Tommy Loughran fight at Yankee Stadium, as did Al Smith, David Belasco, John

McGraw, and half the celebrities of New York. Jack couldn't miss such a show, even if he did have to raise a mustache and sit in an upper deck to avoid recognition. He bet on Loughran, like himself a Philadelphia mick; but Sharkey, the Boston sailor, won.

The crest of his life collapsed with the Hotsy shooting. All he'd been building to for most of a decade—his beer and booze operations, the labor racketeering he built with and inherited in part from Little Augie, his protection of the crooked bucketshops which bilked stock market suckers, an inheritance from Rothstein, his connections with the dope market, and, most ignominiously, his abstract aspiration to the leadership mantle that would somehow simulate Rothstein's—all this was Jack's life-sized sculpture, blown apart by gunpowder.

Dummy, you shoot people in your own club?

Jack got the word from Owney Madden, his old mentor from Gopher days, a quiet, behind-the-scenes fellow who, after doing his murder bit, came out of Sing Sing in 1923 and with a minimum of fanfare became the Duke of New York, the potentate of beer and political power in the city's underworld. Madden brought Jack the consensus sentiment from half a dozen underworld powerhouses: Go someplace else, Jack. Go someplace else and be crazy. For your own good, go. Or we'll have to kill you.

Jack's pistol had punctuated a decade and scribbled a finale to a segment of his own life. He had waged war on Schultz, Rothstein, and half a dozen lesser gang leaders in the Bronx, Jersey, and Manhattan, but he could not war against a consortium of gangs and he moved to the Catskills. I knew some of this, and I was certain Charlie Northrup knew much more, which is why Charlie's spitting beer at Jack and mocking him to his face did not seem, to say the least, to be in Charlie's own best interest.

After Charlie walked out of the Top o' the Mountain House Kiki said she was sick of the place and wanted to go someplace and have fun, and Jack-the-fun-seeker said okay, and we stopped at a hot dog stand, Kiki's choice, and

sought out an aerial bowling alley which intrigued her and
was a first for me. A genuine bowling ball was suspended
on a long cable, and you stood aloof from the pins below
and let the ball fly like a cannon shot. It then truly or falsely
spun through the air and knocked over all the pins your luck
and skill permitted. Kiki scored sixty-eight and almost
brained the pinboy with a premature salvo, Jack got one
fourteen and I won the day with one sixty-four. Jack was
coming to respect my eye at least as much as he respected
my legal acuity.

From bowling we went to miniature golf, where we
played eighteen holes. Some holes you climbed stairs to
and putted downhill. Kiki went first at one of those, and
when you stood to the rear of her, as Jack and I
did—Fogarty and The Goose were consuming soda pop
elsewhere—you had total visibility of the girl's apparatus.
She wore rolled silk stockings with frilly black garters
about five inches above the knee, the sheerest pair of lace
panties I'd theretofore seen, and areas of the most
interesting flesh likely to be found on any mountain
anywhere, and I also include the valleys.

I see her there yet. I see her also crossing and uncrossing
her silkiness, hinting at secret reaches, dark arenas of
mystery difficult to reach, full of jewels of improbable
value, full of the *promise* of tawdriness, of illicitness, of
furtiveness, of wickedness, with possibly blue rouge on the
nipples, and arcane exotica revealed when she slips down
the elastic waistband of those sheerest of sheers. They
infected my imagination, those dark, those sheer, those
elasticized arenas of that gorgeous girl's life.

I did not know that the infection would be prophetic of
Kiki, prophetic of revelations of flesh, prophetic of panties.
Nor did I know that this afternoon, with its sprinkles of rain
interrupting our sport, would be the inspiration for Jack to
initiate his organized shakedown of hot dog stands and
miniature golf courses all over Greene and Ulster counties.

Kiki showed me a clipping once with a coincidence that
made her believe in destiny. It was an item out of Winchell,

which said, "Dot and Dash is a mustache. Yaffle is an arrest. Long cut short is a sawed-off shotgun. White is pure alcohol. Simple Simon is a diamond. . . ." It appeared the day before Kiki met Jack at a nightclub party, and she was just about to go into rehearsal for a new musical, *Simple Simon*.

I look back to those early days and see Kiki developing in the role of woman as sprite, woman as goddess, woman as imp. Her beauty and her radiance beyond beauty were charms she used on Jack, but used with such indifference that they became subtle, perhaps even secret, weapons. I cite the dance floor episode at the Top o' the Mountain House as as example, for she had small interest in whether it was Jack who danced with her or not. Her need was to exult in her profession, which had not been chosen casually, which reflected a self dancing alone beneath all the glitter of her Broadway life. "I must practice my steps," she said numerous times in my presence, and then with a small radio Jack had given her she would find suitable music and, oblivious of others, go into her dance, a tippy-tap-toe routine of cosmic simplicity. She was not a good dancer, just a dancer, just a chorus girl. This is not a pejorative reduction, for it is all but impossible for anyone to be as good a chorus girl as Kiki proved to be, proved it not only on stage—Ziegfeld said she was the purest example of sexual nonchalance he'd ever seen—but also in her photogenicity, her inability to utter a complex sentence, her candor with newspapermen, her willingness to trivialize, monumentalize, exalt, and exploit her love for Jack by selling her memoirs to the tabloids—twice—and herself to a burlesque circuit for the fulfillable professional years of her beauty and the tenacious years of Jack's public name. More abstractly she personified her calling in her walk, in her breathing, in the toss of her head, in her simultaneous eagerness and reluctance to please a lover, in her willingness to court wickedness without approving of it, and in her willingness to conform to the hallowed twentieth-century chorus-girl stereotype that Ziegfeld, George White, Nils T. Granlund, the Minskys, and so many

more men, whose business was flesh, had incarnated, and
which Walter Winchell, Ed Sullivan, Odd McIntyre,
Damon Runyon, Louis Sobol, and so many others, whose
business was to muse and gossip on the ways of this
incarnated flesh, had mythicized. And as surely as Jack
loved pistols, rifles, machine guns—loved their noise, their
weight, their force, the power they passed to him, their
sleekness, their mechanical perfections, their oily surfaces
as balm for his ulcerated gangster soul—so did he cherish
the weaponistic charms of Kiki. And as the guns also
became his trouble as well as his beloved, so became Kiki.
She did not know such ambivalence was possible when she
met Jack, but her time alone with The Goose on the
mountaintop was the beginning of her wisdom, painful
wisdom which love alone could relieve.

A quick summer storm blew up and it started to rain as
Fogarty drove Kiki, Jack, and me back to Haines Falls
after the golf. There was talk of dinner, which I declined,
explaining I had to get back to Albany. But no, no, Jack
wouldn't hear of my leaving. Wasn't I done out of a
champagne lunch by the canary scene? We went to the Top
o' the Mountain House to freshen up before we ate, and
Jack gave me the room The Goose had been using, next to
Kiki's. Jack joined Kiki in her room for what I presumed
was a little mattress action, and I pursued a catnap. But the
walls were thin and I was treated instead to a memorably
candid conversation:

"I'm going back to New York," Kiki said.

"You don't mean it," Jack said.

"I don't care what you do. I'm not staying in this prison
with that goon. He never says a word."

"He's not good at talking. He's good at other things.
Like you."

"I hate having a bodyguard."

"But your body deserves guarding."

"It deserves more than that."

"You're very irritable tonight."

"You're damn right I am."

"You've got a right to be, but don't swear. It's not ladylike."

"You're not so particular in bed about ladylike."

"We're not in bed now."

"Well, I don't know why we're not. I don't see you for two days and you show up with a stranger and don't even try to be alone with me."

"You want a bed, do you? What do you want to put in it?"

"How's this? How does it look?"

"Looks like it's worth putting money into."

"I don't want money in it."

"Then I'll have to think of something else."

"I love to kiss your scars," Kiki said after a while.

"Maybe you'll kiss them all away," Jack said.

"I wouldn't want to do that. I love you the way you are."

"And you're the most perfect thing I've ever seen. I deserve you. And you don't have any scars."

"I'm getting one."

"Where?"

"Inside. You cut me and let me bleed, and then I heal and you leave me to go back to your wife."

"Someday I'll marry you."

"Marry me now, Jackie."

"It's complicated. I can't leave her. She's in a bad way lately, depressed, sick."

"She goes to the movies. She's old and fat."

"I've got a lot of money in her name."

"She could run off with it, wipe you out."

"Where could she run I couldn't find her?"

"You trust her, but you don't trust me alone."

"She's never alone."

"What is she to you? What can she give you I can't?"

"I don't know. She likes animals."

"I like animals."

"No, you don't. You never had a pet in your life."

"But I like them. I'll get a pet. I'll get a cat. Then will you marry me?"

"Later I'll marry you."

"Am I your real lay?"

"More than that."

"Not much more."

"Don't be stupid. I could lay half the town if I wanted to—Catskill, Albany, New York, any town. Unlimited what I could lay. Unlimited."

"I want a set of those Chinese balls. The metal ones."

"Where'd you hear about those?"

"I get around. I get left alone a lot now, but I didn't always."

"What would you do with them?"

"What everybody does. Wear them. Then when nobody's around to take care of me and I get all hot and bothered, I'd just squeeze them and they'd make me feel good. I want them."

"Will you settle for an Irish set?"

"Can I keep them with me?"

"I'll see they don't get out of range."

"Well, see to it then."

"Everything was still incredible with me and Jack back then," Kiki said to me much later, remembering the sweet time. "It was thrilling just to see him from a new angle, his back, or his stomach, any part of his bare skin. He had gouges and scars from knife fights when he was a kid, and where he'd been shot and kicked and beaten with clubs and boards and pipes. I got sad up on the mountain one night looking at them all. But he said they didn't hurt him anymore, and the more I looked at them and touched them, the more they made his body special, the way his head was special. It wasn't an all white and smooth and fatty body like some I've seen but the body of a man who'd gone through a whole lot of hell. There was a long red scar on his stomach just above his belly button, where he'd almost died from a cut in a knife fight over a girl when he was fifteen. I ran my tongue over it and it felt hot. I could almost taste how much it hurt when he'd got it and what it meant now. To me it meant he was alive, that he didn't die easy.

Some people could cut their little toe and give up and bleed to death. Jack never gave up, not his body, not anything.''

Well, we all did have dinner on the mountain, and then I insisted on leaving. "It's been a special day," I told Jack, "but an odd one."

"What's so odd about it?"

"Well, how about buying a paperweight for starters?"

"Seems like an ordinary day to me," he said. I assumed he was kidding. But then he said, "Come to dinner next week. I'll have Alice cook up another roast. I'll call you during the week to set it up. And think about Europe."

So I said I would and turned to Kiki, whom I'd spoken about forty words to all day. But I'd smiled her into my goodwill and stared her into my memory indelibly, and I said, "Maybe I'll see you again, too," and before she could speak Jack said, "Oh you'll see her all right. She'll be around."

"I'll be around he says," Kiki said to me in a smart-ass tone, like Alice's whippy retort had been earlier in the day. Then she took my hand, a sensuous moment.

Everything seemed quite real as I stood there, but I knew when I got back to Albany the day would seem to have been invented by a mind with a faulty gyroscope. It had the quality of a daydream after eight whiskeys. Even the car I was to ride down in—Jack's second buggy, a snazzy, wire-wheeled, cream-colored Packard roadster The Goose was using to chauffeur Kiki around the mountains—had an unreal resonance.

I know the why of this, but I know it only now as I write these words. It took me forty-three years to make the connection between Jack and Gatsby. It should have been quicker, for he told me he met Fitzgerald on a transatlantic voyage in 1926, on the dope-buying trip that got him into federal trouble. We never talked specifically about Gatsby, only about Fitzgerald, who, Jack said, was like two people, a condescending young drunk the first time they met, an apologetic, decent man the second time. The roadster was

long and bright and with double windshields, and exterior
toolbox, and a tan leather interior, the tan a substitute, for
Gatsby's interior was "a sort of green leather conservato-
ry." But otherwise it was a facsimile of the Gatsby
machine, and of that I'm as certain as you can be in a case
like this. Jack probably read *Gatsby* for the same reason he
read every newspaper story and book and saw every movie
about gangland. I know he saw Von Sternberg's
*Underworld* twice; we did talk about that. It was one way of
keeping tabs on his profession, not pretension to culture.
He mocked Waxey Gordon to me once for lining his walls
with morocco-bound sets of Emerson and Dickens.
"They're just another kind of wallpaper to the bum," Jack
said.

I accept Jack's Gatsby connection because he knew
Edward Fuller, Fitzgerald's neighbor on Long Island who
was the inspiration for Gatsby. Fuller and Rothstein were
thick in stocks, bonds, and bucketshops when Jack was
bodyguarding Rothstein. And, of course, Fitzgerald painted a grotesque, comic picture of Rothstein himself in
*Gatsby*, wearing human molar cuff buttons and spouting a
thick Jewish accent, another reason Jack would have read
the book.

I rode with The Goose in Jack's roadster and tried to
make a little conversation.

"You known Jack long?"

"Yeah," said Murray, and then nothing for about three
miles.

"Where'd you meet him?"

"Th'army," said Murray, not spending two words where
one would do.

"You've been working with him since then?"

"No, I did time. Jack, too."

"Ah."

"I got nine kids."

Murray looked at me when he said this, and I guess I
paused long enough before I said, "Have you?" to provoke
him.

"You don't believe me?"

"Sure I believe you. Why shouldn't I?"

"People don't believe I got nine kids."

"If you say it, I believe it. That's a lot of kids. Nobody lies about things like that."

"I don't see them. Once a year. Maybe, maybe not. But I send 'em plenty."

"Uh-huh."

"They don't know what I do for a living."

"Oh?"

Then we had another mile or so of silence, except for the thunder and lightning and the heavy rain, which kept Murray creeping slowly along the snaky road down the mountain. I judged him to be about forty-five, but he was hard to read. He might've seemed older because of the menace he transmitted, even when he talked about his kids. His mouth curled down into a snarleyow smile, his lone eye like a flat spring, tightly coiled, ready to dilate instantly into violent glare. He was obviously the pro killer in the gang, which I deduced as soon as I saw him. Oxie may have had some deadly innings in his career, but he looked more like a strongarm who would beat you to death by mistake. Murray's clothes were a shade too small for him, giving him a puffy, spaghetti-filled look. I thought I detected tomato sauce stains on his coat and pants and even his eyepatch. I choose to believe he was merely a slob rather than inefficient enough to walk around with bloodstains from his last victim. I doubt Jack would have approved of that sort of coarseness.

"You workin' for Jack now?" Murray asked me.

"Tentatively," I said, wondering whether he understood the word, so I added, "for the time being I guess I am."

"Jack is a pisser."

"Is he?"

"He's crazy."

"Is that so?"

"That's why I work for him. You never know what'll happen next."

"That's a good reason."

"He was crazy in the Army. I think he was always crazy."

"Some of us are."

"I said to myself after he done what he done to me, this is a crazy guy you got to watch out for because he does crazy stuff."

"What did he do to you?"

"What did he do to me? What did he do to me?"

"Right."

"I was in the stockade at Fort Jay for raping a colonel's wife, a bum rap. I only did her a favor after she caught me in the house and I rapped her one and she fell down. Her dress goes up and she says, 'I suppose you're gonna strip and rape me,' and I hadn't figured on it, but you take what comes. So I'm in for that, plus burglary and kickin' an MP when Jack comes in to wait for his court-martial.

"'Whatcha in for?' I asked him.

"'Desertion and carrying a pistol.'

"'That's heavy duty.'

"'I figure I'll do a little time,' he said. 'They want my ass.'

"'Likewise,' I said and told him my story.

"'What'd you do before you got in?' he asks me and I tell him, 'I was a burglar.' He got a kick out of that because he done a bit for the same thing when he was a kid. So we talk and Jack gets a pint of whiskey from the corporal who made bedcheck. I don't drink that shit, so Jack asks me if I wanna drink some rain instead. It's raining out just like now, and Jack puts a cup out the window. Took about five minutes to fill it up part way, and by that time Jack's whiskey is most gone and he gets the cup of rain and gives it to me.

"'I don't want no rain,' I says to him. 'It's dirty.'

"'Who says it's dirty?'

"'Everybody says.'

"'They're wrong,' he says. 'Best water there is.'

"'You drink it,' I says, 'I don't want no part of any dirty, shitty rain.'

"'Goddamn it, I told you rain wasn't dirty. You think I'd drink rain if it was dirty?' And he takes a drink of it.

"'Anybody who'd drink rain'd shit in church,' I says to him.

"'Did you say shit in church?'

"'Shit in church and then kick it out in the aisle.'

"'That's a goddamn lie. I'd never shit in church.'

"'If you'd drink rain, you'd shit in church all right.'

"'Not me. I'd never shit in church. You hear that, goddamn it? Never!'

"'All them rain drinkers. They all shit in church.'

"'Not me, no sir. Why do you say that?'

"'I never knew an Irishman wouldn't shit in church if he thought he could get away with it.'

"'Irishmen don't shit in church. I don't believe that.'

"'I seen four Irishmen at the same time, all taking a shit in church.'

"'Polacks shit in church.'

"'I once seen an Irishman shit right in the holy water fountain.'

"'That's a goddamn lie.'

"'Then I seen two Irishmen takin' shits in the confessional boxes and about a dozen more takin' shits up on the altar all at once. I seen one Irishman shit during a funeral. Irishmen don't know no better.'

"I was layin' on my cot while this was going on. Then Jack got up and punched me in the right eye so hard I lost the sight of it. Jesus, that was a crazy thing to do. I didn't even see it comin'. I had to kick him all over the room, broke ribs and stuff. The guards pulled me off him. I woulda killed him if I knew the eye was gone, but I didn't know it then. When I saw him a week later he got down on his knees and asked me to forgive him what he done. I said, 'Fuck you, Jack,' and left him on his knees. But we shook hands before I left and I told him 'Okay, don't worry about it.' But I was still sore about it. I done six years because the MP I kicked died, and when I come out I looked Jack up because I figure he owes me a job. He thought he did a tough thing about the eye, but shit, once you get used to one eye it's just as good as two. And workin' for Jack, you get to do everything you got to do, so I got no complaints."

We were about halfway down the mountain when Murray hit the brakes, but not soon enough, and we skidded into a rock slide and smashed into a boulder that must've just landed because other little rocks kept bouncing off the car. Both of us hit the windshield, and I got a hell of a bump and a four-day headache out of it. Murray's forehead was cut, a horizontal gash like a split seam.

"We better haul ass before another one falls on top of us," Murray said, a thought I hadn't had yet since I was preoccupied with my pain. He tried backing up, but the car made a weird noise and was hard to move. He got out in the rain and so I got out after him. There was about one foot between me and about a four-hundred-foot drop, so I got carefully back inside and out Murray's door. He was pulling on the front left fender, which was smashed and rubbing against the wheel. Murray was a small man but a strong one, for the fender came almost straight at this tug. He cut his right hand on the edge of it, and when I offered him my pocket handkerchief, he shook his head and scooped up a handful of earth and grass and patted it on his forehead and then globbed a wad into his sliced right palm.

"Get in," he said, his face and hand smeared and dripping with bloody mud.

"I'll drive," I told him.

"No, I'll handle it."

"You're in no shape to drive."

"This is not your car, mister," he said in a tone that was unarguably the last word.

"All right, then, back up and turn around. I'll direct you. You're damn near over the edge right there, and it's one hell of a long way down."

It was dark now and I was wet to the underwear, standing in the middle of desolation, maybe about to be buried in a landslide, giving traffic directions to a bleeding, one-eyed psychopath who was, with one hand, trying to drive a mythic vehicle backwards up an enchanted mountain.

I'd come a long way from the K. of C. library.

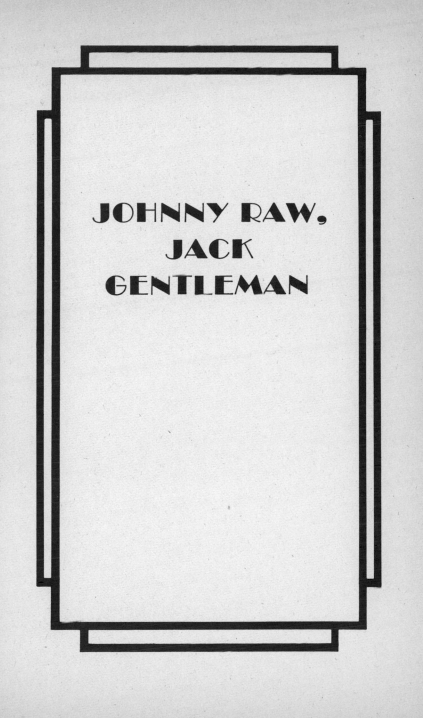

# JOHNNY RAW, JACK GENTLEMAN

Jack came to Albany to see me four days after my time on the mountain. He was full of Europe and its glories, the spas at Bad Homburg and Wiesbaden, the roulette and baccarat in the casinos where croupiers spoke six languages, the eloquent slenderness of the Parisian whore. He came to my office with Fogarty; he was in town on other business we didn't discuss but which I presume was beer supply for his expanding clientele. He handed me five hundred cash as my initial retainer.

"What do I do for this?"

"Buy a ticket to Europe."

"Jack, I've got no good reason to go to Europe."

"You owe it to your body," he said. "All that great wine and great food."

"All right, maybe," I said. But what, really, did I need with this kind of action? Where was the profit? Jack merely said he'd be in touch within the week and that was that.

Then I got a weird call at three the next morning from him, saying he'd decided to go to New York immediately instead of next week and leave for Europe in the afternoon if he got the booking, and was I ready, did I live in control of the quick decision or was I going to take a week to think it over? It meant being in Manhattan in about nine or ten hours and committing myself to the booking and turning off my practice. He kept saying, "Well? Well? What do you think?" And so I said, "All right, yes," against all sane judgment, and he said, "You're a winner, Marcus," and I rolled over and went back for two more hours. Then I closed off my Albany life with four phone calls and caught the ten thirty train to New York.

A fox terrier leaped overboard, an apparent suicide, the day the news broke aboard ship that Charlie Northrup's bloodstained Buick was found in a Sixty-first Street garage near the Brooklyn Army Base. The garage was owned by Vannie Higgins, a pal of Jack's and the crown prince of Long Island rum-runners. Oxie and a Brooklyn couple, the wife a pal of Alice's, were arrested in their apartment with an arsenal: tear-gas grenades, ammo, flares, fountain-pen pistols, bulletproof vests, and enough explosives to blow up a city block. Brooklyn war with Capone, said the papers. Oxie said only that he was sleeping on Jack's porch at Acra when two men he wouldn't identify woke him and offered him fifty bucks to take the Buick to New York and dump it. Cops saw him and the other man near a Fifty-eighth Street pier acting suspiciously, and Oxie admitted that the blocks in the Buick were to be used to run it over the stringpiece.

We were two days out of New York on the *Belgenland,* bound for Plymouth and Brussels, and suddenly our foursome—Jack, Count Duschene, Classy Willie Green, and myself—was the center of all attention. Jack was traveling under the name of John Nolan, a name of notable nautical import, and he got away with it until the radio brought news bulletins from the New York City police commissioner, a feisty old Irishman named Devane, that Jack was fleeing from a foul murder and was now on the high seas, bound for England to buy dope.

He wasn't wanted by the police, but Devane felt it his duty to alert the nations of Europe that a fiend was approaching. The Northrup car was the subject of daily bulletins in the ship's newspaper, and as the mystery of what happened to Charlie intensified, so did Jack's celebrity. Passengers snapped his picture, asked for his autograph, assured him they didn't believe such a nice person as he was would have anything to do with such terrible goings on.

The fox terrier: He appeared as I stood on the sports deck near the rail, while Jack was shooting skeet. I saw nothing chasing the dog, which came at me in a blur of brown and white, but there must have been something, for he was panicky or perhaps suddenly maddened. He took a corner at high speed, dead-ended into a bulkhead, turned around, and leaped through the rail, flailing like a crazy-legged circus clown falling off a tightrope into a net. I saw him surface once, go into a wave, bob up again, and then vanish. I doubt anyone else saw it.

A man finally came toward me at a brisk pace and asked if I'd seen his dog, and I said, yes, I'd just seen it leap overboard.

"Leap overboard?" the man said, stunned by the concept.

"Yes. He leaped."

"He wasn't thrown?"

"Nobody threw him, I can tell you that. He jumped."

"A dog wouldn't leap overboard like that."

He looked at me, beginning to believe I'd killed his dog. I assured him I'd never seen such a thing either, but that it was true, and just then he looked past me and said, "That's Legs Diamond," the dog instantly forgotten, the man already turning to someone to pass along his discovery. In a matter of minutes a dozen people were watching Jack shoot. He had been reloading during my encounter and saw the crowd before he put the shotgun again to his shoulder. He fired, missed, fired, missed. The crowd tittered, but he looked at them and silenced the titters. He fired again, missed again, fired again, missed again, and thrust the gun angrily at the man in charge of lofting the clay pigeons. Then he and I went quickly down to the parlor where Classy Willie and The Count, a dapper pair, were jointly relieving four other passengers of their vacation money in a poker game. I knew neither The Count nor Willie before I boarded the ship with Jack, but it turned out that The Count was Jack's international associate, an expert bottom dealer who spoke French, German, and Spanish and did not lose his head in the presence of too many forks, and that Classy

Willie was a card thief, specializing in ocean liners, who had been hired by Jimmy Biondo to represent him in the dope deal. Willie had a certain suavity behind his pencil-line mustache, but he was also known for his erratic violence on behalf of his employer.

I understood these relationships only much later. At this point in the trip I assumed both men worked for Jack.

I asked Jack about Oxie and the car and he said, "I take no responsibility for mugs like him once they're out of my sight."

"Goddamn it, Jack, you've got me involved in the biggest murder case in upstate New York in Christ knows how long and you give me this evasive routine?"

"Who said you're involved? I'm not even involved."

"You're involved. On the radio is involved."

"Tomorrow there'll be an earthquake in Peru and they'll try to stick me with it."

"Bullshit."

"Shove your bullshit up your ass," he said and walked away.

But he came back an hour later and sat down beside me in a deckchair, where I was brooding on my stupidity and reading Ernest Dimnet on how to think better, and he said, "How's things now?"

"I'm still involved."

"You worry a lot, Marcus. That's a bad sign. Gets you into trouble."

"I'm in trouble now because I didn't worry enough."

"Listen, you got nothing to be afraid of. Nobody's after your ass, nobody wants to put you on the spot. I never knew a fucking lawyer yet couldn't talk his way out of a sandstorm. You'll do all right if you don't lose your head."

"There was blood in that car, and Oxie was with it. And Oxie is your man."

"Somebody could've had a nosebleed. For chrissake, don't fuck me AROUND!" And he walked away from me again.

We didn't speak a direct word to each other, apart from pass the salt, for two days. My plan was to get off at

Plymouth and get the next boat home. I observed him from a distance, seeing people go out of their way for a look at him playing cards in his shirtsleeves. I saw a blond librarian ask him to dance and begin a thing with him. He was a bootlegger and, as such, had celebrity status, plus permission from the social order to kill, maim, and befoul the legal system, for wasn't he performing a social mission for the masses? The system would stay healthy by having life both ways: first, relishing Jack's achievement while it served a function, then slavering sensually when his head, no longer necessary, rolled. This insight softened my hard line of Northrup. Maybe it was all a bootlegger's feud, which somehow made the consequent death okay. Let others assess the moral obliquity in this.

Jack went through a tango with the librarian, who was from Minneapolis, a fetchingly rinsed-out blonde who wore schoolmarmish tweed suits with low-cut blouses beneath. You saw the blouses only when she peeled off the top covering as the dancing went on and on. Jack invited her to eat with us when he started up with her, and he saw to it that none of us lingered over coffee.

Then one day at dinner she wasn't there. Her empty chair went unremarked upon until Jack himself gestured toward it and said, "She wanted my autograph on her briefs," which I thought was a quaint euphemism for Jack.

Everyone laughed at the absurdity, even me.

"I gave her a bullet," Jack said, and I fell into uncertainty until he added, "She says to me, 'It's the right shape but the wrong size.' And I told her, 'Use it sideways.'"

We were swilling duck à l'orange when the librarian came up to the table with her jacket off and put her face inches away from Jack's.

"You turn women into swine," she said.

Jack nodded and bit the duck.

The morning news was that the search for Charlie Northrup had turned into one of the biggest manhunts in New York State history. He was presumed dead, but where? On top of this came a cable from Jimmy Biondo to Classy Willie, precipitating an impromptu meeting of our small quartet in Jack's cabin. Willie arrived, visibly equipped with a pistol for the first time since we boarded ship. Sensing tension, I got up to leave. But Jack said stick around, and so I did.

"Jimmy wants to call off the deal," Willie said to Jack, the first time a deal had been mentioned on the trip.

"Is that so?"

Willie handed the cable to Jack, who read it to us. "Tell our friend we can't stay with him," it said.

"I wonder what he's worried about?" Jack said.

Classy Willie didn't say anything.

"Do you know what he means, Willie?"

"He's talking about the money. Wants me to take it back to him."

"Our money?"

"Jimmy figures it's his money until we make the buy."

"Until I make the buy," Jack said.

"You know what I mean, Jack."

"No, Willie, I can't say that I do. You're a card thief. I never knew a card thief who could talk straight."

"Jimmy must figure you're too hot. The radio says they won't let you into England."

"I wasn't going to England."

"You know what I'm talking about, Jack."

"I suppose I do, Willie. I suppose I do." Jack put on his weary tone of voice. "But I'll tell you the truth, Willie, I'm not even thinking about money. What I'm thinking about is jewels."

"What jewels?"

"I got eighty grand worth and I don't know how to get them off the boat. They'll go through my luggage with a microscope."

"Let your friend Marcus carry them," Willie said. "He's legitimate."

"Not interested, thank you," I said.

"That's not a bad idea, Marcus," Jack said.

"It's a terrible idea, Jack. I want no part of hot merchandise. No part whatever. Not my line of work."

"If Marcus says no, it's no," Jack said. "We'll have to find another way."

I believe Jack already knew what he was going to do with the jewels and was merely testing me for a reaction. My reaction was so instantaneous he didn't even press it a second time. I was more attuned to Classy Willie's problem. If Biondo ever had any sense at all, he wouldn't have sent a dapper thief, a man long known as the Beau Brummell of Forty-eighth Street, to play watchdog to a man as devious as Jack.

"Jimmy wants me to get off at England and come back home with the cash," Willie said. "That was the plan if there was a hitch. He said he talked to you about it."

"I do remember something like that," Jack said. "But how do I know you won't take the cash and hop a boat for the Fiji Islands? I already told you I don't trust card thieves, Willie. I couldn't jeopardize Jimmy's money that way. No. We'll get to Germany and make the deal, and we'll all be a little fatter when we get home. Am I right, Count?"

"The beer is good in Germany," said The Count, a diplomat. "You don't have to needle it."

The façade of the deal was that Jack was to buy booze and wines, and ship them from Bremen to somewhere off Long Island. That's what I was told, by Jack. But Devane was right that Jack was after dope—heroin, which Jack had been buying in Germany since '26 when Rothstein was financing the imports. A federal charge Jack had been dodging successfully since then had come with the bustup of an elaborate smuggling scheme in which Jack was a key figure. The present destination was Frankfurt and, after the deal was wrapped up, a week's vacation in Paris. I remember when we got back to the States that a federal narcotics nabob told the press that Jack's dope smuggling made his booze and beer business look like penny-candy stuff. But people didn't pay attention to such official guff.

Their image of Jack was fixed. He was a bootlegger.
Locking him into dope was only a source of confusion.

I have vivid recollections of Jack and the press meeting
in the hallways of courthouses, at piers and railroad
stations in New York, Philadelphia, Albany, Catskill. I
remember the aggression the newsmen always showed,
persistent in their need to embarrass him with gross
questions, but persistent also in their need to show him
affection, to laugh harder than necessary at his *bons mots,*
to draw ambivalent pleasure from his presence—a man
they loved to punish, a man they punished with an odd kind
of love. When the British newsmen invaded the *Belgenland*
on our arrival in Plymouth, some thirty reporters and
cameramen pushed their way into Jack's stateroom to be
greeted by the presence himself, clad in black slippers,
sky-blue silk pajamas with a white chalk stripe, a navy-blue
silk robe, and a Rameses between index and middle fingers.
The British behaved no differently from their American
brethren, except that Jack's being a foreigner diminished
their need to insult him for the sake of the homeland. But
their self-righteousness shone through in their questions:
Why does America tolerate gangsters? How long have you
been a gangster? Was Mr. Charles Northrup murdered at
your order? Do you think gangsterism will end when
Prohibition ends? How many men have you killed in your
life? What about Capone and your Brooklyn arsenal?

Jack treated them like children, laughing at their requests
for a laundry list of his victims. "First off, boys, I'm not a
gangster, only a bootlegger. There are no gangsters in
America. Too easy to get rich other ways. I'm just a
civilized citizen. Not a dese, dem, and dose guy. Just a man
of the people, trying to make a dollar. Over here getting the
cure. Got some stomach trouble and I was advised to go to
Vichy and Wiesbaden and take the waters. Brooklyn
arsenal? I own nothing in Brooklyn. Capone used to work
for me years ago, driving a truck, but I haven't seen him in
years. That feud is a lot of nonsense. I get along with
people. I'm a legitimate citizen. You newspaper guys

scream at the cops to pick me up, and they hold me a few days and find out I'm clean and let me go. I'm not claiming you treat me wrong, but I never see anybody write big headlines when they tell me the charge don't stick. I'm sick of headlines, boys. I came to Europe to get away from it all for a while. Leave that hubbub behind. Make a kind of grand tour on my own, take the waters and cure what ails me. You can understand that, can't you, fellows?"

Sure they could.

Jack's fame at this point was staggering. About four hundred Englishmen had come to the pier by six thirty just to get a glimpse of him. The press of the whole Western world was following our transatlantic voyage, front-paging it with an intensity not quite up to what they did for Byrd, Peary, and other world travelers, but I'll bet with more reader interest. One English paper was so anxious for a story that it invented a phone interview with Jack two days before our boat reached an English pier. "I'm here in London on a secret mission," they quoted him as saying.

So the newsmen, installing Jack in the same hierarchy where they placed royalty, heroes, and movie stars, created him anew as they enshrined him. They invented a version of him with each story they wrote, added to his evil luster by imagining crimes for him to commit, embellishing his history, humanizing him, defining him through their own fantasies and projections. This voyage had the effect of taking Jack Diamond away from himself, of making him a product of the collective imagination. Jack had imagined his fame all his life and now it was imagining him. A year hence he would be saying that "publicity helps the punk" to another set of newsmen, aware how pernicious a commodity it could be. But now he was an addict, a grotesquely needy man, parched for glory, famished for public love, dying for the chance at last to be everybody's wicked pet.

He called the stateroom press conference to a halt after fifteen minutes and said he had to get dressed. The newsmen waited and he joined them on deck, clad now in his blue pinstriped suit, his wide-brimmed white felt hat, his seven-and-a-half-B black wingtips, his purple tie, and his Knight Templar pin in his lapel.

"Hello, boys," he said, "what else do you want from me?"

They talked for another quarter hour and asked, among other things, about that lapel pin; and a story goes with that.

When we talked after the press left, Jack told me that Charlie Northrup was why he was in the Masons. Back in the Bronx in the mid-twenties Jack was playing cards in the back room of his garish Theatrical Club, orange and black decor, and Charlie was sitting in. For no reason he could remember, Jack wondered out loud what a jack was, the picture card. Charlie told him the symbolic meaning of a knave among kings and queens, and Jack liked the whole idea.

Charlie talked about the Masons and their symbols, and it was like the dawn of a new era for Jack. He pumped Charlie for more, then talked him into proposing him as a candidate in the order. He went through in a whoosh and obviously with attention to all the arcane mumbo jumbo he had to memorize. The Masonic books I inherited from him were well marked and annotated in the margins, in his handwriting.

Alongside one section on an old Templar rite of initiation, a Christly pilgrimage through red, blue, black, and then the final white veils of the temple, Jack had noted: "Good stuff. Sounds like one of my dreams."


Just after meeting the British press Jack complained to me of itching hands, small red dots which gave up a clear fluid when squeezed. The broken pustules then burned like dots of acid. A passenger shot off three of his toes at skeet and blamed Jack for hexing the weapon. Then the Minneapolis librarian cut her wrists, but chose against death and summoned help. Her condition became common knowledge on the ship.

I saw Jack on deck alone after that, toying with a rosary, the first time I knew he carried one. He was not praying—only staring at it, strung like webbing through his fingers, as if it were a strange, incomprehensible object.

The night we were steaming toward Plymouth, a steward came to Jack's room with a message from the captain that the British authorities had definitely proclaimed Jack *persona non grata*. Stay out, you bum. The message jolted him, for it suddenly put our destination in jeopardy. What would Belgium do? And Germany?

Jack came to my stateroom and said he wanted to go up on deck and talk, that he didn't trust the walls. So we walked in the sea-sweetened night along the main deck where a few night walkers took the air, most memorably a rheumatic old aristocratic woman with a belief in the curative power of voyaging that was so religious she left her deckchair only during storms and meals, and to sleep and, I presume, to pee. She chewed tobacco and had a small pewter spittoon alongside her chair which she would pick up and spit her little bloody gobs into in a most feminine manner, that is, through taut, narrow lips.

She was the only witness to my conversation with Jack, and her presence and periodic spitting were the only intrusions on our conversation, apart from the splash of the sea, as we talked and walked, up and then back, in our desolated section of deck. We talked only of Jack's rejection by England until he decided to get to the point.

"Marcus, I want you to do me a favor."

"A legal one?"

"No."

"I thought as much. The jewels. I told you I want no part of it, Jack."

"Listen to me. This is a lot of money. Do you believe in money?"

"I do."

"So do I."

"But I don't want to go to jail to get it."

"How many lawyers you know ever went to jail?"

"A few, and you'd have a point if we were back in Albany."

"I told you a long time ago you were a thief in your heart."

"No, we're still not talking about thievery."

"Right. This is just a proposition. You don't have to take it."

Jack then took from his inside coat pocket a long slender box, and we paused under one of the wall lights so I could view its contents: an array of gems, rings, and necklaces. Some jewel thief had stolen them, fenced them, and they'd found their way to Jack, the internationalist, who would refence them in Europe. I knew he hadn't stolen them. He wasn't above such activity, just afield of it. No longer a burglar. He'd failed at that as a teen-ager and graduated to the activity that conformed to his talent, which was not stealth but menace.

"They don't take up much space," Jack said, and I nodded and made no answer.

"I planned to get rid of them in Brussels, but they're too hot to carry. I mean look at that"—and he held up a ruby for me to admire. "It's kind of famous, I'm told, and where it came from is even more famous."

"I don't think I'm interested."

"My suitcase has special bindings for this stuff. You could get it off the boat and through customs. But not me, not now."

I toyed with it. NOTED UPSTATE LAWYER CAUGHT WITH MRS. ASTOR'S FAVORITE RUBY, Or was it Mrs. Carnegie's? Or that tobacco-chewing lady aristocrat behind us, whoever she might be?

"If you don't handle them, I dump them. Now."

"Dump them?"

"Overboard."

"Christ, why do that? Why not hide them in a chandelier and come back later for them? Isn't that how it's done?"

"Fuck 'em," Jack said. "I don't want anything to do with this goddamn boat again once I get off it. It's a jinx."

"A jinx? You don't really believe in jinxes."

"I'd be fucking well dead if I didn't. Are you game? Yes or no."

"No."

He walked to the railing and I trailed him, expecting the next ploy in the act. A final appeal to my greed.

"You wanna watch?" he said, and so I moved alongside him in time to see him tip the box and see, yes, jewels falling, a few, and disappearing in shadow long before they hit the water. He tipped the box further and a few more plummeted toward the deep, then he shook it empty, looked at me, and, while looking, let the box flutter toward the water. It flipped a few times, made a silent plop we could see because it was white, and was then glommed by the blackness.

Jack was in shirtsleeves, sitting alone at the card table where Classy Willie fleeced the suckers, when I came up for brunch one day. I ate and then watched Jack playing solitaire and losing. I sat across from him and said, "I was planning to get off this tub and go home, but I think I'll stay on for the full treatment."

"Good. What changed your mind?"

"I don't know. Maybe the jewels. But I think I decided to trust you. Is that a mistake?"

"Trust me with anything but women and money."

"I also want a straight answer on Charlie Northrup. Is that asking too much?"

Jack mused, then with high seriousness said, "I think he's dead. But I'm not sure. If he's dead, it wasn't murder. That I am sure of."

"That's straight?"

"That's as straight as I can say it."

"Then I guess I have to believe it. Deal the cards."

He picked them up and shuffled. "Blackjack," he said and, after burying a card, dealt us both a hand. I had eighteen. He had twenty, which he showed me before I could bet. I looked blank and he said only, "Watch," and then dealt six hands, face up. I got between thirteen and seventeen in all six. He got twenty four times and two blackjacks.

"Impressive. Are you always that lucky?"

"They're marked," he said. "Never play cards with a thief." He tossed the deck on the table, leaned back, and looked at me.

"You think I killed Northrup."

"You say you didn't. I told you I accept that."

"You don't convince me."

"Maybe it's the other way around."

He put his coat on and stood up. "Let's go out on deck. I'll tell you a couple of stories." I followed and we found our way back to the desolate spot where he'd dumped the jewels. The old lady was there, and it was still as private as any place on deck.

"How are you today?" Jack said to the old dame, who took the remark first as an intrusion, then looked at Jack as if he were invisible. He shrugged and we walked to the rail and looked down at the waves and at our foamy wake.

"I dumped a guy in the water once over marked cards."

I nodded, waited. He stared out at the ocean and went on: "A card game in a hotel. It was the first time I ever met Rothstein. I was working as a strikebreaker with Little Augie, breakin' heads, just out of jail. A bum. I was a bum. Augie says to me, 'You wanna work strongarm at a card game?' And I said all right and he sent me to this hotel room and there's Rothstein, the cocksucker, and he says to me, 'What happened to your head?' 'Nothin' happened to it,' I said. 'That haircut,' he said. 'You look like a skinned rabbit, skinned by somebody who don't know how to skin. Get a haircut for pity's sake.' Can you imagine that son of a bitch? He's got seventy-six grand in his pocket, he told me so, and he tells me get a haircut. Arrogant bastard. He was right about the haircut. A barber-school job. Awful. I tell you I was a bum on the street and I looked like one. But he made me feel like a zero.

"So the game went on and there's this high roller—let me call him Wilson—who's challenging Rothstein. There's other players, but he wants to beat A. R., who's the king.

And he's doing it. Wins eleven thousand one hand, eight the next, in five thousand-dollar freezeout. Rothstein has two men in the bathroom looking over the decks Wilson brought, and they find the marks, little tits on the design in the corner. First-rate work by the designer. Rothstein hears the news and calls a break but doesn't let on, and then tells me to brain Wilson if he gets out of hand, and I say all right because he's paying me. He bottom-deals Wilson a six and Wilson calls him on it. Then A. R. says never mind about bottom dealing, what about a man who brings paper into a legitimate game? And when Wilson stood up, I brained him. Didn't kill him. Just coldcocked him and he went down. When he came to, they told me to take him someplace he wouldn't be a bother. They didn't say kill him. I took him to the river with a driver and walked him to the edge of a dock. He offered me four grand, all he had left from the game, and I took it. Then I shot him three times and dumped him in. It turned out he had three kids. He was a cheater, but he was complicated. He looked at me and said, 'Why? I give you the four grand.' His life had to be complicated with three kids and I killed him. I wanted the four grand bad and I knew he had it. But I never killed anybody before and I tell you I blame Rothstein. Maybe I wouldn't have killed him if he didn't say that about the haircut, make me feel I was such a bum. I knew I was a bum, but I didn't think it showed so much. With the four grand I wasn't a bum anymore. I bought a new suit and got a haircut at the Waldorf-Astoria.''

The money inspired Jack. He and his brother Eddie met one Ace O'Hagan, who drove for Big Bill Dwyer, the king of Rum Row. Dwyer had the Coast Guard, Jersey City, and part of Long Island on his payroll, and Jack gave Ace fifty to connect him to Dwyer for a job. Ace called Dwyer from the bar where he and the Diamond boys were drinking and found Dwyer was partying and wouldn't be back. Then, in the back of Jack's car, with Eddie driving, Jack had another idea and stuck a pistol in O'Hagan's ear and asked for the location of Dwyer's most vulnerable drop.

"He wouldn't tell me," Jack said, "so I smashed his nose with the pistol and he flooded himself. Bled all the way to the Bronx where I knew we could get a truck. I told him I'd burn his toes to cinders if he didn't tell me, and he told and we packed his nose with toilet paper and headed for Dwyer's smallest drop in White Plains. I cooked up a story that we were sent to load up the truck for a millionaire named Riley, a fellow Dwyer was doing business with, and Ace was the convincer. He talked the two guys guarding the drop into loading the truck with Scotch and champagne, and on the way back to the city, he says to me, 'Dwyer'll kill you.' And I said, 'Bill's a nice guy from what I hear. He wouldn't hurt a fellow with a little ambition.'

"Then we took Ace to the hospital and I paid to get his nose fixed up. We kept him at our rooms till I figured out what to do next, and during the night he says to Eddie, 'He's going to kill me, isn't he?' And Ed told him, 'No, I don't think so. If he was going to kill you, why would he pay for your nose?' "

Jack then went to Rothstein with a proposition.

"Listen, I have quite a lot of booze. I mean quite a lot."

"What are you asking?" Rothstein said, surprised Jack had anything of value besides his pistol.

"The going rate."

"The rate varies. Quality talks."

"Taste it yourself."

"I drink very little. Only at bar mitzvahs and weddings. But I have a friend who drinks nicely and understands what he drinks."

Jack led Rothstein and friend to the West Side garage where the booze truck was parked. The genuine article, said the taster.

"I take it you imported these goods yourself," A. R. said.

"Since when does Arnold Rothstein worry about such details?"

"In some ways, I'm particular about whose pockets my friends pick."

"I'll tell you straight. It's Dwyer's stock."

Rothstein laughed and laughed and laughed.

"That's quite a daring thing, to do this to Big Bill. And I'm laughing also because Bill owes me for several loads of whiskey for which he borrowed a certain sum, and so it's just possible you're trying to sell me goods with a personal interest to me."

"Dwyer doesn't have to know you bought the stuff."

Rothstein laughed again at this devious fellow.

"If I had two more trucks, I could get you this much twice over," Jack said. "That's also part of my proposition. Fit me out with two fast trucks and I'll keep you hip-deep in booze."

"You're moving very fast," said A. R.

"Just a young fellow trying to get ahead," said Jack.

Rothstein came to an end of business dealing with Dwyer as a result of Jack Diamond, the underworld *arriviste*, who, the day after Rothstein bought him two trucks, went back to the White Plains drop and, with his new assistants, and their new shotguns, newly sawed off, cleaned the place out down to the last bottle.

Jack was notorious as a hijacker by 1925, Rothstein's crazy—his own man, however—nabob at his Theatrical Club by then, and making enemies like rabbits make rabbits.

"I felt the pellets hit me before I heard the noise, and I saw the cut barrel sticking out of the window as the car passed before I felt the pain. I scrunched sideways below the bottom level of the window so they couldn't fire another one except through the metal door, and while I was down I heard their wheels scream, and I knew I had to come up to steer when I felt the bullet hit my right heel. I didn't run into anything because there was nothing to hit, just traffic way off and no intersection or parked cars. I was around a Hundred and Sixth Street when I looked up and saw them going away. I knew I had to stop. Make them think I was out of it. I veered off to the curb and put my head back on the seat, like a collapse. Wet with blood, and then the pain

came. Bloody heel. A woman looked in at me, scared, and
ran off. I saw the car away up the block, turning off Fifth,
probably coming back to inspect their work. My car was
stalled by this time. I started it and saw my hat on the floor,
a new straw sailor, the brim half shot off. I lifted my foot,
trying not to let the heel touch the floor, put the car in gear,
clutch, gas. Goddamn but that pain was heavy. People were
out there hiding behind parked cars. I had to get away, so I
turned off Fifth then, touched my head. The blood was
everywhere and the fucking pain was incredible. I headed
for Mount Sinai, the only hospital I knew, a few blocks
back on Fifth. 'Don't let the toes go dead or I'm through
driving. Don't think about the blood. Move the toes.' You
know what else I thought? I wondered could you buy an
artificial heel. They weren't following me. Probably pissed
now that they knew they didn't kill me. My vision was
going on me, the pain getting to where it counted. 'Don't
black out now, tough monkey. Here we go.' Then, Jesus, a
red light. I was afraid if I ran it I'd get hit, and then I'd be
dead for sure. Bleed to death. So I waited for the light, if
you can believe that, a goddamn lake of blood on the floor
and another lake I'm sitting in. My ass floating in blood,
ruining the suit, the hat already ruined. I didn't see the face
behind the muzzle of the shotgun, but I saw the driver. Ace
O'Hagan. He'd be smiling, remembering the night his own
blood flowed all over the seat. Ace would pay. And Ace
would tell me who the shooter was because Ace couldn't
take the pain. I promised I'd make him pick me out a new
suit and hat before I did the son of a bitch. Then I was
almost to the hospital, and I remembered my pistol and
threw it out the window. Didn't want to get caught with that
goddamn thing. I opened the car door and I remember
thinking to myself, is my underwear clean? Imagine that? I
moved the bum leg then, limped toward the door, and I
started to spin. I spun through the doorway and began to
topple and just inside, mother, here comes the floor.

"It was a guinea mob from the Bronx did it. I'd lifted
some of their dope. But I got the bum who led them. He
floated up the East River wearing a stolen watch. The boys

dressed like cops the day they went to his house to get him. O'Hagan, that prick, I got him good, too. The fish ate his fingers. And he named the shooter like I knew he would. A greaseball from St. Louis. I got *him* in a whorehouse.''

It wasn't until after Jack died that I heard the whorehouse story. Flossie told it to me one night at Packy Delaney's Parody Club in Albany, one of Jack's latter-day hangouts. The Floss worked at Packy's as a singer and free-lance source of joy. She and I had no secrets, physical or professional, from each other.

"He was a handsome boy," she began, "with hair like Valentino, shiny and straight and with a blue tint to it because it was so black. Maybe that's why they called him Billy Blue. And they always said from St. Loo whenever they said his name. Billy Blue from St. Loo. I don't think his real name was Blue because he was Italian, like Valentino. He talked and laughed at the bar just like a regular fella, but you know they just ain't no regular fellas anymore, not since I was a kid in school. They all got their specialties. I never would've figured him for what he was. I never even figured him for carryin' a gun. He looked too pretty.

"I was working in Loretta's place on East Thirty-third Street, her own house which she'd lived in alone since her husband was clubbed to death by two fellas he tried to cheat with loaded dice. Loretta had been in the life when she was young and went back to it after that happened. It was a nice place, an old town house with all her old kerosene lamps turned into electric, and nice paintings of New York in the old days, and a whole lineup of teapots she'd collected when she went straight. We were as good as there was in the city and we got a lot of the swells, but we also got a lot of business from hoodlums with big money. Billy was one of those.

" 'What's your name?' he says to me when he come in.

" 'The Queen of Stars, that's my name.'

" 'Beautiful Queen of Stars,' he says to me. 'I'm going to screw love into you.'

"Nobody knew my real name and they never would. And

it's not Flossie neither. My old man would've died of
shame if he knew what I was doin', and I didn't want to
hurt him more than I already done. So I picked Queen of
Stars when Loretta asked me what my name was. I was
thinking of Queen of Diamonds, but I never figured I'd ever
get any diamonds, and I was dead right about that. All I
ever got was rhinestones. So I said Stars because I had as
much right to them as anybody livin'. Then Loretta said
okay and we went from there to business, that lousy
business. You couldn't get out once you were in because
they hooked you. They even charged you for the towels.
And the meals? You'd think it was some swanky place the
way they priced everything. Then they took half what you
made, and by the time you were done payin', what you had
left wasn't worth sockin' away. And try and quit. Marlene
got it with a blackjack in the alley, and she didn't quit
anymore. They even beat up Loretta once after she
complained about how much she had to pay the guys up
above. The only thing to do was forget it. Just work and
don't try to beat 'em out of anything because you couldn't.
They were bastards, all of 'em, and a girl had no chance. I
saved what I could and figured when I got enough money,
I'd make a move. But I never did because I never knew
where to move to.

"So Billy Blue, he called me by my full name anyway.
Some of them called me Queenie and most everybody that
knew me good called me Stars, but he was one of the few
called me the whole thing. I liked him. Most of them I
didn't like, but most I didn't even look at. Billy was pretty
to look at. He got me to sit on the edge of my oak dresser,
and then he walked into me. He had his pistol in his hand
and stuck it in my mouth and told me to suck it. Jeez, that
got me. I was scared as hell. It tasted like sour, oily stuff
and I kept thinking, if he gets too excited when he comes,
he'll blow a hole in my head. But what could I do?

" 'You like my pistol?' he asks me.

"Now what do you say to a goofy question like that? I
couldn't say anything anyway with the thing in my mouth,
but I tried to smile and I give him a nod and he seemed to

like that. You can't understand how a nice-lookin' fella like that could be so bugs. The first bug I ever had stuck a feather duster up his hiney, his own duster he brought with him, and jumped around the room makin' noises like a turkey. All I did was sit on the bed so he could look at me while he did his gobbles.

"So I'm on the table and Billy's doing his stuff and I got the pistol in my mouth when the door opens and in comes Jack Diamond and two other guys, one of them was The Goose with his one eye and the other was fat Jimmy Biondo, and they got guns out, but not Jack, who was just lookin' around with them eyes of his that looked right through doors and walls, and The Goose shoots twice. One bullet hit the mirror of my oak dresser. The other one got Billy in the right shoulder, and he let go the pistol, which fell out of my mouth onto the floor and cut my lip. Billy didn't fall. He just spun around and stared at the men, with nothing on him at all but the safety.

"Jack looked at me and said, 'It's all right, Stars, don't worry about anything.'

"I was scared as hell, but I felt sorry for Billy because he looked so pretty, even if he was bugs. I started to get off the table, but The Goose says to me 'Just stay there,' and so I did, because he was the meanest-looking guy I ever saw. Jack was just lookin' at Billy and gettin' red in the face. You could see how mad he was, but he didn't talk. He just stared, and all of a sudden he takes a gun out of his coat pocket and shoots Billy in the stomach three times, and Billy falls sideways on my bed, bleedin' all over the new yellow blanket I had to pay eleven bucks for after a customer peed all over my other one and the pee smell wouldn't wash out.

"Loretta came runnin' then, and was she mad.

"'Why the hell'd you do that here?' she asked Jack. 'What'm I supposed to do with him? Goddamn it all, Jack, I can't handle this.'

"Billy was moanin' a little bit, so I sat down alongside him, just to be near him. He looked at me like he wanted me to do somethin' for him, get a doctor or somebody, but I

couldn't do anything except look at him and nod my head, I
was so scared. I thought if they decided to leave maybe I
could help him then.

" 'We'll take him with us,' Jack said. 'Wrap him up.'

"The Goose and Biondo walked over to the bed and
stood over Billy. Billy's eyes were still open and he looked
at me.

" 'It's sloppy,' The Goose said, and he took an ice pick
out of his coat and punched it half a dozen times through
Billy's temples, first one side then the other. It happened so
fast I couldn't not look. Then he and Jimmy Biondo
wrapped Billy in my yellow blanket and carried him down
the back way to the alley. Billy was still straight up and still
had the safety on. I'd told him I was clean, that I got regular
checkups, but he wore it anyway. I didn't see The Goose or
Biondo again for years, but I saw Jack quite a lot. He was
our protector. That's what they called him anyway. Some
protector. It was him and his guys beat up Loretta and
Marlene—the bastards, the things they could do and then
be so nice. But they also took care nobody shook us down
and nobody arrested us. I don't know how he did it, but
Jack kept the cops away, and my whole life I never been in
jail except for being drunk. Jack didn't own us, though. I
always heard Arnold Rothstein did, but I never knew for
sure. Loretta never told us anything. Jack did own some
places later and got me a job in a House of All Nations he
was partners in, up in Montreal. I was supposed to be either
a Swede or a Dutchie because of my blond hair. Jack
brought me back down to Albany a couple of years later
and I've been here ever since.

"I really hardly knew him, saw him in Loretta's a few
times, that's all, until he gave Billy Blue his. Then one night
about a month later he come in and buys me a real drink.
None of that circus water Loretta dished us out when the
chumps were buying. Jack bought the real stuff for us.

" 'I'm sorry about that whole scene, Stars,' he said, 'but
we had to settle a score. Your guinea friend tried to kill me
six months ago.'

"Jack took my fingers and ran them over the back of his

head where he said there were still some shotgun pellets. It was very bumpy behind his left ear.

" 'Were you scared, Stars?'

" 'Was I! I been sick over it. I can't sleep.'

" 'Poor kid. I was really sorry to do that to you.'

"He was still holding my hand and then he rubbed my hair. The first thing you know we were back up in my room and we really got to know one another, I'll tell the world."

The Wilson, Rothstein, O'Hagan, and Blue confessions came out of Jack so totally without reservation that I told him, "I believe you about Northrup now."

"Sometimes I tell the truth."

"I don't know as I'm so sure why you've told me all these stories, though."

"I want you to know who you're working for."

"You seem to trust me."

"If you ever said anything, you'd be dead. But you know some people well enough they'd never talk. I know you."

"I take that as a compliment, but I'm not looking for information. Now or ever."

"I know that. You wouldn't get a comma out of me if I didn't want to give it. I told you, I want you to know who I am. And who I used to be. I changed. Did you get that? I come a long way. A long fucking way. A man don't have to stay a bum forever."

"I see what you mean."

"Yeah, maybe you do. You listen pretty good. People got to have somebody listen to them."

"I get paid for that."

"I'm not talking about pay."

"I am. I'm for sale. It's why I went to law school. I listen for money. I also listen for other reasons that have nothing to do with money. You're talking about the other reasons. I know that."

"I knew you knew, you son of a bitch. I knew it that night you cut Jolson up that you talked my language. That's why I sent you the Scotch."

"You're a prescient man."

"You bet your ass. What does that mean?"

"You don't have to know."

"Blow it out your whistle, you overeducated prick."

But he laughed when he said it.

My memories of Jack in Europe during our first stops are like picture postcards. In the first he walks off the *Belgenland* at Antwerp in company of two courteous, nervous Belgian gendarmes in their kicky bucket hats and shoulder straps. He had hoped to sneak off the ship alone and meet us later, but helpful passengers pointed him out to the cops and they nailed him near the gangway.

Down he went but not without verbal battle, assertion of his rights as an American citizen, profession of innocence. In the postcard Jack wears his cocoa-brown suit and white hat and is held by his left arm, slightly aloft. The holder of the arm walks slightly to the rear of him down the gangplank. The second officer walks to their rear entirely, an observer. The pair of ceremonial hats and Jack's oversized white fedora dominate the picture. They led the angry Jack to an auto, guided him into the back seat, and sat on either side of him. A small crowd followed the action. The car turned a corner off the pier into the thick of an army that had been lying in wait for the new invasion of Flanders. Poppies perhaps at the ready, fields of crosses under contract in anticipation of battle with the booze boche from the west. Four armored cars waited, along with six others like the one carrying Jack, each with four men within and at least fifty foot-patrolmen armed with clubs or rifles.

You can see Jack's strong suit was menace.

We left Belgium the next day, the twerps, as Jack called them, finally deciding Jack must be expelled by train. Jack chose Germany as his destination and we bought tickets. The American embassy involved itself by not involving itself, and so Jack was shunted eastward to Aachen, where the Belgian cops left off and the German *Polizei* took over. A pair of beefy Germans in mufti held his arms as he looked over his shoulder and said to me through a frantic, twisted mouth: "Goddamn it, Marcus, get me a goddamn lawyer."

Instead of turning the money over to Classy Willie, Jack gave a hundred and eighty thousand of it to me, some in a money belt, which gave me immediate abdominal tensions, and the rest inside my Ernest Dimnet best seller, *The Art of Thinking,* out of which we cut most of the pages. I carried thirty thousand in thousand-dollar bills in the book and kept the book in the pocket of my hound's-tooth sport jacket until I reached Albany. The money that didn't fit into the book and the money belt we rolled up and slid into the slots in Jack's bag reserved for the jewels. And the bag became mine.

Police were still dragging lakes all over the Catskills. They preferred to do that rather than follow the tip that led to a six-mile stretch of highway near Saugerties that was paved the day after Charlie disappeared.

Jack's home was searched; Alice was nowhere to be found. A shotgun and rifle in a closet were confiscated. Fogarty was seminude with a buxom Catskill waitress of comparable nudity when the raid came.

Life went on.

I noticed that Jack had a luminous quality at certain moments, when he stood in shadow. I suspect a derangement of my vision even now, for I remember that the luminosity intensified when Jack said that I should carry a pistol to protect myself (he meant to protect his money) and then offered me one, which I refused.

"I'll carry the stuff, but I won't defend it," I said. "If you want that kind of protection give it to The Count to take home."

Since that perception of Jack's luminosity, I've read of scientists working to demystify psychic phenomena who claim to have photographed energy emitted by flowers and leaves. They photograph them while they are living, then cut them and photograph them in progressive stages of dying. The scientists say that the intense light in the living flower or leaf is energy, and that the luminous quality fades slowly until desiccation, at which point it vanishes.

I already spoke of Jack's energy as I saw it that memorable Sunday in the Catskills. The luminosity was further evidence of it, and this finally persuaded me of a world run not by a hierarchy of talents but by a hierarchy of shining energetics. In isolation or defeat some men lapse into melancholia, even catatonia, the death of motion a commonplace symptom. But Jack was volatile in his intensifying solitude, reacting with anger to his buffetings, also trying to convince, bribe, sweet-talk, harass his way out. At Aachen he argued with the German cops, saying, yes, he had the same name as the famous gangster, but he wasn't the same man. In protest of their disbelief he did a kind of Indian war dance in the aisle of the first-class coach, a dance at which one could only marvel. Ah, the creative power of the indignant liar.

I remember my own excitement, the surge of energy I felt rising in myself from some arcane storage area of the psyche when I strapped on the money belt. No longer the voyeur at the conspiracy, I was now an accessory, and the consequence was intoxicating. I felt a need to drink, to further loosen my control center, and I did.

At the bar I found a woman I'd flirted with a day or so earlier and coaxed her back to my cabin. I did not wait to strip her, or myself, but raised her dress swiftly, pulled her underclothing off one leg, and entered her as she sat on the bed, ripping her and myself in the process so that we both bled. I never knew her name. I have no recollection of the color of her hair, the shape of her face, or any word she might have said, but I still have an indelible memory of her pubic region, its color and its shape, at the moment I assaulted it.

No one suspected me of carrying The Great Wad, not even Classy Willie. I passed along the sap question to Willie over drinks on the train out of Belgium. "Did Jack ever give you back Biondo's bankroll?'' He gave me a hangdog look that deflated his dapper façade and reduced him forever in my mind to the status of junior villain.

The Berlin lawyer I contacted when Jack was grabbed at Aachen and held for four days was named Schwarzkopf, his name the gift of a German detective who took a liking to Jack and spoke English to him, calling him "der Schack,"'a mythic nickname the German press had invented. (The French called Jack Monsieur Diamant; the Italians, Giovanni Diamante; and he was "Cunning Jackie" to the British.)

Schwarzkopf turned out to be one of Berlin's leading criminal lawyers, but he failed to delay Jack's deportation for even a day. He even failed, when it became clear that Germany was not an open door, to get Jack aboard the liner I'd booked us on out of Bremen. The liner said no.

Nevertheless, Jack commissioned Schwarzkopf with a one grand retainer to sue the German government for mistreatment and expenses, and to grease enough levers to get him back into Germany when the fuss went away. It was typical of Jack not to yield to what other men would consider the inevitable.

When we met Schwarzkopf in the palm garden of the Bremen hotel where Jack was staying, he brought along his nephew, a young, half-drunk playwright named Weissberg, who in turn brought along a gum-chewing, small-breasted, brassiereless, and dirty little whore, dirtier than street whores need to be. She spoke only three words near the end of our conversation, stroking Weissberg's silky black mustache and calling him *"Mein schön scheizekopf."*

Weissberg had written a well-received play about burglars, pimps, and pickpockets in Berlin, but he'd never met anybody in the underworld with the exalted status of Jack and so he'd persuaded Schwarzkopf to arrange a meeting. The violinist and accordion player were sending out Straussian strains suitable to palm gardens as we all drank our dunkelbock and schnapps under an open sky. The tables were small, and so Classy Willie and The Count, who both carried weapons now, sat apart from our quartet, just as Fogarty and The Goose had on the mountain. Jack, like the aristocratic Germans around us, had an acute sense of class distinction.

Jack's German mood, after he was refused first-class passage, seemed, finally, glum. That's how I read it, and I was wrong. He was more disturbed than that, but I was unable to perceive it. I excuse myself for this failure of perception, for I think he was concealing it even from himself. It was Weissberg who brought him to explosion. Weissberg began with questions, not unlike the press, only more penetrating.

"Do you know anyone in the underworld who has a conscience, Herr Diamond?"

"I don't know anybody in the underworld. I'm only a bootlegger."

"What are your feelings about willful murder?"

"I try to avoid it."

"I have known people who would steal and yet would not maim another person. I know people who would maim and yet stop short of murder. And I know of men who claim that they could murder in anger but never in cold blood. Is this the way the underworld is morally structured?"

Jack seemed to like that question. Possibly he'd thought of its import over the years without ever raising the question quite so precisely. He squinted at the playwright, who talked with a cigarette constantly at the corner of his mouth, never removing it, letting the ashes fall as they would, on his chest or into the schnapps, or snorting them away with nasal winds. He was accomplished at this gesture, which I guessed he'd adopted when he first entered the underworld milieu.

"There's always a guy," Jack said to him, "who's ready to do what you won't do."

"What is your limit? What is it you will not do?"

"I've done everything at least twice," Jack said with a satiric snicker, "and I sleep like a baby."

"*Wunderbar!*" said Weissberg, and he threw his arms in the air and arched his body backward in the chair in a physical demonstration of Eureka! We listened to more

waltz music and we drank our legal alcohol and we watched
the playwright commune silently, smilingly, with this
sudden inflation of meaning. He threw off the half inch of
cigarette from his lip and leaned toward Jack.

"I want to write a play about your life," he said. "I want
to come to America and live with you. I don't care what
might happen in your life, and I fully expect you'll kill me if
you think I'm informing on you. I want to see you eat and
breathe and sleep and work and do your bootleg things and
steal and rob and kill. I want to witness everything and
write a great play, and I will give it all to you, all my glory,
all my money. I want only the opportunity to write what I
believe, which is that there are similarities among the great
artist, the great whore, and the great criminal. The great
artist is the work he does which outlives him. The great
whore lives in the memory of ineffable sensual gratification
that outlasts the liaison; she is also the beauty of the parts,
as is art. And she is the perversion of love, as art is the
exquisite perversion of reality. Of course, with both artist
and whore, the rewards are ever-greater recompense,
ever-greater renown. And I see the great criminal shining
through the bold perversion of his deeds, in his willingness
to scale the highest moral barriers (and what is morality to
the whore, the artist?). In all three professions is the
willingness to withhold nothing from one's work. All three,
when they achieve greatness, have also an undeniable high
style which separates them from the pedestrian mobs. For
how could we tell a great criminal from a thug in the alley,
or a great whore from a street slut, if it were not for style?
Yesssss, Herr Diamond, yesssss! It is abandon, first, which
goes without saying, but it is finally style that makes *you*
great and will make *me* great, and it is why we are drinking
here together in this elegant hotel and listening to this
elegant music and drinking this elegant schnapps.

"My little piglet here," he said, turning to his own
whore, who understood no English and whose breasts look
like two fried eggs in my memory, "knows nothing of style
and can never be more than a gutter animal. She is a filthy
woman and I do enjoy this. I enjoy paying her and stealing

back the money. I enjoy infecting her with my diseases and then paying her doctor bills. I enjoy squeezing her nipples until she screams. She is a superb companion, for she is stupid and knows nothing of me. She is not capable of even conceiving of how the great whores of Germany function today. I will have them, too, in time. But now my piglet exalts my young life.

"And you, sir, are a great man and have achieved great things. I can see in your eyes that you have leaped all moral and social barriers, that you are no prisoner of creeds and dogmas. You are intelligent, Herr Diamond. You live in the mind as well as on the street of bullets and blood. I too live in the mind and in the heart. My art is my soul. It is my body. Everything I do contributes to my art. We live, you and I, Herr Diamond, in the higher realms of the superman. We have each overcome our troublesome self. We exist in the world of will. We have created the world before which we can kneel. I speak Nietzsche's words. Do you know him? He says clearly that he who must be a creator in good and evil has first to be a destroyer and break values. We have both destroyed, Herr Diamond. We have both broken old values. We have both gone into the higher planes where the supermen dwell, and we will always triumph over the spirits of defeat that try to pull us down. Will you let me live with you and write your story—our story? Will you do this, Herr Diamond?"

Jack gave it a few seconds, letting it all settle, watching those electric eyes under Weissberg's bushy black brows. Then he went over to The Count's table and came back with The Count's small .25-caliber pistol half-concealed from the two dozen customers who sat in the garden's magical twilight, letting Strauss, the gentle swaying of the potted palms, and the intoxicating mellowness of the afternoon's first drinks lull them into sweet escape. Jack pulled his chair close to Weissberg's until they were knee to knee, and he then showed the playwright the pistol, holding it loosely in his palm. He said nothing at all for perhaps a minute, only held the weapon as a display item. Then suddenly and with eyes turned snakish, with a grimace of hate and viciousness whose like I had never seen before on his face, he nosed the barrel downward and fired one shot into the grass between Weissberg's feet, which were about six inches from each other. The downward course of the firing, the small caliber of the weapon, the shot muffled by pants legs and overwhelmed by music, created a noise that did not disrupt. A few people turned our way, but since we seemed at ease, no disturbance in process, the noise was assumed to be something as trivial as a broken glass. Jack took no notice of any external reaction. He said to Weissberg, "You're a kid, a fool."

The pistol was already in his pocket as he stood up and tossed a handful of deutsche marks on the table to pay for the drinks.

"My beautiful shithead," said the dirty little whore, stroking Weissberg's mustache, which by then was wet with tears, as wet as the front of his pants. Weissberg, the young playwright, had very suddenly liquefied.

Jack was two days out of Hamburg on the freighter *Hannover*, the only passenger, before he heard the strange melodic chaos coming up from below. He went through corridors and down a stairway where he found the forty-five hundred canaries the *Hannover* was bringing to the American bird-cage crowd. The Hartz Mountain birds, yellow and green, stopped singing when Jack entered their prison, and he thought: *They've smelled me.* But canaries are idiots of smell and wizards of hearing and love. The prison was moist and hot and Jack began to sweat. A sailor feeding the birds looked up and said, "I'm feedin' the birds."

"So I see."

"If you don't feed 'em, they drop dead."

"Is that so?"

"They eat a lot of food."

"You wouldn't think it to look at them."

"They do, though."

"Everybody needs a square meal," Jack said.

"Canaries especially."

"Can I help you feed them?"

"Nah. They wouldn't like you."

"What makes you think they wouldn't like me?"

"They know who you are."

"The canaries know me?"

"You saw the way they quit singin' when you come in?"

"I figured they were afraid of people."

"They love people. They're afraid of you."

"You're full of shit," Jack said.

"No, I'm not," said the sailor.

Jack opened a cage to gentle one of the birds. It pecked once at his knuckle. He lifted the bird out and saw it was dead. He put it in his pocket and opened another cage. That bird flew out, silently, and perched on top of the highest stack of cages, beyond Jack's reach unless he used the sailor's ladder. The bird twisted its tail and shat on the floor in front of Jack.

"I told you," the sailor said. "They don't want nothin' to do with you."

"What've they got against me?"

"Ask them. If you know what music is all about, you can figure out what they're sayin'. You know how they learn to sing so good? Listenin' to flutes and fiddles."

Jack listened, but all he heard was silence. The bird shat at him again. Jack yelled, "Fuck you, birdies," to the canaries and went back topside.

Jack heard from the radio operator that he was still steady news across the world, that now everyone knew he was on a ship with forty-five hundred canaries and that the corpse of Charlie Northrup had still not turned up. The sailor who fed the birds came up from below one morning, and Jack detected traces of the Northrup mouth on the man, a semitaut rubber band with the round edges downward turning. No smile, no smile. When the sailor opened the hatch, Jack heard the music of the birds. He inched toward it as it grew more and more glorious. The song heightened his sense of his own insignificance. What song did *he* sing? Yet it unaccountably pleased him to be nothing on the high seas, a just reward somehow; and now the birds were singing of justice. Jack remembered how satisfying it was to be shot and to linger at the edge of genuine nothingness. He remembered touching the Kiki silk and strong Alice's forehead. How rich! How something! And the vibrancy of command. Ah yes, that was *some*thing. Get down, he said to a nigger truck driver one night on the Lake George road; and the nigger showed him a knife, stupid nigger, and Jack fired one shot through his forehead. When Murray opened the door, the nigger fell out. Power! And when they got Augie—the lovely pain under Jack's own heart. Bang! And in the gut. Bang! Bang! Fantastic! Let us, then, be up and doing, with a heart for any fate.

"How's all the birdies?" Jack asked the sailor.

"Very sad," said the sailor. "They sing to overcome their sadness."

"That's not why birds sing," Jack said.

"Sure it is."

"Are you positive?"

"I live with birds. I'm part bird myself. You should see my skin up close. Just like feathers."

"That's very unusual," Jack said.

The sailor rolled up his sleeve to show Jack his biceps, which were covered with brown feathers.

"Now do you believe me?" the sailor asked.

"I certainly do. It's absolutely amazing."

"I used to be a barn swallow before I became a sailor."

"You like it better as a bird or this way?"

"I had more fun as a bird."

"I would've given nine to five you'd say that," Jack said.


A sailor told me a story when I boarded the *Hannover* back in the States.

"A strange man, der Schack, und I like him," the sailor said. "Good company, many stories, full of the blood that makes a man come to life as thousands around him become dead. A natural man. A man who knows where to find Canis Major. I watch him by the railing, looking out at the waves, not moving. He looks, he trembles. He holds himself as you hold a woman. He is a man of trouble. The

captain sends me to his cabin when he does not come to
breakfast, und on the table by the bed are three birds, all
dead. Der Schack is sick. He says he vill take only soup.
For three days he stays in the room und just before
Philadelphia he comes to me und says he wants to buy three
birds to take home. 'They are my friends,' he says. When I
get the birds for him, he wants to pay me, but I say, 'No,
Schack, they are a gift.' In his cabin I look for the three
dead ones, but they are gone.''

I beat Jack home, caught a liner a day and a half after he
left Hamburg, and probably passed his floating birdhouse
before it was out of the English Channel. The money
passed back to America with me without incident, and so, I
thought, had I, for I had been a passive adjunct to Jack's
notoriety, a shadowy figure in the case, as they say. But my
shadow ran ahead of me, and when I returned to Albany
and rented a safe-deposit box for the cash, I found I was
locally notorious. My picture had been taken in Germany
with Jack, and it had smiled all over the local papers. My
legal maneuvering on the Continent, however marginal and
unpublic, had been ferreted out by German newsmen and
duly heralded at home.

I'd told Jack in Hamburg, when we shook hands at the
gangplank, that I'd meet him when he docked in the U. S.
and I'd bring Fogarty with me. But Fogarty, I discovered,
couldn't leave the state, and Jack was coming in to
Philadelphia. The federals had Fogarty on three trivial
charges while they tried to link him to a rum-boat raid
they'd made at Briarcliff Manor, a hundred-and-twenty-
five-thousand-dollar haul of booze, the week before we left
for Europe. This was the first I'd heard of the raid or of
Fogarty's arrest. He'd been waiting in a truck as the boat
docked, and when he spotted a cop, he tried to make a run.
They charged him with vagrancy, speeding, and failing to
give a good account of himself, my favorite misdemeanor.

"They can't tie me to it," Fogarty said on the phone
from Acra. "I never went near the boat. I was in the truck
taking a nap.''

"Excellent alibi. Was it Jack's booze?"

"I wouldn't know."

"As one Irishman to another, I don't trust you either."

So I drove to Philadelphia by myself.

The reception for Jack was hardly equal to the hero welcomes America gives its Lindys, but it surpassed anything I'd been involved in personally since the armistice. I talked my way onto the cutter that was to bring a customs inspector out to meet the *Hannover* at quarantine on Marcus Hook. A dozen newsmen were also aboard, the avant-garde eyeballs of the waiting masses.

We saw Jack on the bridge with the captain when we pulled alongside. The captain called out, "No press, no press," when the customs inspector began to board, and Jack added his greeting: "Any reporter comes near me I'll knock his fucking brains out." The press grumbled and took pictures, and then Jack saw me and I climbed aboard.

"I was just passing by," I said, "and thought I might borrow a cup of birdseed."

Jack grinned and shook hands, looking like an ad for what an ocean voyage can do for the complexion. He was in his favorite suit—the blue double-breasted—with a light gray fedora, a baby blue tie, and a white silk shirt.

"I'm big pals with these birds," he said. "Some of them whistle better than Jolson."

"You're looking fit."

"Greatest trip of my life," he said. The captain was a hell of a fellow, the food was great, the sea air did wonders for his stomach and blah blah blah. Marvelous how he could lie. I told him about the reception he was going to get, some evidence of it already in view: tugs, police launches, chartered press boats, that customs cutter, all of them steaming along with us as we glided up the Delaware toward Pier Thirty-four. Jack's navy.

"I'd estimate three thousand people and a hundred cops," I said.

"Three thousand? They gonna throw confetti or rocks?"

"Palm fronds is my guess."

I told him about Fogarty's travel restrictions, and asked:

"Was that your booze they got on that boat?"

"Mostly mine," he said. "I had a partner."

"A sizable loss—a hundred and twenty-five thousand dollars."

"More. Add another twenty-five."

"Were you on the scene?"

"Not at the dock. I was someplace else, waiting. And nobody showed. My old pal Charlie Northrup worked that one up."

"He was your partner?"

"He tipped the feds."

"Ah. So that's what this is all about."

"No, that's not even half of it. What about Jimmy Biondo?"

"I had a call from him. He wants his money."

"I don't blame him, but he's not going to get it."

"He threatened me. He thinks maybe I've got it. I didn't think he was that bright."

"How did he threaten you?"

"He said he'd make me dead."

"Don't pay any attention to that bullshit."

"It's not something I hear every day."

"I'll fix the son of a bitch."

"Why don't you just give him back his money?"

"Because I'm going back to Germany."

"Oh, Christ, Jack. Don't you learn?"

When he talked to Schwarzkopf about greasing the way for a return trip, I took it as the necessary response of an angry reject. I couldn't imagine him really risking a second international fiasco. But I was making a logical assumption and Jack was working out of other file cabinets: his faith in his ability to triumph over hostility, his refusal to recognize failure even after it had kicked him in the crotch, and, of course, his enduring greed. As a disinterested observer I might have accepted all but the greed as admirable behavior, but now with Biondo on my back as well as Jack's, such perseverance struck me as an open invitation to assassination.

"Let's get it straight, Jack. I'm not comfortable."

"Who the hell is?"

"I used to be. I want to get rid of that money and I want to get rid of Jimmy Biondo. I went along for the ride, but it's turned into something else. You don't know how big this Northrup thing is. In the papers every day. Biggest corpse hunt in years, which raises our old question again. Is he or isn't he? I've got to know this time."

We were on the forward deck, watching the boats watch us. The captain and his sailors were nowhere near us, but Jack looked behind and then spoke so no breeze would carry the words aft.

"Yeah," he said.

"Great. Jesus Christ, that's great news."

"It wasn't my fault."

"No?"

"It was a mistake."

"Then that makes everything all right."

"Don't fuck around with this, Marcus. I said it was a mistake."

"It's a mistake I'm here."

"Then get the fuck off."

"When it's over. I don't quit on my clients."

I think I knew even as I said it that there would be no quitting. Certainly I sensed the possibility, for just as Jack's life had taken a turning in Europe, so had mine. Our public association had done me in with the Albany crowd. They could do beer business all year long with Jack, but after mass on Sunday they could also tut-tut over the awful gangsterism fouling the city. It followed they could not run a man for the Congress who was seeking justice for an animal like Jack. Forget about Congress, was the word passed to me at the Elks Club bar after I came home from Germany. When I think back now to whether the Congress or the time with Jack would have given me more insight into American life, I always lean to Jack. In the Congress I would have learned how rudimentary hypocrisy is turned into patriotism, into national policy, and into the law, and how hypocrites become heroes of the people. What I learned from Jack was that politicians imitated his style without comprehending it, without understanding that their venality was *only* hypocritical. Jack failed thoroughly as a hypocrite. He was a liar, of course, a perjurer, all of that, but he was also a venal man of integrity, for he never ceased to renew his vulnerability to punishment, death, and damnation. It is one thing to be corrupt. It is another to behave in a psychologically responsible way toward your own evil.

The police came aboard, just like Belgium, with a warrant for Jack as a suspicious character. Jack was afraid of the mob, afraid he was too much of a target, but the cops formed a wedge around him and moved him through. The crowd pushed and broke the wedge, calling out hellos and welcome backs to Jack; and some even held up autograph books and pencils. When all that failed, the fan club began to reach out to feel him, shake his hand. A woman who couldn't reach him hit his arm with a newspaper and apologized—"I only wanted to touch you, lover"—and a young man made a flying leap at Jack's coat, got a cop's instead, also got clubbed.

"Murderer," someone called out.

"Go home. We don't want you here."

"Don't mind them, Jack."

"You look great, Legs."

"He's only a bird in a gilded cage."

"Give us a smile, Legs," a photographer said and Jack swung at him, missed.

"Hello, cuz!" came a yell and Jack turned to see his cousin William, an ironworker. Jack asked the cops to let him through, and William, six four with major muscles and the facial blotch of a serious beer drinker, moved in beside the car where Jack was now ringed by police.

"Lookin' snappy, Jack," William said.

"Wish I could say the same for you, Will."

"What's that you got there in the lapel?"

"Knight Templar pin, Will."

"Son of a bitch, Jack, ain't that a Protestant bunch?"

"It's good for business, Will."

"You even turned on your own religion."

"Ah shit, Will, have you got anything to tell me? How's Aunt Elly?"

"She's fit."

"Does she need anything?"

"Nobody needs anything from you."

"Well, it was nice seeing you, Will. Give my regards to the worms."

"We know who the worm in this family is, cousin."

And Jack got into the car.

"What do you think of the killing of the dry agent yesterday at the Rising Sun Brewery in Newark?" a reporter asked through the window.

"First I heard of it, but it's the most foolish thing in the world. It'll cramp business for a month."

"Can you whistle for us?" another reporter asked.

"Up your whistle, punk," Jack said, and the reporter faded.

"How did you find Europe?"

"I got off the boat and there it was."

"Who was the blonde you were with in Hamburg?"

"A Red Cross nurse I hired to take my pulse."

"How well did you know Charlie Northrup?"

"A personal friend."

"The police think you killed him."

"Never trust what a cop or a woman thinks."

No longer amused, the cops shoved the reporters back and made a path for the car. Jack waved to me as it pulled away, smiling, happy to be vulnerable again. My subconscious works in musical ways at times and as I wrote that last sentence I heard an old melody float up and I couldn't say why. But I trust my music and when I sang it all the way through I could hear a jazz band playing it in raucous ragtime, Jack giving me that going-away smile on the pier forty-two years ago, soothed by the music, which I hear clearly, with a twist all my own:

It goes Na-Da, Na-Da,
Na-Da-Na-Da nil-nil-nil.

Jack was twenty hours in jail. His aunt sent him a box of molasses cookies, and I sent him two corned beefs on rye. Commissioner Devane in New York had asked Philadelphia to hold Jack, but they found nothing to prosecute and by midmorning I'd worked out a release arrangement. We'd announce we were leaving town, assuring the citizenry that no carpetbaggers would invade the territory of the local hoodlums. Jack wanted only two hours to visit relatives and the judge said all right, so we went through a four-minute court ritual. But the judge found it necessary to give Jack a dig: "This court considers the attention you have received from the press and from the vast numbers of people who gathered at the pier to witness your arrival, to be twin aberrations of the public mind, aberrations which find value in things that are worth nothing at all. I speak for the decent people of this city in saying that Philadelphia doesn't want you any more than Europe did. Get out of this city and stay out."

In the car, Jack looked like a man trying to see through a rain of cotton balls. The reporters tailed us, so he said, "Skip the relatives, head for New York." We lost the last of the press about thirty miles out of the city. It was a decent fall day, a little cloudy, but with a lot of new color in the world. But then it started to drizzle and the road got foggy. The fog seemed to buoy Jack's spirits and he talked about his women. He'd left his canaries on the ship and now wanted to buy something for Alice and Kiki, so we stopped at Newark, which he seemed to know as well as he knew Manhattan.

"Dogs," he said. "Alice loves dogs."

We went to three pet shops before we found a pair of gray Brussels griffons. They appealed to Jack because he could claim he'd bought them in Belgium. There were four in the litter and I suggested another pair for Kiki.

"She'd lose them or let them die," he said, and so we found a jewelry store and he bought her an eight-hundred-dollar diamond, elaborately set ("A diamond from my Diamond," she quickly dubbed it).

I'd expected him to emphasize one or the other woman

when he arrived, depending on his mood: horny or homey. But he balanced them neatly, emphasizing neither, impatient to see them both, moving neither away from one nor toward the other but rather toting one on each shoulder into some imagined triad of love, a sweet roundelay which would obviate any choice of either/or and would offer instead the more bountiful alternative of both. More power to you, old boy.

But his mood was not bountiful at the moment. We came out of the jewelry store and got in the car, and he looked at me and said, "Did you ever feel dead?"

"Not entirely. I woke up once and felt my leg was dead. Not pins and needles but genuinely dead. But that's as far as I ever got."

"I feel like I died last week."

"You've had a pretty negative experience. It's understandable."

"I didn't even feel like this when I *was* dying."

"Go someplace and sleep it off. Always works for me when I hit bottom."

"Some cocaine would fix my head."

"I'll stop at the next drugstore."

"Let's get a drink. Turn right, we'll go to Nannery's"—and we hunted down a small speakeasy where Jack knew the doorman and got the biggest hello of the week from half the people in the place.

"I just heard about you on the radio ten minutes ago," Tommy Nannery told him, a spiffy little bald-headed Irishman with oversize ears. He kept clapping Jack on the back and he put a bottle of rye in front of us. "They sure gave you a lot of shit over there, Jack," Nannery said.

"It wasn't so bad," Jack said. "Don't believe all that horseshit you read in the papers. I had a good time. I got healthy on the ocean."

"I didn't believe any of it," Nannery said. "Talkin' here the other night about it I says to a fellow, they don't shove Jack Diamond around like that, I don't care who they are. Jack has got friends a way up. Am I right?"

"You're right, Tommy. Here's to my friends."

Jack drank about three straight ones while I was getting halfway through my first. He put a twenty on the bar and said he'd take the bottle.

"My treat, Jack, my treat," Nannery said. "Glad to see you back in Newark."

"It's nice to have good friends," Jack said. "Tommy, it's nice."

He had another two fast ones before we left, and in the car he sat with the bottle between his legs, swilling it as we went. When I got into Manhattan, he was out of his depression with a vengeance, also out of control with good old Marcus at the wheel. I'd every intention of dropping him in the city and going straight on to Albany with a demarcating flourish. The end. For the peculiar vanity that had first sent me to Catskill on that odd summer Sunday, the need for feeding the neglected negative elements of my too-white Irish soul, the willful tar-and-feather job on my conscience, all that seemed silly now. Childish man. Eternal boy. Bit of a rascal. Unpredictable Marcus. The wiping away of my political future, however casually I'd considered it in the past, the prospect of assassination, and my excursion into quasi-rape convinced me my life had changed in startling ways I wouldn't yet say I regretted. But what would I do with such developments? Underneath, I knew I was still straight, still balancing the either/or while Jack plunged ahead with diamonds and doggies toward the twin-peaked glory of bothness. I felt suddenly like a child.

I looked at Jack and saw him whiten. Was that a bad bit of barley he was swilling? But the bottle was two-thirds down. He was suddenly quite drunk, and without a sound or a move toward the door, he puked in his lap, onto the seat, onto the gearshift, the floormat, the open ashtray, my shoes, my socks, my trousers, and the Philadelphia *Inquirer* I'd bought before going to court, Jack's face in closeup staring up from it at Jack, receiving mouth-to-mouth vomit.

"Fucking ocean," Jack said, and he collapsed backward with his eyes closed, lapsing into a ragged flow of mumbles as I looked frantically for a gas station. He rattled on about being offered fifteen hundred a month to perform in a German cabaret, and twenty-five thousand by an English news syndicate for his life story and a blank check by the *Daily News* for the same thing. I'd heard all this in Germany and was now far more interested in any sign of the flying red horse on Eleventh Avenue, steed that would deliver me from puke.

"'Magine 'em asking Rothstein?" Jack said, eyes closed, words all tongued. "'Magine him packin' 'em in?"

"No, I can't imagine it," I said, distracted still. Jack opened his eyes when I spoke.

"Wha'?"

"I said I couldn't imagine it."

"'Magine wha'?"

"Rothstein onstage."

"Where?"

"Forget it."

"They wouldn't put that bum onstage," he said and he closed his eyes. He snapped to when I hosed down his lap and shoes at the gas station, and by the time we got to the Monticello Hotel where Kiki was waiting, he was purged, stinking and still drunk but purged of salt air and European poisons, cured by America's best home remedy. And good old Uncle Marcus was still there, guiding him with as little guidance as possible toward the elevator. Upstairs, Jack could lie down and think about puke and poison. He could discover in quiet what his body already understood: that his fame hadn't answered the basic question he had asked himself all his life, was still asking.

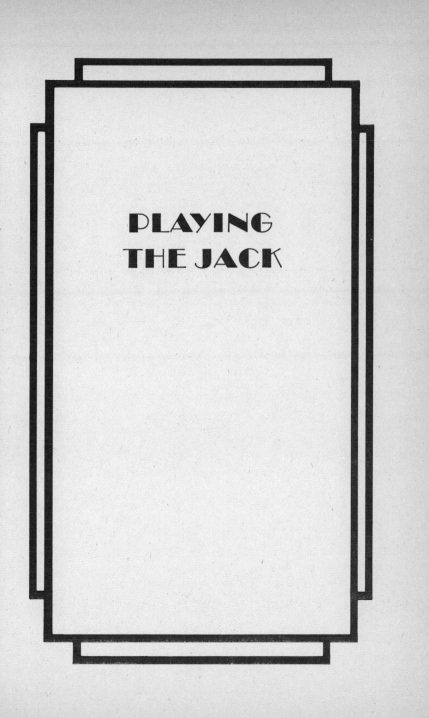

# PLAYING
# THE JACK

Jimmy Biondo visited Kiki three hours before we knocked on her door. The result was still on her face. She'd met him with Jack frequently, and so, when he knocked, she let him in. He then dumped his froggy body into the only easy chair in the room, keeping his hat on and dripping sweat off his chin onto his bow tie.

"Where's your friend Diamond?"

"He hasn't called me yet."

"Don't lie to me, girlie."

"I don't lie to people and don't call me girlie, you big lug."

"Your friend's got trouble."

"What kind of trouble?"

"He's gunna grow great big holes in his belly."

"He better not hear you say that."

"He'll hear it all right. He'll hear it."

"Listen, I don't want to talk to you and I'll thank you to leave."

"I'll tank you to leave."

"So get lost."

"Shut up, you dumb cunt."

"Oh! I'm tellin' Jack."

"Just right. And tell him I want my money and tell him he shouldn'a done what he done to Charlie Northrup."

"He didn't do anything to Charlie Northrup."

"You dumb cunt, what do you know? You think he's a nice guy, wouldn't hurt anybody? I wanna tell you what a nice guy your boyfriend is and what nice guys he's got workin' for him. You ever hear of Joe Rock? Your boyfriend's pals took him up inna woods, and when he said he wooden pay off the ransom, Murray the Goose pulls himself off inna cloth and rubs it in Joe's eyes and ties the rag on the eyes and Joe goes bline because The Goose has got the clap and the syph, both kinds of diseases, and that's your boyfriend Jack Diamond. I tell you this because Joe Rock was a business associate of mine. And after your boyfriend burns up Red Moran inna car over inna Newark dump and finds out Moran's girl knows who done it, he ties her up with sewer grates and dumps her inna river while she's still kickin'. That's your boyfriend Jack Diamond. How you like your boyfriend now, you dumb cunt?''

"Oh, oh, oh!" said Kiki as Joe left the room.

After we heard her story Jack shoved a fifty into my hand with the suggestion: "How you like to take a pretty girl out to dinner?" He called somebody and went out with word to us that he'd be back in a few hours and was gone before I found the way to tell him we were quits. I can't say the idea of Kiki's company repelled me, but I was intimidated. I've talked about her beauty, and it was never greater than at that moment. She'd been primping for Jack, calling up all her considerable wisdom of sex and vanity, and had created a face I've since thought of as The Broadway Gardenia. It was structured with eyebrow pencil, mascara, an awareness of the shape of the hairline and the fall of the loose curl. It was beauty that was natural and artificial at once, and the blend created this flower child of the Follies. No carefree Atlanta belle, no windblown, wheat-haired Kansas virgin, no Oriental blossom, or long-stemmed Parisian rose could quite match her. Beauty, after all, is regional. I remember the high value the Germans put on their rose-cheeked Fräuleins. And to me the cheeks were just blotchy.

"Are you leaving me alone?" Kiki said as Jack kissed her.

"I'll be back." He had sobered considerably in less than ten minutes.

"I don't want to be alone anymore. He might come in again."

"Marcus is here."

That's when he gave me the fifty and left. Kiki sat on the bed looking at the door, and when she decided he was definitely gone, she said, "All right, goddamn it," and went to the mirror and looked at her face and took out some black wax I've since learned is called beading and heated it in a spoon and dabbed it on her eyelids with a toothpick. Her eyes didn't need such excess, but when she looked at me, I saw something new: not excess but heightening. Magic beyond magic. I've never known another woman in the world who used that stuff and only one who even knew what it was. It was an object out of Kiki's mystical beauty kit like all her other creams and powders and soft pencils and lip brushes, and as I looked at the bottles and jars on the dressers, they all illuminated something central to her life: the studied passivity of being beautiful, of being an object to be studied, of being Jack's object. Her radio was on the dresser and exaggerated the passivity for me—lying there waiting for Jack, always waiting for Jack, and letting the music possess her as a substitute; the pink rubber douche equipment on top of the toilet tank—more proof of Kiki as Jack's vulnerable receptacle.

She stood, after she finished her eyebrows, and lifted her dress over her head, a navy-blue satin sheath with silver spangles on the bodice—Jack loved spangles. Her slip went part way up, and there flashed another view of some of the underneath dimension, to which I reacted by saying, memorably, "Whoops." She laughed and I stood up and said, "I'll meet you in the lobby."

"Why?"

"Give you a little privacy."

"Listen, I'm all fed up with privacy. Stick around. You won't see half what you'd see if I was in one of my costumes. I'm just changing my dress."

She moved around in her slip, sat down at the dressing table and combed the hair she had mussed, then turned quickly, faced me, giving me a full central view of upper, gartered thigh, and I thought, oh, oh, if I do what I am being tempted to do, I will end up with very substantial trouble; thinking also: vengeful concubine. But I was wrong there.

"You know," she said, "I don't know why I'm here."

"In this room or on this earth?"

"In this room waiting for that son of a bitch to come and see me whenever he goddamn feels like it, even after I tell him a story like I told him about Jimmy Biondo."

I sensed she was talking to me this way because she had taken her dress off and felt powerful. She was a sexual figure without the dress and merely a vulnerable beauty with it. Sitting there giving me an ample vision of her hinterlands was a gesture of power. Tenors shatter glassware. Strongmen bend iron bars. Sexual powerhouses show you their powersources. It reassures them in the place where they are strongest, and weakest, that they are significant, that the stares that automatically snap toward that sweet region of shadow are stares of substance and identification. With this stare, I thee covet. Desirable. Yes, yes, folks, see that? I'm desirable and everything is going to be all right. Feeling powerful, she could talk tough.

"Do you work for him all the time now, Mr. Gorman?" That "Mr." destroyed my fantasy of being seduced. A disappointment and a relief.

"I've done some things for him."

"Do you remember Charlie Northrup from that day up on the mountain?"

"I do indeed."

"Do you think Jack really did something to him? Hurt him?"

"I have no firsthand information on that."

"I don't think Jack would kill him like that Biondo man said. And what he said about that man's eyes and that girl in the river. Jack wouldn't do that stuff."

"I'm sure he wouldn't."

"I couldn't stay with him if he did that stuff."

"I understand."

"I'd leave right now if I thought he did that stuff. You think I could love a man who could do something to somebody's eyes like that?"

"Didn't you say it was Murray who did that?"

"That's what Biondo said, but he said Jack knew about it."

"Well, you can't believe Biondo."

"That's just what I think.

"I know Jack liked Charlie Northrup. When he spit that beer at Jack up on the mountain, Jack told me that night, 'If I didn't like that guy, he'd be in a lot of trouble.' Everybody thinks Jack is such a tough guy, but he's really sweet and gentle and never hurts nobody. I never even saw him pop the guts on a fly. Jack is a gentleman always and one of the tenderest, sweetest human persons I've ever come across, and I've come across my share of persons and they're not all human, I'll tell you that. I saw him with Charlie Northrup up in the mountains, and they were talking together and walking around the front yard. So I know Jack wouldn't hurt him. It's a bunch of lies what's in the papers because I know what I saw."

"That happened *after* that day we were all on the mountain?"

"Five days after. I counted the days. I always count the days. At Biondo's farm up there. Jack said staying up on the mountain was too far away for me, and he moved me down to the farm for a few days."

"What about dinner?"

"Jesse cooked for me. The old nigger man who runs the still."

"I mean now."

"Oh, now. All I have to do is put my dress on."

She closed her gates of power and stood up.

"You know," she said, "I like you. I could talk to you. Don't take this the wrong way now."

"I take it as a statement of friendship."

"That's just what I mean. Some people you talk to them and ka-zoom, it's a pass, just because you said something nice."

"You like me because I didn't make a pass?"

"Because you wanted to and didn't and you had such a good chance."

"You're a perceptive girl."

"What's that mean?"

"You see inside people."

"I see how they look at me, that's all."

"Not many people see that much."

"You see, I knew I could talk to you. You don't make me feel like a dumb bunny."

The night I went to dinner with Kiki, Tony (The Boy) Amapola was shot through the head and neck four times and dumped outside Hackensack. The papers said he was a close pal of Jimmy Biondo's and that Biondo was Capone's man in town, which wasn't true. Another victim of another beer war, was the consensus, but I suggest he was a victim of Jimmy's bad manners toward ladies.

I sat talking with Kiki that night until Jack came back around midnight, and then I drove to Albany without telling him I was all through. A call from Jesse Franklin was waiting for me when I got to the office the next day, asking me to come and see him. I don't think I'd have remembered him if Kiki hadn't mentioned him as her cook at the farm the night before. I called him back and got a hotel which turned out to be a flophouse for Negroes in Albany's South End. I told him to come and see me, but he said he couldn't, and would I come to see him? I never met a client in a flophouse before, so I said I would.

It turned out to be the ground floor of an old converted livery stable with a dozen cots, two of which were occupied: one by a man wheezing and ranting in a drunken, mumbly wine coma, and the other by Jesse, who sat on his cot like a bronze sculpture of despair, a weary old man with nubby white hair, wearing ratty overalls and staring downward, watching the roaches play around his muddy shoes. He hadn't been out of the flop in three weeks except to go to a corner store and buy food, then come back and sleep and wait.

"You remember me, Mr. Gorman?"

"I was talking about you with Kiki Roberts only last night."

"Pretty lady."

"That's her truth all right."

"She didn't see nothin' what I seen, what I wants to tell you 'bout. Nobody seen what I seen."

"Why do you want to tell me about it?"

"I got some money. I can pay."

"I would expect it."

"I sent my boys away but I don't wanna go myself, don't know where to go. Only one place to go I know of is back to the farm and work for Mr. Jack, but I don't wanna go back there. Can't go back to that old place after what I seen. I fear 'bout those men. I know the police lookin' for me too 'cause they askin' Mr. Fogarty 'bout me before he go to jail and I don't want no police, so I highfoots it up to Albany 'cause I know they got coloreds up here plenty and nobody know me, and then I know I gonna run out of money and have to be on the road and I gonna get picked up sure as Jesus. So I been sittin' here thinkin' 'bout what I gonna do and I remember Mr. Jack got a lawyer friend in Albany. I been sittin' here three weeks tryin' to 'member your name. Then yesterday this old bum he fall right in front of me, right there by them little roaches, and he got a newspaper in his pocket and I seen your picture and Mr. Jack's picture and I say, that's my man all right, that's my man. Man who runs this place got me your phone number all right. I gets picked up you goin' help me?"

"I'll help you if I can, but I've got to know what this is all about."

"Yep. I gonna tell you but nobody else. No how. What I see I don't want no more part of. I see it when I just about finished at the still for about five hours, sun goin' down and I throwed down my head to sleep off the miseries when I heerd this automobile pull up in front of the barn. I sleeps in the back of the house, so I look out and see Mr. Fogarty openin' the barn doors and other fellas Mr. Jack have around him all the time in the car and they drives right inside. Now I never did see this before. Mr. Jack use that barn for storage and he don't want no automobiles drivin' in and out of where he keep his beer and his whiskey 'cept for loadin' and that ain't no loadin' car I see. But Jesse ain't about to tell them fellas they can't use Mr. Jack's barn. Bye'em bye, Mr. Fogarty he come in the house and then he and Miss Kiki go out with Mr. Jack. I spies out the window

at the gay-rage and I sees the light on there. I don't see
nobody comin' or goin' out of that old place so I figure it
ain't none of Jesse's business and I tries to go back and
sleep. Bye'em bye, I hear that car again and it's dark now
and in a little bit Mr. Fogarty comes in and gets some old
newspapers and calls up to Jesse, is you up there and I say I
is and he say Mr. Jack say for me not to go near the still
tonight and I say okay by me and I don't ask why because
Jesse ain't a man who asks why to Mr. Jack and his friends.
Mr. Fogarty carries them papers back out and about twenty
minutes go by and I heerd that car again and I sits right up
in the bed and says, well they's done whatever they's done
and I look out the window and they's no light in the
gay-rage and I call down the stairs to Mr. Fogarty, but he
don't say nothin' back and nobody else does neither, and I
know my boys won't, 'cause they sleep like fishbones on
the bottom of a mud pond, and so I think of what they been
doin' in the gay-rage and I can't figure it out. But I say to
myself, Jesse, you ought to know what's goin' on
hereabouts since this is where you livin' and maybe they up
to somethin' you don't want yourself fixed up in. So I takes
my flashlight and I spokes quiet like down them stairs and
out into the backyard and they's no light in the gay-rage so I
sprites 'round by the back in case somebody pull up. And
inside it's the same old gay-rage, a couple three newspapers
on the floor 'longside the wheelbarra. Coolin' room's the
same as usual and Mr. Jack's tahger's on the back wall's
the same as usual and all the tools on the bench. I can't see
no difference nowhere. Then I see in the corner of the
coolin' room a big piece of somethin' all wrapped up and I
knows this wasn't there before and I knows what I think it
is soon as I sees it. And I shines the light on it. It look like a
rug all rolled up 'cept it ain't no rug. It's canvas we throwed
over the beer barrels first time the roof leaked. And I goes
over and touches that canvas with my toe and it is solid. It
feel just like I 'spect it to feel. And Jesse beginnin' to worry
what gonna happen if he caught here with this thing alone.
But I got to make sure it's what I think, so I puts my whole
foot on it and feel how it feels, and it ain't exactly like what

I 'spect, so I touches it with my hand. And that ain't exactly
like I 'spect either and so I opens one end of the canvas to
peek inside and see what is this thing that ain't like what it
ought to be like, and out come this here head. All by itself.
It roll out just a little bit, and I tell you if I ain't 'lectrified
dead now, I don't know why I ain't. And I highfoots it out
of that barn and back into the house and up them stairs and
back to my own room and under the covers so's I can think
by myself what I ought to do. And I thinks. And I thinks.
And I don't hear nobody comin' back. Then I say to
myself, Jesse, if somebody do come back, you is in mighty
trouble. Because that head ain't where it ought to be and
they is goin' to know somebody been out peekin' into that
canvas. And first thing, they comin' back in here and say to
you, Jesse, why you foolin' around with that head out in
that barn? What you say then, old man? So bye'em bye, I
sits up, and gets up, and goes downstairs and out to the
gay-rage and what scare me now ain't that head, but them
lights of the car if they come shootin' back in the road. But
I say to myself, Jesse, you got to go put that head back
where you got it. So I goes back in the coolin' room and
shines the light down and sees the old head lookin' up at me
three feet out from the end of the canvas where it rolled.
And I gets a good look at that face which I can't reckonize
and maybe nobody on this earth gonna reckonize over
again, because it been beat so bad it ain't no face at all. It
just a head full of beat-up old flesh. I feels sorry for that
poor fella 'cause he got his. No doubt 'bout that. But I say,
Jesse, feel sorry for this man when you gets back to your
bed. Right now, get yourself busy puttin' that head back in
with the rest of him. Now I don't like it nohow, but I pick
up that old head and opens up the canvas so's I can put it
back in and, oh God A'mighty, there's two hands and a foot
side by side like the Lord never intended nobody's hands
and foot to be put together. And I opens up the canvas
wider and oh God A'mighty, they ain't one whole piece of
that poor fella no more. He is in ten, fifteen pieces, oh my
Jesus, I gonna die. I put that head back where it used to be
and fold that canvas up the way it used to be. Then I look

around on the floor for any little blood drippin's I might of spilt, but I can't see none. I can't see none they might of left either, so I guess they got it all mopped up with them newspapers Mr. Fogarty picked out. Oh, sweet Jesus. And I go back out of the coolin' room then, and back into the house. I ain't worried now whether they gonna find me out there, because they ain't. It just like it was before I seen it the first time. Now I'se worryin' about somethin' else, which is how I gonna get myself and the boys out of this here butcher shop. I sure can't do it right away or they gonna know I knows more'n I s'pose to know. So I lays there thinkin' 'bout how long it'd be before it be right for me to go my own way and take my boys with me. And wonderin' where we gonna go, 'cause we ain't had no job good as this in mighty a year. But I ain't worryin' now 'bout no job. I worryin' 'bout the jailhouse gettin' me, and what my boys gonna do then? I'se still thinkin' 'bout this when I hears the car pull into the yard and I looks out and there comes Mr. Murray and somebody I can't see and they pulls in the gay-rage again but with one of Mr. Jack's trucks and stays 'bout five minutes and they back out and close the door. Then good-bye. They gone. I know the canvas and the head and the rest of the pieces of that poor ol' boy done gone too, but I don't move, 'cause it's daylight just beginnin', and ain't nobody gonna see Jesse Franklin in that barn today. Not any of those fellas, not Mr. Jack, not any stranger, not Jesse hisself. Jesse is gonna stay clear of that ol' gay-rage till somebody come who got business to do in it. And when it all simmer down, Jesse gonna take his boys and he goin' waaaay 'way from here. These is bad people, cut a man up like that. How he gonna make it all back together again come judgment time? Bad people, doin' that to a man."

It was Fogarty who told me how Charlie Northrup got it, told me later when he was figuring out where his life went, still drunk, still ready to muzzle any pussy that showed itself. He never changed and I always liked him and I knew all along why Jack kept him on—because he was the

opposite of Murray. He was Fogarty, the group's nice guy.
I liked him in that context, probably because of the
contrast. I no longer think it strange that Jack had both
kinds—Fogarty kind, Murray kind—working for him. Jack
lived a long time, for Jack, and I credit it to his sense of
balance, even in violent matters, even in the choice of
killers and drivers, his sense that all ranges of the self must
be appeased, and yet only appeased, not indulged. I make
no case for Jack as a moderate, only as a man in touch with
primal needs. He read them, he answered them, until he
stopped functioning in balance. That's when the final
trouble began.

Charlie Northrup drove his car to the Biondo farm at
dusk to keep his appointment with Jack. Fogarty said
Murray and Oxie were on the porch, rocking in the
squeaky, green rockers while Jack waited inside.

"I don't go inside," Charlie said at the foot of the steps.

"Then you wait there," Murray said, and he went for
Jack, who came out through the screen door and walked
down the stairs and put his hand out to shake Charlie's
hand. But it wasn't there.

"Never mind jerking me off," Charlie said. "Get to the
point."

"Don't talk nasty, Charlie," Jack said, "or I'll forget
we're brothers."

"Brothers. You got some rotten fucking way of being a
brother. What you done to me, you're a bum in my book, a
bum in spades."

"Listen, Charlie. I got something to say to you. I ought
to blow your face off. Anybody talks to the federals has a
right to get their face blown off, isn't that so?"

Fogarty said Charlie shut up at that point, that he
obviously didn't think Jack knew.

"I got some good friends who happen to be federals,"
Jack said.

Charlie kept quiet.

"But the way I look at it, Charlie, I blow your face off
and I lose all that money I'd have had if the federals didn't
pick up my cargo. And what I figure is, set up a working

relationship with Charlie and he'll pay me back what I lost. All we do is cooperate and the problem is solved."

"Cooperate," said Charlie, "means I give you my shirt and kiss your ass for taking it."

"Partners, Charlie. That's what I got in mind. Partners in an expanding business. I produce the business, you provide the product. We split seventy-thirty till you pay off the debt, then we reduce it, fifty-fifty, because we're brothers. Business doubles, triples at higher prices and a locked-up market. It's brilliant, Charlie, brilliant."

"You know I got partners already. They're nobody's patsies."

"I take the risk about your partners."

"I don't want no part of you," Charlie said. "I wouldn't hold onto you in an earthquake."

Charlie stopped walking. They were under the maples, a few feet from the porch, Jack in a tan suit and Charlie in his sweat shirt.

"I said it before, Jack. Stuff it up your ass. You're not talking to a man without power. Play with me you're not playing with some apple-knocker up here, some dummy saloonkeeper. You know my friends. I'm done talking about it."

He walked away from Jack, toward his car.

"You stupid fucking donkey," Jack said, and he looked up at Oxie and Murray, who stood up and pointed their pistols at Charlie. Fogarty remembered only his own rocker squeaking at that point. He kept rocking until Murray gave him the gesture and then he got out of the chair and in behind the wheel of Northrup's car and drove it back into the garage with Oxie and Murray inside it holding their pistols against Charlie's belly. Fogarty remembered Jack climbing the porch steps and watching them all get in the car.

"Now, Charlie," he said, "you got to get a lesson in manners."

Murray always wore steel-toed shoes and I never knew that either until Fogarty told me this whole story. He used a gun or the long, pointed, three-cornered file he carried (his improvement on the ice pick Flossie remembered) when necessary, but he used his feet when he could. The story is he took lessons from a French killer he met in jail and who used to box savate style. Murray had the rep of being able to kill you with one kick.

He kicked Charlie in the belly as soon as they got out of the car. Charlie doubled up but charged Murray head down, two hundred and forty pounds of wild bull. Murray sidestepped and kicked Charlie in the leg. Charlie crashed into a wall and bounced off it like a rubber rhino. Murray the shrimp gave a high kick and caught Charlie under the chin, and as Charlie wobbled, Murray kicked him in the kneecap and he went down. Murray kicked him in the groin, creased his face, crunched his nose with the side of his shoe. He danced around Charlie, kicking elbows, ribs, shins, calves, and thighs, kicking ass and back and then kicking Charlie's face lightly, left foot, right foot, lightly but still a kick, drawing blood, rolling the head from side to side like a leaky soccer ball.

Fogarty left the garage and went inside the house. He poured himself a double whiskey and stood looking at a fly on the front screen door. Jack and Kiki came down the stairs, Jack carrying Kiki's suitcase.

"Can I see you, Jack?" he said and they went out on the porch, and Fogarty said, "I don't need that stuff going on back there. That cocksucker's not going to leave any face on the man."

"All right. The Goose and Oxie can handle it alone."

"The Goose is a fucking maniac. He oughta be in a cage."

"The Goose knows what he's doing. He won't hurt him too bad."

"He's gonna kill him. You said you didn't want to kill him."

"The Goose won't kill him. He's done this before."

"He's a sick son of a bitch."

"Listen, don't get your balls out of joint. Drive us to

town. Have a drink in the village while we have dinner. Change your mood."

So Fogarty drove them in, and Jack checked Kiki in at the Saulpaugh to get her away from the farm. He moved her around like a checker. Fogarty drove Jack back to his own house at midnight and went to sleep himself on the porch sofa where he was awakened at two in the morning by the private buzzer, the one under the second porch step. Jack was at the door almost as soon as Fogarty got himself off the soda. Jack was wide awake, in his red silk pajamas and red silk robe. It was Oxie at the door.

"Northrup's shot," Oxie said.

"Who shot him?"

"Murray."

"What the hell for?"

"He had to. He acted up."

"Where are they?"

"In Northrup's car, in the driveway."

"You half-witted cocksucker, you brought him here?"

"We didn't want to leave him no place."

"Get him over to the farm. I'll meet you there in ten minutes."

Fogarty pulled up behind the Northrup car which Oxie had parked in shadows on the farm's entrance road.

"He looks dead," Jack said when he looked at Charlie's crumpled frame in the back seat. The seat was full of blood near his head.

"He ain't peeped," Murray said. "I think he's a cold fishy."

Jack picked up Charlie's hand, felt it, dropped it.

"What happened?"

"I was past Newburgh when he got the rope off," Murray said.

"Who tied him up?"

"Me," said Murray.

"He got free and swung a tire iron and hit me in the neck," Murray said. "Almost broke my neck."

"I was followin' in our car and I saw him swerve, almost go in a ditch," Oxie said.

"Where'd he get a tire iron?"

"It musta been down behind the seat," Murray said. "It wasn't on the floor when we put him in."

Jack kept nodding, then threw up his hands in a small gesture.

"You had to shoot him?"

"It was only one shot, a fluke. What am I supposed to do about a guy with a tire iron?"

"You're a fucking maniac. You know what this could cost me? Front pages. Not to mention a fucking war." He hit the roof of the car with his fist.

"What do we do with him?" Oxie asked.

"Get some weights, we'll put him in the river," said Murray.

"Goddamn this," Jack said. He kicked Northrup's fender. Then he said, "No, the river he could float up. Take him in the woods and bury him. No, wait, they could still find the son of a bitch. I want no evidence on this. Burn him."

"Burn him?" Fogarty said.

"Use the fire out at the still. You can make it as big as you want, nobody pays attention." And then he said to Fogarty, "If he's dead, he's dead, right? A lump of mud."

"What about Jesse and his kids?"

"Go see them. Tell them to stay away from the still tonight."

"You can't burn a man's body in that pit out there," Fogarty said. "It's big but not that big."

"I'll take care of that," Murray said. "I'll trim off the edges."

"Christ Almighty."

"Try not to burn down the woods," Jack said. "When you're done, let me know. And you won't be done till there's nothing left, even if it takes two days. And then you clean out the pit and sift the ashes and smash the teeth and the bones that don't burn, especially the teeth. And scatter the pieces and the dust someplace else."

"Gotcha," said Murray. It was his kind of night.

"Speed, you better give 'em a hand," Jack said. "Drive

and stand guard. He don't have to touch anything," Jack told Murray.

"What does he ever touch?" Murray said.

Fogarty's stomach was burbling as he drove Northrup's car inside the barn. Murray said he needed a lot of newspapers, and so Fogarty went into the house and got some and told Jesse to stay clear of the still until he was told he could go back. Fogarty walked slowly back to the barn, feeling like he might puke. When he saw what Murray had already done to Charlie with the hatchet, it shot out of him like a geyser.

"Tough guy," Murray said.


"Marcus," Kiki said from the other end of the phone, and it was the first time she called me that, "I'm so damn lonely."

"Where's your friend?"

"I thought you might know."

"I haven't seen him since the night I took you to dinner."

"I've seen him twice since then. Twice in seventeen days. He's up in the country with her all the time. Christ, what does he see in that fat old cow? What's the matter with me? I wash my armpits."

"He's all business these days. He'll turn up."

"I'm getting bedsores waiting. What he don't know is I'm not waiting anymore. I'm going into a new show. I just couldn't cut it anymore, sitting, waiting. Maybe he sees me dancing again he'll think twice about playing titball with his fat-assed wife. I bet when she takes off her brassiere they bounce off her toes."

Kiki was tight, another road to power.

"What's the show and when does it open? I wouldn't miss that."

"*Smiles* is the name of it, and I do one routine by myself, a tap number. It's swell, Marcus, but I'd rather make love."

"Sure. Had any more visits from Jimmy Biondo?"

"Nobody visits me. Why don't you come down to the

city and see me? Just to talk, now. Don't let the little lady give you the wrong impression."

"Maybe I will," I said, "next time I'm down there on business."

I had no pressing business in New York, but I made it a point to go, and I presume it was for the same reason I'd helped old Jesse frame a new identity for himself and then got him a job in Boston—because I was now addicted to entering the world of Jack Diamond as fully as possible. I was unable not to stick around and see how it all turned out. And yes, I know, even as a spectator, I was condoning the worst sort of behavior. Absolute worst. I know, I know.

I called Jack when I decided to go down, for I had no wish to put myself in the middle of the big romance.

"Great," he said. "Take her to a movie. I'll be down Friday and we'll all go out."

"You know I still have some of your belongings."

"Hang onto them."

"I'd rather not."

"Only for a little while more."

"A very little while."

"What's the problem? They taking up too much room?"

"Only in my head."

"Clean out your head. Go see Marion."

So I did and we went to dinner and talked and talked, and then I took her to see Garbo in *Flesh and the Devil* in a place that hadn't yet converted to talkies. Kiki was a Garbo fanatic and looked on herself as a *femme fatale* even though she was nothing of the sort. The main thing she had in common with Garbo was beauty. There is a photo of Garbo at fifteen that has something of Kiki about it, but after that the ladies were not playing the same game. "The spiritually erotic rules over the sensually erotic in her life," an astrologist once said of Garbo, which was a pretty fair critical summary of her movie self at least.

Kiki was something else: a bread-and-butter sensualist, a let's-put-it-all-on-the-table-folks kind of girl. She actually enjoyed the feeling of being wicked. In the movie Garbo rushes to save her two loves from a duel, repentant that she started it all as a way of simplifying her choice between them. She falls through the ice on the way and it's good-bye Greta. Kiki leaned over to me and whispered, "That's what you get for being a good girl."

Kiki started out with the glitter dream, a bathing beauty at fifteen, a Follies' girl at eighteen, a gangster's doll at twenty. She yearned for spangles and got them quickly, then found she didn't really want them except for what they did for her head. They preserved her spangly mood. She was in spangles when she met Jack at the Club Abbey during his fugitive time, and he loved them almost as much as he loved her face.

"I always knew exactly how pretty I was," she told me, "and I knew I could write my own ticket in show business, even though I don't dance or sing so great. I don't kid myself. But whatever you can get out of this business with good looks, I'm going to get. Then when I met Jack it changed. My life started going someplace, someplace weird and good. I wanted to feel that good thing in me, and when I did it with Jack, I knew I didn't care about show business except as a way to stay alive and keep myself out front. I'm Jack's girl, but that's not all I am, and supposing he drops me? But I know he won't do that because what we have is so great. We go out, me and Jack, out to the best places with the best people, rich people, I mean, society people, famous people like politicians and actors and they fall all over us. I know they envy us because of what we've got and what we are. They all want to make sex with us and kiss us and love us. All of them. They look up my dress and down my front and touch me any place they can, stroke my wrist or hair or pat my fanny and say excuse me, or take my hand and say something nice and stupid, but it's all an excuse to touch. And when practically everybody you come across does this to you, women too, then you know you're special, maybe not forever, but for now. Then you go home and he puts it up in you and you wrap around him and you come and he comes, and it mixes up together and it's even greater than what was already great, but it's still

the same fantastic thing. You're in love and you're wanted
by everybody, and is anything ever better than that? One
night, when Jack was in me, I thought, Marion, he's not
fucking you, he's fucking himself. Even then I loved him
more than I'd ever loved anything on earth. He was
stabbing me and I was smothering him. We were killing
everything that deserved to die because it wasn't as rich as
it could be. We were killing the empty times, and then we'd
die with them and wake up and kill them again until there
wasn't anything left to kill and we'd be alive in a way that
you can never die when you feel like that because you own
your life and nothing can ruin you.

"And then he leaves me here for seventeen days and
keeps track of everygoddamnbody I buy a paper off or
smile at in the lobby, and so I stay in and practice my dance
steps and listen to Rudy Vallee and Kate Smith, and I don't
even have a view of the park because Jack doesn't want to
be a target from the trees. This is a nice little suite and all,
and do I mean little. Because you can lose your mind
staying in two rooms, and so I fix my hair and pluck my
eyebrows. I know when every hair in my eyebrows first
pokes its way out. I watch it grow. I take a hot bath and I
rub myself off to forget what I want. One day I did that four
times and that's not healthy for a young person like me and
I'll tell you straight, I'm to the point where I'm not going to
be so damn particular who's inside me when I want to feel
that good thing. But I never cheated on him yet, and I don't
want to. I don't want to leave him, and that's the God's
truth. I almost said I can't leave him, but I know I can. I can
leave if I want. But I don't want to leave. That's why I took
the job in *Smiles*. To show him I can leave him, even when I
don't want to."

At 9:30 P.M. on Saturday, October 11, 1930, three men,
later identified as members of the Vincent Coll gang,
walked into the Pup Club on West Fifty-first Street in
Manhattan. One walked up to the short one-eyed man at the
bar and said softly to him, "Murray?" The one-eyed man
turned on his stool and faced two guns.

"You're out, Murray," the man who had spoken to him said, and the other two fired six bullets into him. Then they left.

An hour and a half later, in an eighth-floor room at the Monticello Hotel, across the hall from the room occupied by Marion Roberts, two men stepped off the elevator at the same time that two others were touching the top step of the stairs leading to the eighth floor. The four fanned out into the cul-de-sacs of the hallways and returned to the elevator with an all clear, and Jimmy Biondo stepped out past a blanched elevator man. The five men, Jimmy at the center, walked down the hall to Room 824 and knocked three times, then twice, then once, and the door opened on Jack Diamond in shirtsleeves, a pistol on the arm of the chair he was sitting in. Count Duschene said he stood to Jack's left, and at other points around the room were the men who had confronted Murray earlier in the evening: Vincent Coll, Edward (Fats McCarthy) Popke, and Hubert Maloy.

"Hey, Jimmy," Jack said. "Glad you could come. How you getting along?"

Pear-shaped Jimmy, still mistrusting the room, stared at all faces before settling on Jack's and saying, "Whatayou got to offer aside from my money?"

"Sit down, Jimmy, chair there for you. Let's talk a little."

"Nothing to talk about. Where's the money?"

"The money is in good hands. Don't worry about that."

"Whose good hands?"

"What's the difference if it's safe?"

"Never mind the horseshit, where's the money?"

"What would you say if I told you it's on its way back to Germany?"

"I'd tell you you ain't got very fucking long to live."

"I'm going back there, Jimmy, and this time I'll get in. Don't you like instant seven-to-one on your money?"

"I like my money."

"We made a deal. I want to keep my part of the bargain is all."

"No deal. Tony Amapola knows how you deal. Charlie Northrup knows how you deal."

"I knew you'd think of me when Tony got it. But I had nothing to do with that. I like Tony. Always did. As for Charlie I do know what happened. It was a free-lance job. Charlie made enemies up in the country. But Charlie and I were as close as you and Tony. We were like brothers."

"Charlie had a different story. He said you were a fuckhead."

"You don't believe me, ask any of these boys who it was gave it to Charlie."

Jimmy looked around, settled on Fats McCarthy. Fats nodded at him.

"Murray The Goose," Fats said. "He give it to Charlie."

"You heard yet what happened to Murray The Goose?" Jack asked Jimmy.

"No."

"Somebody just dealt him out, up in the Pup Club. Walked in and boom-boom-boom. Cooked The Goose. Somebody got even for Charlie is how I read it. Now how do you like your friends?"

"It's a fact," The Count said. "I happened to be in the club at the time."

"There's a coincidence for you," Jack said.

"Puttin' it on The Goose don't mean he was even in the same state."

"Ask around. Don't tell me you didn't hear the rumors."

"I hear nothin'."

"You oughta listen a little instead of talking so much about money. There's more to life than money, Jimmy."

"Fuck life. I been listenin' too long. I been listenin' to your bullshit here five minutes, and I don't see no money onna fuckin' table. I tell you what—you got a telephone I make a call to an old frienda yours. Charlie Lucky."

"Always glad to say hello to Charlie."

"He be glad to say hello to you too because half the two hundred come outa his pocket. Whataya think of that, you Irish fuck?"

"I'll tell you what, you guinea fuck, call Charlie. He tells me it's half his I'll have it for him in the morning."

Jimmy moved his elbow at one of his young gunmen: early twentyish, pencil-line mustache. The gunman dialed, said something in Italian, waited, handed the phone to Jimmy.

"That you, Charlie?" Jimmy said. "I'm with our friend. He wants to know were you my silent partner. Okay. Sure." He handed Jack the phone.

"Charlie, how you doin'? You staying thin? Right, Charlie, that's the only way. You were. You did. So. Yeah. Now I get it. You're not saying this just for Jimmy. You wouldn't con me after all these years. Right. I understand. Let's have a drink one of these days, Charlie. Any time. Beautiful."

Jack hung up and turned to Jimmy. "He said he loaned you twenty grand at fourteen percent."

"He don't say that."

"I just talked to the man. Did you hear me talk to him? What am I, a guy who makes up stories you see with your own eyes?"

"He's in for half, no interest."

"I tell you what, Jimmy. I'll have twenty available in the morning. I'll call you and tell you where to pick it up and you can pay Charlie back. Meantime we still got a deal with what's left."

"Charlie, give me a hundred, you fuckheaded fuck!" Jimmy screamed and stood up, and everybody's pistol came out at the same time. Jack didn't touch his. All the pistols were pointed at all the other pistols. Anybody moved it was ten-way suicide.

"We don't seem to be getting anyplace," Jack said. He lit a Rameses and sat down and crossed his legs. "Why don't you go have a drink and think about life, Jimmy? Think about how rich you'll be when I come back with all that beautiful white stuff. A million four. Is that hard to take or is that hard to take?"

"I'm talkin' to a dead man," Jimmy said.

"Dead men pay no debts, Jimmy."

"Keep lookin' for me," Jimmy said.

"Watch yourself crossing the street," Jack said.

These were atrocious melodramatics, and I would not give them the time of day, despite my trust in Fogarty, except that when Jimmy and his friends left the Monticello and walked down West Sixty-fourth Street, a car came in their direction at low speed and two shotgun blasts from a back window blew apart two of Jimmy's shooters. Jimmy and the other two escaped with only a certain loss of dignity.

Count Duschene later remembered Jack's reaction when he heard the news: "Mustache cocksuckers. Fast as you knock 'em off they bring in another boatload." The rest of the news came out in the morning paper: Murray, with six bullets in him, was not yet dead.

Kiki said that the positively worst time of her life was when she was hiding at Madge's apartment and the knock came on the door and Madge turned to her and said, "Get in the bedroom and hide." So she went first behind Madge's big Morris chair, but then she said to herself, Gee, they'd look here right away, and so she started to roll under Madge's canopy bed with the beaded curtain, but then she said to herself, Won't they look under here, too? And so she stood in the closet behind Madge's summer and winter dresses and coats until she realized that anybody opening the door would look right through the hangers into her great big beautiful brown eyes, and so she took Madge's dyed muskrat everybody thought was mink off the wooden hanger and covered herself with it and rolled into the smallest ball she could make out of herself and faced the wall with her rounded back to the door so they would think the coat had fallen off the hanger on top of a pile of shoes and little boxes and galoshes. And then they'd go away. Yes. Go away. Let me alone.

Right then, Kiki would have said if anyone had asked her, she ordinarily didn't like to be alone. But now it was quite necessary, for she had to figure out what she was going to do with her life. She never had to hide in a closet before, ever. Jack's fault. Her fault too for staying with him, waiting for him. She had decided to leave him for good, truly leave this time and not just go back into show business or take a train home to Boston with her mad money. No. This was the end. Nothing on earth could make her stay with Jack Diamond for another day because he truly did kill people.

She had read all the news stories when he was in Europe, but she didn't read past the parts where they began to say things about him. She'd just throw the papers in the bottom of her closet for Jack because she knew how he loved to save clippings about himself. And what a big stack it got to be! She didn't even read any of the long series of articles they wrote about him because the first one began by calling him Eggs Diamond. Because eggs are yellow. And though she knew Jack wasn't yellow, she didn't really know what color he was. She didn't know anything really deep about him except what he said and what she wanted him to say and what he said was "You're gorgeous in my life" and "You're the most beautiful thing in the world. I deserve you." And she said to that, "And I deserve you, too." And they went into their silk cocoon then. Her warm bed with the pink silk sheets and her white silk nightgown and Jack in his yellow silk pajamas with the green dragon on them, and slowly they took the silk off one another and just smothered themselves in the cocoon and fucked and fucked and fucked. And when they were all through they went to sleep and woke up, and then they fucked and fucked some more and took a shower and went to see Jolson again in *Mammy,* and had dinner and came back to the cocoon, and didn't they fuck even more? They certainly did. Oh, wasn't that the cat's knickers? Vo-de-oh-do! There was never anything like that in her life before Jack, though she knew about fucking all right, all right. But fucking is one thing and fucking with Jack was another thing altogether. It was not the glitter. Sometimes when you fucked it was just to get something or because you thought you ought to or because you liked his looks and he was nice to you and it was expected of you and you wanted to do what was

expected. It was your role to fuck men who were nice
because you're only young once, isn't that so? Isn't that
why you wanted to be in the glitter dream? To glitter by
yourself? And what better way to glitter than to fuck
whenever you felt like it? Fuck the best people, the most
beautiful people. Do you like to fuck? Oh, I love it, don't
you?

But then she met Jack and she didn't want anybody but
him. Now it wasn't just liking to fuck. It was liking to fuck
Jack. And it was feeling wanted and taken and also taking
and also wanting, which was the key to the thing that
changed in her. She wanted in a new way. Jack taught her
that. She wanted not just for the moment or the hour or the
day, but she wanted permanently.

"We'll always live in the cocoon, won't we?"

"Sure, kid."

"We'll make love even when you're seventy-five, won't
we?"

"No, kid. I'm not going to live to be seventy-five. I didn't
expect to make it to thirty-three."

And that changed her again. She wanted him and wanted
what he gave her forever and ever, but now she had to think
about outliving him, of this maybe being that last time she
would ever put her arms around him and bite his ear and
play with his candy cane because then he might get up and
get dressed and go out and die. Well, then she wanted him
more than ever. She didn't know why. She just called it
love because that's what everybody else called it. But it
wasn't only that, because now she wanted not just Jack
himself but Jack who was going to die. She wanted to kiss
and fuck somebody who was going to die. Because when he
died, then you had something nobody else could ever get
again.

And then Jimmy Biondo came and talked to her and she
said she didn't believe what he said about Jack being so
awful. But she went and read all the papers she was saving
in the closet and oh, the things they said that Jack did all his
life, and she couldn't believe her eyes because they were so
awful, so many killings and torturing people and burning

prostitutes with cigarettes. Oh, oh, oh! And so she knew
then she would leave him. She knew it and she knew it and
she knew it all Saturday night even after he came to her
room and they went into the cocoon killing the bad things.
She forgot while that was happening that she was going to
leave him, for how can you leave a person when they're
making you forget the bad things? But when it was over she
remembered and when she went to sleep alongside him she
thought of it and she was still thinking about it when she
woke up and saw him drinking the orange juice he'd
ordered for them both, with toast and eggs and coffee and a
steak for him, and she thought of it while he ate the steak in
his blue pajamas with the red racehorses on them. I am
seeing you eat your last piece of steak. I am seeing you
wear your last pajamas. She would kill him in her mind and
that would be the end of Jack Diamond for Marion Roberts.
So long, Jackie boy. I loved your candy. Gee it was swell.
But you're dead now for me. You're mine forever. Marion
Roberts is not going to go on living her life as a gangster's
doll, a gangster's moll. Marion Roberts is her own woman
and she is not going to live for fucking. She is not going to
live for any one man. She is not going to live for killing
because she knows better. She knows how good life is and
how hard it is to make life good. She's going to move on to
something else. She can go on dancing. She will find a way
to live out her life without gangster Jackie.

But then she wondered: What is it about a gangster like
him? Why did I take up with him? Why didn't I believe
what everybody said about him, that I might wind up in the
river, that I might get shot in bed with him, that he might
ruin my face if he ever caught me cheating? Because
gangsters are evil and don't care about anybody but
themselves. Why didn't she believe those things? Because
she wanted it all out of life, all all all there was to get. The
top, the tip, the end, the reach, the most, the greatest, the
flashiest, the best, the biggest, the wildest, the craziest, the
worst.

Why did Kiki want the worst? Because she was a
criminal too? A criminal of love? Birds of a feather,

Marion. You knew even as you were saying that you were leaving him that you wouldn't leave. You knew as you read about the torture he did and the killing he did that you wouldn't give him up because you knew about the other side of that glorious man, with his candy up in your sweet place and his mouth on yours. You wouldn't give that up.

Even when those men came to the hotel this morning and Jack went to meet them and said to them while you were lying there in the half-empty cocoon, even when he said: "Hello, boys, how are you? Be right with you," and said to you that he'd only be a few minutes, and that he had some business to finish up, and went out in the hallway still in his blue pajamas with the red racehorses and the darker blue robe with the white sash and the white diamond embroidered on the breast pocket, even then you knew.

You got up and went into the shower and you let it smother you like you smothered him and you were standing in that sweet heat after love in the morning when you heard the shots: two, four, six, then none, then three more and another and another and another. And you froze in all that heat because you said to yourself (Oh, God forgive you for saying it), you said: That murdering bastard, he's killed somebody else.

Later, when she started to dance, she remembered looking at her feet and said to herself: These are going to be the most famous legs on Broadway. And she danced on that for five minutes to the piano man's rippling repetition of a tune of four-four tempo whose name she couldn't remember any more than she could remember the piano man's name or the director's name or the name of the musical itself. Black mesh stockings enveloped her most famous legs. White trunks covered her most famous hips. A white blouse tied at the midriff covered her most famous breasts. And black patent leather tap shoes covered her most famous toes, which nobody realized yet were famous. She thought of how people would behave when they found out how famous they were and tried to let that thought crowd out the rest. But she couldn't. Because her mind

went back to what it was that was going to make her toes so
famous and she stopped dancing, seeing it all again, seeing
herself see it this time and knowing she was webbed in
something that wasn't even going to be possible to get out
of. So she looked at the piano man and then at the director,
and while the other girls went on dancing, she decided to
fall down.

The next thing she knew she was sitting at her mirror
with all her theatrical makeup on the table in front of her,
and the calico kitten Jack had won for her at the Coney
Island shooting gallery, all cuddly and sleepy in the middle
of the table. In the mirror she saw Madge Conroy sitting on
a chair beside her, and Bubble, the chorus boy who had
helped Madge pick her off the floor. They both stared at
her.

"She finally blinked," Bubble said.

"You all right?" Madge asked.

"Close your eyes, for heaven's sake," Bubble said,
"before they explode all over us."

The mirror was outlined by a dozen bare bulbs, all
illuminating her face, so famous to be, so unknown to even
its own exploding eyes. Why aren't you running away,
pretty lady in the brilliant mirror? What brought you to the
theater? Is it that you don't know what to be afraid of yet?
Do you think the theater will protect you? Do you think the
mirror will?

Bubble said, "Mirror, mirror on the wall, who's got the
Kikiest eyes of all?"

"Shut up," Madge said, "and get her a drink someplace." Madge rubbed Kiki's wrists as Bubble went away.

"Oh, Madge, I just got to talk to somebody."

"I had a hunch you did. I kept watching you dancing out
there. You looked like somebody kidnapped your brain.
Like a zombie."

"Honest to God, Madge, it's something awful. It's so
awful."

Bubble came back with an unlabeled half-pint. Madge
grabbed it and looked at it, smelled it and poured Kiki a
drink. She capped the bottle, set it on Kiki's table, and told
Bubble, "Will you please, please, please get lost?"

"What's the *matter* with her?"

"I'll find out if you let us be."

"Yes, nursie."

"You oughta be rehearsing out there," Kiki said to Madge.

"They can do without me. I know the routine."

"It was so awful. Honest to God, this is the worst thing that ever happened to me."

"What? What the hell happened?"

"I can't tell you here. Can we go someplace? I don't know what to do, Madge. Honest to God I don't."

"We can go over to my apartment. Change your clothes."

But it took so much effort for Kiki to take off her trunks that she left on the rest, her mesh stockings and the rehearsal blouse and only put on her skirt and street shoes. She threw her other street clothes and the trunks and tap shoes into her red patent-leather hatbox and saw, as she did, her street makeup and her purse, the only things she took when she ran out of the hotel.

"I'm ready," she said to Madge.

"You better buy a paper," Kiki told Madge when they came to a newsstand at Broadway and Forty-seventh. And as Madge did and after Kiki saw her utter a small "Oh" and throw her face into the paper, Kiki turned to see an old man in a gray bowler, with a yellowing white walrus mustache and pince-nez specs, wearing a frock coat with lapel gardenia and a brocaded yellow vest across which dangled an old watch chain and fob in the design of a mermaid. Blank cards, an ink bottle, and a quill pen lay in front of him on a table that folded into a suitcase. Samples of his script-for-sale, tacked to the table's drop-leaf front, were splendid with antique swirls, curlicues, and elegant hills, valleys, and ovals.

"I hope you're in show business, young lady," the old gent said to her over his pince-nez.

"As a matter of fact, I am."

"It's the only safe place for talentless beauty, miss."

"You've got some crust saying I don't have any talent."

"Anywhere else you'll be destroyed."

"As a matter of fact, I'm quitting show business."

"A disastrous move."

"But none of *your* business."

"Forgive me for speaking so freely, but you look to me like a bird wounded in the heart, the brain, and between the legs, and we in the Audubon Society do what we can for the wounded. My card."

"I'm Jack Diamond's girl. What about that?"

"Ah, then, ah. I had no way of knowing"—and the old man retrieved his card and handed her another. "Jack Diamond is an entirely safe place. You have nothing to fear, my dear, as long as you have a role in Jack Diamond's hilarious tragedy."

She looked at the card and saw in the obsolete glory of his pen strokes the biography of her vampy, bondaged, satin-slippered addiction. The card read: "There is no good and bad in the elfin realm." When she looked up, the man had packed his table and was halfway down the block.

Kiki looked over Madge's shoulder at the headline which read: JACK DIAMOND SHOT FIVE TIMES BY GUNMEN IN 64TH STREET HOTEL.

"I was there," Kiki told Madge.

"You didn't shoot him, did you?"

"Oh, Madge, I love him."

"What's that got to do with it? Come on, we've got to get you off the street."

And so they took a cab to Madge's place and Kiki had a stiff drink, a very stiff one, and then she started to weep. So Madge held her hand and Kiki knew that even though Madge was her friend that she was touching her because she was a special person. Because Madge never touched her like that before, stroking the back of her hand, patting it with her fingertips; and Kiki felt good because somebody was being nice to her and she finally told Madge then how she heard the shots as she stood in the shower. And she thought somebody would come in and shoot her. And she would die in the bathtub, her blood going down the drain.

Maybe Jack would be the one to shoot her. Why did Kiki think that about Jack?

Then she heard the running in the corridor, and she said to herself, why, Jack wouldn't run away and leave me, and so she quickly got into her pink robe and went next door to Jack's own room and saw the door open and Jack on the floor with his eyes open but not moving, looking up at her. And she said, "Oh, Jackie, you're dead," but he said, "No I'm not, help me up," and they were just the best old words she'd ever heard and she put her arms under him and lifted him and he put one of his hands over his stomach and the other over his chest to hold in the blood where they'd shot him. Blood was coming down his face and all down his blue pajamas so you couldn't even see the red racehorses anymore.

"Get the whiskey," Jack told her when she had him sitting on the bed, and she looked around the room and couldn't see it, and Jack said, "In the bathroom," and when she got it, he said, "In my mouth," and she wiped the blood off his lips and poured in the whiskey. Too much. He choked and coughed and new blood spurted out of one of the holes in his chest, and like a little fountain turned on and off by the pumping of his heart, it flowed down over his fingers.

"Get The Count," he said, "across the hall," and she knocked on The Count's door until her knuckles hurt and he came to Jack's room and Jack said to her then: "Get the hell out of here and don't come back and don't admit you were here or you're all washed up." And Kiki nodded but didn't understand and said to Madge, "How would I be washed up, Madge? Did he mean in show business?" And Madge said, "Go on," so she said The Count called a doctor as she was leaving and then took Jack to another room in the hotel, down the hall, because Jack said the killers might come back to see if they did the job right. And Kiki, still in her pink robe, backed down the hallway toward her own room, and watched The Count walking and holding Jack, who was bent like a wishbone, and in they went to another room, which was when Kiki decided she would go to the theater and behave like nothing at all had happened. And things went along perfectly well, didn't they? They went along fine, just fine until she saw it all again while she was dancing. What she saw was that little spurt of blood coming out of Jack's chest like a fountain after she gave him too much whiskey. That was when she decided to fall down.

Madge read in the paper that two gunmen came running out of the hotel about the time Jack was shot and got into a car with its motor running and its door open and drove off with their New Jersey license plates. Those men, awful men, had shot Jack two places in the chest and once in the stomach and once in the thigh and once in the forehead, and the doctor said he was certainly not going to be able to go on living with all those holes in himself. The paper made no mention of the pretty little lady who was the first to see it all, but Kiki knew that her time of attention was going to come.

She caught the faintest smell of mothballs in Madge's closet, and she thought of marriage because only married people need mothballs. Kiki would never keep anything long enough to worry about moths unless she happened to be married. Last year's things? She stuck them away and bought new ones and let the moths have their fun. Kiki never thought of herself as married, even though she and Jack talked about it all the time. She talked about it and Jack tried to change the subject, is more like it.

"I'll marry you someday, kid," he told her once, but she didn't believe that and wasn't even sure she wanted to believe it. Kiki doing the wash. Kiki beating the rugs. Kiki making fudge. It was certainly a laughing matter.

When the second knock on the door came, just seconds after Madge told her to hide in the bedroom (and she was in the closet by then, under the muskrat and smelling the mothballs by then), she heard Madge say to somebody, "What the hell are you bothering me for? You have no right to come in here." But they didn't go away. Kiki heard them walking in the rooms and heard them just outside the door, so she breathed so silently that not even a moth would have known she was there.

Who are those men is what Kiki wanted to know. Are they after me? And at that the light flashed into the closet and the muskrat unwrapped itself from her back and a hand grabbed her and two great big faces stared down at her.

"Go away," she said. "I don't know you men." And she pulled one of Madge's dresses over her face. She could hear Madge saying, "I had no idea she was involved in any shooting. I certainly wouldn't have brought her into my own home if I thought she was mixed up in any sort of nasty shooting business. I don't want this kind of publicity."

But they put Madge's picture in the papers too. With her legs crossed.

Jack didn't die. He became more famous than ever. Both the *News* and the *Mirror* ran series on him for weeks. The *News* also ran Kiki's memoirs: How I went from bathing beauty to the Ziegfeld chorus to Jack Diamond's lap. She and Jack were Pyramus and Thisbe for the world and no breakfast table was without them for at least a month. Kiki overnight became as famous as most actresses, her greatest photo (that gorgeous pout at the police station) on every page one.

Jack recovered at Polyclinic Hospital, and when he came to and saw where he was, he asked to be moved into the room where Rothstein had died. The similarities to this and A. R.'s shooting, both shot in a hotel, both mysterious about their assailants, money owed being at the center of both cases, and Jack being A. R.'s man of yore, were carefully noted by the press. You'd think it was the governor who'd got it, with all the bulletins on conditions and the endless calls from the public. The hospital disliked the limelight and worried too about the bill until a delivery boy brought in an anonymous thirty-five hundred dollars in crumpled fifties and twenties and a few big ones with a note: "See Jack Diamond gets the best." This the work of Owney Madden.

Of course Jack never said who shot him. Strangers he could never possibly identify, he told Devane. Didn't get a good look at them. But the would-be assassins were neutral underworld figures, not Jack's enemies and not in Biondo's or Luciano's circle (nor Dutch Schultz's either, who was generally credited with the work at the time). Their neutrality was why Jack let them in.

Their function was to retrieve Charlie Lucky's money, but Jack refused to give it back, claiming finally that Luciano was lying about his role in the transaction. This was not only Jack's error, but also his willful need to affront peril. The visitors' instructions were simple: Get *all* the money or kill him.

He was sitting on the bed when they took out their guns. He ran at them, swinging the pillow off the bed, swinging in rage and terror, and though both men emptied their pistols, the pillow deflected both their attention and their aim so that only five of twelve bullets hit him.

But five is a lot. And the men ran, leaving him for dead.

The Count called me to say that Jack mentioned me just before he went unconscious from his wounds. "Have Marcus take care of Alice and see she doesn't get the short end from those shitkickers up in the country," he told The Count. Then when Alice called me from the hospital and said Jack wanted to see me, I went down, and it turned out he wanted to make his will: a surreptitious ten thousand to Kiki, a token bequest, no more; everything else to Alice. The arrangement seemed to speak for itself: Alice, the true love. But Jack wasn't that easy to read even when he spelled it out himself. Money was only the measure of his guilt and his sense of duty, a pair of admitted formidables, but not his answer to his enduring question.

He was in good spirits when I saw him, his bed near the window so he could hear the city, the roar of the fans spiraling upward from Madison Square Garden during the fights, all the cars on Broadway squealing and tooting, the sirens and bells and yells and shouts of the city wafting Jackward to comfort him, the small comfort being all he would have for two and a half months, for Jack Diamond the organism, was playing tag with adhesions, abscesses and lungs which had the congenital strength of tissue paper.

Jack's mail came in sacks and stacks, hundreds upon

hundreds of letters during the first weeks, then dwindling to maybe a steady twenty-five a day for a month. A good many were sob stories, asking for his money when he shuffled off. Get well wishes ran second, and dead last were the handful who wanted him dead: filthy dog, dirty scum. Women were motherly, forgiving, and, on occasion, uninhibited: "Please come to my home as soon as you are up and around and I will romp you back to good health. First you can take me on the dining room table, and then in the bathroom on our new green seat, and the third time (I know you will be able to dominate me thrice) on my husband's side of the bed."

"Please when you are feeling better I would like you to please come and drown our six kittens," another woman wrote. "My husband lost everything in the crash. We cannot afford to feed six more mouths, and children come before cats. But I am much too chickenhearted to kill them myself and know you are strong enough to oblige."

"I have a foolproof plan for pass-posting the bookie I bet with," wrote a horseplayer, "but, of course, I will need protection from his violence, which is where you come in as my partner."

"Dear Mr. Legs," a woman wrote, "all my life I work for my boy. Now he gonna go way and leave his momma. He is no dam good. I hope he die. I hope you shoot him for me. I will pay what you think up to fifty-five dollars, which is all the extra I got. But he deserve it for doing such a thing to his momma who gave him her life. His name is Tommy."

"Dear Sir," wrote a man, "I read in the papers where you have been a professional killer. I would like to hire you to remove me from this life. I suppose a man in your position gets many requests like this from people who find existence unbearable. I have a special way I would prefer to die. This would be in lightly cooked lamb fat in my marble bathtub with my posterior region raised so you may shoot several small-caliber bullets into my anus at no quicker than thirty-second intervals until I am dead."

A package came which the police traced, thinking someone was trying to make good on the numerous threats

that Jack would never leave the hospital alive. An
eight-year-old girl from Reading, Pennsylvania, had sent
it—an ounce of holy oil from the shrine of Ste. Anne de
Beaupré.

"I read about Mr. Diamond being shot and how his arm is
paralyzed, and I have been taught in school to help those
who are down and out," the child told police.

"Punk kid," Jack said. "What does she mean down and
out?"

On the street in front of Polyclinic little clusters of Jack's
fans would gather. A sightseeing bus would pass and the
announcer would say, "On your right, folks, is where the
notorious Jewish gangster Legs Diamond is dying," and all
would crane but none would ever see the lip quivering as he
slept or the few gray hairs among all the chestnut, or the
pouches of experience under his eyes, or the way his ears
stuck out, and how his eyes were separated by a vertical
furrow of care just above the nose, or that nose: hooked,
Grecian, not Jewish, not Barrymore's either, merely a
creditable piece of work he'd kept from damage, now
snorting air. He was twelve pounds under his normal one
fifty-two and still five ten and a half while I sat beside his
bed with his last will and testament in my pocket for his
signature. And he wheezed just like other Americans in
their sleep.

I'd been fumbling through a prayer book on Jack's
bedside table while he slept and I had turned up a credo I no
more accepted as mere coincidence than I did the
congruence of his and my pleasure in Rabelais; which is to
say I suspected a pattern hovering over our relationship.
The credo read:

> You work much harm in these parts, destroying and
> slaying God's creatures without his leave; and not only have
> you slain and devoured beasts of the field but you have
> dared to destroy and slay men made to the image of God:
> wherefore you are worthy of the gallows as a most wicked
> thief and murderer; all folk cry out and murmur against you.
> But I would make peace, Brother Wolf, between them and

you, and they shall obtain for you so long as you live, a
continual sustenance from the men of this city so that you
shall no more suffer hunger, for well I know that you have
done all this harm to satisfy your hunger. . . .

This paraphrased perfectly my private plot to forget
Charlie Northrup the way everybody else was forgetting
him. He was gone off page one, only a subordinate clause in
Jack's delightful story. Charlie, thanks for giving us so
much of your time. Such fun having a cadaver in the
scenario, especially one we can't locate. But, Charl, please
excuse us while we say a little prayer for Jack.

I remember also the passing thought that maybe it would
be better if Jack never woke up, and then I remember
seeing him wide awake, swathed in hospital-white hygienic
purity.

"Hey, Marcus," he said, "great to wake up to a friendly
face instead of some snooping cop. How's your ballocks?"

"Friendly toward ladies," I said, and when he laughed he
winced with pain.

"I been dreaming," he said. "Talking to God. No joke."

"Uh-oh."

"Why the hell is it I'm not dead? You figured it out?"

"They were bum shooters? You're not ready to die?"

"No, it's because I'm in God's grace."

"Is that a fact? God told you that?"

"I'm convinced. I thought I was just lucky back in '25
when they hit me. Then when Augie got it, I thought maybe
I was as strong as a man can be, you know, in health. But
now I think it's because God wants me to live."

He was not quite sitting up in bed, his prayer book there
all soft and black on the white table and his rosary twined
around the corner post of his bed, shiny black beads
capturing the white tubing. Did he appreciate the contrast?
I'm convinced he created it.

"You've got the disease of sanctity," I told him.

"No, that's not it."

"You've got it the way dogs get fleas. It's common after
assassination attempts. It accounts for the closeness
between the church and aging dictators. It's a kind of

infestation. Look at this room." Alice had hung a crucifix
over the bed and set a statue of the virgin on the
windowsill. The room had been priest-ridden since Jack
moved into it, the first a stranger who came to hear his
confession and inquired who shot him. Even through
quasi-delirium Jack recognized a Devane stooge. The next,
a Baltimore chum of Alice's who dropped in without the
press learning his name, comforted Jack, blessed him
through opiated haze, then told newsmen: "Don't ask me
to tell you anything about that poor suffering boy in there."
And then came good Father Skelly from Cairo, indebted to
Jack for the heavenly music in his church.

"God won't forget that you gave us a new organ," said
the priest to the resurrecting Jack.

"Will God do the same for us when ours gets old?" Jack
asked.

The priest heard his confession amid the two bouquets of
roses Alice renewed every three days until Jack said the
joint smelled like a wake, and so she replaced them with a
potted geranium and a single red wax rose in a vase on the
bedside table.

"I thought you'd given up the holy smoke," I said. "I
thought you had something else going for you."

"What the hell am I supposed to do after people keep
shooting me and I don't die? I'm beginning to think I'm
being saved."

"For dessert? Looks classic to me, Jack. Shoot a man
full of bullets and he's a candidate for blessedness."

"What about you and your communion breakfasts?
Big-shot Catholic."

"Don't be misled. That's just part of being an Albany
Democrat."

"So you're a Democrat and I got fleas. But it turns out I
don't mind them."

"I can see that, and it all ties in. Confession, sanctity,
priests. Yes, it goes with having yourself shot."

"Come again?"

"The shooting. I've assumed all along that you rigged
it."

"You're not making sense."

"Could it have happened without your approval? You saw them alone, you know what they were. I know what such go-betweens can be, and I'm not even in your business. And you never had any intention of turning over that money. You asked for exactly what you got. Am I exaggerating?"

"You got some wild imagination, pal. I see why you score in court."

But when he looked at me, that furrow of care between his eyes turned into a question mark. He ran his fingertips along the adhesive tape of his chest bandage, pleasurably some might say, as he looked at the author of the bold judgment. Jack Diamond having himself shot? Ridiculous. He fingered the rosary entwined over his right shoulder on the bed, played the beads with his fingertips as if they were keys on an instrument that would deliver the music he wanted to hear. Organ music. A sound like Skelly's new machine. No words to it, just the music they play at benediction after the high mass. Yes, there are words. From a long time ago. The *"Tantum Ergo."* All Latin words you never forget, but who the hell knows what they mean? *"Tantum ergo sacramentum, veneremur cernui; et antiquum documentum, Novo cedat ritui."*

A bridge.

A certain light.

Something was happening to him, Jack now knew.


"I want you to talk for me," he said. He had recovered from my impertinence, was restoring the client-attorney relation, putting me in my place. "I want you to talk to some people upstate. A few judges and cops, couple of businessmen, and find out what they think of my setup now. Fogarty's handling it, but he can't talk to those birds. He's too much of a kid. I got through to all those bastards personally, sent them whiskey, supported their election campaigns, gave 'em direct grease. All them bums owe me favors, but the noise in the papers about me, I don't know now whether it scares 'em or not."

" 'Pardon me, your honor, but are you still in the market for a little greasy green as a way of encouraging Jack Diamond with his bootlegging, his shakedowns, and his quirky habit of making competitors vanish?' Is that my question?"

"Any fucking way you like to put it, Marcus. You're the talker. They all know my line of work. It'll be simpler if I still got the okay, but I don't really give a goddamn whether they like it or not. Jack Diamond's got a future in the Catskills."

"Don't you think you ought to get straight first?"

"You don't understand, Marcus. You can carve out a whole goddamn empire up there if you do it right. Capone did it in Cicero. Sure there's a lot of roads to cover, but that's all right. I don't mind the work. But if I slow now, somebody else covers those roads. And it's not like I got all the time in the world. The guineas'll be after me now."

"You think they won't ride up to the Catskills?"

"Sure, but up there I'll be ready. That's my ball park."

I've often vacillated about whether Jack's life was tragic, comic, a bit of both, or merely a pathetic muddle. I admit the muddle theory moved me most at this point. Here he was, refocusing his entire history, as if it had just begun, on the dream of boundless empire. It was a formidable readjustment and I considered it desperate, but maybe others would find it only confused and ridiculous. In any case, given the lengths he was willing to go to carry it off, it laid open his genuine obsession.

I might have credited the whole conversation about the Catskills to Jack's extraordinary greed if it hadn't been for one thing he said to me. It took me back to 1928 when Jack was arrested with his mob in a pair of elegant offices on the fourteenth and fifteenth floor of the Paramount Building, right on Times Square. Some address. Some height. Loftiness is my business, said the second-story man.

Now Jack gave me a wink and ran his hand sensuously along the edge of the chest bandage that was giving him such pleasure. "Marcus," he said, "who else do you know collects mountains?"

I've been in Catskill maybe a dozen and a half times, most of those visits brief, on behalf of Jack. I don't really know the place, never needed to. It's a nice enough village, built on the west bank of the Hudson River about a hundred or so miles north of the Hotsy Totsy Club. Henry Hudson docked near this spot to trade with the Indians and then went on up to Albany, just like Jack. The village had some five thousand people in this year of 1931 I'm writing about. It had a main street called Main Street, a Catskill National Bank, a Catskill Savings Bank, a Catskill Hardware and so on. Formal social action happened at the IOOF, the Masonic Temple, the Rebekah Lodge, the American Legion, the PTA, the Women's Progressive Club, the White Shrine, the country club, the Elks. Minstrel shows drew a good audience and visiting theater companies played at the Brooks Opera House. The local weekly serialized a new Curwood novel at the end of 1931, which Jack would have read avidly if he'd not been elsewhere. The local daily serialized what Jack was doing in lieu of reading Curwood.

Catskill was, and still is, the seat of Greene County, and just off Main Street to the north is the four-story county jail, where Oxie Feinstein was the most celebrated resident on this particular day. Before I was done with Jack, there would be a few more stellar inmates.

The Chamber of Commerce billed the village as the gateway to the Catskills. The Day Line boats docked at Catskill Landing, and tourists were made conscious of the old Dutch traditions whenever they were commercially applicable. A Dutch friend of mine from law school, Warren Van Deusen, walked me through the city one day and showed me, among other points of interest, the home of Thomas Cole on Spring Street. Cole was the big dad of the nineteenth-century's Hudson River school of painting, and one of his works "Prometheus Bound," a classic landscape, I remember particularly well, for it reminded me of Jack. There was this giant, dwarfed by the landscape, chained to his purple cliff in loincloth and flowing beard (emanating waves of phlogiston, I'll wager) and wondering when the eagle was going to come back and gnaw away a few more of his vitals.

. I called Van Deusen, who was involved in Republican county politics, as a way of beginning my assignment for Jack. In the early days of our law practice, his in Catskill, mine in Albany, I recommended him to a client who turned into very decent money for Van, and he'd been trying for years to repay the favor. I decided to give him the chance and told him to take me to lunch, which he did. We dined among men with heavy watch chains and heavier bellies. Warren, still a young man, had acquired a roll of well-to-do burgher girth himself since I'd last seen him, and when we strolled together up Main Street, I felt I was at the very center of America's well-fed, Depression complacency. It was an Indian summer day, which lightened the weight of my heavy question to Warren, that being: "What does this town think of Jack Diamond?"

"A hero, if you can believe it," Van said. "But a hero they fear, a hero they wished lived someplace else."

"Do you think he's a hero?"

"You asked about the town's feelings. My private theory is he's a punishment inflicted on us for the sins of the old patroons. But maybe that's just my Dutch guilt coming out."

"You know Jack personally?"

"I've seen him in some of our best speakeasies and roadhouses. And like most of the town, I at least once made it a point to be passing by that little barbershop right across the street there when he and his chums pulled up at eleven o'clock one morning. They always came at eleven for their ritual daily shave, hair trim, shampoo, hot towels, shoe shine, and maybe a treatment by the manicurist from up the street."

"Every day?"

"Whatever else I say about him, I'll never accuse him of being ill-groomed."

"I can't imagine this being the extent of your knowledge, a political fellow like yourself."

Van gave me a long quiet look that told me the subject

was taboo, if I wanted to talk about a subsidy from
Jack—that he was not in the market and knew no one who
was.

"I know all the gossip," he said, finessing it. "Everybody does. He's the biggest name we've had locally since
Rip Van Winkle woke up. I know his wife, too; I mean, I've
seen her. Alice. Not a bad-looking woman. Saw her awhile
back at the Community Theater, as a matter of fact. They
change the movie four times a week and she sees them all.
People seem to like her, but they don't know why she stays
with Diamond. Yet they kind of like him, too—I suppose in
the same way you find him acceptable."

"I accept him as a client."

"Sure, Marcus, And what about that European jaunt?
Your picture even made the Catskill paper, you know."

"Someday when I understand it all better, I'll tell you
about that trip. Right now all I want to know is what this
town thinks."

"What for?"

"Grounding purposes, I suppose. Better my understanding of the little corner of the world where my candle burns
from time to time."

Van looked at me with his flat Dutch face that seemed as
blond as his hair. He was smiling, a pleasant way of calling
me a liar. Van and I knew each other's facial meanings
from days when our faces were less guarded. We both
knew the giveaway smirks, the twitches, puckers, and
sneers.

"Now I get it," he said. "It's him. He wants to know if
the town's changed, how we take to his new notoriety. Is he
worried?"

"What are you talking about?"

"All right, Marcus, so you won't play straight. Come on,
I want to show you something."

We walked awhile, Van singling out certain landmarks
for my education: There stood the garage the Clemente
brothers used before Jack terrorized them out of the beer
business. Over that way is a soft drink distributor's
warehouse, which Diamond also took over. This was news

to me. But I suppose when you set out to corner the thirst market, you corner it all.

Then Van turned in at the Elks' Club and led me to the bar. I ordered a glass of spring water and Van a beer, and then he motioned to the bartender, a man who might have been twenty-eight or forty-five, with a muscular neck; large, furlable ears; and a cowlick at the crown of his head. His name was Frank DuBois and Van said he was a straight arrow, a countryman of old Huguenot stock, and a first-class bartender.

"I was just about to tell Marcus here about your visit from the Diamond boys," Van said to him, "but I know you tell it better."

DuBois snuffed a little air, readying his tale for the four-hundredth telling, and said, "They come in all right, right through that door. Come right behind the bar here, unhitched the beer tap and rolled the barrel right out the door. 'Say,' I says to 'em, 'what'd ya do that for?' And one of them pokes me with a gun and says it's because we wasn't buying the good Canadian beer and they'd deliver us some in the mornin'. 'Yeah,' I says, 'that's just fine, but what about tonight? What do the fellas drink tonight?' 'Not this,' said one of 'em, and he shoots a couple of holes in the barrels we got. Not a fella I'd seen around before, and don't want to see him again either. Then they went out back, two of 'em, and shot up the barrels out there. Took me and Pete Gressel half a day to get the place mopped up and dried out. Dangdest mess you ever saw."

"You know the fellow who poked the gun at you?" I asked.

"I knew him all right. Joe Fogarty. Call him Speed, they do. Nervous fella. Been around this town a long time. I seen him plenty with the Diamond bunch."

"When was all this?"

"Friday week, 'bout eleven at night. Had to close up and go home. No beer to serve. No people neither, once they saw who it was come in."

"Is that the right kind of beer Van's drinking now?"

"You betcha, brother. Nobody wants no guns pokin' at

them they can help it. Membership here likes peace and quiet. Nobody lookin' for trouble with Legs Diamond. He's a member this here club, you know. In good standin' too. Paid up dues and well liked till all this happen. Don't know what the others think now.''

It was tidy. If Jack let his men point a gun at his own club, what other club could be safe? DuBois moved up the bar and Van said quietly, ''A lot of people aren't just accepting this kind of thing, Marcus.''

''I don't know what that means, not accepting.''

''I'll let you use your imagination.''

''Vigilantes?''

''That's not impossible but not likely either, given the people I'm talking about. At least not at the moment.''

''What people *are* you talking about?''

''I have to exercise a little discretion too, Marcus. But I don't mean helpless people like Frank here.''

''Then all you've got for me is a vague, implied resistance, but without any form to it. People thinking how to answer Jack?''

''More than vague. More than thinking about it.''

''Van, you're not telling me much. I thought I could count on your candor. What the hell good are riddles?''

''What the hell good is Jack Diamond?''

Which was the same old question I'd been diddling with since the start. Van's expression conveyed that he knew the answer and I never would. He was wrong.

# JOHN
# THOMSON'S
# MAN

When the police went through Jack's house in one of their fine-combings near the end, somebody turned up a piece of plaster, one side covered with the old-time mattress ticking wallpaper. The paper was marked with twenty-five odd squiggles, which the police presumed were some more code notations of booze deliveries; and they saved the plaster along with Jack's coded notebooks and file cards on customers and connections all over the United States and in half a dozen foreign countries.

I asked Alice about the plaster before she was killed, for it turned up in the belongings they returned to her, through my intervention, after Jack died. When she saw it she laughed a soft little laugh and told me the squiggle marks were hers; that she'd made them the first weekend she and Jack were married; that they stayed in an Atlantic City hotel and hardly went out except to eat and that they'd made it together twenty-five times. After number five, she said, she knew they'd only just started and she kept the score on the wall next to the bed. And when they checked out, Jack got the tire iron from the car and hacked out the plaster with all the squiggles on it. They kept it in their dresser drawer until the police took it away. Alice made Jack give the hotel clerk twenty-five dollars for the broken wall. A dollar a squiggle. Half the price of professional action.

I thought of Warren Van Deusen telling me people didn't understand why Alice stayed with Jack. She had her reasons. Her memories were like those squiggles. She was profoundly in love with the man, gave him her life at the outset and never wanted anyone else. She was in love with loving him too, and knew it, liked the way it looked. She won a bundle of psychic points sitting at his bedside after the Monticello, cooing into his ear while the reporters listened at the door and the nurses and orderlies carried messages to tabloid snoops. Alice heroine. Sweet Alice. Alice Blue. When the crash comes they always go back to their wives. Faithful spouse. Betrayed, yet staunch. Adversity no match for Alice. The greatest of the underworld women. Paragon of wifely virtue. Never did a wrong thing in her life. The better half of that bum, all right, all right.

Texas Guinan let her have a limousine, with chauffeur, all the time she was in New York, so she wouldn't have to worry about hawking taxis to and from Jack's bedside. The press gave Kiki the play at first, but then they caught up with Alice at the police station (that's where Kiki and Alice first met; they glowered at each other, didn't speak). The press boys tried to make her the second act of the drama, but Alice wouldn't play.

"Did you know the Roberts girl?"

"No."

"Did you know any of his friends?"

"He had many friends, but I'm not sure I knew them."

"Did you know his enemies?"

"He didn't have any enemies."

Alice was no sap, had no need for publicity. Not then. It was all happening in her ball park anyway, whether she talked or not.

"You know," she said to me after the shooting, "I hardly even brought up the subject of Marion with him. Only enough to let him know I wasn't going to die over it, that I was bigger than that. I was just as sweet as I could be. Gave him the biggest old smile I could and told him I remembered the squiggles and let him lay there and fry."

She said she was thinking about her Mormon dream and how it didn't make any sense when she had it, even after she told John about it and they talked about him having another wife. It was in the time of the roses, after he was shot the first time, on Fifth Avenue, when he was afraid he would die before he had done what he set out to do. He saw girls at his Theatrical Club. She knew that. But that was a trivial thing in the life of Alice Diamond because she had John as a husband, and that superseded any girl. Alice Diamond was bona fide. The real thing. A wife. And don't you forget it, John Diamond. A wife. For life.

She sat on the arm of his chair one night in the living room and told him she dreamed he'd brought home a second wife. He stood alongside the woman in the dream and said to Alice, "Well, we'll all be together from now on." And Alice said, "Not on your Philadelphia tintype." But even as she said no to him she knew it was not no. Never a total no to anything John wanted. Then the other wife came in and started taking over little things Alice used to do for John. But after Alice told him the dream, he said, "Alice, I love you, nobody else." And Alice said to him, "No, you've got another wife." And they both laughed when he said to her, "Alice, we'll be together as long as we live."

Alice did not think her dream would ever come true. Maybe he'd see a woman now and then. But to move into a hotel, to keep a woman permanently, to see her just hours after he'd seen Alice, and maybe even after he'd *been with* Alice, was terrible. It was not incomprehensible. How, after all, could *anything* be incomprehensible to a person like Alice, who knew what everybody along Broadway thinks, wants, does, and won't do? Alice was as smart about life as anybody she ever came up against. She knew the worst often happened, worse than the worst you can imagine, and so you made provisions. Her prayer book helped her make provision for the worst: for the sick, the dying, for a happy death, for the departed, for the faithful departed, for the souls in Purgatory, for the end of man, for release from Purgatorial fire. Even a special one for John. She knew she was deceived by John's capacity for passion, and so she sat by his bed and read the *Prayer to Overcome Passions and to Acquire Perfection:* "Through the infinite

merits of Thy painful sufferings, give John strength and
courage to destroy every evil passion which sways his
heart, supremely to hate all sin, and thus to become a
saint.''

Saint John of the Bullets.

"Alice, there you are, Alice,'' Jack said when he woke
up and saw her. The beginning and the end of his first
coherent sentence.

She smiled at him, picked up the wax rose she'd brought
him, the one rose, the secret nobody else knew, and said,
"It's wax, John. Do you remember?'' The corners of his
mouth eased upward and he said, "Sure,'' so softly she
could barely hear it. Then she ran her fingers ever so softly
through his hair. Bittykittymins. Sweet baby. Son of a
bitch. Bittykittymins. And when he was really awake for
the first time, when he'd even had a little bouillon and she'd
combed his hair and they put a new hospital gown on him,
she said to him in her silent heart: I wish you had died.

"How are you, kid?'' she said out loud, the first time in a
long, long while she called him kid, the code word.

"I might make it.''

"I think you might.''

"They got me good this time.''

"They always get you good.''

"This time it hurt more.''

"Everybody got hurt this time.''

Alice was hurt, and she knew why. Because she loved an
evil person and always would. She now wondered about
her remarkable desire to see Jack dead. She had at times
wished death to bad persons. Because Alice was good.
Alice would not stay long in Purgatory. Because she was
good. But now she wanted to die herself when she wished
John dead and saw how deeply evil she herself was. She
prayed to Jesus to let her want John to live. Let me not
think that he's evil. Or me either. I know he's a good man in
certain ways. Don't tell me I should've married somebody
pure and holy. They would've bored the ass off me years
ago. After all, I didn't marry a priest, Jesus. I married a

thief. And landed on the front pages alongside him. My hubbydubbylubbybubby. People asking me questions. Coming for interviews. Forced to hide. Hide my light under the bushel. It will shine brighter for all that hiding. Light polishes itself under the bushel. What an awful thing for Alice to think: polishing up her own private brilliance through the troubles of Johnny-victim-on-the-boat. Oh, Alice. How awful you really are. It is so enormously wrong and wicked and evil and terrible, loving John for the wrong reasons; wanting him dead; profiteering from your marriage. Alice was evil and she truly hated herself.

But listen, kiddo, Alice knew she was married to one of the rottenest sons of bitches to come along in this century. Just the fact that she was able to sit there stroking his fingers and the back of his hand and running her hand through his bittykittymins gave her the evidence of her moral bankruptcy. Yet she was still trying to reform John. She didn't want him to be a Mason on the square. She wanted a genuine four-cornered Catholic. Four corners on my bed. Four angels overhead. Matthew, Mark, Luke, John. Bless the bed we all lie on. She put a rosary around his neck while he lay under the influence of drugs to invoke grace and secret blessings God couldn't possibly deliver publicly to such a person. Hypocrisy for her to do that. Yes, another sin, Alice. But she knew that without being a hypocrite she could never love John.

Knowing this, knowing how evil she was for being married to evil, she therefore knew she must stay married to it, knew she must suffer all the evil that evil brings. For how else could a girl, an Irish Catholic girl brought up to respect grace and transubstantiation, ever get to heaven? How else could a girl hold her head up in her family? How else could a girl ever show her face among her peers, let alone her sneering inferiors, unless she expiated her awfulness, that black terribleness of marrying and loving evil, except by staying married to it?

Suffer the evil to come unto me, said doughty Alice. Perhaps she enjoyed that evil too much. More than she could ever expiate. Perhaps she will merit longer and more excruciating punishment than she can yet imagine. Yes, the very worst may be in store for this little lady.

But she sat there with the villain, stroking, cooing, telling the Good Lord Above: Go ahead and do me, Lord. I can take it.


Sitting beside his hospital bed watching him breathe perhaps the final breaths of his life, she knew he was unquestionably hers now forever. Nothing and nobody could part them. She had withstood the most scandalous time and had not stopped loving him. She was the victim of love: sucker and patsy for her own sloppy heart. But from suckerdom comes wisdom the careful lover never understands.

"I'm sorry what this is doing to you," John said to Alice.

"Are you, John? Or is that just another apology?"

"It's a bad time for you, Al, I know. But this ain't exactly a great big bed of roses I got myself into."

"You'll get out of it."

"We both will. We'll have a special time when I get my ass up out of here."

"Give your ass a rest."

"Anything you say."

"Give everybody's ass a rest."

"Whose ass you talking about now?"

"Maybe you could figure it out if you live long enough."

"I'm in no condition to tire anybody out."

"That's a nice change. I also mean no visitors. I already put up with more than I can stand, but I won't put up with her here."

"She hasn't shown up yet. And if she does, it won't be my doing. But she won't."

"The police won't let her out of custody, that's why she won't."

"She knows better. She knows her place."

"Oh? And just what the hell *is* her place?"

"No place. Nothing. She knows she's got no hold on me."

"That's why you kept her in the hotel."

"I was doing her a favor."

"How often? Twice a night?"

"I saw her now and then, no more. A friend. A date when I was in town looking for company."

"The whole world's got it figured out, John. Don't start with the fairy tales."

She was talking to him as if he had the strength of a healthy man, but he was only an itty-bitty piece of himself, a lump of torn-up flesh. Why did Alice talk so tough to a sick lump? Because she knew the lump was tough. She was tough too. A pair of tough monkeys, is how John always said he saw this husband-wife team. Yes, it's why we get along, was Alice's way of looking at this toughness. She always treated him this way, even when he was most vulnerable, told him exactly what she thought. There now. See? See his hand move off the sheet and onto her knee? See his fingers raise the hem of her skirt? Feel him touch her with his fingertips on the flesh above her stocking? Home territory. Jack is coming home. Jack is not discouraged by her tough line. Tough monkey, my husband.

When Alice felt these fingers on herself she looked at the single wax rose on the bedside table and remembered the early growth of the rose. There will always be a wax rose in our life, Alice now insisted, and in his own way Jack remembered it too. With a tea rose in his lapel when he wore his tux. Never a gardenia. Never a white carnation. Always the red, red rose.

It was after the Fifth Avenue shooting in 1925 and he sat in the living room of their house on 136th Street in the Bronx with the top and back of his head shaved and bandaged, wearing the old blue wool bathrobe with the holes in the elbows, sitting alone on the sofa, looking at the floor and drinking coffee royals because he liked their name and potency; eating saltine crackers with peanut butter but no meals, awake all night for a week but saying almost nothing, just making soft whimpering sounds like a dog dreaming of his enemies. Keeping Alice awake until her ear got used to the rhythms of the whimpers. When the rhythm was right, she could always sleep.

She had tried the rosary, but he wasn't ready for that, and so it only sat on the coffee table alongside the wax roses in the orange and black Japanese vase. She had tried to calm him, too, by reading from the prayer book, but he wouldn't listen. He was as far from religion as he'd ever been. Alice told him he should take the shooting as a warning from God to get out of the rackets or die in the bullet rain.

"I don't want to be like that woman in Brooklyn who lost a husband and two sons in the gang wars," Alice said to him. But that had no effect. Alice didn't know what would have any effect.

"Come on out, boy," she had said one day, a little whisper in his ear. "We all know you're hiding in there."

But all he ever asked was did you call in my numbers: 356, 880, and 855. Jackie, Jack and John out of the dream book. Jack always played numbers, from the time he ran them as a teen-ager. Now he played five dollars on each number and she never knew whether he hit them or not. Her game was not played with numbers.

She would also turn the radio on for him, but when she'd leave the room, he'd turn it off.

"Jesus, they really almost got me, almost wiped me out," he said one night and shook his head as if this were an incredible possibility, some wild fancy that had nothing to do with the real life and potential of John Thomas Diamond. That was when Alice knew he was not going to quit the rackets, that he was committed to them with a fervor which matched her own religious faith.

"They can't keep me down forever" had been his phrase from when she first knew him. She hoped he would find another way up, but this thought still was the central meaning of his whimpers.

The bridge lamp was on the night Alice got out of bed, unable to accept the animal noises John was making. They had become more growls than whimpers or the whisperings of troubled sleep. She saw him on the floor where he'd slid off the couch. He was pointing his pistol at the Japanese vase.

"Are you going to shoot the roses, John?"

He let his hand fall, and after a while she took the pistol. She helped him back onto the sofa and then knelt in front of him in her nightgown, not even a robe over it, and herself visible right through the sheer silk. Her amply visible self.

"I can't sleep no more," he said to her. "I close my eyes and I see my mother screaming every time she breathes."

"It's all right, boy. It's going to be all right."

And then Alice rose half up out of her kneeling position, but without sitting either, stretched herself lengthwise and leaning, a terribly uncomfortable position as she recalls it. But John could see all of her very private self that way, feel her all along his arm and his hip and his good leg that wasn't shot. And without the pistol his hand was free. First she said the Our Father to him just to put the closeness of God into his head again and then she maneuvered herself until her perfect center was against the back of his hand. Then she moved ever so slightly so he could feel where he was, even if he couldn't see it or didn't sense it.

Did this maneuvering work? Alice put an arm around his neck and kissed him lightly on the ear. He turned his hand so the knuckles faced away from her. Then, with a little bit of help, that sheer silk nightgown rose to the demands of the moment. John said she smelled like grass in the morning with dew on it, and she said he smelled like a puppyduppy, and with both their hands where they had every right in the world to be, Mr. and Mrs. John Diamond fell asleep on the sofa in their very own parlor. And they slept through the night.

When they killed Alice, she was sitting at the kitchen table of her Brooklyn apartment looking at old clippings of herself and Jack. One clip, of which she had seven copies, showed her beside his bed of Polyclinic pain. She sat beneath her cloche hat in that old clip, a few tufts of blond hair (not yet dyed Titian to match that of Kiki, The Titian-Haired Beauty of the tabloids; not yet dyed saffron to glamorize her for her Diamond Widow stage career) sticking out from underneath. She was all trim and tailored in the gray tweed suit Jack had helped her choose. "My hero!" was what Alice had written on the clipping.

I imagine her in her final kitchen remembering that bedside scene and all that came later up in Acra when Jack left the Polyclinic bed: Alice nursing her John back to health, massaging his back with rubbing alcohol, taking him for walks in the woods with some of the boys fanning out ahead and behind them, making him toddies and cooking him beef stew and dumplings and tapioca pudding. Now he was more handsome than he'd ever been in his life. Oh, brilliant boy of mine! Hero of the strife! From New Year's Day, 1931, when he left the hospital, on through early April, she possessed him exclusively. Oh, rapturous time! Nothing like it ever before, ever again. What a bitter cup it was for Alice to leave him after that.

She told me she left him the day after Lew Edwards and I paid a curious visit to idyllic Acra. Lew was a Broadway producer, dead now, who grew up next door to me in North Albany, became the impresario of most of Public School 20's undergraduate productions, and went on to produce plays for Jeanne Eagels, Helen Morgan, and Clifton Webb. Lew knew Jack casually, knew also my connection with Jack, and called me with an idea. I told him it was sensational and would probably die at first exposure to Jack. Lew said it was worth the chance and we met at the Hudson train station. I drove down from Albany to pick him up, we had lunch in Catskill, took a short walk to buy the papers, a fateful purchase, and then drove out to Jack's.

The chief change from my summer visit was the set of outside guards at the house, a pair of heavies I'd never seen before who sat in a parked Packard and periodically left the driveway to explore the road down toward Cairo and up toward South Durham for visitors who looked like they might want to blow Jack's head off. When that pair drove off, another pair on duty on the porch took up driveway positions in a second car, and a set from the cottage took up posts on the porch as inside guards.

"Just like Buckingham Palace," Lew said.

Alice gave me a big hello with a smooch I remember. That tempting appleness. Fullness. Pungent wetness I remember thee well. But she meant nothing by such a lovely kiss except hello, my friend. Then she said to me: "Marcus, he's wonderful. He looks better than he has in years. I swear he's even handsomer now than when I married him. And it's better other ways too."

She shook Lew's hand and took my arm and walked me into the living room and whispered: "He's all through with her, Marcus, he really is. He hasn't seen her since the shooting, only once. She came to the hospital one day when I wasn't there, but I heard about it. Now she's all a part of the past. Oh, Marcus, you can't imagine how glorious it's been these past few months. We've been so damned happy you wouldn't believe we were the same people you saw the last time you were here."

She said he was upstairs napping now, and while she went up to rouse him, Cordelia, the maid, mixed us a drink. Jack came down groggy—and in shirtsleeves, baggy pants and slippers—and gave us a few vague minutes. Then we were a group—Jack and Alice on the sofa with Alice's pair of long-legged dolls in crinoline between them, his hand in hers across the dolls, Lew and I in the overstuffed chairs as witnesses to this domestic tranquillity.

"So you've got a deal," Jack said, and Lew immediately went for his cigar case to get a grip on something. Jack had met Lew five years back when Lew butted aggressively into a bar conversation Jack was having, without knowing who Jack was. That's another story, but it turned out Lew gave Jack a pair of theater tickets that introduced him to Helen Morgan, who became one of Jack's abstract passions. He never could understand why Morgan was so good, why she moved him so. It was perverse of him to want to understand the secrets of individual talent, to want secret keys to success. He was still talking about La Morgan the night he died.

"I got a million-dollar idea for you, Jack," Lew said, stuffing a cigar in his mush but not lighting it.

"My favorite kind."

"And you don't have to do a thing for a year."

"It gets better."

"I like it too," said Alice.

"You've got to be one of the most famous, pardon the expression, criminals in the East, am I right?"

"I wouldn't admit to any wrongdoing," Jack said. "I just make my way the best I can."

"Sure, Jack, sure," said Lew. "But plenty of people take you for a criminal. Am I right?"

"I got a bad press, no doubt about that."

"Bad press is a good press for this idea," said Lew. "The more people think you're a bad-ass bastard, the easier we make you a star."

"He's already a star," Alice said. "Too much of a one."

"You mean a Broadway star?" Jack asked. "I carry a tune, but I'm no Morgan."

"Not Broadway. I mean all of America. I can make you the biggest thing since Billy Sunday and Aimee Semple McPherson. An evangelist. A preacher."

"A preacher?" Jack said, and he gave it the big ho-de-ho-ho.

"A preacher how?" Alice said, leaning forward.

Lew said, "If you'll excuse me for saying it, there's about a hundred million people in this country know your name, and they figure you're one mean son of a bitch. Is this more or less true or am I mistaken?"

"Go on," Jack said. "What else?"

"So this mean son of a bitch, this Legs Diamond, this bootlegger, this gang leader, he gives it all up. Quits cold. Goes straight. And a year later he hears the voice of the Holy Spirit. He is touched by a whole damn flock of flaming doves or tongues or whatever the hell they send down to touch guys with, and he becomes an apostle for the Big Fellow. He goes barnstorming, first on a shoestring. A spiritual peanut vendor is all he is. A man with a simple commitment to God and against Satan and his works. He talks to anybody who'll sit still for half an hour. The press picks him up immediately and treats him like a crazy. But also it's a hell of a story for them. Whatsisname, on the

road to Damascus. You know the routine. Doesn't care
about gin, gangs, guns, gals or gelt anymore. All he wants is
to send out the word of God to the people. The people!
They'll sell their kids for a ticket. Tickets so scarce you've
got to hire a manager, and pretty soon you, he, winds up on
the vaude circuits, touches every state, SRO all over. A
genuine American freak. Then he gets word from God he
shouldn't play theaters with those evil actors. Oughta talk
in churches. Of course the churches won't have him. Fiend
turned inside out is still a fiend. And a fake. A show biz
figure. So he has to play stadiums now, and instead of six
hundred he draws maybe twenty thousand and winds up in
Yankee Stadium with a turnaway crowd, a full orchestra,
four hundred converts around him, the best press agent in
town, and the first million-dollar gate that isn't a heavy-
weight fight. More? Sure. He builds his own temple and
they come from all over the world to hear him speak. Then,
at his peak, he moves off to Paris, London, Berlin. And
hey. Rome.''

Lew fell against his chairback and lit the cigar he'd been
using as a pointer, a round little man with a low forehead,
thick black hair, and a constant faceful of that stogie. He
worked at being a Broadway character, structured comic
lines to deliver ad lib at the right moment: "Jack Johnson
got the worst deal of any nigger since Othello'' is one of his
I never forgot.

Lew had bought the New York *Daily Mirror* and read bits
of it in the car on the way to Jack's, and now he pulled it out
of his right coat pocket in a gesture he said later was caused
by discomfort from the bulk, and tossed it onto the coffee
table. Jack opened it, almost as a reflex, and skimmed the
headlines while all the silence was drumming at us. Jack
turned the pages, barely looking at them, then stopped and
said to Lew: "How the hell could I preach anything
anybody'd believe? I haven't made a speech since high
school when I did something from Lincoln. I'm no speaker,
Lew.''

"I'd make you one," Lew said. "I'd get you drama
coaches, speech coaches, singing teachers. Why, for

Christ's sake, you'd be a voice to reckon with in six months. I seen this happen on Broadway.''

"I think it's a fantastic idea," Alice said. She stood up and paced in front of the couch nervously.

"You know the power you'd have, Jack?" Lew asked. "Hell, we might even get a new American church going. Sell stock in it. I'd buy some myself. A man like you carrying the word to America what the rackets are all about, giving people the lowdown on the secret life of their country. Jesus, I get the shivers thinking how you'd say it. Snarling, by God. Snarling at those suckers for God Almighty. Your stories don't have to be true but they'll sound true anyway. Jesus, it's so rich I can hear the swoons already. I could put together a team of writers'd give you the goddamnedest supply of hoopla America ever heard. Force-feed 'em their own home-grown bullshit. Tell 'em you've gotten inside their souls and know what they need. They need more truth from you, that's what they need. Can't you see those hicks who read everything they can lay hands on about crooks and killers? Organ music with it. 'The Star-Spangled Banner.' 'Holy, Holy, Holy.' You know what Oscar Wilde said, don't you? Americans love heroes, especially crooked ones. Twenty to one you'd get a movie. Maybe they'd even run you for Congress. A star, Jack, I mean a goddamn one hundred percent true-blue American star. How does it grab you?''

Alice exploded before Jack could say anything at all.

"John, it's absolutely perfect. Did you ever believe anybody'd ask you to do anything as marvelous as this? And you can do it. Everything he said was true. You'd be wonderful. I've heard you talk when you're excited about something and I know you can do it. You know you can act, you did it in high school, oh, I know it's right for you.''

Jack closed the newspaper and folded it. He crossed his legs, left foot on right knee and tapped the paper on his shoe.

"You'd like to do a little barnstorming, would you?" he said to her.

"I'd love to go with you.''

Alice's faith. Love alone. She really believed Jack could do anything. Such an idea also had pragmatic appeal: saving herself from damnation. Show business? So what? As to the stardom, well, the truth is, Alice could no longer get along without it. Yet this promised stardom without taint. Oh, it was sweet! The promise of life renewed for Alice. And her John the agent of renewal.

"What's your reaction, Marcus?" Jack said. And when I chuckled, he frowned.

"I can see it all. I really can see you up there on the altar, giving us all a lesson in brimstone. I think Lew is right. I think it'd work. People would pay just to see you sit there, but if you started saving their souls, well, that's an idea that's worth a million without even counting next month's house." And I laughed again. "What sort of robes would you wear? Holy Roman or Masonic?"

Maybe that did it, because Jack laughed then too. He tapped Alice lightly on the knee with the newspaper and tossed it on the coffee table in front of her. It's curious that I remember every move that newspaper made, not that Alice would've missed its message without us, although I suppose that's possible. The point is that Lew and I, on our mission for American evangelism, were innocent bearers of the hot news.

Jack stood up. "It's a joke," he said.

"No," said Lew, "I'm being straight."

"Make a funny story back in Lindy's if I said yes."

"Jack," said Lew, who was suddenly drained of facial blood by the remark, "this is an honest-to-God idea I had and told nobody but Marcus and now you and your wife. Nobody else."

Jack gave him a short look and figured out from his new complexion that he wasn't practical-joking.

"Okay, Lew. Okay. Let's say it's a nice try then. But not for me. Maybe it'd make a bundle, but it rubs me wrong. I feel like a stool pigeon just thinking about it."

"No names, Jack, nobody's asking for names. Tell stories, that's all. It's what you know about how it all works."

"That's what I mean. You don't tell the suckers how the game is played."

Alice picked up the *Mirror* and slowly and methodically rolled it into a bat. She tapped it against her palm the way a cop plays with a sap. I thought she was going to let Jack have a fast one across the nose. Good-bye barnstorm. Good-bye private Diamond altar. Good-bye salvation, for now.

Her crestfallen scene reveals to me at this remove that she really didn't understand Jack as well as I thought she did. She knew him better than anyone on earth, but she didn't understand how he could possibly be true to his nature. She really thought he was a crook, all the way through to the dirty underwear of his psyche.

"It'd be fun, Lew," Jack said, starting to pace now himself, relaxed that it was over and he could talk about it and add it to his bag of offers. "It'd be a hell of a lot of fun. New kind of take. And I know I got a little ham in me. Yeah, it'd be a good time, but I couldn't take it for long. I couldn't live up to the part."

Alice left the room and carried the newspaper with her. It looked like a nightstick now. I can see her unrolling it and reading it in the kitchen, although I was not in the kitchen. She turns the pages angrily, not seeing the headlines, the photos, the words. She stops at Winchell because everybody stops there and reads him. She is not really reading. Her eyes have stopped at his block of black and white, and she stares down at it, thinking of getting off the train in Omaha and Denver and Boston and Tallahassee and spreading the word of John and God and standing in the wings holding her John's robe, making him tea, no more whiskey, washing his socks, answering his mail, refusing interviews. Damn, damn, damn, thinks Alice, and she sees his name in Winchell.

In the living room, standing on his purple Turkish rug, framing himself against the blue silk he'd stolen from a Jersey boxcar eight years before, Jack was saying he couldn't be a hypocrite.

"That sound funny coming from me, Lew?"

"Not a bit, Jack. I understand." But I could see Lew too, watching a million-dollar idea curl up in the smoke of another Broadway pipe dream.

"Hypocrite? What the hell was he talking about?" Lew asked me later when we were on the way back to the Hudson station. "Does he think I don't know who he is?"

"He had something else in mind, I'm sure," I said. "He knows you know who he is. He knows everybody knows. But he obviously doesn't think what he's doing is hypocritical."

Lew shook his head. "All the nuts ain't on the sundaes."

Lew too. Victim of tunnel vision: A man's a thief, he's dishonest. What we didn't know as we listened to Jack was that he was in the midst of a delicate, supremely honest balancing act that would bring his life together if it worked, let it function as a unified whole and not as warring factions. Maybe Jack thought he was being honest in his retreat from page one, in his acquiescence to Alice's implorings that he become a private man, a country man, a home man, a husband. This behavior generated in Lew's head the idea that if Jack could only stay down long enough, he was fodder for American sainthood.

But Lew's conversion plan was false because Jack's behavior in retreat was false. Jack wasn't a private but a public man, not a country squire but a city slicker, not a home but a hotel room man, not a husband but a cocksmith, not an American saint but an insatiable extortionist. ("Fuck 'em," he said when I told him about Warren Van Deusen's vigilantes.) And he was not the sum of all these life-styles either, but a fusion beyond them all.

In a small way this was about to be demonstrated. Shirtsleeved, Jack shook our hands, walked us to the front door, apologized for not standing there with us, but said he didn't want to make it too easy for any passing shooters, and thanked us for livening up his afternoon.

The liveliness was just beginning.

The Winchell item in the *Mirror* read: "Stagehands in the Chicago theater where Kiki Roberts is dancing in 'Flying

High' under the name of Doris Kane can set their watch by
the phone call she gets every night at 7:30. You guessed the
caller: Legs Diamond. . . ."

"You son of a bitch, you said you weren't talking to
her."

"Don't believe everything you read."

"You're always out of the house at that hour."

"Doesn't mean a thing."

"You promised me, you bastard. You promised me."

"I talked to her once in four months, that's all."

"I don't believe that either."

"Believe Winchell then."

"I thought you were being straight with me."

"You were right. I was. I didn't see her, I didn't see
nobody."

"After all the goddamn nursing and handholding."

"I'm fond of the girl. I heard she was having some
trouble and I called her. She's all right."

"I don't believe that. You're a liar."

"What's that on your housedress?"

"Where?"

"By the pocket."

"A spot."

"A spot of what?"

"What's the difference what the spot is. It's a spot."

"I paid to have that housedress cleaned and pressed and
starched. The least you could do is keep it clean."

"I do keep it clean. Shut up about the housedress."

"I pay for the laundry and you put these things on and
dirty them up. Goddamn money going down the goddamn
laundry sink."

"I'm leaving."

"What's that in your hair?"

"Where?"

"Behind your right ear. There's something white. Is that
gray hair?"

"It might be. God knows I've got a right to some."

"Gray hair. So that's what you've come to. I spend

money so you can get your hair bleached half the colors of
the goddamn rainbow and you stand there and talk to me
with gray hair."

"I'm going upstairs to pack."

"What's that on your leg?"

"Where?"

"Right there on the thigh."

"Don't touch me. I don't want you to touch me."

"What is it?"

"It's a run in my stocking."

"Goddamn money for silk stockings and look what
happens to them."

"Get your hand away. I don't want to feel you. Go on,
get it away. I don't want your hand there. No. Not there
either. No. You won't get it that way anymore. Not after
this. No. Don't you dare do that to me with Cordelia in the
kitchen and after what I just read. You've lied once too
often. I'm packing and nobody on God's earth can do
anything to stop me."

"What if I moved her in with us?"

"Oh."

"We could work it out."

"Oh!"

"She's a great girl and she thinks the world of you. Sit
down. Let's talk about it."


Kiki lay naked on the bed that was all hers and which
stood where Alice's had stood before Jack had it taken out
and bought the new one. She was thinking of the evening
being unfinished, of the fudge that hadn't hardened the last
time she touched it, and of Jack lying asleep in his own
room, his heavy breathing audible to Kiki, who could not
sleep and who resented the uselessness of her nakedness.

They had been together in her bed at early evening,
hadn't eaten any supper because they were going to have
dinner out later. The fudge was already in the fridge then.
Jack was naked too, lying on his back, smoking and staring
at the wall with the prints of the Michelangelo sketches, the
punishment of Tityus and the head of a giant, prints Jack

told her he bought because Arnold Rothstein liked them and said Michelangelo was the best artist who ever brushed a stroke. Jack said Kiki should look at the pictures and learn about art and not be so stupid about it. But the giant had an ugly head and she didn't like the one with the bird in it either, so she looked at Jack instead of dopey pictures. She wanted to touch him, not look at him, but she knew it wouldn't be right because there was no spark in him. He was collapsed and he had tried but wasn't in the mood. He started out in the mood, but the mood left him. He needed a rest, maybe.

He wouldn't look at her. She kept looking at him but he wouldn't look back, so she got up and said, "I'm going downstairs and see if that fudge is hard yet."

"Put something on."

"I'll put my apron on."

"Take a housecoat. There may be somebody on the porch."

"They're all out in the cottage playing pool or in the car watching the road. I know they are."

"I don't want you showing off your ass to the hired help."

She put on one of Alice's aprons, inside out so it wouldn't look too familiar to Jack, and went downstairs. She looked in the mirror and knew anybody could see a little bit of her tail if there was anybody to see it, but there wasn't. She didn't want clothes on. She didn't want to start something and then have to take the clothes off in a hurry and maybe lose the spark, which she would try to reignite when she went back upstairs. She wanted Jack to see as much of her as he could as often as he could, wanted to reach him with all she could reach him with. She had the house now. She had beaten Alice. She had Jack. She did not plan to let go of him.

The fudge was still soft to her touch. She left another fingerprint in it. She had made it for Jack, but it wasn't hardening. It had been in the fridge twenty-eight hours, and it wasn't any harder now than it was after the first hour.

"What do you like—chocolate or penuche?" she had asked him the day before.

"Penuche's the white one with nuts, right?"

"Right."

"That's the one."

"That's the one I like too."

"How come you know so much about fudge?"

"It's the only thing I ever learned how to cook from my mother. I haven't made it in five or six years, but I want to do it for you."

The kitchen had all the new appliances, Frigidaire, Mixmaster, chrome orange juice squeezer, a machine for toasting two slices of bread. But, for all its qualities, Kiki couldn't find the ingredients she remembered from her mother's recipe. So she used two recipes, her own and one out of Alice's *Fanny Farmer Cook Book,* mixed them up together and cooked them and poured it all into a tin pie plate and set it on the top shelf of the fridge. But it didn't harden. She tasted it and it was sweet and delicious, but it was goo after an hour. Now it was still goo.

"It's all goo," she told Jack when she went back upstairs. She stood alongside him and took off her apron. He didn't reach for her.

"Let's go out," he said, and he rolled across the bed, away from her, and stood up. He put on his robe and went into his own room to dress. Even when Alice was there he had had his own room. Even at the hotel he had kept his own room to go to when he and Kiki had finished making love.

"Are you angry because the fudge didn't harden?"

"For crissakes, no. You got other talents."

"Do you wish I could cook?"

"No. I cook good enough for both of us."

And he did, too. Why Jack made the best chicken cacciatore Kiki ever ate, and he cooked a roast of lamb with garlic and spices that was fantastic. Jack could do anything in life. Kiki could only do about three things. She could dance a little and she could love a man and she could be pretty. But she could do those things a thousand times better than most women. She knew about men, knew what men told her. They told her she was very good at love and that she was pretty. They also liked to talk about her parts. They all (and Jack too) told her she was lovely everyplace. So Kiki didn't need to learn about cooking. She wasn't going to tie in with anybody as a kitchen slave and a fat mommy. She wore an apron, but she wore it her way, with nothing underneath it. If Jack wanted a cook, he wouldn't have got rid of Alice. Kiki would just go on being Kiki, somebody strange. She didn't know how she was strange. She knew she wasn't smart enough to understand the reasons behind that sort of thing. I mean I know it already, she said to herself. I don't have to figure it out. I know it and I'm living it.

Kiki thought about these things as she was lying naked in her bed wishing the fudge would harden. Earlier in the night, after Jack had rolled out of her bed, they'd gone out, had eaten steaks at the New York Restaurant in Catskill, one of the best, then had drinks at Sweeney's club, a good-time speakeasy. It was on the way home that everything was so beautiful and quiet. She felt strange then. She and Jack were in the back seat and Fogarty was driving. She was holding Jack's hand, and they were just sitting there, a little glassy-eyed from the booze, yes, but that wasn't the reason it was so beautiful. It was beautiful because they were together as they deserved to be and because they didn't have to say anything to each other.

She remembered looking ahead on the road and looking out the window she'd rolled down and feeling the car was moving without a motor. She couldn't hear noise, couldn't see anything but the lights on the road and the darkened farmhouses and the open fields that were all so brightly lighted by the new moon. The stars were out too, on this silent, this special night. It was positively breathtaking, is how Kiki later described the scene and the mood that preceded the vision of the truck.

That damn truck.

Why did it have to be there ahead of them?

Why couldn't Joe have taken another road and not seen it?

Oh, jeez, wouldn't everything in her whole life have been sweet if they just hadn't seen that truck?

When he saw the old man in the truck, got a good look and saw the side of his face with its bumpkin stupid smile, Jack felt his heart leap up. When Fogarty said, "Streeter from Cairo—he hauls cider, but we never caught him with any," Jack felt the flush in his neck. He had no pistol with him, but he opened the gun rack in the back of the front seat and unclipped one of the .38's. He rolled down the window on his side, renewed.

"Jack, what's going to happen?" Kiki asked.

"Just a little business. Nothing to get excited about."

"Jack, don't get, don't get me, don't get . . ."

"Just shut up and stay in the car."

They were on Jefferson Avenue, heading out of Catskill when the trucker saw Jack's pistol pointing at him. Fogarty cruised at equal speed with the truck until Streeter pulled to the side of the road across from a cemetery. Jack was the first out, his pistol pointed upward. He saw the barrels on the truck and quick-counted more than fifteen. Son of a bitch. He saw the shitkicker's cap, country costume, and he hated the man for wearing it. Country son of a bitch, where Jack had to live.

"Get down out of that truck."

Streeter slid off the seat and stepped down, and Jack saw the second head, another cap on it, sliding across the seat and stepping down, a baby-faced teen-ager with a wide forehead, a widow's peak, and a pointy chin that gave his face the look of a heart.

"How many more you got in there?" Jack said.

"No more. Just me and the boy."

"Who is he?"

"Bartlett, Dickie Bartlett."

"What's he to you?"

"A helper."

Streeter's moon face was full of rotten teeth and a grin.

"So you're Streeter, the wise guy from Cairo," Jack said.

Streeter nodded, very slightly, the grin stayed in place and Jack punched it, cutting the flesh of the cheekbone.

"Put your hands up higher or I'll split your fucking head."

Jack poked Streeter's chest with the pistol barrel. The Bartlett boy's hands shot up higher than Streeter's. Jack saw Fogarty with a pistol in his hand.

"What's in the barrels?"

"Hard cider," said Streeter through his grin.

"Not beer or white?"

"I don't haul beer, or white either. I ain't in the booze business."

"You better be telling the truth, old man. You know who I am?"

"Yes, I know."

"I know you too. You been hauling too many barrels."

"Haulin's what I do."

"Hauling barrels is dangerous business when they might have beer or white in them."

"Nothing but cider in them barrels."

"We'll see. Now move."

"Move where?"

"Into the car, goddamn it," Jack said, and he slapped Streeter on the back of the head with his gun hand. He knocked off the goddamn stinking cap. Streeter bent to pick it up and turned to Jack with his grin. He couldn't really be grinning.

"Where you taking that cider?"

"Up home, and some over to Bartlett's."

"The kid?"

"His old man."

"You got a still yourself?"

"No."

"Bartlett got a still?"

"Not that I know of."

"What's all the cider for then?"

"Drink some, make vinegar, bottle some, sell some of

that to stores up in the hollow, sell what's left to neighbors. Or anybody."

"Where's the still?"

"Ain't no still I know of."

"Who do you know's got a still?"

"Never hear of nobody with a still."

"You heard I run the only stills that run in this county? You heard that?"

"Yes siree, I heard that."

"So who runs a still takes that much cider?"

"Ain't that much when you cut it up."

"We'll see how much it is," Jack said. He told Kiki to sit in front and he put Streeter and Bartlett in the back seat. He pulled their caps down over their eyes and sat in front with Kiki while Fogarty drove the truck inside the cemetery entrance. Fogarty was gone ten minutes, which passed in silence, and when he came back, he said, "Looks like it's all hard cider. Twenty-four barrels." And he slipped behind the wheel. Jack rode with his arm over the back seat and his pistol pointed at the roof. No one spoke all the way to Acra, and Streeter and Bartlett barely moved. They sat with their hands in their laps and their caps over their eyes. When they got out of the car inside the garage, Jack made them face the wall and tied their hands behind them. Fogarty backed the car out, closed the door, and took Kiki inside the house. Jack sat Streeter and Bartlett on the floor against a ladder.

Shovels hung over the old man's head like a set of assorted guillotines. Jack remembered shovels on the wall of the cellar in The Village where the Neary mob took him so long ago when they thought he'd hijacked a load of their beer—and he had. They tied him to a chair with wire around his arms and legs, then worked him over. They got weary and left him, bloody and half conscious, to go to sleep. He was fully awake and moved his arms back and forth against the wire's twist until he ripped his shirt. He sawed steadily with the wire until it ripped the top off his right bicep and let him slip his arm out of the bond. He climbed up a coal chute and out a window, leaving pieces of the bicep on the twist of wire, and on the floor: skin, flesh, plenty of blood. Bled all the way home. Bicep flat now. Long, rough scar there now. Some Nearys paid for that scar.

He looked at the old man and saw the ropes hanging on the wall behind him, can of kerosene in the corner, paintbrushes soaking in turpentine. Rakes, pickax. Old man another object. Another tool. Jack hated all tools that refused to yield their secrets. Jack was humiliated before the inanimate world. He hated it, kicked it when it affronted him. He shot a car once that betrayed him by refusing to start. Blew holes in its radiator.

The point where the hanging rope bellied out on the garage wall looked to Jack like the fixed smile on Streeter's face. Streeter was crazy to keep smiling. He wasn't worth a goddamn to anybody if he was crazy. You can kill crazies. No loss. Jack made ready to kill yet another man. Wilson, the first one he killed. Wilson, the card cheat. Fuck you, cheater, you're dead. I'm sorry for your kids.

In the years after he dumped Wilson in the river Jack used Rothstein's insurance connections to insure family men he was going to remove from life. He made an arrangement with a thieving insurance salesman, sent him around to the family well in advance of the removal date. When the deal was sealed, give Jack a few weeks, then bingo!

"You got any insurance, old man?"

"No."

"You got any family?"

"Wife."

"Too bad. She's going to have to bury you best she can. Unless you tell me where that still is you got hid."

"Ain't got no still hid nowheres, mister. I told you that."

"Better think again, old man. You know where the still is, kid?" Dickie Bartlett shook his head and turned to the wall. Only a kid. But if Jack killed one, he would have to kill two. Tough break, kid.

"Take off your shoes."

Streeter slowly untied the rawhide laces of his high

shoe-boots without altering his grin. He pulled off one shoe
and Jack smelled his foot, his sweaty white wool sock, his
long underwear tucked inside the sock. Country leg,
country foot, country stink. Jack looked back at the grin,
which seemed as fixed as the shape of the nose that hovered
above it. But you don't fix a grin permanently. Jack knew.
That old son of a bitch is defying me, is what he thought.
He hasn't got a chance and yet he's defying Jack
Diamond's law, Jack Diamond's threat, Jack Diamond
himself. That grinning façade is a fake and Jack will remove
it. Jack knows all there is to know about fake façades. He
remembered his own grin in one of the newspapers as he
went into court in Philadelphia. Tough monkey, smilin'
through. They won't get to me. And then in the courtroom
he knew how empty that smile was, how profoundly he had
failed to create the image he wanted to present to the
people of Philadelphia, not only on his return but all his life,
all through boyhood, to live down the desertion charge in
the Army, and, worse, the charge that he stole from his
buddies. Not true. So many of the things they said about
Jack were untrue and yet they stuck.

He was a nobody in the Philadelphia court. Humiliated.
Arrested coming in, then kicked out. And stay out, you
bum. I speak for the decent people of this city in saying that
Philadelphia doesn't want you any more than Europe did.
Vomit. Puke, puke. Vomit. Country feet smelled like
vomit. Jack's family witnessing it all in the courtroom. Jack
always loved them in his way. Jack dumped about eight
cigarettes out of his Rameses pack and pocketed them. He
twisted the pack and lit it with a loose match, showed the
burning cellophane and paper to Streeter, who never lost
his grin. Jack said, "Where's the still?"

"Jee-zus, mister, I ain't seen no still. I ain't and that's a
positive fact, I tell you."

Jack touched the fire to the sock and then to the edge of
the underwear. Streeter shook it and the fire went out. Jack
burned his own hand, dropped the flaming paper and let it
burn out. Fogarty came back in then, pistol in hand.

"Kneel on him," Jack said, and with pistol pointed at

Streeter's head, Fogarty knelt on the old man's calf. The pistol wasn't loaded, Fogarty said later. He was taking no chances shooting anybody accidentally. It had been loaded when they stopped Streeter's truck because he felt when he traveled the roads with Jack he was bodyguard as well as chauffeur, and he would stand no chance of coping with a set of killers on wheels if his gun was empty. But now he wasn't a bodyguard anymore.

"He's a tough old buzzard," Jack said.

"Why don't you tell him what he wants to know?" Fogarty said conspiratorially to Streeter.

"Can't tell what I don't know," Streeter said. The grin was there. The flame had not changed it. Jack knew now he would remove that grin with flame. Finding the still was receding in importance, but such a grin of defiance is worth punishing. Asks for punishing. Will always get what it asks for. The Alabama sergeant who tormented Jack and other New York types in the platoon because of their defiance. "New Yoahk mothahfucks." Restriction. Punishment. KP over and over. Passes denied. And then Jack swung and got the son bitch in the leg with an iron bar. Had to go AWOL after that, couldn't even go back. That was when they got him, in New Yoahk. Did defiance win the day for Jack? It was satisfying, but Jack admits it did not win the day. Should have shot the son bitch in some ditch off-post. Let the rats eat him.

"Where's that still, you old son bitch?"

"Hey, mister, I'd tell you if I knew. You think I'd keep anythin' back if I knew? I dunno, mister, I just plain dunno."

Jack lit the sock, got it flaming this time, and the old man yelled, shook his whole leg again and rocked Fogarty off it. The flame went out again. Jack looked, saw the grin. The old man is totally insane. Should be bugged. Crazy as they make 'em. Crazy part of a man that takes any kind of punishment, suffers all humiliations. No pride.

"You old son bitch, ain't you got no pride? Tell me the goddamn answer to my question. Ain't you got no sense? I'm gonna hang your ass off a tree you don't tell me what I want to know."

But you can't really punish a crazy like that, Jack. He loves it. That's why he's sitting there grinning. Some black streak across his brain makes him crazier than a dog with his head where his ass oughta be. He's making *you* crazy now, Jack. Got you talking about hanging. You can't be serious, can you?

"All right, old man, get up. Speed, get that rope."

"What you got in mind, Jack?"

"I'm gonna hang his Cairo country ass from that maple tree outside."

"Hey," said Streeter, "you ain't really gonna hang me?"

"I'm gonna hang you like a side of beef," Jack said. "I'm gonna pop your eyes like busted eggs. I'm gonna make your tongue stretch so far out you'll be lickin' your toes."

"I ain't done nothin' to nobody, mister. Why you gonna hang me?"

"Because you're lyin' to me, old man."

"No, sir, I ain't lyin'. I ain't lyin'."

"How old are you right now?"

"Fifty."

"You ain't as old as I thought, but you ain't gonna be fifty-one. You're a stubborn buzzard, but you ain't gonna be fifty-one. Bring him out."

Fogarty led the old man outside with only one shoe, and Jack threw the rope over the limb of the maple. He tied a knot, looped the rope through the opening in the knot—a loop that would work like an animal's choker chain—and slipped it over Streeter's neck. Jack pulled open a button, one down from the collar, to give the rope plenty of room.

"Jack," Fogarty said, shaking his head. Jack tugged the rope until he took up all the slack and the rope rose straight up from Streeter's neck.

"One more chance," Jack said. "Where is that goddamn still you were headed for?"

"Jee-zus Keh-ryst, mister, there just ain't no still, you think I'm kiddin' you? You got a rope around my neck. You think I wouldn't tell you anything I knew if I knew it? Jee-zus, mister, I don't want to die."

"Listen, Jack. I don't think we ought to do this."

Fogarty was trembling. The poor goddamn trucker. Like watching a movie and knowing how it ends, Fogarty said later.

"Shitkicker!" Jack yelled. "Where is it? SHITKICKER! SHITKICKER!"

Before the old man could answer, Jack tugged at the rope and up went Streeter. But he had worked one hand loose and he made a leap as Jack tugged. He grabbed the rope over his head and held it.

"Retie the son of a bitch," Jack said, and Fogarty knew then he was party to a murder. Full accomplice now and the tied-up Bartlett kid a witness. There would be a second murder on this night. Fogarty, how far you've come under Jack's leadership. He tied the old man's hands, and Jack then wound the rope around both his own arms and his waist so it wouldn't slip, and he jerked it again and moved backward. The old man's eyes bugged as he rose off the ground. His tongue came out and he went limp. The Bartlett kid yelled and then started to cry, and Jack let go of the rope. The old man crumpled.

"He's all right," Jack said. "The old son of a bitch is too miserable to die. Hit him with some water."

Fogarty half-filled a pail from an outside faucet and threw it on Streeter. The old man opened his eyes.

"You know, just maybe he's telling the truth," Fogarty said.

"He's lying."

"He's doing one hell of a good job."

Jack took Fogarty's pistol and waved it under Streeter's nose. *At least he can't kill him with that,* Fogarty thought.

"It's too much work to hang you," Jack said to Streeter, "so I'm gonna blow your head all over the lawn. I'll give you one more chance."

The old man shook his head and closed his eyes. His grin was gone. I finally got rid of that, is what Jack thought. But then he was suddenly enraged again at the old man. You made me do this to you, was the nature of Jack's accusation. You turned me into a goddamn sadist because of your goddamn stinking country stubbornness. He laid

the barrel of the pistol against the old man's head and then
he thought: *Fogarty.* And he checked the cylinder. No
bullets. He gave Fogarty a look of contempt and handed
him back the empty pistol. He took his own .38 from his
coat pocket, and Streeter, watching everything, started to
tremble, his lip turned down now. Smile not only gone, but
that face unable even to remember that it had smiled even
once in all its fifty years. Jack fired one shot. It exploded
alongside Streeter's right ear. The old man's head jerked
and Jack fired again, alongside the other ear.

"You got something to tell me now, shitkicker?" Jack
said.

The old man opened his eyes, saucers of terror. He
shook his head. Jack put the pistol between his eyes, held it
there for seconds of silence. Then he let it fall away with a
weariness. He stayed on his haunches in front of Streeter,
just staring. Just staring and saying nothing.

"You win, old man," he finally said. "You're a tough
monkey."

Jack stood up slowly and pocketed his pistol. Fogarty
and one of the porch guards drove Streeter and Bartlett
back to their truck. Fogarty ripped out their ignition wires
and told them not to call the police. He drove back to Acra
and slept the sleep of a confused man.


When Speed had brought her from the car into the house,
Kiki had said to him, "What's going to happen with those
men?"

"I don't know. Probably just some talk."

"Oh, God, Joe, don't let him hurt them. I don't want to
be mixed up in that kind of shit again, please, Joe."

"I'll do what I can do, but you know Jack's got a mind of
his own."

"I'll go and see him. Or maybe you could tell him to
come in. Maybe if I asked him not to do anything, for me,
don't do it for me, he wouldn't do it."

"I'll tell him you said it."

"You're a nice guy, Joe."

"You go to bed and stay upstairs. Do what I tell you."

"Yes, Joe."

Kiki was thinking that Joe really and truly was a nice guy and that maybe she could make it with him if only she wasn't tied up with Jack. Of course, she wouldn't do anything while she was thick with Jack. But it was nice to think about Joe and his red hair and think about how nice he would be to play with. He was nicer than Jack, but then she didn't love Jack because he was nice.

She worried whether Jack had killed the two men when she later heard the two shots and the screaming. But she had thought the worst at the Monticello, thought Jack had killed *those* men when they had really tried to kill him. She didn't want to think bad things about Jack again. But she lived half an hour with uncertainty. Then Jack came into her room and said the men were gone and nobody got hurt.

"Did you get the information you wanted?" she asked.

"Yeah, I don't want to talk about it."

"Oh, good. Are you done now?"

"All done."

"Then we can finish the evening the way we intended."

"It's finished."

"I mean really finished."

"And I mean really finished."

He kissed her on the cheek and went to his bedroom. He didn't come back to see her or ask her to come to him. She tried to sleep, but she kept wanting to finish the evening, continue from where she and Jack had left off in the car in the silence and the chilliness and the brightness of the new moon on the open fields. She wanted to lie alongside Jack and comfort him because she knew from the way he was behaving that he had the blues. If she went in and loved him, he would feel better. Yet she felt he didn't really want that, and she rolled over and tossed and turned, curled and uncurled for another hour before she decided: Maybe he really does want it. So then, yes, she ought to do it. She got up and very quietly tiptoed into Jack's room and stood naked alongside his bed. Jack was deeply asleep. She touched his ear and ran her fingers down his cheek, and all

of a sudden she was looking down the barrel of his .38 and
he was bending her fingers back so far she was screaming.
Nobody came to help her. She thought of that later. Jack
could have killed her and nobody would have tried to stop
him. Not even Joe.

"You crazy bitch! What were you trying to do?"

"I just wanted to love you."

"Never, never wake me up that way. Don't ever touch
me. Call me and I'll hear it, but don't touch me."

Kiki was weeping because her hand hurt so much. She
couldn't bend her fingers. When she tried to bend them, she
fainted. When she came to, she was in a chair and Jack was
all white in the face, looking at her. He was slapping her
cheek lightly just as she came out of it.

"It hurts an awful lot."

"We'll go get a doctor. I'm sorry, Marion, I'm really
sorry I hurt you."

"I know you are, Jack."

"I don't want to hurt you."

"I know you don't."

"I love you so much I'm half nuts sometimes."

"Oh, Jackie, you're not nuts, you're wonderful and I
don't care if you hurt me. It was an accident. It was all my
fault."

"We'll go get the doc out of bed."

"He'll fix me up fine, and then we can come back and
finish the evening."

"Yeah, that's a swell idea."

The coroner was Jack's doctor, and they got him out of
bed. He bandaged her hand and said she'd have to have a
cast made at the hospital next day, and he gave her pills for
her pain. She told him she'd been rehearsing her dance
steps and had fallen down. He didn't seem to believe that,
but Jack didn't care what he believed, so she didn't either.
After the doctor's they went back home. Jack said he was
too tired to make love and that they'd do it in the morning.
Kiki tossed and turned for a while and then went down to
the kitchen and checked the fudge again, felt it with the

fingers of her good hand. It was still goo, so she put it out
on the back porch for the cat.

Clem Streeter told his story around Catskill for years. He
was a celebrity because of it, stopped often by people and
asked for another rendition. I was being shaved in a Catskill
barber chair the year beer came back, and Jack was, of
course, long gone. But Clem was telling the story yet again
for half a dozen locals.

"The jedge in Catskill axed me what I wanted the pistol
*per*mit for," he said, "and I told him 'bout how that Legs
Diamond feller burned my feet and hung me from a sugar
maple th'other night up at his garage. 'That so?' axed the
jedge. 'I jes told you it were,' I said. People standin' 'round
the courthouse heard what we was sayin' and they come
over to listen better. 'You made a complaint yet against this
Diamond person?' the jedge axes me. But I tell him, only
complaint I made so far was to the wife. That jedge he
don't know what to do with hisself he's so took out by what
I'm sayin'. I didn't mean to upset the jedge. But he says, 'I
guess we better get the sheriff on this one and maybe the
DA,' and they both of 'em come in after a little bit and I tell
'em my story, how they poked guns outen the winders of
their car and we stopped the truck, me and Dickie Bartlett.
They made us git down, but I didn't git fast enough for
Diamond, so he hit me with his fist and said, 'Put up your
hands or I'll split your effin' head.' Then they hauled us up
to Diamond's place with our caps pulled down so we
wouldn't know where we was goin', but I see the road
anyway out under the side of the cap and I know that place
of his with the lights real well. Am I sure it was Diamond,
the jedge axes. 'Acourse I'm sure. I seen him plenty over at
the garage in Cairo. He had a woman in the car with him,
and I recognized the other feller who did the drivin' 'cause
he stopped my truck another night I was haulin' empty
barrels 'bout a month back.' 'So this here's Streeter, the
wise guy from Cairo,' Diamond says to me and he cuffs me
on the jaw with his fist, just like that, afore I said a word.

Then up in the garage they tried to burn me up. 'What'd they do that for?' the jedge axes me, and I says,"Cause he wants to know where there's a still I'm s'posed to know about. But I told Diamond I don't know nothin' 'bout no still.' And the jedge says, 'Why'd he think you did?' And I says, "Cause I'm haulin' twenty-four barrels of hard cider I'd picked up down at Post's Cider Mill.' 'Who for?' says the jedge. 'For me,' I says. 'I like cider. Drink a bunch of it.' 'Cause I ain't about to tell no jedge or nobody else 'bout the still me and old Cy Bartlett got between us. We do right nice business with that old still. Make up to a hundred, hundred and thirty dollars apiece some weeks off the fellers who ain't got no stills and need a little 'jack to keep the blood pumpin'. That Diamond feller, he surely did want to get our still away from us. I knew that right off. Did me a lot of damage, I'll say. But sheeeeee. Them fellers with guns is all talk. Hell, they don't never kill nobody. They just like to throw a scare into folks so's they can get their own way. Son of a bee if I was gonna give up a hundred and thirty dollars a week for some New York feller."

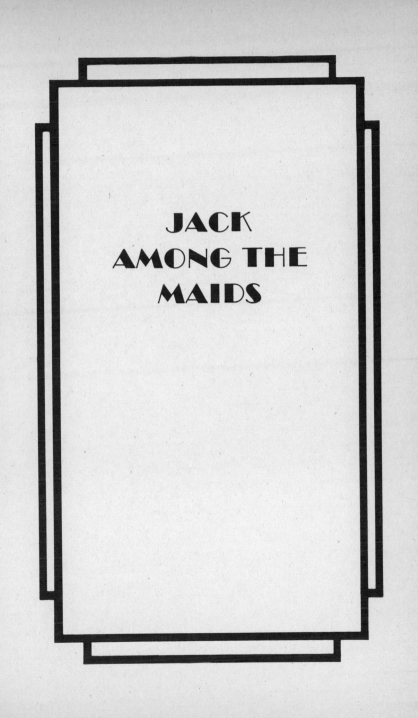

# JACK
# AMONG THE
# MAIDS

The Streeter incident took place in mid-April, 1931. Eight days later, the following document was released in the Capitol at Albany:

Pursuant to section 62 of the Executive Law, I hereby require that you, the Attorney General of this state, attend in person or by your assistants or deputies, a regular special and trial term of the Supreme Court appointed to be held in and for the County of Greene for the month of April, 1931, and as such term as may hereafter be continued, and that you in person or by said assistants or deputies appear before the grand jury or grand juries which shall be drawn and sit for any later term or terms of said court for the purpose of managing and conducting in said court and before said grand jury and said other grand juries, any and all proceedings, examinations and inquiries, and any and all criminal actions and proceedings which may be taken by or before said grand jury concerning any and all kinds and—or—criminal offences, alleged to have been committed by John Diamond, also known as Jack (Legs) Diamond and—or—any person or persons acting in concert with him, and further to manage, prosecute and conduct the trial of any indictments found by said grand jury or grand juries at said term or terms of said court or of any other court at which any and all such indictments may hereafter be tried, and that in person or by your assistants or deputies you supersede the district attorney of the County of Greene in all matters herein specified and you exercise all the powers and perform all the duties conferred upon you by Section 62 of the Executive Law and this requirement thereunder; and that in such proceedings and actions the District Attorney of Greene County shall only exercise such powers and perform such

duties as are required of him by you or by the assistants or
deputies attorney general so attending.

Franklin Delano Roosevelt
Governor of the State of New York

Jack thus became the first gangster of the Prohibition Era
to have the official weight of an entire state, plus the gobble
of its officialese, directed at him. I find this notable.

I did what little I could to throw a counterweight when
the time came. I cited the whole affair as a cynical political
response to the harsh spotlight that Judge Seabury, his
reformers, and the Republican jackals were, at the
moment, shining on the gangsterism and corruption so
prevalent in New York City's Tammany Hall, with
Democratic Gentleman Jimmy Walker the chief illuminated
goat. FDR, I argued when I pleaded Jack's case in the
press, was making my client the goat in a Republican
stronghold. I voiced particular outrage at superseding the
Greene County District Attorney.

But my counterweight didn't weigh much. Jack went to
jail and I understood the spadework done in Albany by Van
Deusen's vigilantes. FDR even sent his personal bodyguard
to Catskill as an observer when the swarm of state police
and state attorneys moved toward Jack's jugular.

Knute Rockne told his men: "Don't be a bad loser, but
don't lose."

Fogarty got me out of bed to tell me Jack had been
arrested and that he himself was going into hiding. Jack and
Kiki were in the parlor at Acra, and Fogarty was playing
pool in the cottage when the trooper rang the bell under the
second step. Three times. Jack's straight neighbors thought
three was the insider's ring, but it was the ring only for
straights.

Jack tried to talk the trooper into letting him surrender in
the morning by himself, avoid the ignominy of it, but the
trooper said nix, and so Jack wound up on a hard cot in a
white-washed third-floor cell of the county jail. Tidy and

warm, not quite durance vile, as one journalist wrote, but
vile enough for the King Cobra of the Catskills, as he was
now known in the press.

I worked on the bail, which was a formidable twenty-five
thousand dollars: ten each for assaulting Streeter and
Bartlett, five for the kidnapping. Uh-oh, I said, when I
heard the news, heard especially how young Bartlett was.
What we now are dealing with, I told Fogarty, and Jack too,
is not a bootleggers' feud, which is what it was in a
left-handed way, but the abduction of children in the dead
of night. Not a necessary social misdemeanor, as most
bootlegging was contemporaneously regarded, but a high
crime in any age.

I called Warren Van Deusen to see if I could pry Jack
loose by greasing local pols, but found him haughtily
supporting the state's heavy anti-Jack thrust. "Kidnapping
kids now, is he? I hear he's holding up bread truck drivers
too. What's next? Disemboweling old ladies?" I wrote off
Warren as unreliable, a man given to facile outrage, who
didn't understand the process he was enmeshed in.

It has long been my contention that Jack was not only a
political pawn through Streeter, but a pawn of the entire
decade. Politicans used him, and others like him, to carry
off any vileness that served their ends, beginning with the
manipulation of strikebreakers as the decade began and
ending with the manipulation of stockbrokers at the end of
the crash, a lovely, full, capitalistic circle. Thereafter the
pols rejected Jack as unworthy, and tried to destroy him.

But it was Jack and a handful of others—Madden,
Schultz, Capone, Luciano—who reversed the process, who
became manipulators of the pols, who left a legacy of
money and guns that would dominate the American city on
through the 1970's. Jack was too interested in private goals
to see the potential that 1931 offered to the bright student of
urban life. Yet he was unquestionably an ancestral
paradigm for modern urban political gangsters, upon whom
his pioneering and his example were obviously not lost.

I hesitate to develop all the analogies I see in this, for I
don't want to trivialize Jack's achievement by linking him

to lesser latter-day figures such as Richard Nixon, who left significant history in his wake, but no legend; whose corruption, overwhelmingly venal and invariably hypocritical, lacked the admirably white core fantasy that can give evil a mythical dimension. Only boobs and shitheads rooted for Nixon in his troubled time, but heroes and poets followed Jack's tribulations with curiosity, ambivalent benevolence, and a sense of mystery at the meaning of their own response.

Fogarty, sitting at a bar and waiting for a female form to brighten his life, and meanwhile telling a story about a gang-bang, felt alive for the first time in a week, for the first time since they hauled Jack in and he took off up the mountain. A week in a cabin alone, only one day out for groceries and the paper, is enough to grow hair on a wart, shrivel a gonad.

Fogarty found solitude unbearably full of evaporated milk and tuna fish, beans and cheese, stale bread and bad coffee, memories of forced bed-rest, stultifying boredom with one's own thought. And then to run out of candles.

The old shack on stilts was down the mountain from Haines Falls, half a mile in an old dirt road, then a quarter of a mile walk with the groceries. He walked down from the cabin to his old car every morning and every night to make sure it was still there and to start it. Then he walked alone in the woods looking at the same trees, same squirrels, same chipmunks and rabbits, same goddamn birds with all that useless song, and came back and slept and ate and thought about women, and read the only book in the cabin, *The World Almanac*. He related to the ads—no end to life's jokes:

Last Year's Pay Looks Like Small Change to These Men Today; Raised Their Pay 500% When They Discovered Salesmanship . . . Have YOU Progressed During the Past Three Years? . . . Ask Your Dealer for Crescent Guns, 12-16-20-410 Gauge . . . A Challenge Made Me Popular! . . . This Man Wouldn't Stay Down . . . It Pays to

Read Law . . . Success—Will You Pay the Price? . . . Finest of All Cast Bronze Sarcophagi.

Fogarty closed the book, took a walk in the dark. A wild bird call scared him, and he retreated to the cabin to find only half a candle left, not enough to get him through the night. It's time, he said. It was ten o'clock. The Top o' the Mountain House would have some action and he needed a drink, needed people, needed a look at a woman, needed news. His old relic of a Studebaker started all right. Would he ever again see his new Olds, sitting back in the shed behind his house in Catskill? No chance to take it when he left Jack's in such a hurry.

There were four men at the bar, two couples at one table in the back room. He checked them all, knew nobody, but they looked safe. The bartender, a kid named Reilly he'd talked to, but never pressured, was okay. Fogarty ordered applejack on ice. He made it, sold it, liked it. Jack hated it. He had three and was already half an hour into a conversation with Reilly, feeling good again, telling about the night he and eight guys were lined up in a yard on 101st Street for a girl named Maisie who was spread out under a bush, taking on the line.

"I was about fourth and didn't even know who she was. We just heard it was on and got in line. Then when I saw her, I said to myself, 'Holy beazastards,' because I knew Maisie, and her brother Rick is my pal and he's in line right behind me. So I said to him, 'I just got a look, she's a dog, let's beat it,' and I grabbed his arm and pulled, but he was ready, you know, and I couldn't talk him out of it. He had to see her for himself. And when he saw her, he pulled off the guy on her and whipped him, and then beat hell out of Maisie. Next day everybody had trouble looking Rick in the eye. Guys he knew were there all said they were behind him in the line and didn't know who she was either. Maisie was back a couple of nights later, and we all got her without Rick breaking it up."

Fogarty paused nostalgically. "I got in line twice."

The barman liked the story, bought Fogarty a drink, and

said, "You know, was a guy in here last night askin' about your friend Diamond. Guy with a bandage on his eye."

"A bandage? You don't mean an eyepatch?"

"No, a bandage. Adhesive and gauze stuff."

"What'd he want?"

"Dunno. Asks has Jack Diamond been in much and when was the last time."

"You know him?"

"Never seen him before."

"You remember a guy named Murray? Called him The Goose."

"No."

"Nuts."

"You know this guy with the eye?"

"I don't know. Could be he's a friend of ours. Your phone working?"

"End of the bar."

Fogarty felt the blood rise in his chest, felt needed. Reilly had told him Jack was out on bail, so it was important for him to know Murray was around, if he was. All week in the woods Fogarty had cursed Jack, vowed to quit him, leave the country; that if this thing straightened out, he'd find a new connection; that he couldn't go on working with a man who wasn't playing with a full deck. Northrup first, then Streeter. Crazy. But now that feeling was gone, and he wanted to talk to Jack, warn him, protect his life.

"Don't touch that phone."

Fogarty turned to see old man Brady, the owner, standing alongside him with his hand on a pistol in his belt.

"Get out of here," Brady said.

"I just want to make a call."

"Make it someplace else. You or none of your bunch are welcome here. We're all through kissing your ass."

Brady's beer belly and soiled shirt pushed against the pistol. The spiderweb veins in Brady's cheeks Fogarty would remember when he was dying, for they would look like the crystalline glaze that covered his own eyes in his last days. Brady with the whiskey webs. Old lush. Throwing me out.

"If it wasn't for your father," Brady said, "I'd shoot you now. He was a decent man. I don't know how in the hell he ever got you."

Fogarty would remember that drops of sweat had run off Brady's spiderwebs one day long ago, the day Fogarty stood in front of him at the bar and told him how much of Jack's beer he would handle a week. Told him. Two of Jack's transient gunmen stood behind him to reinforce the message.

"You're lucky I don't call the troopers and turn you in," old Brady said to him now, "but I wouldn't do that to a son of your father's. Remember the favor that decent man did for you from his grave, you dirty whelp. You dirty, dirty whelp. Go on, get out of here."

He moved his fingers around the butt of his pistol, and Fogarty went out into the night to find Jack.

Fogarty stopped the car and loaded his pistol, Eddie Diamond's .32. If he saw Murray, he would shoot first, other things being equal. He wouldn't shoot him in public. Fogarty marveled at his own aggression, but then he knew The Goose, knew Jack's story of how The Goose stalked a man once who went to the same movie house every week. The Goose sat in the lobby until the man arrived, then shoved a gun in his face, and blew half the head off the wrong man. A week later he was in the same lobby when the right man arrived, and he blew off half the correct head. Jack liked to tell Goose stories, how Goose once said of himself: "I'm mean as a mad hairy." What would The Goose have done to Streeter? Old man'd be stretched now, and the kid too. Was Fogarty the difference between life and death on that night?

He wanted to buy a paper, find out what was happening. He hadn't asked many questions at the bar, didn't want to seem ignorant. But he knew from a conversation with Marcus after Jack's arrest, plus something Reilly said, that the state was sitting heavily on Jack. Old man Brady's behavior meant everybody'd be tough now. Jack is down and so is Fogarty, so put on your kicking shoes, folks.

Was it all over? No more money ("The boss needs a loan") coming in from the hotels and boardinghouses? No more still? Yes, there would be beer runs. There would always be beer runs. And there were the stashes of booze, if nobody found them. Reilly said four of Jack's men, all picked up at the cottage, were booked on vagrancy, no visible income. But they couldn't say that about Fogarty with his three bank accounts, fifteen thousand dollars deposited in one during the past six months. But he couldn't go near them until he knew his status.

Yet he knew what that had to be. Fugitive. They'd try to hang him by the balls. Jack's closest associate. Jack's pal. Jack's bodyguard. A laugh. But he did carry a loaded gun, finally, just for Jack. Why did Joe Fogarty feel the need to protect Jack Diamond? Because there was a bond. Friendship. Brothers, in a way. Jack talked about Eddie, gave him Eddie's pistol, and they swapped TB stories. Eddie was a bleeder. Always had the streak in his sputum the last year of his life, almost never out of bed or a wheelchair except when he came to New York to help Jack during the Hotsy. No wonder Jack loved him. Jack cried when he talked about Eddie: "He used to bleed so bad they put ice on his chest, made him suck ice too, and the poor guy couldn't move."

Fogarty knew. He'd seen all that, spent five and a half years in sanitariums, twenty-eight months in bed for twenty-four hours a day. Got up only when they made the bed, a bed bath twice a week. Galloping TB is what Fogarty had, and if they hadn't used the pneumo he'd have been dead long ago. Blew air into his lungs, collapsed it, pushed up the poison. Hole in the bronchus, and when the air went in, the pus came up and out his mouth. A basinful of greenish-yellow pus. But after five months that didn't work anymore and the pus stayed in, and he had to lie still for those years.

Death?

Joe Fogarty wasn't afraid of death anymore, only bleeding. He died every day for years. What he was afraid of was lying still and not dying.

"Remember your fibrosis," the nurses would say. "Don't raise your arms above your head. Don't even move when you do pee-pee."

The woodpeckers would come around and tap his chest with stethoscopes and fingers, listen to his percussion. "Cough and say ninety-nine." It must heal, you know. Give yourself a chance to heal. Terrific advice. Bring your tissue together. Heal. Oh, nice. Fight off the poison. Of course. Then show a streak in the sputum and they don't let you brush your teeth by yourself anymore. A long time ago, all that; and Fogarty finally got well. And met Jack. And did he then make up for those months in bed doing nothing? Ahhhhhh.

"So you think The Goose is back?" Jack said.

"Who else?"

"Maybe you're right. But maybe it was just a one-eyed tourist. Tourists always asking about me."

"You want to take that chance?"

"Not with The Goose. He'll find a way if he's up here. I should stay away from the window."

"You been going out?"

"No, just sticking close here. But we'll go out now."

"Take me with you," Kiki said. She was alone on the couch, knees visible, no stockings, slippers on. But sweeeet lover, did she look good to the Speeder.

"No," said Jack. "You stay home."

"I don't want to be here alone."

"I'll call the neighbor."

"That old cow, I don't want her here."

"She'll be company. We won't be long."

"Where you going?"

"Down the road, make some calls, then we'll be back."

"You'll be out all night."

"Marion, you're a pain in the ass."

"I'm going back to Chicago."

"That show closed."

"You think that show is the only offer I got out there?"

"You can't come with us. I'll bring home spaghetti."

"I want to do something."

"We'll do something when I get back. We'll eat spaghetti."

"I want to hear some music."

"Turn on the radio. Put on a record."

"Oh, shit, Jack. Shit, shit, shit."

"That's better. Have a sherry."

Fogarty finished his double rye and Jack swigged the last of his coffee royal, and they went out the back door. Jack stopped, said, "We'll take your car. Nobody'd look for me in that jalop."

"Nobody looking for me at all?"

"Not yet, but that don't mean they won't be out with a posse tomorrow. They'll get to you, all right, but tonight you're a free citizen. Take it from me, and Marcus. He's down at the Saulpaugh while this stuff is going on. We talked before you got here. Joe, I'm glad you came down."

Jack clapped him on the shoulder. The old jalop was wheezing along. Fogarty smiled, remembered his plan to break with Jack. What a crazy idea.

Jack had taken a rifle from the hall closet, loaded it with dum-dums, and thrown it on the back seat. He wouldn't carry a pistol with all the heat on. He'd also put on his gray topcoat, fedora, and maroon tie with a black pearl tie tack. Fogarty, you bum, you wore a linty black sweater and those baggy slacks you slept in all week.

"It's like a dog race," Jack said.

"What is?" Fogarty asked, thinking immediately of himself as a dog.

"This thing. I'm the rabbit. And who'll get it first?"

"Nobody gets those rabbits. The dogs always come up empty."

"The feds are coming into it. The state, all the goddamn cops in the East, Biondo and his guinea friends, Charlie Lucky's pals, and now maybe Murray out there, driving around, trying to make a plan. The good thing about Murray is he can never figure out how to get near anybody. Once he gets near you, so long. But unless you figured it out for him, he could think all month without getting the idea to maybe ring the doorbell.''

"Maybe you ought to get away from here.''

"They're all keeping track of me. Let's see what news we come up with. Hey, you're heating up.''

The temperature gauge was near two twenty when they pulled into the parking lot at Jimmy Wynne's Aratoga Inn on the Acra-Catskill Road. Fogarty unscrewed the radiator cap and let it breathe and blow, and then they went inside, Fogarty with his two pistols Jack didn't even know he had. Fogarty was ready for Murray, who was absent from the gathering of twelve at the bar. It was quiet, the musicians on a break. Fogarty asked Dick Fegan, the bartender, bald at twenty-five, if he'd seen Murray. Fegan said he hadn't seen Murray in months, and Jack went for the telephone. Fogarty dumped four quarts of water into the car radiator and went back in to find Jack off the phone with a Vichy water in front of him, talking about heavyweights to the clarinet player. Heavyweights. "I lost seven grand on Loughran," Jack was saying. "I thought he was the best, gave seven to five, and he didn't last three rounds. Sharkey murdered him. He says, 'Let me sit down, I don't know where I am,' and then he tried to walk through the ropes. Last time I ever bet on anybody from Philadelphia.'' Jack will talk to anybody about anything, anytime. Why shouldn't people like him?

"Seven grand," said the clarinet player.

"Yeah, I was crazy.''

It seemed like a slip, Jack mentioning money. He never got specific about that, so why now? Must be nervous. Jack went back to the phone and made another call.

"He said he lost seven grand on one fight," the clarinetist said to Fogarty.

"Probably did. He always spent.''

"But no more, eh?''

It sounded to Fogarty like a line at a wake. That man in the coffin is dead. Fogarty didn't like the feeling he got from shifting from that thought to a thought about Murray walking in the door. But Murray would have to come through the inn's glassed-in porch. Plenty of time to see him. What made Fogarty think he'd pick the one spot in the mountains where Jack happened to be at this odd moment? Did he think maybe he followed the car? Or that he'd been waiting near here for Jack to show up?

"He's probably still got a few dollars in his pocket," Fogarty said to the clarinetist.

"I wouldn't doubt that."

"You sounded like you did."

"No, not at all."

"You sounded like you were saying he's a has-been."

"You got me wrong. I didn't mean that at all. Listen, that's not what I meant. Dick, give us a drink here. I was just asking a question. Hell, Jesus, it was just a goddamn silly question."

"I get you now," Fogarty said.

Wasn't it funny how fast Fogarty could turn somebody's head around? Power in the word. In any word from Fogarty. In the way people looked at him. But it was changing. Maybe you wouldn't think so, sitting here at the Aratoga, and Jack being respected and Fogarty being respected, with maybe that hint of new tension in the air. But it definitely was changing. Little signs: Jack's living room being different, messy, papers on the floor, the chairs not where they used to be. Authority slipping away from Fogarty, authority that he knew Jack well, could talk all about him, talk for him. Dirty dishes on the dining room table. Picture of Eddie on the coffee table never there before, which meant something Fogarty didn't understand. The parties at Jack's; they were over too, at least for now. Even priests used to come. Neighbors, sometimes a cop or a judge from the city, actors and musicians and so many beautiful women. Women liked Jack and the feeling rubbed off to the benefit of Jack's friends. Jack the pivot man at every party. Funny son of a bitch when he gets a few drinks in. Fogarty couldn't remember one funny joke Jack ever told, but all his stories were funny. Just the way he used his voice. Yes. The story about Murray shooting the wrong man. Split your gut listening to Jack tell it. A good singing voice, too. Second tenor. Loves barbershop. "My Mother's Rosary." A great swipe in the middle of that. One of Jack's favorites.

"Well, that's some kind of news," Jack said, sitting back down beside Fogarty. "Somebody saw him at the Five O'Clock Club last night."

"Last night? He must've gone back down."

"If he was ever up here."

"Don't you think he must've been?"

"After this, maybe not. He's not the only one-eyed bum in the state. The point is, where is he now? Last night is a long time ago. He could be here in a few hours. They're still checking him out. Give me a small whiskey, Dick."

And he went back to the phone. Everybody was watching him now. Silence at the bar. Whispers. The clarinetist moved away and stayed away. Dick Fegan set up Jack's drink and moved away. They're watching you, too, Joe. Jack's closest associate. Fogarty drank alone while Jack talked on the phone. The whiskey eased his tension, but didn't erase it. Jack came back and sipped his whiskey, all eyes on him again. When he looked up, they looked away. They always watched him, but never with such grim faces. More finality. Man dying alone in an alley. There's Jack Diamond over there, that vanishing species. That pilot fish with him is another endangered item.

"I can't sit still," Jack said, and he stood up behind the barstool. "I been like this for two days."

"Let's go someplace else."

"They're going to call me. Then we'll move."

The musicians started up, a decent sound. "Muskrat Ramble." Sounds of life. Memories of dancing. Like old times. Memories of holding women. Got to get back to that.

Three-quarters of an hour passed, with Jack moving back and forth between the bar and the phone, then pacing up and down, plenty nervous. If Jack is that nervous, it's worse than Fogarty thought. Pacing. Jack's all alone and he

knows it. And you know what that means, Joe? You know
who else is alone if Jack is?

On his deathbed, when fibrosis was again relevant to him,
Fogarty would recall how aware he was at this moment, not
only of being alone, but of being sick again, of being
physically weak with that peculiar early weakness in the
chest that he recognized so quickly, so intimately. He
would recall that he saw Dick Fegan pick up a lemon to
squeeze it for a whiskey sour a customer had ordered. The
customer was wearing a sport coat with checks so large
Fogarty thought of a horse blanket. He would remember he
saw these things, also saw Jack move out of his sight, out
onto the porch just as the first blast smashed the window.

Fogarty ordered a hot dog and a chocolate milk and
watched a fly that had either survived the winter or was
getting an early start on the summer. The fly was inspecting
the open hot dog roll.

"Get that goddamn fly off my bun," Fogarty told the
Greek.

The Greek was sweaty and hairy. He worked hard. He
worked alone in the all-night EAT. Fogarty has a loaded
pistol in his pocket, which is something you don't know
about Fogarty, Greek. The fly could be a cluster fly. Crazy.
Flies into things. Fast, but drunk. Few people realize where
the cluster fly comes from. He comes from a goddamn
worm. He is an earthworm. A worm that turns into a fly.
This is the sort of information you do not come by easily.
Not unless you lie on your back for a long, long time and
read the only goddamn book or magazine or newspaper in
the room. And when you've read it all and there's nobody
to talk to you, you read it again and find plenty of things
you missed the first time around. All about worms and flies.
There is no end to the details of life you can discover when
you are flat on your back for a long, long time.

"That goddamn fly is on my bun."

There is a certain amount of sadness in an earthworm
turning into a fly. But then it is one hell of a lot better than
staying an earthworm or a maggot.

"You gonna let that goddamn fly eat my bun, or do I have to kill the goddamn thing myself?"

The Greek looked at Fogarty for the first time. What he saw made him turn away and find the flyswatter. Naturally the goddamn fly was nowhere to be found.

Fogarty had parked his 1927 Studebaker in front of the EAT, which was situated on Route 9-W maybe eight or nine miles south of Kingston at a crossroads. The name of the EAT was EAT, and the Greek was apparently the one-man Greek EAT owner who was now looking for the fly while Fogarty's hot dog was being calcified.

"That's enough on the dog," Fogarty said to the Greek, who was at the other end of the counter and did not see the fly return to the bun. Fogarty saw and he heard his pistol go off at about the same moment the bullet flecked away slivers from the EAT's wooden cutting board. There was a second and then a third and a fourth report from the pistol. The fourth shot pierced the hot dog roll. None of the shots touched the fly. The Greek fled to a back room after the first shot.

Fogarty rejected the entire idea of a hot dog and left the EAT. He climbed into his Studebaker and nosed onto 9-W, destination Yonkers, his sister Peg's, which he knew was a bad idea, but he'd call first and get Peg's advice on where else he might stay. He could stay nowhere in the Catskills. That world exploded with the ten shotgun blasts from a pair of Browning automatic repeaters, fired at Jack as he paced in and out of the porch of the Aratoga. A pair of shooters fired from the parking lot, then stopped and drove away. Somebody snapped out the lights inside at the sound of those shots and everybody hit the floor. Fogarty heard: "Speed, help me," and he crawled out to the porch to see Jack on his stomach, blood bubbling out of holes in his back.

"Bum shooting," Jack said. "Better luck next time."

But he was flat amid the millions of bits of glass, and hurting, and Fogarty got on the phone and called Padalino, the undertaker, and told him to send over his hearse because he was not calling the cops in yet.

When it was obvious the shooting was over, the musicians and customers came out to look at Jack on the floor of the porch and Dick Fegan went for the phone. But Fogarty said, "No cops until we get out," and everyone waited for Padalino.

"Find Alice, keep an eye on her," Jack said to Fogarty.

"Sure, Jack. Sure I will."

"They're putting me in the meat wagon," Jack said when Fogarty and Fegan lifted him gently, carefully into the hearse. By then Fogarty had cut Jack's shirt away and tied up the wounds with clean bar towels. He kept bleeding, but not so much.

"I'll follow you," Fogarty told Padalino, and when they were near Coxsackie, he parked his Studebaker at a closed gas station and got into the hearse alongside Jack. He fed Jack sips of the whiskey he had the presence of mind to take from the bar, tippled two himself, but only two, for he needed to be alert. He kept watching out the window of the rear door. He thought the hearse was being followed, but then it wasn't. Then it was again and then, outside Selkirk, it wasn't anymore. He sat by the rear door of the hearse with a gun in each hand while Jack bled and bled. I know nothing about shooting left-handed, Fogarty thought. But he held both guns, Jack's and Eddie's, a pair. Come on now, you bastards.

"Hurts, Speed. Really hurts. I can't tell where I'm hit."

They'd hit him with four half-ounce pellets. They'd fired ten double-ought shells with nine pellets to a shell. Somebody counted eighty some holes in the windows, the siding, and the inside porch walls. Ninety pellets out of two shotguns, and they only hit him with four, part of one shell. It really *was* bum shooting, Jack. You ought to be dead, and then some.

But maybe he is by this time, Fogarty thought, for he'd left Jack at the Albany Hospital, checked him into emergency under a fake name, called Marcus and got Padalino to take him back to his car at Coxsackie. Then, with the leftover whiskey in his lap, he headed south, only to have a fly land on his hot dog bun. Bun with a hole in it now.

The temperature gauge on the Studebaker was back in the red, almost to 220 again. He drove toward the first possible water, but saw no houses, no gas station. When the needle reached the top of the gauge and the motor began to steam and clank, he finished the whiskey dregs, shut off the ignition, threw the keys over his shoulder into the weeds and started walking.

Four cars passed him in fifteen minutes. The fifth picked him up when he waved his arms in the middle of the road, and drove him three miles to the roadblock where eight state troopers with shotguns, rifles, and pistols were waiting for him.

> *Poem from the Albany* Times-Union
>
> Long sleeping Rip Van Winkle seems
> At last arousing from his dreams,
> And reaching for the gun at hand
> To drive invaders from his land.
> The Catskills peace and quiet deep
> Have been too much disturbed for sleep.
> The uproars that such shootings make
> Have got the sleeper wide awake.

Fogarty called me and asked me to appear for him at the arraignment, which I did. The charges had piled up: Kidnapping, assault, weapons possession, and, in less than two weeks, the federal investigators also charged both him and Jack with multiple Prohibition Law violations. His bail was seventeen thousand five hundred dollars and climbing. He said he knew a wealthy woman, an old flame who still liked him and would help, and I called her. She said she'd guarantee five thousand dollars, all she could get without her husband knowing. Fogarty had more in the bank, enough to cover the bail, but unfortunately his accounts, like Jack's and Alice's, were all sequestered.

Two of Jack's transient henchmen—a strange, flabby young man who wore a black wig that looked like linguine covered with shoe polish, and a furtive little blond rat named Albert—also inquired after my services, but I said I was overloaded.

"What are you going to do about bail?" I asked Fogarty, and he suggested Jack. But Jack was having trouble raising his own, for much of his cash was also impounded.

Beyond Jack, the woman, and his own inaccessible account, Fogarty had no idea where to get cash. His new Oldsmobile was repossessed for nonpayment a week after his arrest.

"How do you plan to pay me?" I asked him.

"I can't right now, but that money in the bank is still mine."

"Not if they prove it was booze profits."

"You mean they can take it?"

"I'd say they already have."

I liked Joe well enough—a pleasant, forthright fellow. But my legal career was built on defending not pleasant people, but people who paid my fee. I follow a basic rule of legal practice: Establish the price, get the money, then go to work. Some lawyers dabble in charity cases, which, I suspect, is whitewash for their chicanery more often than not. But I've never needed such washing. It was not one of Jack's problems either. What he did that had a charitable element to it was natural, not compensatory behavior. He liked the woman whose cow needed a shed, and so he had one built. He disliked old Streeter and showed it, which cost him his empire. I've absorbed considerable outrage over Jack's behavior with Streeter, but few people consider that he didn't *really* hurt the old man. A few burns to the feet and ankles are picayune compared to what might have happened. I understand behavior under stress, and I know Streeter lived to an old age and Jack did not, principally because Jack, when tested, was really not the Moloch he was made out to be.

Seeing events from this perspective, I felt and still feel justified in defending Jack. Fogarty took a fall—twelve and a half to fifteen, but served only six because of illness. I feel bad that anyone has to go to prison, but Fogarty was

Jack's spiritual brother, not mine, and I am neither Jesus Christ nor any lesser facsimile. I save my clients when I can, but I reserve the right of selective salvation.

Jack took pellets in the right lung, liver, and back, and his left arm was again badly fractured. The pellet in his lung stayed there and seemed to do him little harm. The papers had him near death for three days, but Doc Madison, my own physician, operated on him and said he probably wasn't even close to dying. He beat off an infection, was out of danger in ten days, and out of the hospital in four and a half weeks. One hundred troopers lined the road for forty-seven miles between Albany and Catskill the day he left the hospital for jail, to discourage loyalists from snatching away FDR's prize. New floodlights were installed on the Greene County jail (lit up the world wherever he went, Jack did), and the guard trebled to keep the star boarders inside: Jack, Fogarty, and Oxie, who had gained fifty pounds in the eight months he'd been there.

The feds indicted Jack on fourteen charges: coercion, Sullivan Law and Prohibition Law violations, conspiracy etc., and it was two weeks before we could raise the new bail to put him back on the street. It really wasn't the street, but the luxurious Kenmore Hotel in Albany, a suite of rooms protected by inside and downstairs guards.

The troopers and the revenue men continued their probing of the mountains. They found Jack's books with records of his plane rentals, his commissioning the building of an oceangoing speedboat. They found the empty dovecotes where he kept his carrier pigeons, his way of beating the phone taps. They found his still on the Biondo farm, and, from the records and notations, they also began turning up stashes of whiskey, wine, and cordials of staggering dimension.

The neatly kept files and records showed Jack's tie-in with five other mobs: Madden's, Vannie Higgins', Coll's, and two in Jersey; distribution tie-ins throughout eighteen counties in the state; brewery connections in Troy, Fort Edward, Coney Island, Manhattan, Yonkers, and Jack's (formerly Charlie Northrup's) plant at Kingston; plus dozens of storage dumps and way stations all through the Adirondacks and Catskills, from the Canadian border to just west of Times Square.

The first main haul was evaluated at a mere $10,000 retail, but they kept hauling and hauling. Remember these booze-on-hand statistics the next time anyone tells you Jack ran a two-bit operation. (Source, federal): 350,000 pints and 300,000 quarts of rye whiskey, worth $4 a pint retail, or about $3.8 million; 200,000 quarts of champagne at $10 a bottle, or $2 million; 100,000 half-kegs of wine worth $2.5 million, plus 80,000 fifths of cordials and miscellany for a grand estimated total of $10 million. Not a bad accumulation for a little street kid from Philly.

Catskill was looking forward to Jack's trial, which was going to be great for tourism. The first nationwide radio hookup of any trial in American history was planned, and I think somehow they would've sold tickets to it. A hundred businessmen, many of them hotel and boardinghouse operators, paying up to three hundred dollars in seasonal tribute to the emperor, held a meeting at the Chamber of Commerce, a meeting remarkable for its anonymity. Fifty newsmen were in town covering every development, but none of the hundred attendees at that meeting were identified.

What they did was unanimously ratify a proclamation calling on one another not to be afraid to testify against Jack and the boys. Getting tough with the wolf in the cage. There was even talk around town of burning down Jack's house. And finally, what Warren Van Deusen had been trying and not trying to tell me about Jack was that half a hundred people had written FDR letters over the past two months, detailing Jack's depredations. It was that supply of complaints, capped by the Streeter episode, which fired old Franklin to do what he did. That and politics.

The abandoned getaway car of Jack's would-be killers turned up with a flat tire on Prospect Avenue in Catskill, behind the courthouse. The Browning repeaters were still in it, along with a Luger, a .38 Smith and Wesson, and two

heavy Colt automatics with two-inch barrels, all fully
loaded. The car had a phony Manhattan registration in the
name of Wolfe, a nice touch, and when perspective was
gained, nobody blamed Murray for the big do. Too neat.
Too well planned. A Biondo job was Jack's guess.

My chief contribution to the history of these events was
to snatch the circus away from the Catskill greed mob.
They squawked that Jack was robbing them again, taking
away their chance to make a big tourist dollar. What I did
was win us a change of venue on grounds that a fair trial
was impossible in Greene County. The judge agreed and
FDR didn't fight us. He hopscotched us up to Rensselaer
County. With Troy, the county seat, being my old stamping
grounds, I felt like Br'er Rabbit being tossed into the briar
patch.

Attorney General Bennett paid homage to Jack at the
annual communion breakfast of the Holy Name Society of
the Church of St. Rose of Lima in Brooklyn. In celebration
of Mother's Day he said that if men of Diamond's type had
listened to the guidance of their mothers, they would not be
what they were today.

"One of the greatest examples of mother's care," the
attorney general said, "is the result which the lack of it has
shown in the life of Legs Diamond. Diamond never had a
mother's loving care nor the proper training. Environment
has played a large part in making him the notorious
character he is today. A mother is the greatest gift a man
ever had."

Alice came out of the elevator, walked softly on the rich,
blue carpet toward the suite, and saw a form which stopped
all her random thought about past trouble and future
anguish. The light let her see the hairdo, and the hair was
chestnut, not Titian; and the face was hidden under half a
veil on the little clawclutch of a maroon hat. But Alice
knew Kiki when she saw her, didn't she? Kiki was locking
the door to the room next to Alice's. Then she came toward
the elevator, seeming not to recognize Alice. Was it her?
Alice had seen her in the flesh only once. She was smaller

now than her photos made her out to be. And younger. Her face looked big in the papers. And at the police station. She had sat there at the station and let them take her picture. Crossed her legs for them.

She passed within inches of Alice, explaining herself with the violent fumes of her perfume. It *was* her. But if it truly was, why didn't she give some form of recognition, some gesture, some look? Alice decided that, finally, Kiki didn't have the courage to say hello. Coward type. Brazen street slut. Values of an alleycat. Rut whore. Was it really her? Why was she here? Would Jack know?

Kiki saw Alice coming as soon as she stepped out of the room, and she immediately turned away to lock the door. She recognized the fat calves under the long skirt with the ragged hem. On the long chance Alice wouldn't recognize her, Kiki chose to ignore her, for she feared Alice would turn her in. Kiki the fugitive. But would Alice run that risk? Jack would kill her for that, wouldn't he? Kitchen cow.

Why did life always seem to be saltwater life for Kiki, never life with a sweetness? Violence always taking Jack away. Violence always bringing back the old sow. Meat and potatoes pig. Why was fate so awful to Kiki? And then for people to say she had put the finger on Jack. What an awful thing to think. The cow passed her by and said nothing. Didn't recognize her. Kiki kept on walking to the elevator, then turned to see Alice entering the room next to Kiki's own. But how could that be? Would Alice break into Kiki's room? But for what? Why would she rent a room next to Kiki's? How would she know which one Kiki was in? Kiki would tell Jack about this, all right. But, Fat Mama, why are you here?

The Kenmore had status appeal to Jack: historic haven of gentility from the mauve decade until Prohibition exploded the purple into scarlet splashes. Its reputation was akin to Saratoga's Grand Union in Diamond Jim's and Richard Canfield's day. It was where Matthew Arnold stayed when he came to Albany, and Mark Twain too, on the night he lobbied for osteopathy in the Capitol. It was where Ulysses S. Grant occasionally dined. Al Smith's son lived there when Al was governor, and it was the dining room where any governor was most likely to turn up in the new century. It boasted eventually of Albany's longest bar, always busy with the chatter of legislators, the room where a proper gentleman from Albany's Quality Row could get elegantly swozzled among his peers.

Sure Jack knew this, even if he didn't know the details, for the tradition was visible and tangible, in the old marble, in the polished brass and mahogany, in the curly maple in the lobby, in the stained glass, and the enduring absence of the hoi polloi. Jack was always tuned in to any evidence of other people's refinement.

He dominates more memories of the place even now than Vincent Lopez or Rudy Vallee or Phil Romano or Doc Peyton or the Dorsey Brothers or any other of the greater or lesser musicians who held sway in the Rain-Bo room for so long, but whose light is already dim, whose music has faded away, whose mythology has not been handed on.

Jack didn't create the ambience that made the Kenmore so appealing, but he enhanced it in its raffish new age. He danced, he laughed, he wore the best, and moved with the fastest. But I well knew he had conceived that style long ago in desperation and was bearing it along cautiously now, like a fragile golden egg. He was frail, down eighteen pounds again, eyes abulge again, cheekbones prominent again, left arm all but limp, and periodically wincing when he felt that double-ought pellet bobbling about in his liver. But more troubling than this was the diminishing amount of time left for him to carry out the task at hand: the balancing of the forces of his life in a way that would give him ease, let him think well of himself, show him the completion of a pattern that at least would look *something* like the one he had devised as a young man: Young Jack—that desperate fellow he could barely remember and could not drive out.

Empire gone, exchequer sequestered, future wholly imperfect, it occurred to Jack that the remaining values of his life inhered chiefly in his women. Naturally, he decided

to collect them, protect them, and install them in the
current safe-deposit box of his life, which at the moment
was a six-room second-floor suite in the Kenmore.

"Marcus, you won't believe what I'm saying, but it's a
true. I'm in the kitchen one day and the boss come in and
says, Sal, you busy? I say no, not too much. He says, I
gotta friend of mine in such and such a room and his name
is Jack Legs Dime. Have you heard him? Well, I say, in the
newspape, yes. He says you wanna be his waiter from now
on while he stays uppa here? You go upstays every morning
eight thirty breakfast, noon if he's a call, maybe sandwich
now and then, don't worry dinner. Take care of him and his
friends and he pay you. I say, sure, it's all right with me. So
every morning I used to knock on the door with the same
breakfast—little steak and egg overlight for Jack, coffee,
toast, buns, some scramble eggs for everybody, some
cornflakes, milk, plenty potsa coffee, all on the wagon, and
Hubert, this rough-lookin' bast with a puggy nose, he's got
a goddama gun in both hands. I say Hubert, you son um a
bitch I won't come up here no more if you don't put them
guns away. I talk to him like that more for joke than
anything else. So I see Jack Dime and I give him the
breakfast and sometime breakfast for two, three extra
people they call to tell me about and Jack call to somebody
and says, hey, give Sal twenty-five dollar. He says to me,
will that be enough? I say Yeah, Legs, plenty. More than
what I expect. Just take care a me and my friends and you
down for twenty-five a day, how's that? Beautiful. Jesa
Christ, them days twenty-five dollar, who the hell ever seen
twenty-five dollar like that? Every day was a different five,
six new people, I guess they talking about Jack's trial
coming up. And one day Jack call the next room and say,
hey, Coll, you wanna eat some breakfas? I gotta breakfas
here. Hey, Legs, I say, that Vince Coll? He supposed to be
you enemy it says in the pape. Jack says no, he's a good
friend a mine. And I pour Coll a coffee and some toast.
Then three, four weeks later I met another fellow, Schultz.
I say, Hey, Legs, you and Schultz, you supposed to be the

worst enemies. And he says no, only sometimes. Now we
get along pretty nice. So I pour Schultz a coffee and some
toast. I say, Hey, Jack, they's a big fight tonight, who you
like, we bet a dollar. Nah, he says, them fighters all crooks.
Punks, no good. Then how about baseball, I says. Yeah, he
says, I bet you a dollar. I take the Yanks. Legs like Babe
Ruth and Bill Dickey. Then one day he says to me, Sal, I
want you to meet my wife, Mrs. Jack Legs Dime. I say it's
a pleasure, and then another day I go up and he says, Sal, I
want you to meet my friend, Miss Kiki Roberts. And Kiki
she says hello and I say it's a pleasure. Jesa Christ, I
wonder how the hell Jack Dime got these women together. I
see them sit down together, have breakfast, and then go out
together and shop down the stores on Pearl Street while
Jack stay home. I say to Freddie Robin, the detective
sergeant who sits in the lobby looking for punks who don't
look right and who ask funny quetions about Legs and I
say, Freddie, son um a bitch, it's magic. He got the both
women up there. Freddie says you think that's something
you ought to see them Sunday morn. All in church together.
No, I say. Yeah, Freddie say. All in the same pew, seven
o'clock mass Saint Mary's. No, I say. Don't tell me no,
Freddie says, when I get paid to go watch them. So I says
this I got to see for myself and next Sunday seven o'clock
mass son um a bitch they don't all come in, first Kiki, then
Alice, then Jack, and little ways back in another pew,
Freddie. Alice goes a communion and Jack and Kiki sit
still. Then later every Friday I see the monsignor come into
the hotel and go upstairs. To hear the confessions, Freddie
says, and he thinks sometimes they go to communion right
in the room. Hey, I says to Freddie, I don't know nobody
gets a communion in this hotel. How they get away with
that when they all living together in the same rooms? I took
a peek one day, the women got a room each, and Legs, he
got a room all his own and the bodyguards got a room and
they got other rooms for people in and out, transaction
business. Course when I was up there, everything was
mum. Nobody say anything, and when I go back for the
dishes and the wagon Legs is maybe getting a shave and a

haircut, every day, saying the rosary beads. They got a candle in every room, burn all day long, and a statue of Saint Anthony and the Blessed Virgin, which, I figure out, maybe is through Alice, who is on the quiet side, maybe because she got too damn much on her mind. She don't smile much at me. Hello, Sal, good morning, Sal, always nice, but not like Kiki, who says, Sal, how are you this morning, pretty good? Howsa weather outside? She liked to talk, some girl, Kiki. Wow! Freddie says to me, Sal, you think they all wind up in bed together? I laugh like hell. Freddie, I say, how the hell anybody going to do anything with a woman when another woman alongside you? No, that's not it. Bad as the guy might be, if I had a swear, put my hands to God and say would the guy do anything like that, I would say no. Maybe he got a desire to stay with his wife, then he call his wife into his room. He gotta desire to stay with his girlfriend, he call his girlfriend. It's the only thing I can see. Nine time out of ten I would say his girlfriend. On the other hand, he had to take care of his wife too. She wasn't so bad-looking, and after all it was a legitimate wife. You ask me was he an animal, a beast—I say no. He was a fanat. If he wasn't a fanat, why the hell he got Saint Anthony up there? He must've had some kind of good in him, I gotta say it. Not for the moneywise he gave me. I wouldn't judge him for that. But I couldn't say nothing bad toward the guy. I never even hear him curse. Very refine. Pardon me, pardon me. If he sneeze sometime, it's pardon me, tank you, see ya tomorra. But, actually speaking, who's a know what the hell really goes on upstays?"

The night I went to dinner with Jack, Alice, and Kiki at the Kenmore, the ménage seemed to be functioning the way Jack wanted it to function. He'd called me to come down and see him, talk about the trial, and, more important, he wanted to pay me. I'd already told him I was fond of him as a friend, even though I disagreed with some of his behavior, and I enjoyed his company. However, I said, all that has nothing to do with business. If I work for you, I expect to get paid, and now that you've got your bank accounts under government lock and key, what are you going to do about my fee, which, I explained, would be ten thousand dollars payable in advance? I knew two aspiring criminal lawyers who waited until after trial for their pay and arc waiting yet.

"Jack, let's face it," I said, "you're a crook."

He laughed and said, "Marcus, you're twice the crook I'll ever be," which pleased me because it implied prowess in a world alien to me, even if it wasn't true. What he was really doing was admiring my willingness to structure an alibi for his trial, give it a reasonableness that smacked lovingly of truth. I had fifteen witnesses lined up three weeks before we went to trial, and all were ready to testify, in authenticatingly eccentric and voluminous detail, that Jack had been in Albany the night Streeter and the kid were abducted. Waiters saw him, a manicurist, a desk clerk, a physiotherapist, a car salesman, a bootblack, a barber, a garment executive from the Bronx, and more.

I arrived at Jack's Kenmore suite half an hour ahead of schedule and was let in by Hubert Maloy, the plump Irish kid from Troy whom Jack had hired away from Vincent Coll as his inside guard. Hubert knew me and let me sit in the parlor. I immediately caught the odor of exotic incense and saw a wisp of smoke curling upward from an open door to one of the bedrooms. I glimpsed Alice on her hands and knees with a brushbroom, pushing a lemon back and forth on the rug in front of the incense, which burned in a tin dish. The scene was so weird it embarrassed me. It was like intruding on someone's humiliating dream. Alice was in her slip and stocking feet, a long run in the stocking most visible to me. Her hair was uncombed and she was without the protection of makeup. I quietly got up from the chair and moved to another one, where I wouldn't be able to see her room.

Jack arrived with Kiki about ten minutes later, and Alice emerged from the incense room like a new woman, hair combed, lipstick in place, lovely wildflower housecoat covering slip and run. She kissed Jack on the check, kissed me too, and said to Kiki: "Your black dress came from the cleaners, Marion. It's in the closet."

"Oh terrific, thanks," said a smiling, amiable, grateful Kiki.

Such was the nature of the interchanges I observed, and I won't bore you further with the banality of their civility. Jack took me aside, and when we'd finished updating the state of the trial, and of our witnesses (our foreboding reserved not for this but for the federal trial), Jack handed me a white envelope with twenty five-hundred-dollar bills.

"That suit you?"

"Seems to be in order. I'll accept it only if you tell me where it came from."

"It's not hot, if that's your worry."

"That's my worry."

"It's fresh from Madden. All legitimate. My fee for transferring some cash."

The cash, I would perceive before the week was out, was the ransom paid for Big Frenchy DeMange, Owney Madden's partner in the country's biggest brewery. Vincent Coll, Fats McCarthy, and another fellow whose name I never caught, whisked Big Frenchy off a corner in midtown Manhattan and returned him intact several hours later after the delivery of thirty-five thousand dollars to Jack, who, despite being on bail, left the state and drove to Jersey to pick it up. Madden knew Coll and McCarthy were basically cretins and that Jack was more than the innocent intermediary in such a neat snatch, and so Madden-Diamond relations were sorely, but not permanently, ruptured. I had little interest in any of that. I merely assured Jack he would now have the best defense money could buy.

Kiki had flopped into the chair from which I'd witnessed Alice's lemon brushing, and she said to Jack when he and I broke from conference: "I wanna go eat, Jackie." I saw Alice wince at the "Jackie." Jack looked at me and said, "Join us for dinner?" and I said why not and he said, "All right, ladies, get yourself spiffy," and twenty minutes and two old-fashioneds later we were all in the elevator, descending to the Rain-Bo room, my own pot of gold tucked away in a breast pocket, Jack's twin receptacles on either side of him, exuding love, need, perfume, promise, and lightly controlled confusion; also present: Hubert, the troll protecting all treasures.

For purposes of polite camouflage, Kiki clutched my arm as we moved toward Jack's corner table in the large room. "You know," she said to me softly, "Jack gave me a gift just before we came down."

"No, I didn't know."

"Five hundred dollars."

"That's a lovely gift."

"In a single bill."

"A single bill. Well, you don't see many of them."

"I never saw one before."

"I hope you put it in a safe place."

"Oh, I did, I'm wearing it."

"Wearing it?"

"In my panties."

Two days later Kiki would take the bill—well stained by then not only with her most private secretions, but also with Jack's—to Madame Amalia, a Spanish gypsy crone who ran a tearoom on Hudson Avenue, and paid the going fee of twenty-five dollars for the hex of a lover's erstwhile possession, hex that would drive the wedge between man and wife. Knowing whose wife was being hexed and wedged, Madame Amalia was careful not to make the five-hundred-dollar bill disappear.

"Did you see the new picture of me and Jack?" Alice asked me across the table.

"No, not yet."

"We had it taken this week. We never had a good picture of us together, just the ones the newspapermen snap."

"You have it there, do you?"

"Sure do." And she handed it over.

"It's a good picture all right."

"We never even had one taken on our honeymoon."

"You're both smiling here."

"I told Jack I wanted us to be happy together for always, even if it was only in a picture."

Despite such healthy overtness, the good Alice had pushed the lemon back and forth in front of the incense for three months, a ritual learned from her maid Cordelia, a child of Puerto Rico, where the occult is still as common as the sand and the sea. The lemon embodied Alice's bitter wish that Jack see Kiki as the witch Alice knew her to be, witch of caprice and beauty beyond Alice's understanding; for beauty to Alice was makeshift—nice clothing, properly colored hair, not being fat. And Kiki's beauty, ineffable as the Holy Ghost, was a hateful riddle.

When Jack's lucky blue suit came back from the hotel cleaners, a silver rosary came with it in the key pocket. I always suspected Alice's fine Irish Catholic hand at work in that pocket. The night of our Rain-Bo dinner Jack pulled out a handful of change when he sent Hubert for the *Daily News*, and when I saw the rosary I said, "New prayer implement there?" which embarrassed him. He nodded and dropped it back into his pocket.

He had examined it carefully when it turned up in that pocket, looked at its cross, which had what seemed to be hieroglyphics on it, and at the tiny sliver of wood inside the cross (which opened like a locket), wood that might well, the monsignor suggested, have been a piece of the true cross. The hieroglyphics and the sliver had no more meaning for Jack than the Hail Marys, the Our Fathers, and the Glory Bes he recited as his fingers breezed along the beads. His scrutiny of the cross was a search for a coded message from his mother, whose rosary, he was beginning to believe, had been providentially returned to him. For he remembered clearly the silver rosary on her dresser and, again, twined in her hands when she lay in her coffin. He studied it until its hieroglyphics yielded their true meaning: scratches. The sliver of wood, he decided, was too new to have been at Calvary. Piece of a toothpick from Lindy's more like it. Yet he fondled those silver beads, recited those holy rote phrases as if he, too, were rolling a lemon or hexing money, and he offered up the cheapjack stuff of his ragged optimism to the only mystical being he truly understood.

Himself.

No one else had the power to change the life at hand.

How does a mythical figure ask a lady to dance? As if Jack didn't have enough problems, now he was faced with this. Moreover, when he has a choice of two ladies, which one does he single out to be the first around whom he will publicly wrap what is left of his arms as he spins through waves of power, private unity, and the love of all eyes? These questions shaped themselves as wordless desires in Jack's head as he read his own spoken words about his own mythic nature.

When Hubert came back with four copies of the *Daily News*, everyone at the table opened to the first of a three-part interview with Jack by John O'Donnell. It was said to be Jack's first since all his trouble, and he corroborated that right there in the *News'* very bold type:

> **"I haven't been talking out of vanity—the fact that I've never given out my side before would show pretty clearly that I'm not publicity mad."**

Reasonable remark, Jack. Not publicity mad anymore. Too busy using interviews like these to generate sympathy for your cause, for the saving of your one and only ass, to worry about publicity for vanity's sake. Jack could be more pragmatic, now that he's a myth. But was he really a myth? Well, who's to say? But he does note a mythic development in his life in that bold, bold *Daily News* type:

> **"Here's what I think. This stuff written about me has created a mythical figure in the public mind. Now I'm Jack Diamond and I've got to defend myself against the mythical crimes of the mythical Legs."**

Legs. Who the hell was this Legs anyway? Who here in the Rain-Bo room really knows Legs?

"Hello, Legs."

"How ya doin', Legs?"

"Good luck on the trial, Legs."

"Glad to see you up and around, Legs."

"Have a drink, Legs?"

"We'd like you to join our party if you get a minute, Mr. Legs."

Only a handful in the joint really knew him, and those few called him Jack. The rest clustered 'round the mythic light, retelling stories of origins:

"They call him Legs because he always runs out on his friends."

"They call him Legs because his legs start up at his chest bone."

"They call him Legs because he could outrun any cop at all when he was a kid package thief."

"They call him Legs because he danced so much and so well."

*Shall we dance! Who first?*

"This is a good interview, Jack," said Marcus. "Good for the trial. Bound to generate some goodwill somewhere."

"I don't like the picture they put with it," Alice said. "You look too thin."

"I am too thin," Jack said.

"I like it," Kiki said.

"I knew you would," Alice said.

"I like it when your hat is turned up like that," Kiki said.

"So do I," Alice said.

" Find your own things to like," Kiki said.

*Who first?*

Dance with Alice and have the band play "Happy Days and Lonely Nights," your favorite, Jack. Dance with Marion and have them play "My Extraordinary Gal," your favorite, Jack.

"Is it true what he says there about Legs and Augie?" Kiki asked.

"All true," Jack said.

"As a matter of fact I was never called Legs until after that Little Augie affair. Look it up and see for yourself. It don't make much difference, but that's a fact. My friends or my family have never called me Legs. When the name Legs appeared under a picture, people who didn't know me picked it up and I've been called Legs in the newspapers ever since."

O'Donnell explained that Eddie Diamond was once called Eddie Leggie ("Leggie," a criminal nickname out of the nineteenth-century slums) and that somehow it got put on Jack. Cop told a newsman about it. Newsman got it wrong. Caption in the paper referred to Jack as Legs. And there was magic forever after.

"I didn't know that," Kiki said. "Is it really true, Jackie?"

"All the garbage they ever wrote about me is true to people who don't know me."

The music started again after a break, and Jack looked anxiously from woman to woman, faced once again with priority. Did his two women think of him as Legs? Absurd. They knew who he was. If anybody *ever* knew he was Jack Diamond and not Legs Diamond, it was those two ladies. They loved him for his own reasons, not other people's. For his body. For the way he talked to them. For the way he loved them. For the way his face was shaped. For the ten thousand spoken and unspoken reasons he was what he was. It wasn't necessary for Jack to dwell on such matters, for he had verified this truth often. What was necessary now was to keep the women together, keep them from repelling each other like a matched pair of magnets. This matched pair would work as a team, draw the carriage of Jack's future. Fugitive Kiki, wanted as a Streeter witness, needed the protection of Jack's friends until the charge against her went away. She would stick, all right. And Alice? Why, she would stick through anything. Who could doubt that at this late date?

A voluptuous woman in a silver sheath with shoulder straps of silver cord paused at the table with her escort.

"This one here is Legs," she said to the escort. "I'd

know him anywhere, even if he is only a ridiculous bag of bones.''

"Who the hell are you?" Jack asked her.

"I saw your picture in the paper, Legs," she said.

"That explains it."

She looked at Alice and Kiki, then rolled down the right strap of her gown and revealed a firm, substantial, well-rounded, unsupported breast.

"How do you like it?" she said to Jack.

"It seems adequate, but I'm not interested."

"You've had a look anyway, and that counts for something, doesn't it, sweetheart?" she said to her escort.

"It better, by God," said the escort.

"I can also get milk out of it if you ever feel the need," she said, squeezing her nipple forward between two fingers and squirting a fine stream into Jack's empty coffee cup.

"I'll save that till later," Jack said.

"Oh, he's so intelligent," the woman said, tucking herself back into her dress and moving off.

"I think we should order," Kiki said. "I'm ravished."

"You mean famished," Jack said.

"Yes, whatever I mean."

"And no more interruptions," said Alice.

Jack signaled the waiter and told him, "A large tomato surprise."

"One for everybody?"

"One for me," Jack said. "I have no power over what other people want."

The waiter leaned over and spoke into Jack's face so all could hear. "They tell *me* you've got the power of ten thousand Indians."

Jack picked up his butter knife and stared at the waiter, prepared to drive the blade through the back of that servile hand. He would take him outside, kick him down the stairs, break his goddamn snotty face.

"The way I get it," the waiter said, backing away, speaking directly to Jack, "you know it all. You know who the unknown soldier is and who shot him."

"Where do they get these people?" Jack asked. But

before anyone could respond, the waiter's voice carried across the room from the kitchen, "A tomato surprise for the lady killer," and the room's eyes swarmed over Jack in a new way.

Jack straightened his tie, aware his collar was too big for his neck, aware his suit had the ill fit of adolescence because of his lost weight. He felt young, brushed his hair back from his ears with the heels of both hands, thought of the work that lay ahead of him, the physical work adolescents must do. They must grow. They must do the chores of life, must gain in strength and wisdom to cope with the hostile time of manhood. The work of Jack's life lay stretched out ahead of him. On the dance floor, for instance.

He started to get up, but Alice grabbed his arm and whispered in his ear: "Do you remember, Jack, the time you stole the fox collar coat I wanted so much, but then I took it back and you insisted and went back and stole it all over again? Oh, how I loved you for that."

"I remember," he said softly to her. "I could never forget that coat."

Kiki watched their intimacy, then leaned toward Jack and whispered, "I've got my legs open, Jackie."

"Have you, kid?"

"Yes. And now I'm opening my nether lips."

"You are?"

"Yes. And now I'm closing them. And now I'm opening them again."

"You know, kid, you're all right. Yes, sir, you're all right."

He stood up then and said, "I'm going to dance."

Alice looked at Kiki, Kiki at Alice, the ultimate decision blooming at long last. They both looked to Jack for his choice, but he made none. He got up from his chair at last and, with his left arm swinging limply, his right shoulder curled in a way to give his movement the quality of a young man in full swagger, he headed for the dance floor where a half dozen couples were twirling about to a waltz. When Jack put a foot on the dance floor, some, then all couples stopped and the band trailed off. But Jack turned to the bandstand, motioned for the music to continue. Then he looked at Kiki and Alice, who stood just off the edge of the floor.

"My arm, Marion," he said. "Take my arm."

And while Alice's eyes instantly filled with tears at the choice, Kiki gripped Jack's all but useless left hand with her own and raised it. As she moved toward him for the dancer's embrace, he said, "My right arm, Alice," and Alice's face broke into a roseate smile of tears as she raised Jack's right hand outward.

The women needed no further instruction. They joined their own hands and stepped onto the dance floor with their man. Then, as the orchestra broke into the waltz of now and forever, the waltz that all America, all Europe, was dancing to—"Two Hearts in Three-Quarter Time," its arithmetic obviously calculated in heaven—Alice, Marion, and Jack stepped forward into the music, into the dance of their lives.

"One-two-three, one-two-three, one-two-three, one-two-three," Jack counted. And they twirled on their own axis and spun around the room to the waltz like a perfect circle as the slowly growing applause of the entire room carried them up, up, and up into the ethereal sphere where people truly know how to be happy.

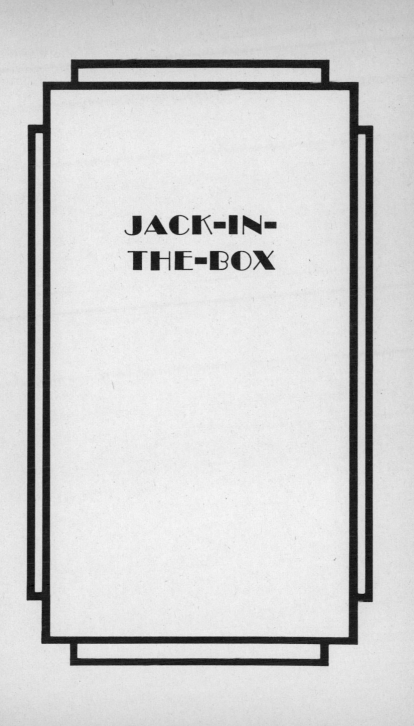

# JACK-IN-THE-BOX

I'll spare you the details of the summer's two trials, which produced few surprises beyond my own splendid rhetoric and, in the Troy trial, a perjury indictment for one of our witnesses whose vigorous support of Jack's alibi was, alas, provably untrue. I presume the July verdict must be counted a surprise, being for acquittal of Jack on a charge of assaulting Streeter. The courtroom burst into applause and shouts when the verdict was read. Alice ran down the aisle in her lovely pink frock with the poppy print and her floppy picture hat, leaned over the rail and gave Jack a wet one with gush. "Oh, my darling boy!" And three hundred people standing outside the Rensselaer County courthouse in Troy, because there were no seats left in the courtroom, sent up a cheer heard 'round the world. Moralists cited that cheer as proof of America's utter decadence and depravity, rooting for a dog-rat like Diamond. How little they understood Jack's appeal to those everyday folk on the sidewalk.

I must admit that the attorney general lined up an impressive supply of witnesses to prove conclusively to any logician that Jack was in Sweeney's speakeasy in Catskill the night Streeter was lifted. But once I identified Streeter as a bootlegger, the issue became a gangster argument about a load of booze, not the torture of innocence. And Jack was home free.

It wasn't so easy to confuse the issue at the federal trial in Manhattan. All that the federal lawyers (young Tom Dewey among them) had to do was connect Jack with the still, which wasn't much of a problem, and *they* were home

free. The Catskill burghers, including my friend Warren
Van Deusen, spouted for the prosecution, and so did some
of Jack's former drivers; but most damning was Fogarty,
who called Jack a double-crossing rat who wouldn't put up
money for a lawyer, who let this poor, defenseless,
tubercular henchman, who had trusted him, take the rap
alone and penniless. Alice was in court again, with Eddie's
seven-year-old son, a marvelously sympathetic prop, and
Jack broke into genuine tears when a newsman asked him
in the hallway if the boy really was his nephew. But those
feds nailed our boy. My rhetoric had no resonance in that
alien courtroom: too many indignant businessmen, too
much faceless justice, too far from home, too much
Fogarty. In an earlier trial at Catskill, the state had
managed to convict Fogarty on the same Streeter charge
Jack was acquitted of, which was poetic justice for the
turncoat as I see it. Jack drew four years, the maximum,
and not really a whole lot, but enough of a prospect to spoil
the summer.

Jack had been making plans to merge with Vincent Coll
and Fats McCarthy, substitute their mob for his own,
refurbish the Catskill scene, and maybe put a toe in the
door of the Adirondacks. But Johnny Broderick and a
squad of New York dicks followed Coll's crowd up from
Manhattan and raided them in Coxsackie, hauling in about
a dozen. They missed Coll and McCarthy, who along with a
few stragglers holed up in an artist's home in Averill Park, a
crossroads summer town east of Troy, where Jack and Coll
occasionally met and tried to cook up a future for
themselves.

It was a depressing time for Jack. Kiki had to take an
apartment away from the Kenmore when the state police
began to breathe heavily around the lobby, and Alice was
delighted to get rid of the competition. But Jack took Kiki
out regularly and brought her back to the hotel for visits
after the first trial, and Alice finally said good-bye forever,
folks, and went to live in her Manhattan apartment on
Seventy-second Street.

The acquittal in Troy came in early July, the federal

conviction in early August, and the state announced it
would try Jack on a second Streeter charge, kidnapping, in
December. It was a very long, very hot summer for all of
us, but especially Jack, like the predator wolf pushed ever
farther from civilization by angry men, who was learning
the hard way how to die.

Jack's federal conviction drove a spike of gloom into
everybody. Jack insisted on trying to buy a retrial, his
hangover from the days when Rothstein had money in
everybody's mouth, all the way up to the Presidential
cabinet. That money had bought Jack a delay on a federal
charge of smuggling heroin for Rothstein, the noted
bowling pin case, and Jack died without ever having to face
up to the evidence against him.

"The fuckers are all the same, all the way to the top," he
said to me one night. "They'll do you any favor you can
pay for."

But times had changed to a certain unpredictable degree
in Manhattan, especially for people like Jack. The new
federal crowd was young, imbued with Seaburyism, and
still unbuyable. Even if we had found somebody to buy,
there was the case of the diminishing bankroll. The first
thing Jack did after he got out of the Catskill jail on bail was
to take the one hundred and eighty thousand dollars I'd
held for him in safe deposit. That still seemed like a lot of
money to me, but it wasn't for Jack. He owed everybody:
me, the hospital, the doc, his barber, his waiter, the hotel,
his driver, Hubert the bodyguard, infinite numbers of
bartenders who would now and in the future provide him
with service. He was keeping apartments in Troy,
Watervliet, Albany, East Greenbush, a house in Peters-
burg, and probably six or eight other cities I don't know
about. He was keeping Kiki. He was subsidizing Alice in
Manhattan. And, and most costly of all, he was paying off
politicians everywhere to keep his freedom, keeping them
from infecting him with further trouble. The one hundred
and eighty thousand dollars went in a few months, or so
Jack said, though I think he must have kept a secret nest

egg somewhere, and if he did, of course, he kept it utterly
to himself. He didn't leave the egg with me. I also know
Vincent Coll offered him a loan of ten thousand dollars
after a nifty Coll snatch of a Saratoga gambler, and a
handsome ransom of sixty-five thousand dollars; and Jack
took it.

He coped with the money problem like the pragmatist he
had come to be. He went back to work. I met him at the
Albany Elks Club bar on a steamy August evening after a
day at Saratoga had given me nothing but the aesthetic
boredom of picking losers under the elms of the track's
stylish old clubhouse and paddock. I came back to town
alone, feeling curiously empty for no reason I could
explain. The emptiness was a new development. I decided,
after six beers, that I hadn't felt this way since that day I
was sitting alone in the K. of C. library. And when this
thought registered, I knew the problem was Jack-related.
My life was far from empty professionally. Since Jack's
acquittal in Troy the calls were flooding in and I could name
my price for trial work. Was it, then, the loss of a political
career? Like an amputated leg, that particular part of me
did pain, even though it wasn't there, and yet I was
simultaneously relieved at never having to be a politician. It
was such a vapid way to spend your life, and a slavish
game, too, slavish to the political clubroom crowd, even to
the Elks Club where I was standing, a superb fragment of
all I found stagnant, repulsive, and so smugly corrupt in
Albany. The Democratic bagman, though it was two
months till election, was already in his corner of the card
room (two city detectives watching the door), accepting
tithes from everybody who fed at the county courthouse or
city hall troughs—janitors, lawyers growing fat from the
surrogate court, vendors, bankers, cops, firemen, secretar-
ies, clerks, contractors. The pattern was consistent with
Jack's notion of how an empire should be run. Everybody
pays.

Just as I liked Jack, I also liked the old bagman. He was a
dandy and a curmudgeon and a wily and wise old Irishman

who had read his Yeats and Wilde as well as his Croker and Tweed. I also liked the men who were next to me at the bar. They were men I'd been raised with, men who knew my father and my uncles: tradesmen and sportswriters and other lawyers and politicians and factory hands who liked pinochle and euchre and salesmen who liked to bowl and drink beer, and, of course, of course, Jack.

Most of the Elks who talked frankly with me were confused by his presence. They knew what his minions had done at the Elks Club in Catskill, which bothered them far more than the kidnapping of Streeter or making Charlie Northrup disappear. They didn't really want Jack around. But they were also awed when he walked in, flattered when he bought them a drink, and marked forever when he put his arm on their shoulder and talked baseball with them. Hello, Bill! Hello, Jack! Brotherrrrrrrrrrrrr!

"Counselor," Jack said to me when he moved in alongside me at the bar, "I'm going to buy you a new hat."

"So you're at that again," I said.

"The heat must've got to it, Marcus. It's dead for sure. Take a look."

I looked at my trusty old Panama, which had aged considerably since I last examined it, I must admit.

"Well, it's getting old, Jack, but then so are we all. And I do feel compassion for things that are deteriorating visibly."

"Whataya say, you want to take a ride?"

"Sounds sinister, Jack. My father warned me about taking rides with strange gangsters."

"Little business trip, and what the hell, it's too goddamn hot to stand here smelling armpits. The air'll do you good. Blow the stink off you."

"You're right, I could stand a change. Who's driving?"

"Hubert."

"Ah, Hubert. I still find it hard to believe you've got somebody named Hubert in your employ."

"Good kid, Hubert. Does what he's told."

We left the bar and walked out to the top of the club's

stone stoop, which faced on State Street. It was middle evening, the streetlights on, but the sun still making long shadows. We looked up toward Capitol Park, where Hubert went for the car, where General Philip Sheridan, another Albany Irishman, sat astride his horse, riding into eternity. There were only the two of us on the stoop, which struck me as unnecessarily foolish, given the recurring rumor of gunmen out to get Jack.

"We make nice targets for your friends here," I said.

"Fuck it. You can't live like a rat in a hole forever."

I could only agree with that, which straightened my back. How little encouragement it takes to place oneself in jeopardy.

"What's this business trip you've got planned?"

"A small delivery to a customer."

"You don't mean you want me to join you on a booze run."

"Relax, would I do that to you? We won't be in the same vehicle with the stuff. And it's only beer. We'll follow the truck, well back. Plenty safe. Up to Troy, back down to Packy Delaney's. It's a favor for Packy and I'm glad to do it. I like The Pack."

"I do myself."

"I'm glad for the ride, too," Jack said. "Jesus, I get bored easy lately."

"We've got the same affliction."

Hubert pulled up and we headed for Stell's, a busy Troy brewery run by a gang of beer-savvy Dutchmen Jack had been doing business with for years. But the pickup and delivery of the moment would be a departure for Jack: made in a borrowed truck by the man himself, notable status reduction. His excuse was he was doing Packy a favor. "He's in a bind with his Albany supplier, hates the beer he has, but he's gotta take it." It proved to be the other way around, Packy responding to Jack's request for a loan with a pragmatic substitute—a deal. Packy would buy the beer at Jack's price, even though he didn't need it; Jack would show a profit, Packy would avoid making a cash loan that would probably never be repaid, and Packy would have the beer, at least, to show for his investment.

We drove up Broadway and through North Albany, past the streets of my own neighborhood: Emmett, Albany, Mohawk, Genesee, Erie, then the park in front of Sacred Heart Church on Walter and North Second Streets, a view which provided me with a pang of recognition and a sliver of insight which made this trip worth recording. I remembered how my father looked, sitting on a park bench in the years just before his death, teeth too prominent, like a skull's mindless grin, his brain almost as white as his hair, watching the trolleys go to Troy and back. I tried to imagine what that man, who never stole a nickel in his life, would make of his son being on Jack's payroll, a speculation which, I know, reveals more of me than of the old man.

My father was not a religious man in his youth and middle years. He routinely did his Easter duty, kept the Commandments, but often slept through the Sunday slate of masses. Yet he ended his days at daily mass, even serving for the priest when the altar boy of the day overslept. I've long tried to persuade myself that his final conversion to piety was more than simplistic fear of the next, for my father was complex, a teacher, a Latin scholar who named me for his favorite Stoic. Remembering him, then, at that moment by the park when I was also conscious of how Jack was regularly telling his beads, and when I was questioning my own irrational reading of Aquinas long after I'd lost my faith, I knew all three of us were hounded by religious confusion: Jack out of Saint Anne's, both my father and I out of Sacred Heart, products all of the ecclesiastical Irish sweat glands, obeisant before the void, trying to discover something.

And as we passed Sacred Heart, I looked at Jack and said to him, "My old man used to sit in that park and watch the world go by when he got old."

Jack craned his neck for a look, smiling at the thought. His own yellowing skin, and his teeth with too much prominence, gave me back the face of my father. And I thought then that I knew what they were both looking for. I thought: They have misplaced tomorrow and are looking for it. And the search is ruining today.

We stopped at a garage on Fourth Street in Troy to pick up the truck Jack was borrowing from a fellow named Curley, who once drove for him. Curley had gone off on his own and now had a fleet of Macks and Reos which did heavy duty on the highways on behalf of public thirst. Hubert got the keys for our truck and drove it from a back lot to the gas pump in front of the garage, where a kid attendant in overalls gassed us up with Socony.

"You want any cupcakes tonight, Legs?" the kid asked.

"Why not?" Jack said and gave him a ten-dollar bill. When the tank was full, the kid ran across the street to an old lady's grocery and came back with three cupcakes in cellophane and an opened bottle of sarsaparilla. Jack ate a cake and sucked at the soda for the kid, who wanted to be near Jack, do things for him.

"You think you can beat that federal rap on an appeal, Legs?"

"A sure thing, kid. Don't bet against me."

The kid—with his freckles, his large Irish teeth, and a cowlick his barber didn't understand—laughed and said, "Bet against you? Never do that."

"Listen, kid," Jack said, and I can hear Cagney telling Billy Halop almost the same thing years later, "don't get the wrong idea about me. I'm not going to live much longer. I got more metal in me than I got bones. Stay in school. The rackets are a bum life. There ain't no heroes in the rackets."

"I heard you were on the spot," the kid said. "That true?"

Jack gave him a happy grin. "I been on the spot all my life."

"I heard a rumor there's guys around want to get you."

"The word's even out to the kids," Jack said to me.

"I wouldn't tell 'em nothing if they come here," the kid said.

"Attaboy," Jack said.

"You know I didn't say nothin' about the panel truck."

"I know that."

"I heard one of the guys looking for you is called Goose."

"Yeah? What else do you hear?"

"That they were asking questions up in Foley's last week."

"Nothing since then?"

"Nothing."

"I heard about that," Jack said. "It's all over with. The Goose flew south."

"It's okay then," the kid said. "Good news."

"Give your old lady some good news, kid. Don't mess in the rackets."

"Okay, Legs."

Jack tipped him five and got behind the wheel of his Lincoln, which he was buying on time. Within a month he'd be too broke to keep it. I got in and we followed Hubert to the brewery, where Jack paid for the beer and saw it loaded. Then we headed for Packy's in downtown Albany. We took a back road from Troy through North Greenbush and into Rensselaer, a town like Albany, where Jack was safe passing through with wet goods, across the Dunn Bridge and up to Packy's on Green Street.

"What was that panel truck the kid mentioned?" I asked when we were rolling again.

"Heavy load of booze. We parked it there one night we were being chased. Oxie sat in it all night with a machine gun."

"That was nice advice you gave the kid. But I can't believe you don't want disciples in your own image, like the rest of us."

"Kid's too soft," Jack said. "If he was tougher, I'd tell him, 'Go ahead kid, see how tough you really are,' line him up behind all the other tough guys waiting to die young, let him take his chances. Sure I'd tell him about the easy money, easy pussy, living high. But I like that kid."

"You liked Fogarty too. Why'd you take him in?"

"He reminded me of Eddie."

"But you let him sink."

"Did I? You had more say over that than me."

"I told you I get paid for what I do. And it was you who said the hell with him, that he was never any good."

"He wasn't. You saw he turned stool pigeon. He was a weak sister. What'd he expect me to do, mother him? Rothstein not only dumped me, he tried to kill me. But I never blew the whistle on him. Never trust a pussy freak. Fogarty's cock ran ahead of him like a headlight. Made a sucker of a good guy. Why not let him sink? I'd let anybody sink except Eddie. And Alice and Marion. I'd even let you sink, Marcus."

"I know. And I'd do the same for you, Jack. But the difference is that I'm just a businessman and you're a prick in your heart."

"Pricks are the only ones got it made in this world."

"That's a chump's line."

"Maybe. I look like a chump these days."

"Chumps never know who their real friends are."

"Friends," said Jack. "I got no friends. You and me, we're just knockin' around, passing the time. You're all right, Marcus, and I always said so, but I only had one friend my whole goddamn life. My brother Eddie. Came down from Saranac when he was dying to help me during the Hotsy thing. Christ, we set up a meeting in the subway, Twenty-eighth Street, and he was all dressed up, coconut straw, brown palm beach, and a new white silk shirt with a lemon tie, looked like a million except you could've got two other guys inside the suit with him. He wanted to make collections for me, wanted to run the operation while I was hiding out. Said he'd do anything and the poor bastard could hardly breathe. We talked an hour, and when we got up to go, I was holding him and he started giving me the Holy Roller malarkey. He got religion up in Saranac and they were calling him The Saint. Used to go around visiting in his wheelchair, seeing guys who couldn't move a muscle, who were afraid to fucking breathe. Really selling me hard, and so I said to him, forget that guff, Ed, it's not my style.

You'll come around, he said, and I say in a pig's whistle, and he keeps at it, so I finally say will you for crissake shut up about it? And we're up in the street by then, so I hailed a taxi to get him back to the Commodore where he had a room. And when I let go of his arm, he fell down and Christ Jesus, he let out a cough I thought his whole insides was liquid. Death rattle is what it was. Fantastic horrible goddamn gurgle. He only lasted a couple of months more. Shortened his life coming down to help me out. Couldn't do a goddamn thing for anybody, but he tried, the son of a bitch tried with all he fucking had. That's what's friends, Marcus. That's what I call friends."

Jack, the gush, was crying.

Old Joe Delaney opened The Parody Club in 1894 to appease a capricious thirst that took hold of him at odd hours, often after the city's saloons had closed. He ran it until 1919 and dated his retirement to the day a hod carrier swooned at the bar and crumpled like a corpse. Delaney's son Packy (né Patrick), apprenticing as a bartender after a stint with the AEF, looked the hoddy over, kicked his ass, and yelled in his ear, "Get up and go home, you stewbum."

"A born saloonkeeper," the elder Delaney rejoiced, yielding swiftly then to the pull of retirement in his favorite chair, where he died five years later with a bent elbow and foam on his handlebars.

Music greeted us when we walked through the old swinging doors, original doors that led to the Delaney time capsule. We walked under a four-globed chandelier and a four-bladed ceiling fan, past photos on the walls of old railroad men, old politicians, old bare-knuckle fighters, dead Maud Gonne's likeness sketched on a handbill announcing her appearance at Hibernian Hall to raise funds for a free Ireland, defunct Hibernian Society marching down State Street on a sunny Saint Patrick's Day in '95, disbanded private fire companies standing at attention in front of their pumpers, K. of C. beer drinkers, long in their graves, tapping a keg at a McKown's Grove clambake. I went back to Packy's now and again until the place burned down in 1942, when fire dumped all that old history of faces into the powdery ashpit. Nothing ever changed there, till then.

Flossie was making the music when we walked in, the piano being her second talented instrument of pleasure. Flossie was a saucy blond cupcake then, not working directly out of Packy's, where sins of the flesh were traditionally prohibited on premises. But she was advertising from the piano bench and specializing in private sessions to augment her income after her musical workday. Ah, Floss. How well I remember your fingers, so educated to the music of joy.

She was jangling away at the keyboard while Packy and another man delivered up some two-part harmony, not half-bad, of "Arrah-Go-On, I'm Gonna Go Back to Oregon," a song from the war years.

"Now this is something like it," Jack said, and he walked ahead of me past the crowded bar toward an empty back table that gave a view of the door. Hubert, having deposited the truck for unloading inside Packy's garage, followed us; but Jack told him, "Watch the door and the street." And without a word Hubert went to the end of the bar and stood there alone while Packy pined for Oregon, where they'd call him Uncle Pat, not Uncle John. He gave Jack a smile on that line and an extended left arm that welcomed and introduced the hero to the customers who hadn't yet recognized him; Jack waved to half a dozen men at the bar looking our way.

"You know those fellows?" he asked me.

"I guess I've seen one or two around town."

"All thieves or hustlers. This is a good place to buy yourself a new suit or a new radio cheap."

Jack bought the drinks himself at the bar, then settled into a chair and gave full attention to Flossie's piano and Packy's baritone. Packy came to the table when his harmony ran out.

"Fellow singing with me says he knows you, Jack."

"I don't place him."

"Retired railroad cop and not a bad fellow for a cop. Nice tenor too, and he carries a tune. Hey, Milligan."

The tenor came over and looked at us through cataract lenses. His hair was pure white and standing tall, and his magnified eyes and cryptic smile gave him the look of a man in disguise.

"You don't remember me," he said to Jack.

"Give me a clue."

"Silk. New Jersey. 1924."

"Ah, right. I make you now. You pinched me."

"You've got it. You were stealing the railroad blind, you and your brother."

"I remember. You were in the house when I came home. Sure, I remember you now, you son of a bitch. You sapped me."

"Only after you tried to kick me in the balls."

"I forgot that."

"You were out of jail quicker than I put you in."

"I had some classy political connections in those days."

"I know all about it. You remember anything else about that night? Remember singing a song coming up the stairs?"

"A song."

"It was a favorite of mine and I said to myself, now this can't be such a bad fellow if he knows a song like that. Just about then you saw me and tried to kick me in the crotch."

"I can't remember any song, Milligan, that your name?"

"Milligan's right. You were drunk and howling it out like a banshee. Listen, see if you remember."

He backstepped and put his hand on his stomach, then gave us:

> There's an old time melody,
> I heard long ago . . .

"I damn well remember that," Jack said. "One of my favorites."

> Mother called it the rosary,
> She sang it soft and low . . .

Jack nodded, grinned, sat back, and listened as most of the customers were also listening now, not merely to Milligan, but to Milligan singing for Legs Diamond.

> Without any rhyme,
> I mean without any prose,
> I even forgot
> How the melody goes  . . .

Flossie found Milligan's key and trilled some soft background chords, a flicker of faint melody.

> But ten baby fingers  . . .

And then Jack could hold it back no longer and added a spoken line: "And ten baby toes  . . ." And then together he and Milligan finished the song:

> She'd watch them by the setting sun,
> And when her daily work was done,
> She'd count them each and every one,
> That was my Mother's ro-sa-reeeeeeee.

Flossie gave them a re-intro, and with Jack on melody, Milligan on first tenor, and Packy on baritone, the harmonizers sang mournfully, joyously, and profoundly out of the musical realm of their Irish Catholic souls. They sang for all the children who ever had mothers, for all the mothers who ever had children, and when it was over, Jack called out, "Flossie, love, let's do it again."

"Anything for you, Jack. Anything you want."

And the harmonizers moved closer together, their arms on each other's shoulders, and began once more:

> There's an old time melody,
> I heard long ago  . . .

We sang songs that way for three hours and drove everybody out of the bar, including the bartender. Packy made our drinks and Flossie stayed and played for us, long after her advertising day had ended without a client. But I think the Floss anticipated things to come, and rejected all Johns who had no hint of transcendence about their requests. I was drinking beer and Jack was not quite reckless, but was at the boilermakers. And so both of us were a little slow on the uptake when Hubert, back in from a reconnaissance walk up the block, quick-stepped over to our table and spoke his first words of the musical evening: "There's a guy in a car across the street, Jack. Two guys, in fact. One at the wheel looks like he's got that eyepatch you been looking for."

"Would that be The Goose?" Packy asked. "I heard he was around asking questions about you."

"Probably him," Jack said.

"Then we've got to get you out of here," said The Pack.

Of our little group of six, only Milligan did not know The Goose. But he asked no questions. The song was over, and Flossie's face showed it. Jack, on the other hand, seemed without tension, which, of course, he was not. Yet his control under the circumstances was almost equal to having none.

"It's tricky with The Goose," he said. "He might break in here any minute and start blasting. That's nonprofessional, but he's crazy all the way now. People have to remember that."

"Sure he's crazy," said Packy. "In and out of town all summer asking questions."

"He's made a game of it," Jack said. "He wants me to sweat."

"But now he's outside," Hubert said, understandably perplexed by a discussion at such a moment. My own first thoughts were to evacuate the uninvolved from the premises, myself included. Yet it seemed cowardly to think of running away from only the possibility of somebody else's trouble. Yet there *was* the Hotsy to recall, where innocents were nicked by crossfire. So if you didn't run away, you might eventually be obliged to duck. It was the price of being Jack's companion.

"Oh, sweet mother," Flossie said when the reality of The Goose hit her. Her face collapsed then, perhaps into a vision of Billy Blue. She was having a good time just before Billy got it, too.

"I'll call the dicks, have 'em come down and pick him up," said Packy, nerve ends flaring, spinning on a proprietor's understandable confusion.

"Pick him up for what?" Jack said. "Sitting in a car?"

"I can think of half a dozen charges if necessary," I said. "Getting them here seems to be the priority."

Packy was already at the phone. Hubert locked the front door and said the two men were still in the maroon sedan, fifty feet from The Parody, across the street.

"Maybe you should just stay here all night," I said.

Jack nodded, aware of that possibility. Milligan pushed his chair away from the table, but didn't get up, an ambiguous gesture which suited an ex-cop in such a situation.

"You don't know if they'll come or not," Packy said after his call. "I got Conlon on the desk, the prick. You never know what they're gonna do for you. Or to you. He said the lieutenant was at a big fire up in the West Albany railroad shops. He'll try to tear a car loose. The prick, the prick."

"They want me dead, too," Jack said.

"I never liked that Conlon," Milligan said, "but I never took a backstep from him or any of them up there. I'll call him."

"It's not your problem, Milligan," Jack said, amused by the old man's concern.

"I always try to keep down violence in the city," said Milligan. "Valuable citizens involved here"—and he gave me a quick eye and a wink and went to the phone. I was left to look at Jack, who'd barely been able to move a shotglass with his left arm all night. He was living mainly by the use of one hand, a liability, should he be forced to confront The Goose in any physical way. Hubert was a good shot, which was one reason Jack hired him; but so was The Goose, and who knew about his faceless helper? Jack would be on the short end of any fight, a fact I was just coming to understand.

Milligan came back. "I called Cap Ronan, but no answer. Maybe he's out at the fire, too. Then I called Conlon again and told him the trouble here personally. He got the message." Milligan sat down and waited, though he was free to leave. But he would then miss how it all came out, miss the test of cop-to-cop influence.

No police came. Sorry, Milligan.

I've since concluded Jack was right. They would have welcomed his assassination, were perhaps even aware one was impending. The police were called often about Jack during this period: Did Diamond get it yet? . . . He's going to get it tonight. I sensed then, my innocence on such matters at last thinning out, that Jack was not really an enemy of the police as much as he was an object of their envy. I can imagine a roomful of them talking about ways to annihilate his privilege.

Hubert announced from the door: "They put their headlights on. They're moving."

"Thank God," said the Floss.

"They're probably not going anyplace," Jack said. And he was right again. Within a few minutes they had parked facing the opposite direction, on The Parody side of the street now, still about fifty feet away.

"They just wanted to look in," Jack said.

The car movement prodded all of us except Jack into standing up and moving around. We turned our attention to each other, and finally, one by one, to Jack for the decision was his alone. Go or stay? Barricade or open season? Packy would probably resent, but maybe not resist a barricade fight. Damage would be minimal, apart from any death, but the legend would be immortal, a shrine of gold established in perpetuity.

Only Hubert lacked doubt about what he was to do. His pistol was already part of our little group because of the way he kept fingering it inside his coat pocket. Jack knew what he was doing when he hired Hubert.

"You have an extra pistol?" Jack asked Packy.

"How many? I got a collection."

"Two then, and shells."

Packy unlocked a closet beneath the back bar and brought out a pair of unmatched handguns, one an old Smith and Wesson .32 which I came to know well, its patent dating to 1877, an ugly little bone-handled, hammerless bellygun that was giving in to rust and had its serial number at the base of the butt filed away. No serious gunfighter would have given it room in the cellar. Packy had probably bartered it for beer. Useless, foolhardy, aggravating weapon. It had a broken mechanism behind the firing pin then and still has, but under ideal circumstances it would fire, and it still will. Ugly, deformed little death messenger, like a cobra on a crutch.

"This is insane," I finally said. "We sit here watching a man prepare for a gun battle, and we know damn well there are other ways to solve the problem. The whole world hasn't gone nuts. Why not call the *state* police?"

"Call the governor," Jack said. "He'll want to keep me healthy."

"Not a bad idea," I said.

"Call my relatives in Philadelphia," Jack said. "Call your own relatives. Call all your friends and tell them we've got an open house here, free booze. Build up a mob in fifteen minutes."

"Another brilliant idea," I said.

"But what do I do tomorrow night?" Jack said.

He loaded one of Packy's pistols while we thought about that one. Flossie decided she was not ready for fatalism.

"If you go upstairs, he'll never find you," she said.

"Where upstairs?"

"My upstairs. Where I go in a pinch."

"You got a place upstairs?"

"A place, yeah. But not really a place."

"He comes in here, don't you figure he'll look upstairs?"

"He'd never find my place, that's the whole point. If you're up there and we go, and the place is dark, he'd never find you in a thousand years. It ain't even in this same building."

"The Goose is thick, but thorough," Jack said. "I wouldn't trust him not to find it."

"Then let's go meet the Polack son of a bitch on the street," Hubert said. "Goddamn fucking sitting ducks here, the hell with it."

"None of this makes sense," I said. "Going, staying, not getting any help, not even trying to get any."

"One night at a time," Jack said. "You work it out slow. I know a lot of dead guys tried to solve a whole thing all at once when they weren't ready. And listen. It's also time you all cleared out."

"I think I'll have another beer," I said, and I sat down at the end barstool farthest from the door. Milligan sat alongside me and said, "I'll have one for the road."

"I'll be closing up after one drink," Packy said, going behind the bar. "I'll put the lights out and leave. I'll get a cop down here if I have to drag him down with a towrope."

Jack shrugged.

"Upstairs then," he said to Flossie. "I guess that's the place."

"Follow me," she said.

"Is there a way back down except through here?"

"Two stairways," Packy said. "It's an old loft. They used to have a peanut butter factory up there."

"Jesus, a peanut butter factory?"

"It faces the other side, on Dongan Avenue, and there's no windows. Flossie is right. Nobody'd ever think we were connected to it. Just a quirk of these antique buildings. They made connections you wouldn't believe in these old relics."

"Nothing'll happen if The Goose *doesn't* come in here," I said. "Isn't that right?"

"I don't think he'll come inside anyplace," Jack said, "and he don't want to hurt anybody but me. But he's a maniac, so how do you know anything he'll do? You all should wait for Flossie to come back down and then clear the hell out of here. Hubert and I can wait it out."

That seemed workable. But I said, "I'll keep you company," and Jack laughed and laughed. I didn't think it was that funny, but he said, "All right, let's move," and I took my bottle of beer and followed him and Hubert to the place where there was no longer any peanut butter.

Flossie led us up an unsafe staircase, through musty corridors, through a rough doorway in the brick wall of another building, and through still more corridors, all in darkness, each of us holding the hand of the other. When she finally lit a kerosene lamp, we were in the loft, a large empty space with a warped floor, a skylight with some of its panes broken and now an access route to a pigeon perch. The pigeons had created a pair of three-inch stalagmites with their droppings, rather brilliant aim, as I remember it. The room held only an old Army cot with an olive-drab blanket and a pillow without a pillowcase. A raw wooden box stood alongside the bed for use as a table, and a straight-back wooden chair stood alongside that. There was nothing else in the room except for the cobwebs, the dust, the rat leavings, and a plentiful scatter of peanut shells.

"You know, Jack," Flossie said, "I never use this place except in special emergencies that can't wait. I keep a sheet downstairs. I could go get it."

"Maybe another time, kid," Jack said, and squeezed her rump with his good hand.

"You haven't grabbed me in years, Jack."

"I'd love to think about getting back to that."

"Well, don't you neglect it. Oh, sweet Jesus, look at that."

She pointed to a wall behind Jack where an enormous rat, bigger than a jackrabbit I'd say, looked out at us, his eyes shining red in the light, white markings under his jaw. He was halfway out of a hole in the wall, about four feet from the floor. He looked like a picture on the wall. As the light reached him, we could see he was gray, brown, and white, the weirdest, handsomest rat I ever saw, and in the weirdest position. A bizarre exhibit, if stuffed, I thought.

"I never saw *him* up here before," Flossie said.

The rat watched us with brazen calm.

"He was here first tonight," Jack said, and he sat on the bed and took off his suit coat. Flossie put the lamp on the box table and told us, "I'll come back and let you know what's going on. I don't know if Delaney's going out, but I'm damn well staying."

"Lovely, Flossie, lovely," said Jack.

"He'd never find his way up here, Jack," she said. "Just stay put."

"I want Hubert to check all the stairs. Can he be seen from outside if he walks with the lamp?"

"Not a chance."

Flossie took the lamp, leaving Jack and me in darkness, the stars and a bright moony sky the only source of our light.

"Some great place to wind up," Jack said.

"I'm sitting down while I consider it," I said and groped toward the chair. "I mean while I consider what the hell I'm doing here."

"You're crazy. I always knew it. You wear crazy hats."

Flossie came back with the kerosene lamp and put it back on the box.

"I lit one of my candles and gave it to Hubert," she said. "I'll be back."

Some moths joined us in the new light and Jack sat down on the cot. The rat was still watching us. Jack put the two pistols Packy gave him on the box. He also took a small automatic out of his back pocket. It fit in his palm, the same kind of item he fired between Weissberg's feet in Germany.

"You've been carrying that around?"

"A fella needs a friend," he said.

"That'd be lovely, picked up with a gun at this point. How many trials do you think you can take?"

"Hey, Marcus, I'm tryin' to stay alive. You understand that?"

"Let Hubert carry the weapons. That's what he's for."

"Right. Soon as I hear The Goose is gone. Long as he's in town there's liable to be shooting, and I might stay alive if I can shoot back. You on tap for that?"

He picked up the Smith and Wesson and handed it to me.

"The Goose only wants me, but he'd shoot anything that moved or breathed. I don't want to make it tough for you, old pal, but that's where you're livin' right this minute. You're breathing."

He had a point. I loaded the weapon. In a pinch I could say I pocketed the pistol when we all fled from the maniac.

Jack fell backward on Flossie's dusty cot and said to me, "Marcus, I decided something. Right now there's nothing in the whole fucking world I want to steal."

I thought that was a great line and it was my turn to

laugh. Jack laughed, too, then said, "Why is that so funny?"

"Why? Well, here I am, full of beer and holding a gun, joined up with a wild man to hide from a psychopath, watching the stars, staring at a red-eyed rat, and listening to Jack Diamond, a master thief of our day, telling me he's all through stealing. Jesus Christ, this is an insane life, and I don't know the why of any of it."

"Well, I don't either. I don't say I'm swearing off, because I am what I am. But I say I don't want to steal anything now. I don't want to make another run. I don't want to fight The Goose. I suppose I will, sooner or later, him or some other bum they send."

"Who is they?"

"Take your pick. They get in line to shoot at me."

"But you won't shoot back anymore?"

"I don't know. Maybe, maybe not."

"The papers would eat this up. Jack Diamond's vengeance ends in peanut butter factory."

"Anybody can get revenge. All it costs is a few dollars. I don't want to touch it anymore, not personally."

"Are you just tired? Weary?"

"Maybe something like that."

"You don't believe in God, so it's not your conscience."

"No."

"It's caution, but not just caution."

"No."

"It's self-preservation, but not just that either."

"You could say that."

"Now I've got it. You don't know what's going on either."

"Right, pal."

"The mystery of Jack Diamond's new life, or how he found peace among the peanut shells."

I was too tired, too hot, too drunk to sit up any longer. I slid off the chair onto the floor, clutching the remnants of my beer in my left hand, the snotty little Smith and Wesson in my right, believing with an odd, probably impeachable faith, that if I survived this night I would surely become rich somehow and that I would tell the story of the red-eyed rat to my friends, my clients and my grandchildren. The phrase "If I survived" gave me a vicious whack across the back of the head. That was a temporary terror, and it eventually left me. But after this night I knew I would never again feel safe under any circumstances. Degeneration of even a marginal sense of security. Kings would die in the bedchambers of their castles. Assassination squads would reach the inner sanctum of the Presidential palace. The lock on the bedroom window would not withstand the crowbar.

Such silly things. Of course, this goes on, Marcus, of course. Mild paranoia is your problem.

Yes. That's it. It goes on and finally I know it. I truly know it and feel it.

No. There is more to it than that. Jack knows more.

Flossie came running. Cops down in the street. Taking Goose away. You can come down. Packy's buying. Milligan got through.

Six detectives, oh, yes. How lovely.

Jack leaped off the bed and was gone before I could sit up.

"Are you comin' too, love? Or can't you move?" the Floss asked me. In my alcoholic kerosene light she was the Cleopatra of peanut-butterland. Her blond hair was the gold of an Egyptian sarcophagus, her eyes the Kohinoor diamond times two.

"Don't go, Flossie," I said and stunned her. I'd known the Floss now and again, sumptuous knowledge, but not in a couple of years. It was past, my interest in professionals. I had a secretary, Frances. But now Flossie's breasts rose and fell beneath her little cotton transparency in a way that had been inviting all of us all night long, and when she had half turned to leave, when my words of invitation stopped her, I caught a vision of her callipygian subtleties, like the ongoing night, never really revealed to these eyes before.

She came toward me as I lay flat on my back, ever so little bounce in the splendid upheaval of her chest, vision too of calf without blemish, without trace of muscular impurity. None like Floss on this earth tonight, not for Marcus.

"Do you want something from me?" she said, bending forward, improving the vision fiftyfold, breathing her sweet, alcoholic whore's breath at me. I loosened my hand from the beer and reached for her, touched her below the elbow, first flesh upon first flesh of the evening. Client at last.

"Come up on the cot, love," she said, but I shook my head and pulled the blanket to the floor. She doubled it as the moon shone on her. The rat was watching us. I raised the pistol and potshot it, thinking of it dying with a bullet through its head and hanging there on the wall; then thinking of framing it or stuffing it in that position, photographing the totality of the creature in its limp deathperch and titling it "Night Comes to the Peanut Butter Factory."

My shot missed and the rat disappeared back into the wall.

"Jesus, Mary, and Holy Saint Joseph," Flossie said at the shot, which sounded like a cannon. "What are you doing?"

"Potting the rat."

"Oh, honeyboy, you're so drunk. Give us that pistol."

"Of course, Flossie"—and she put it on the table out of my reach. The stars shone on her then as she unbuttoned her blouse, unhooked her skirt, folded the clothes carefully and lay them at the foot of the cot. She wore nothing beneath them, the final glory. She helped prepare me as the men moved in with the peanut butter machine and the women arrived to uncrate the nuts.

"It's been a while, hasn't it?" the Floss said to me.

"Only yesterday, Floss, only yesterday."

"Sometimes I feel that way, Marcus, but not tonight."

"It's always yesterday, Floss. That's what's so great."

"Tonight is something else."

"What is it?"

"It's better. It's got some passion in it."

"Lovely passion."

"I don't get at it very often."

"None of us do."

The rat came back to his perch and watched us. The sodden air rose up through the skylight and mated with the nighttime breezes. The machine began to whirr and a gorgeous ribbon of golden peanut butter flowed smoothly out of its jaws. Soon there were jars of it, crates of jars, stacks of crates.

"Isn't it lovely?" said Flossie, flat on her back.

"It's the most ineffable of products," I said. "The secret substance of life. If only the alchemists knew of this."

"Who were the alchemists?" she asked.

"Shhhh," I said.

And instead of talking, Flossie made me a peanut butter sandwich, and we fortified ourselves against the terror.

# JACK O' THE CLOCK

Jack walked up Second Street in Troy, dressed in his double-breasted chinchilla coat and brown velour fedora, walked between his attorney and his wife, a family man today, Kiki discreetly tucked away in the love nest. Jack walked with his hands in his pocket, the press swarming toward him as he was recognized. How do you feel, Legs? Any statement, Mr. Gorman? Do you have faith in your husband's innocence, Mrs. Diamond?

"You guys are responsible for all this," Jack said to the newsmen. "I wouldn't be in trouble if it wasn't for you sonsabitches."

"Keep out the cuss words, boys," I said to the press. I smiled my Irish inheritance, easing the boys.

"What'll you make your case on, counselor?" Tipper Kelly said. "Same as the first trial? An alibi?"

"Our case is based wholly on self-defense," I said.

Self-defense against a kidnapping charge. Jack laughed. His loyal wife laughed. The newsmen laughed and made notes. A *bon mot* to start the day.

"How do you feel about all this, Mrs. Diamond?"

"I'll always be at his side," said Alice.

"Don't bother her," said Jack.

"She's just a loyal wife to a man in trouble," I said. "That's why she's here."

"That's right," said Alice. "I'm a loyal wife. I'll always be loyal, even after they kill him."

"We mustn't anticipate events," I said.

The gray neo-classical Rensselaer County courthouse,

with its granite pillars, stood tall over Legs Diamond: legs of Colossus, as this peanut man walked beneath them. Birds roosted on the upper ledges. A stars and stripes snapped in the breeze. As Legs brushed the wall with his shoulder, dust fell from the pillars.

The Pathé News cameraman noted the action and the consequence and asked Legs to come back and do it again. But, of course, Legs could not commit precisely the same act a second time, since every act enhanced or diminished him as well as the world around him. Yet it was that precise moment, that push, that almost imperceptible fall of dust, the cameraman wanted on film.

As the crowd moved into the courtroom the cameraman exercising a bit of creative enterprise, lifted Legs Diamond's coat and hat from the cloakroom. He dressed his slightly built assistant cameraman in the garments and sent him up the stairs to brush the wall for a repeat performance.

The Pathé News cameraman then filmed it all. Inspecting the floor for a closeup, he discovered that the dust that fell was not dust at all, but pigeon shit.

In the crowded hallway of the courthouse, during a brief moment when no one was holding his arm, a youth Jack did not know separated himself from the mob and whispered, "You're gonna get it, Diamond, no matter what happens here. Wanna take it now?" Jack looked at the kid—maybe nineteen, maybe twenty-two, with a little fuzz on his lip and a bad haircut—and he laughed. The kid eased himself back into the crowd, and Jack, pulled by me toward the courtroom, lost sight of him.

"Kid was braggin'," Jack said, telling me about the threat. "He looked like a hundred-dollar pay killer. Too green to be in the big money." Jack shook his head in a way I took to be an amused recognition of his own lowly condition. *They send punk kids after me.*

But I also saw a spot of white on his lower lip, a spot of bloodlessness. He bit at the spot, again and again. The bite hardened his face, as if he were sucking the blood out of the point of his own fear, so that when the threat became tangible it would not bleed him into weakness. It struck me as a strange form of courage, but not as I knew it for myself: no intellectual girding, but rather a physiological act: a Jack Diamond of another day, recollected not by the brain but by the body, his back to a cave full of unexplored dangers of its own, staring out beyond a puny fire, waiting for the unspecified enemy who tonight, or tomorrow night, or the next, would throw a shadow across that indefensible hearth.

By eight o'clock on the evening of the first day of Jack's second Troy trial, both the prosecution and the defense attorneys had exhausted their peremptory challenges and the final juror was at last chosen. He was an auto mechanic who joined two farmers, a printer, an engineer, a mason, a lumber dealer, an electrical worker, two laborers, a merchant, and a plant foreman as the peers, the twelve-headed judge, of Legs Diamond. I had sought to relieve the maleness by accepting two female jurors, but Jack's appeal to women had been too widely documented for the prosecution to take such a risk, and both were challenged.

The prosecution's chief trial counsel was a man named Clarence Knought, who wore a gray, hard-finish, three-button herringbone with vest, gray tie, watch chain, and rimless glasses. His thin lips, receding hairline, gaunt figure, and voice, which lacked modulation but gained relentless moral rectitude through its monotony, provided the jury with the living image of New York State integrity, American Puritanism, and the Columbian quest for perfect justice. He spoke for twenty minutes, outlining the case against Legs Diamond, whom he called Diamond. He recapitulated the kidnapping of Streeter and Bartlett in his opening summary, savoring the punching of Streeter, the death threats, the burning and the hanging, details which landed on the jurors' faces like flying cockroaches. The recapitulation set off an uncontrollable twitching in one juror's cheek, dilated just about every eye, wrinkled eyebrows, and dried up lips. Having filled the jurors with terror, Knought congratulated them.

"You are privileged," he told them. "You have the chance to rid this nation of one of its worst scourges. You have the chance to put behind bars this man Diamond, this figure of unmitigated evil, this conscienceless devil who has been arrested twenty-five times for every crime from simple assault to foul, vicious murder, whose association with the worst men of our time has been widely reported in the press and whose record of having cheated justice again and again is an appalling blot on our national image. Shall this nation be ruled by the rod? Shall this ogre of bestial behavior paralyze every decent man's heart? You twelve can end this travesty, put him in the penitentiary where he belongs."

Knought breathed fury, thumped the railing of the jury box with his fist, then walked to his chair and sat down in a cloud of legitimized wrath.

I rose slowly from my chair alongside Jack, this thought in my head as I did: *O priggish stringbean, thank you for befouling my client with your excremental denunciation, with the ordurous funk of your morality, for you now give me the opportunity to wipe this beshitted countenance clean and show the human face beneath the fetid desecration.*

My image before the jury was calculatedly bumpkinish, my clothes workingman's best, aspiring to shabby genteel. I tweaked my bow tie and ran my fingers through my unruly head of hair, which I was told, seemed as gifted with wild statement as the brain it covered. The head was leonine, the mane controlled just this side of bushy frazzle. I wore an apple-red vest, high contrast to my baggy-kneed brown tweed suit. I tucked thumbs in vest and unleashed the major weapon of the defense—my voice—that timbre of significance, that resonant spume of the believer, that majestic chord of a man consecrated to the revelation of boilingly passionate truths. I said:

"I expect low blows from the prosecution's lawyers—all

seven of them. Are you aware, my friends, that the state
has seven lawyers climbing over one another in a frantic
effort to railroad one frail man into jail? Yes, I expected
their low blows, but never such base name calling as we
have just heard—'figure of unmitigated evil,' 'conscienceless devil,' 'ogre of bestial behavior.' I would never have
dreamed of telling you what I am about to tell if this
champion of self-righteousness had not been so vitriolic a
few moments ago, so full of acid and poison toward my
client. But I will tell you now. I will tell you of the little old
lady—no, I won't disguise her vocation, not now. A little
old Catholic nun, she was, and she came to this courtroom
less than an hour ago to talk with Jack Diamond, only a few
steps from where you are seated. She didn't see him, for he
was otherwise occupied. She saw me, however, and I will
see to it that she gets her wish, for she came here for one
reason only—to see the man who was once a boy at her
knee. Jackie Diamond was the name she knew him by, a
boy she described as one of the most devout Catholic
children she has ever known. She sees that boy still in the
face of the man you know as Legs Diamond, that mythical
figure of unmitigated evil the prosecutor has invented. This
woman had heard such cruel insults hurled before at the
boy she knew. She had heard them for years. She had read
them in the newspapers. But that little old woman, that
creature of God Almighty's very own army, sat down in
that room with me for five minutes and talked to me about
Jackie Diamond's prayers, his prayers for his mother, a
woman who died too early, about the Diamond home and
family in Philadelphia. And when she was through with her
reminiscing she told me precisely what she thought about
all those accusations against the boy whose gaunt, troubled
face she hardly recognized when she saw it across the
room. 'They're all lies. Mr. Gorman,' she said to me,
'fiendish lies! Now that I have seen his face for myself I
know those were lies, Mr. Gorman. I teach children, Mr.
Gorman, and I have boys and girls in my charge who delight
in drowning puppies and stabbing cats and watching them

slowly perish, and I know evil when I see it in the eyes of a human being. I came here today to see for myself whether my memory had deceived me, whether I knew good when I saw it, whether I knew evil. I have now seen the eyes of Jack Diamond in this room and I am as certain as I am of God's love that whatever on earth that man may have done, he is not an evil man. I have verified this for myself, Mr. Gorman. I have verified it.' "

When I finished the rest of my oratory and sat down at the table, Jack leaned over and whispered: "That nun business was terrific. Where did you dig her up?"

"She wandered in during the recess," I said, eyes downcast, scribbling a businesslike doodle on a yellow pad. "She's a regular in the courthouse. Collects nickels for the poor."

"Does she really know anything about me?"

I looked at my client, astounded.

"How the hell should I know?" I retorted.


The trial proceeded as the first one had in July, with two parades of witnesses for and against Jack. We used fewer for the defense, treading lightly after the perjury indictment from the first trial.

I made two points I remember fondly. The first was a countercharacterization of Streeter, who had been dubbed "a son of the soil," by the prosecution. I had not thought to say it in July, but we rise to our challenges, and I said he might better be called a son of the apple tree, which once again reduced the kidnapping to a bootleggers' feud.

I also asked a juror, a wretched little popinjay, whether he thought God loved Legs Diamond. "God made little green apples," he said to me crisply, "but he also put worms in 'em." He got a laugh at Jack's expense, but I liked his theology and kept him. He wore an orange shirt and I knew my man. He'd have been in line for Jack's autograph if he hadn't been on the jury. He turned out to be a vigorous partisan for acquittal. Jack was, of course acquitted, December 17, 1931, at 8:03 P.M. The crowd in the street sent up its usual cheer.

I was standing at Keeler's Men's Bar in Albany a week after the trial, talking to the barman about Jack, and I resurrected a story he told me about a day in 1927 when he was walking in Central Park with his brother Eddie and Eddie's baby boy. Jack had the boy in his arms, and they'd paused on a hill which I can picture even now. Jack was tossing the boy and catching him when he saw a car coming with a gun barrel sticking out its window, a vision to which he had been long sensitized. He tossed the baby feet-first into a bushy blue spruce, yelling the news to brother Ed, and both dove in the opposite direction from the baby as the machine gun chopped up the sod where they'd been standing.

Nobody was hit: the baby bounced off the tree and rolled to safety under a lilac bush. And after I'd told this tale, a fellow tippler at the bar asked, "How many people did he kill?" I said I didn't know, and then, without apparent malice, without actually responding to my baby story, the fellow said, "Yeah, I remember a lot of otherwise intelligent people used to think he was a nice guy."

I told the man he was a horse's ass and walked to the other end of the bar to finish my drink. Intelligent people? The man was an insurance salesman. What could he possibly know about intelligent people?

I am bored by people who keep returning life to a moral plane, as if we were reducible, now, to some Biblical concept or its opposite, as if all our history and prehistory had not conditioned us for what we've become. It's enough to make a moral nigger out of a man. The niggers are down there, no doubt about it. But Jack didn't put them there and neither did I. When we get off the moral gold standard, when the man of enormous wealth is of no more importance to anybody than the man in rags, then maybe we'll look back at our own day as a day of justifiable social wrath.

Meantime, the game is rising, not leveling.

Jack taught me that.

Cured me.

(Brother Wolf, are you listening?)

Dove Street runs north and south in Albany through what for years was the rooming house district on the fringe of downtown. Number 67 sits on the west side of the street between Hudson Avenue and Jay Street, a two-story brick building with a six-step wooden stoop, a building not unlike the house on East Albert Street in Philadelphia where Jack lived as a child. The basement shoemaker, the druggist up the block, the grocery and garage at the corner of Hudson Avenue, the nurses and the masseuse next door and across the street and all other life-support systems in the neighborhood were dark at 4:15 A.M. on Friday, December 18, 1931, when Jack pulled up in front of 67 Dove in his hired cab, Frankie Teller at the wheel.

Teller parked and ran around to open the passenger door, took Jack's arm, helped him out. Teller held the arm while Jack stood up, and together they walked raggedly up the stoop. Jack found his key, but it remained for Teller to open the door with it. The two men then walked up the stairs together and into the room at the front of the house, overlooking the street. Jack took off his hat, and then, with Teller's help, his coat, and sat on the side of the bed, which was angled diagonally, foot facing the windows that looked down on the street.

"Frankie," Jack said. And he smiled at his driver.

"Yeah, Jack."

"Frankie, I'll duke you tomorrow."

"Sure, Jack, don't worry about it."

"Duke you in the morning."

"Sure, Jack, sure. Anything else I can do for you? You all right here alone?"

"Just get outa here and let me sleep."

"Right away. Just want you settled in all right."

"I'm in."

"Tomorrow, then."

"Tomorrow," Jack said.

Frankie Teller went downstairs and got into his car and drove south on Dove Street, back to Packy's to carry the news that Jack was tucked in. A block to the north on the west side of the street a dark red sedan idled with its lights out.

During the eight hours and fifteen minutes that elapsed between his acquittal and the moment when he sat on the bed and looked into the mirror of the scratched and flaking oak dresser in his Dove Street room, Jack had been seeking an antidote to false elation. The jury foreman's saying not guilty created an instant giddiness in him that he recognized. He'd felt it when he saw Streeter's truck in front of him on the road, and he felt it on the ship when he decided not to give Biondo back his money. He could drown in reasons for not yielding the cash and for giving Streeter the heat. But none explained why a man would keep anything that brought on that much trouble, or why a man would jeopardize his entire setup in life for a truckload of cider. And so he feared the giddiness, knew it was to be resisted.

When he'd tossed his forty-dollar brown velour hat onto the bed, it had hit the threadbare spread and rolled off. He folded his brown chinchilla coat (two grand, legitimately acquired) over the footboard, and it too slipped to the floor. When he left the courthouse and saw the newsmen backing away from him in the corridor, saw them on the steps and in the streets with their cameras, he had the impulse to reach into his coat pocket and find the rotten eggs to throw at the bastards. And this was the Jack Diamond who once hired a press agent to get his name around.

He sat on the bed, unable to see the condition of his eyes, which were heavy-lidded with whiskey—too little light in the room and in his brain. He squinted at the mirror, but saw only his squint returned. He felt an irritation of the penis from his lovemaking and adjusted his shorts where they rubbed. He remembered Alice's kiss before he left the party, a wet one. She opened her mouth slightly, as she always did when she had a few whiskeys in. He reached into his pocket, felt a card, and looked at it. Packy's speakeasy card. The Parody Association, members only. Jack had seen it on the bar during the party, never owned one, never needed one, but picked it up and pocketed it out of habit. There was a time when he could enter any speakeasy on his name alone, but now people imitated him, even made collections in his name. I'm Legs Diamond. Oh sure, and I'm Herbert Hoover. He used the cards now because he no longer even looked like his own pictures.

Fifty people were in The Parody when Marcus gave his victory toast, the words floating now somewhere behind Jack's squint.

"To Jack Diamond's ability to escape from the clutches of righteous official indignation, which would so dearly love to murder him in his bed. . . ."

Fifty people with glasses in the air. Would've been more, but Jack said keep it small, it ain't the circus. But it was, in its own way, what with Packy and Marcus and Sal from the Kenmore, and Hubert and Hooker Ryan the old fighter, and Tipper Kelly the newsie, and Flossie, who came with the place.

Jack told me to bring Frances, my secretary, who still thought Jack was the devil, even though he'd been acquitted twice. "Show her the devil face to face," Jack said, but when he saw her he mistrusted her face. Lovely Irish face. Reminded Jack of his first wife, Katherine, he married in '17. Army bride. Prettiest Irish kid you ever saw, and she left him because he used coke. Crazy young Jack.

Crazy Jack owes Marcus. Five grand. Coming in the morning from Madden. Where would Jack Diamond be without Uncle Owney? Pay you in the morning, Marcus. Meet you at your office at eleven. Cash on the barrelhead. Jack would be a semifree man, walking Albany's streets, a little less intimidated by the weight of his own future. Maybe his head would clear now that he'd won a second acquittal. They could go on trying him on gun charges, but Marcus said the state boys were whipped, would never try him again with Streeter the adversary witness. The federals were the problem, with four years facing him and no end of other charges pending. No end, even if he reversed the conviction with an appeal. But Jack would worry about the federals when he got well. The immediate future lay in South Carolina. A beachfront spot where he'd holed up when Rothstein and Schultz were both gunning for him in

'27. Beautiful old house on a sand dune back from the ocean. Sea air good for the lungs.

Lung talk: Do you know why Jack Diamond can drink so much whiskey? Because he has TB and the fever burns up the alcohol. Facts. Left lung is congested. But, Jack, really now, you never had TB in your life. What will jail do to your lungs? What will it do to your brain, for that matter? Bore you? You'll have to play a lot of dominoes in jail. Boring dominoes. But you knew that. You were always ready to play dominoes, right? That's part of the game, right?

Wrong. Not part of Jack's game.

Jack took off the coat of his lucky blue suit and hung it on the back of the chair. Suit needs a pressing, Marcus told him, even before the trial began. But Jack told Marcus, told the press boys too: "This is my lucky suit and I'm not parting with it. If we win, I'll get it pressed to celebrate." The suit coat fell to the floor in a pile.

Jack took the change out of his pants pockets, his nail file and comb, his white monogrammed handkerchief, and put them on top of the dresser that one of his obituary writers, Meyer Berger, would describe as tawdry. Jack's ethereal mother, starched and bright in a new green frying pan apron, held up Jack's bulletproof vest. "You didn't wear this," she said. "I told you not go out without it, Jackie. Remember what happened to Caesar?" They rendered old Caesar, Jack was about to say when he felt a new surge of giddiness. It was bringing him a breakthrough perception. I am on the verge of getting it all wrapped up, he said to the steam heat that hissed at him from the radiator. I hear it coming. I have been true to everything in life.

"I toast also to his uncanny ability to bloom in hostile seasons and to survive the blasts of doom. Jack, we need only your presence to light us up like Times Square in fervid and electric animation. You are the undercurrent of our lives. You turn on our light. . . ."

Freddie Robin, the cop, who stopped in for a quick one, had the glass in his hand when good old Marcus started the toast. And Milligan, the railroad dick alongside him, had a glass in the air, too. Pair of cops toasting Jack's glorious beswogglement of law and order. Hah! And alongside them the priest and the screwball.

"Who the hell is that screwball, anyway?" Jack said to Hubert, who began sniffing. The screwball was talking to everybody, wanted to meet everybody at the party. Looks like a killer to you, does he, Jack? No. But maybe like a cop. Like a federal stooge. They like to crash my parties.

Hubert got his name. He was Mr. Biswanger from Buffalo. A lightning rod salesman. What's he doing at your party, Jack? Trying to hustle you a sample to wear behind your ear? He came with the priest, Hubert reported. And the priest came to Albany to see Marcus. Is that true, Marcus? Marcus says yes, but adds, "He just tagged along, Jack, after a legal chat. I didn't bring the clergy. But they have an affinity for you, like cops. The underside of everybody's life, is what you turn out to be, Jack."

Jack undid his tie, blue with diagonal white stripes, and hung it on the upright pole of the dresser mirror. It slid off. Priests and cops toasting Jack. It's like those Chinese bandits, Jack. Nobody can tell the good from the bad. China will always have bandits, right? So, fellow Chinks, let's sit back and enjoy them.

"To his talent for making virtue seem unwholesome and for instilling vicarious amorality in the hearts of multitudes. . . ."

Alice gave Flossie the fish eye when she kidded Jack about pigeons in the loft and fondled his earlobe. Then Frances gave Flossie the fish eye when the Floss kidded Marcus about pigeons in the loft and fondled his earlobe. The Floss moved alongside the piano, and while the pianoman played "It's a Sin to Tell a Lie," she shook her ass to that sweet and gracious waltz, turning, pivoting, shaking. Disgusting. Gorgeous. Oh, Floss, ya look like Mae West. Harpy. Sweetmeat. Goddess of perfume.

"Who is she?" Alice asked.

"Flossie, she works here," Jack said

"She knows you pretty well to play with your ear."

"Nah, she does that with all the boys. Great girl, the Floss."

"I never knew anybody who liked ears like that."

"You don't get around, Alice. I keep telling you that."

"I know you think I'm jealous of all the harpies in the world, but I'm really not, John. Just remember that the truest love is bright green. Avoid substitutes."

From Buffalo the hunger marchers began their walk toward Washington. John D. Rockefeller, in Ormond, Florida, told newsreel microphones that "better times are coming," and he wished the world a Merry Christmas. In Vienna a grand jury unanimously acquitted Dr. Walter Pfrimer and seven other Fascist Party leaders of charges of high treason stemming from an attempted putsch. A speedy recovery was predicted for Pola Negri.

Jack took off the signet ring that no longer fit, that had been bothering him all day. He wore it because it was lucky, like his suit, gift from the old man in high school: *D* is also for Dear Daddy. Dead Dad. Defunct Diamond. Sorry, old fellow. Jack listened to the candles burning on the altar of Saint Anne's church. They made the sound of leaves falling into a pond where a calico cat was slowly drowning. In the shadow of the first pillar the old man cried as the candles danced. When the mass was ended, when Jack the small priest had blown out the authenticating candle of his mother's life, the old man stood up and turned to pity, politics, and drink. And, oh, how they laughed back in Cavan. Publicans did not complain when the laughter died and you threw your arms around yourself in a fit of need. "Nobody knows what it's like until they lose their wife," old Jack said. "Then you eat Thanksgiving dinner alone." Young Jack looked on. "Just a weak old man. He cried more than I did. I cried only once."

Jack dropped the signet ring with a clunk into the tawdry dresser alongside two holy pictures (Stephen and Mary) Alice had brought him from New York, alongside the letters, the holy fan mail. Jack kept one letter: "God bless you, son, from a mother with a large family." And God bless you too, mother, going away.

The giddiness was turning to smiles. Jack looked at himself in the mirror and smiled at the peeling mercury. His smile was backward. What else was backward? He was. All. All backward in the mirror image. Nobody would ever know which image was the real Jack. Only Jack knows that, and he giggled with the knowledge that he alone was privy to the secret. What a wonderful feeling! A vision of the Jack nobody knows. Fuck that stupid Legs, right Jack? What'd he ever do for you?

One of Marcus' law partners came to the party to meet Legs Diamond—a kid with wide eyes when he shook the hand that shook the Catskills. Hubert brought two poker players from Troy, and they talked to Jack about a little game some night. Love to, boys. Packy had rounded up the musicians, piano, banjoman, drummer. Marcus asked Alice to dance and then Jack took an armful of Frances and foxtrotted around to "Ain't Misbehavin'."

"I must say you're a wonderful dancer," said Frances.

And why, miss, must you say it? Jack dancing with yesterday in his arms. Thank you, young woman out of yesterday.

"You know I never think of you as dancing or doing anything like this."

"What *do* you think of me doing?"

"Terrible things," she said. She spoke sternly. Scolded, Jack relaxed, touched her hair with his fingertips, remembering his Army bride.

"Your hair reminds me of Helen Morgan," he said.

Frances blushed.

Doc Madison pulled his wife to her feet, stepped into a snappy foxtrot with the same certainty he revealed when he removed the filling from Jack, all those double-ought pellets, restoring life to the dying frame. We're all so full of life now, Doc. And ain't it great? So many thanks, Doc.

". . . perhaps you all noticed the lofty stained-glass windows of the court house annex this afternoon as the sun streamed through, as the light fell about our Jack's

frail but sturdy shoulder, illuminating in those windows
both New York's and Jack's splendid virtues . . . in-
dustry, law, peace, learning, prosperity . . .''

The courtroom felt like a church still, old Presbyterian
palace desanctified years ago; choir loft over Jack's head,
judges sitting where the pulpit used to be, truncated suns
over the door, ecclesiastical fenestration and only the faces
on the walls different now: clergy and the Jesus crowd
replaced with jurists. But retributionists all.

Frankie Teller, of course, came to the party, and so did
one of the Falzo boys who ran four houses on The Line in
Troy, squiring one of his beauties. Jack asked Johnny
Dyke, the Albany bookie, to come by, and Mushy Tarsky
too, who ran the grocery on Hudson Avenue where Jack
bought ham and cheese sandwiches for three weeks when
he and two boys never went off the block because of The
Goose. Jack's Uncle Tim, who had hung on at Acra since
the roof fell in, waiting for Jack to return to the homestead,
came up for the celebration.

Tuohey and Spivak, the bagmen detectives from the
gambling squad, dropped in for a look and brought
greetings from the Democratic organization.

Marion did not come.

Couldn't do that. Alice would've blown up if she
showed. Jack sent Hubert and Frankie Teller up with a pint
of whiskey to keep her happy, but she was gone. Note on
the door: "Going to Boston to see Mama." Frankie brought
the note back, and Jack said, "Go look for her, she's on the
street. Try the station, and find her. She wouldn't go
without seeing me." It took Frankie and Hubert an hour,
and they found her walking back up Ten Broeck Street
toward her apartment house, Number Twenty-one,
upstairs. Hubert says he told her, "Jack is worried about
you, Marion," and then she said, "You tell him I'm
goddamn good and mad. I'll stay till the morning, but then
I'm leaving; I'm not putting up with this. One of the biggest
nights of his life, and he leaves me alone four hours while

he sits around partying with his cow, and I have to go to the talkies to keep myself busy. The talkies on a night like this."

So Hubert called Jack with the news, and Jack went back to the table and told Alice a fib. Bones McDowell, a newsman, calling with death-threat information. Gotta go see him, Al. But she'd been waiting for this, Jack. She knows you, Jack, you and your fake excuses. Then Jack said, "Listen, Al, I know you're having a good time, but why don't you come with me? It's business, but Bones is only a newspaperman with some maybe important dope, and it ain't big business or trouble, and I won't be long. Come with me."

She believed that and gave Jack the wet one with the lips apart, he can see them now, and her tongue just dancing and saying, Come on in, boy, and she smiled too and winked at him, and he let his hand slide down and pat her on the benevolent behind, secretly, so the priest wouldn't be scandalized, so that all the eyes that were never off either of them all night would see something, yes, but not enough to talk dirty about such a sweet, clean woman. And then he let go of her. And she leaned back and gave him a smile, a real smile, crinkling her blue-green eyes and saying, "No, I'll stay here with Kitty and Johnny," Ed's wife and the boy alongside her, family lady to the end, the end. He gave her one final peck and looked at her green cloche hat with the little wispy curls of Titian, color of winners, sticking out from underneath.

"Don't be long," she said. "It's such a swell party."

"I'll be back in half an hour," Jack said, running his fingertips lightly down her cheek. "You can count on that."

He stood up then. It was one o'clock and thirty people still at the party when he turned his back on the crowd and walked the length of the bar, past all the enduring dead on the walls, and then out through Packy's swinging doors.

*Now Playing in Albany, December 18, 1931*
    STRAND: (The clearest picture, the best sound in New York State), George Bancroft in *Rich Man's Folly*.

HARMANUS BLEECKER HALL: (Albany's Palace of Entertainment), Ronald Colman in *The Unholy Garden.*

LELAND: (Where the talkies are better), Billie Dove in *The Age for Love.*

PALACE: (Showplace of The Capital), Leo Carillo in *The Guilty Generation.*

MADISON: Mae Clarke in *Waterloo Bridge.*

COLONIAL: Ann Harding in *Devotion.*

PARAMOUNT: Wheeler and Woolsey in *Hook, Line and Sinker.*

PARAMOUNT: Marian Nixon and Neil Hamilton in *Ex Flame* (a modernized version of *East Lynne*).

ALBANY: Wheeler and Woolsey in *Caught Plastered.*

Jack, sitting on his bed in the rooming house, took off the blue pants, pulled them over the scuffy black shoes, the dark-blue socks with the white clocks. He hung the pants on the open drawer of the tawdry dresser, and they stayed there a few seconds before they fell to the floor. Jack had drunk too much with too many. And yet he was lucid when he left the party, pushed by the whiskey into clarity and anticipation of the sweets of love; that face of perfect worship, the excitement of the body of perfect satisfaction, so wholly Jack's, so fully responsive to his touches, his needs. Climbing the stairs to her apartment, he already relished the look of her, the way she would smile when he greeted her with a kiss, the sweetness of presence alone when they sat and faced each other. This did not change. The power of sweetness had not faded in the almost two years he'd known her.

"They tell me you're going to Boston."

"I really am."

"Without even saying good-bye?"

"What's another good-bye? We're always saying that."

"You're not going anyplace. Tomorrow we'll go down to the mountains, have a drink with old Brady up at Haines Falls. Weather's still pretty good."

"You say that, but we won't go."

"Sure. I'll have Frankie pick you up at noon and meet me at Marcus' office, and we'll go from there."

"What about your darling Alice?"

"I'll send her out shopping."

"Something'll happen and we won't go."

"Yes, we'll go. You can count on it. You got my word."

Jack, euphoric now, opened Marion's robe, gazed on her garden of ecstasy. Always a vision. Now better than ever. Jack had been down. He had hit bottom. But like an astral rubber ball, he was bouncing back toward the stars. When he held Marion in his arms, he felt the giddiness. "Top of the goddamn world," he said into her ear. "I'm on top of the goddamn world."

"That's nice, Jackie."

"I'm a winner again."

"That's really nice."

Jack knew that winners celebrated with biological food. You found the most beautiful woman on the Eastern Seaboard. You took your body to where she waited. You turned off her radio, then gave her body to your body. Your body would thank you for such a gift. Your body would be a happy body.

Jack laughed out loud, once, in his bed, a resonant "Haw!"

Moonshine was down to thirty-five cents a pint, and kids were sipping it with two straws. Iced beer was down to five dollars a gallon, and you could get it delivered home. College girls were pledging not to call for drinks costing more than a nickel when their boyfriends took them out for a good time. Dorothy Dix found this a step in the right direction, for matrimony was waning in popularity, a direct result of the high cost of living.

Jack remembered the night he penetrated to the center of Kiki's treasure at Haines Falls and struck something solid.

"What the hell is that?"

"A cork," she said.

"A cork? How'd it get up there?"

"I took it off a gallon of dago red and put it up there. It's my Italian chastity cork."

"What the hell's the matter with you?"

"I'm not taking it out till you promise to marry me."

But she got over that, and when he entered her on this euphoric night in Albany there was no cork, no ultimatum; no climax either. Jack erected, Marion lubricious, they could've danced all night. But Jack wearied of the effort, and Marion ran out of her capacity to groan with pleasure. They rolled away from each other and let the sweat slowly cool, the breathing return to normal, the artifacts dry.

He pulled off one shoe without opening the laces, let it drop. He took off the second shoe, noted its scuffiness and remembered the night he surrendered on the Hotsy charges. He walked into the Forty-seventh Street station house in his navy-blue chesterfield with the velvet lapels, white on white silk scarf, the midnight-blue serge double-breasted, the gray and black dragon tie, and the shoes so highly polished they could pass for patent leather, the derby heightening the tone of his special condition. Jack was on top that night, too, remembering Vinnie Raymond from East Albert Street, who walked by the Diamond house every night in *his* derby and *his* high-polish shoes and spats, on his way to life. The image of that man's perfection was still in the mind that controlled the scuffed shoe, down at the heel. Then he let it too, drop.

Jack heard the horn blowing in the street outside Marion's Ten Broeck Street apartment. He raised the window.

"It's gettin' late, Jack," Frankie Teller called up to him. "You said half an hour. It's going on two hours. You know what Alice told me. You get him back here to this party, back here to me."

But no partying remained in Jack. He would not return to any festive scene, festive drunks, festive Alice. He closed the window and looked at Marion, who had wrapped herself in a beige floor-length silk robe, gift from Jack six months ago when he had money for anything. The gown had one large brown flower below the knee, same color as the stripe around the small lapel. So gorgeous. Will ever a woman look more gorgeous to Jack than this one?

"You treat women like animals," Marion said.

"Ah, don't fight me tonight, baby. I'm feelin' good."

"Like cats. You treat us like damn old cats. Pet us and pussy us up and scratch our neck."

Jack laughed, fell back on the pillow of his own rooming house bed and laughed and laughed and laughed. She was right. You look a cat in the eye and demand a love song. It sits there, and if it likes you at all, it doesn't run away. It wants its goddamn neck scratched. Wants you to play with its whiskers. Give it what it wants, it turns on its motor. He laughed and raised his feet off the floor and saw his socks, still on.

He sat up and took off one sock, dropped it onto one shoe, missed.

". . . I toast his defiance, his plan not to seduce the world but to terrify it, to spit in the eye of the public which says no Moloch shall pass . . ."

Jack would not begin life again in the same way. Adirondacks? Vermont? Maybe. But Coll was in jail, his mob busted up after a shoot-out in Averill Park and a roundup in Manhattan. Jack would have to recruit from scratch, and the prospect was wearying. So many dead and gone. Mike Sullivan, Fatty Walsh, Eddie. He reached for the second sock, remembering all the old boys, friends and enemies. Brocco. Babe. Frenchy. Shorty. Pretty. Mattie. Hymie. Fogarty. Dead, gone off, or in jail. And he seemed to himself, for the first time, a curiously perishable item among many such items, a thing of just so many seasons. When does the season end? He has survived again and again to another day, to try yet again to change what he had never been able to change. Would Jack Diamond ever really change? Or would he wake tomorrow out of this euphoria and begin to do what he had done every other day of his senior life? Was there any reason to doubt that recurring pattern? In the morning he would pay Marcus what he owed and take Kiki for a ride and hustle Alice and keep her happy somehow and try to figure out what next. Where was the money coming from? Something would come up.

He would solve it—he, Jack Diamond, who is what was designed, what was made this morning, yesterday, and the day before out of his own private clay.

Ah. What was designed.

This perception arrived as Jack dropped his second sock to the floor and leaned toward the dresser and saw the rosary in the top drawer. He thought then of saying it again. But no. No rosary. No prayer. No remorse. Jack is so happy with his perception of being what was designed, so released from the struggle to change, that he begins with a low rumble that rises from the sewers of madness; and yet he is not mad, only enlightened, or could they be the same condition? The rumble grows and rises to his throat where it becomes a cackle, and then into his nose where he begins to snort its joy, and into his eyes which cry with this pervasive mirth. Now his whole being—body, mind, and the spirit of nothing that he has at last recognized in the mirror—is convulsed with an ecstasy of recognition.

". . . Jack, when you finally decide to go, when you are only a fading memory along Broadway, a name in the old police files and yellowing tabloids, then we will not grieve. Yet we will be empty because our friend Jack, the nonpareil, the nonesuch, the grand confusion of our lives, has left us. The outer limit of boldness is what your behavior has been, Jack, and even if Christ came to town, I'm not sure He'd be seen on the same hill with you. Nevertheless, I think I speak for all when I say we're rooting for you. And so here's to your good health, and to ours, and let me add a safe home, Jacko, a safe home."

Jack heard the cheer go up out in the street in front of the courthouse. But he knew they were cheering for the wrong man.

"I know that son of a bitch," Jack said as he entered his final dream. "He was never any good."

Mrs. Laura Woods, the landlady at 67 Dove, said she heard two men climb the carpeted stairs past the potted

fern and enter the front room where the noted guest, who
had originally rented the room as Mr. Kelly, was sleeping.
She heard the shots, three into Jack's head, three into the
wall, and then heard one man say, "Let's make sure. I been
waiting a long time for this." And the second man said,
"Oh, hell, that's enough for him."

Mrs. Woods telephoned The Parody Club where she
knew Mrs. Diamond was partying. It was 6:55 A.M. before
the family notified the police and by then Doc Madison had
said yes, death seemed to have at last set in for Jack. When
the detectives arrived, Alice was holding a bloody
handkerchief, with which she had wiped the face of the
corpse with the goggle eyes.

"Oh, my beloved boy," she was saying over and over, "I
didn't do it, I didn't do it."

". . . Months ago," Winchell wrote, "we called him
'On His Last Legs' Diamond. . . ."

Jack wore his tuxedo and signet ring and held his rosary
at the wake, which was given at the home of Alice's
relatives in Maspeth, Long Island. The family sent four
floral tributes, and I paid for one-third of the fifth, a pillow
of red roses, the other two-thirds kicked in by Packy and
Flossie, and signed, "Your pals." An eight-foot bleeding
heart was dedicated to "Uncle John," and Alice sent a
five-and-a-half-foot-high floral chair of yellow tea roses and
lilies of the valley. On a gauze streamer in two-inch gold
letters across the chairback she had inscribed: VACANT
CHAIR, TO MY OWN, AFTER ALL, YOUR LOVING WIFE.

Owney Madden paid for the coffin, a dark mahogany box
worth eight hundred dollars. Jack had seven hundred
dollars' worth of industrial insurance once, but the
company canceled it. The plan was to bury Jack in Calvary
Cemetery alongside Eddie, but the church wouldn't let him
be put in consecrated ground. Wouldn't allow a mass
either. And the permission for the final prayer by a priest at
the wake house, which I negotiated with Cardinal Hayes,

was withdrawn at the last minute, putting the women in tears. A thirteen-year-old cousin of Jack's said the rosary in place of the priest, as a thousand people stood outside the house in the rain.

It rained yellow mud into the grave. A couple of hundred of Jack's fans went to the cemetery with the family and the press. Somebody from the undertakers picked up a shovel and tried to drive the photographers away from the graveside, but none of them gave an inch, and when the man screamed at them, the photographers chased him up a tree. Jack belonged to them.

It was all over quickly. Alice, heavily veiled, said, "Good-bye, boy, good-bye," when they began to fill the grave, and then she walked away with a single red rose in her hand. Ten minutes later most of the flowers on the grave were gone. Souvenirs.

When Kiki began her five-a-day stint at the Academy of Music on Fourteenth Street ("See Kiki, the Gangster's Gal"), fifteen hundred people were in line before the theater opened at eleven in the morning, and the manager sold two hundred and fifty SRO tickets. "She is better box office than Peaches Browning," the manager said, "and Peaches was the best I ever had here." Sidney Skolsky reported Alice was in the balcony at the opening to see the wicked child (she was just twenty-two) tippy-tap-toe to the tune of twin banjos, then take four bows and never mention Jack. But Sidney was wrong. Alice didn't see the show. I called her to offer a bit of consolation after I'd read about Kiki's success.

"Only eighteen days, Marcus," Alice said. "He's dead only eighteen days and she's out there with banjos, dancing on his grave. She could at least have waited a month."

My advice was to stop competing with Kiki for a dead man, but it was an absurd suggestion to a gladiator, and the first time I made the mistake of thinking Jack was totally dead. Alice had already hired a writer and was putting together a skit that would be staged, thirty-five days after

Jack's murder, on the boards of the Central Theater in the Bronx. The theme was crime doesn't pay. In one moment of the drama Alice interrupted a holdup, disarmed the gunman, and guarded him with his own gun until the police arrived. Then she said to the audience, "You can't make a dime with any of them. The straigh aand narrow is the only way," which brought to mind the era when she banked eighteen thousand dollars in about six months at Acra. Ambivalence, you're beautiful.

Kiki and Alice both took their acts on the road, in vaudeville and on the Minsky burlesque circuit, outraging any number of actors, the Marx Brothers among them. "A damn shame and a disgrace," said Groucho of Kiki's sixteen-week contract, "especially when so many actors are out of work. For what she is getting they could have hired five good acts, people who know their business. She's nothing but a gangster's moll."

The girls both played the same big towns, and both scandalized the smaller ones, Alice barred from Paterson, Kiki hustled out of Allentown, Alice presuming to teach a moral lesson with her act, Kiki the successful sinner against holy matrimony. Who drew the crowds? Ah.

By spring Kiki was still traveling, but Alice was no longer a serious road attraction. Alice and I talked a few times because she was having money problems, worried about the mortgage on the Acra house. She said then she was going to open at Coney Island and she chided me for never seeing her perform. So I said I'd come and catch her opener.

There is a photograph of her as she looked on the day her show opened on the boardwalk. I was standing behind the news cameraman as he caught her by surprise, and I remember her face before, during, and after the click: the change from uncertainty to hostility to a smile at me. Her hair is parted and wavy, falling over her forehead and covering her ears. A poster behind her advertises Siamese twins joined at the shoulder blades, and there is a girl outlined by a dozen long-bladed knives. A midget is in the photo, being held aloft by a man with dark, oily hair and a pencil-thin mustache. The sign says SIDE SHOW in large letters and to the right: BEAUTIFUL MRS. JACK LEGS DIAMOND IN PERSON.

The weather was unseasonably warm that afternoon, mobs on the boardwalk in shirtsleeves and unnecessary furs, camp chairs on the sand, and young girls blooming in summer dresses as Beautiful Mrs. Jack walked onto the simple unpainted board stage.

From the other direction came the tuxedo man with the little mustache. He introduced Alice, then asked if she wanted to say anything at the start.

"Mr. Diamond was a loving and devoted husband," she said. "Much that was stated and printed about him was untrue."

"People find it difficult to understand why a woman would stay married to a gangster," said the tuxedo man.

"Mr. Diamond was no gangster. He wouldn't have known how to be a gangster."

"It's been said he was a sadistic killer."

"He was a man in love with all of nature, and he celebrated life. I never saw him kill even a fly."

"How, then, would you say he got the reputation for being a gangster and a killer?"

"He did some very foolish things when he was young, but he regretted them later in life."

So it went. The sixteen customers paid ten cents each to enter, and after the show Alice also sold four photos of herself and Jack, the one with "my hero" written on the clipping found in her apartment a year later when they put a bullet in her temple. The photos also sold for a dime, which brought the gross for the first performance to two dollars.

"Not much of a crowd," she said to me when she came off the stage. Her eyes were heavy and she couldn't manage a smile.

"You'll do better when the hot days come along."

"The hot days are all over with, Marcus."

"Hey, that's kind of maudlin."

"No, just honest. Nothing's like it used to be. Nothing."

"You look as good as ever. You're not going under, I can see that."

"No, I don't go under. But I'm all hollow inside. If I went in for a swim I'd float away like an old bottle."

"Come on, I'll buy you a drink."

She knew a speakeasy a few blocks off the boardwalk, upstairs over a hot dog stand, and we settled into a corner and talked over her travels, and her fulfilling of her own fragment of Lew Edwards' dream: John the Priest on the boards of America. He was there. The presence within Alice.

"Are you staying alive on this spiel?" I asked her.

"You mean money? No, not anymore. But I've got a little coming in from a dock union John did some favors for. One of his little legacies to me was how and why he did the favors, and who paid off. And when I told them what I had, they kept up the payments."

"Amazing."

"What?"

"That he's still taking care of you."

"But she's living off him, too. That's what galls me."

"I know. I read the papers. Did you ever catch her act?"

"Are you serious? I wouldn't go within three miles of her footprints."

"She stopped by to see me when she played a club in Troy. She spoke well of you, I must say. 'The old war-horse,' she said to me, 'they can't beat her.'"

Alice laughed, tossed her hair, which was back to its natural color—a deep chestnut—but still a false color, for after Jack died, her roots went white in two days. But it looked right, now. Authentic Alice. She tossed that authentic hair in triumph, then tossed off a shot of straight gin.

"She meant *she* couldn't beat me."

"Maybe that's what she meant. I only agreed with her."

"She never knew John, not till near the end. When she moved into Acra she thought she had him. Then, when I walked out of the Kenmore she thought she had him again. But she didn't know him.''

"I thought *she* left the Kenmore."

"She did. The police came looking and John put her in a rooming house in Watervliet, then one in Troy. He moved her around, but he kept bringing her back to the Rain-Bo room and I refused to take it. I told John that the day I left. I wasn't gone three days when he called me to come back up and set up a house or an apartment. But I didn't want Albany anymore, so he came to New York when he wanted to see me. It must've killed her.''

I remember Jack telling a story twice in my presence about how he met Alice. "I pulled up to a red light at Fifty-ninth Street and she jumped in and I couldn't get her out.''

In its way it was a true story. Jack couldn't kick her out of his life; Alice couldn't leave. Her wish was to be buried on top of him, but she didn't get that wish either. She had to settle for a spot alongside; and buried, like Jack, without benefit of the religion she loved so well. Her murderers took her future away from her, and that, too, was related to Jack. She was about to open a tearoom on Jones' Walk at Coney, which would have been a speakeasy within hours, and was also lending her name to a sheet to be called *Diamond Widow's Racing Form*. She'd gotten the reputation of being a crack shot from practicing at the Coney shooting galleries and practicing in her backyard with a pistol too, so went the story. And in certain Coney and Brooklyn bars, when she was escorted by gangsters who found her company improved their social status, she would announce with alcoholic belligerence that she could whip any man in the house in a fight. They also said she was threatening to reveal who killed Jack, but I never believed that. I don't think she knew any more than the rest of us. We all had our theories.

I remember her sitting at that Coney table, head back, laughing that triumphant laugh of power. I never saw her again. I talked to her by phone some months later when she was trying to save Acra from foreclosure and she was even talking of getting a few boys together again to hustle some drink among the summer tourists. But she just couldn't put that much money together (sixty-five hundred dollars was due) and she lost the house. I did what I could, which was to delay the finale. She wrote me a thanks-for-everything note, which was our last communication. Here's the last paragraph of that letter:

> Jack once told me when he was tipsy that "If you can't make 'em laugh, don't make 'em cry." I don't know what in hell he meant by that, do you? It sounds like a sappy line he heard from some sentimental old vaudevillian. But he said it to me and he did mean something by it, and I've been trying to figure it out ever since. The only thing I can come up with is that maybe he thought of himself as some kind of entertainer and, in a way, that's pretty true. He sure gave me a good time. And other people I won't name. God I miss him.

She signed it "love and a smooch, just one." She was dead a month later, sixty-four dollars behind in her thirty-two-dollar-a-month rent for the Brooklyn apartment. Her legacy was that trunkful of photographs and clippings, the two Brussels griffons she always thought Jack bought in Europe, and a dinner ring, a wedding ring, and a brooch, all set with diamonds.

She was a diamond, of course.

They never found her killers either.

I saw Marion for the last time in 1936 at the old Howard Theater in Boston, another backstage encounter. But then again why not? Maybe Jack hit the real truth with that line of his. The lives of Kiki and Alice were both theatrical productions; both were superb in their roles as temptress and loyal wife, and as leading ladies of underworld drama. Marion was headlining a burlesque extravaganza called *The Pepper Pot Revue* when I read the item in the *Globe* about her being robbed, and I went downtown and saw her, just before her seven o'clock show.

She was sitting in one of the Howard's large dressing rooms, listening to Bing Crosby on the radio crooning a

slow-tempo version of "Nice Work If You Can Get It."
She wore a fading orchid robe of silk over her costume,
wore it loosely, permitting me a glimpse of the flesh-colored
patches which made scant effort to cover her attractions.
She worked on her toes with two ostrich-feather fans, one
of which would fall away by number's end, revealing
unclothed expanses of the whitest of white American
beauty flesh. She billed herself out front as "Jack (Legs)
Diamond's Lovely Light o'Love," a phrase first applied to
her after the Monticello shooting by a romantic caption
writer. Her semipro toe dance, four a day, five on
Saturday, was an improvement over her tippy-tap-toe
routine, for the flesh was where her talent lay.

"You're still making the headlines," I told her when the
stage doorman showed me where she was.

Her robe flowed open, and she gave me a superb hug, my
first full-length, unencumbered encounter with all that
sensual resilience, and after the preliminaries were done
with, she reached in a drawer, put a finger through an
aperture in a pair of yellow silk panties with a border of
small white flowers and dangled them in front of me.

"That's the item?"

"That's them. Isn't it ridiculous?"

"The publicity wasn't bad, good for the show."

"But it's so . . . so cheap and awful." She broke down,
mopped her eyes with the panties that an MIT student had
stolen from her as a fraternity initiation prank. He left an
ignominious fifty-cent piece in their place, saying, when
they nabbed him at the stage door with the hot garment in
his pants pocket, "I would've left more, only I didn't have
change."

I was baffled by her tears, which were flowing not from
the cheapness of the deed, for she was beyond that, inured.
I then considered that maybe the fifty cents was not
enough. But would five or fifty dollars have been enough
for the girl who once wore a five-hundred-dollar negotiable
hymen inside another such garment? No, she was crying
because I was witness to both past and present in this actual
moment, and she hadn't been prepared to go over it all

again on such short notice. She knew I remembered
Ziegfeld and all her promise of greater Broadway glory,
plus a Hollywood future. But Ziegfeld turned her down
after Jack died, and Will Hays wouldn't let her get a
foothold in Hollywood: No molls need apply. And finally,
as we talked, she brought it out, tears gone, panties there to
haunt both of us (I remembered the vision at the miniature
golf course, in her Monticello room, and I thought, Pursue
it now; nothing bars the way now; no fear, no betrayal
intervening between you and that bound-to-be-lovely by-
way), and she said: "It's so shitty, Marcus. It seems once
fate puts the finger on you, you're through."

"You're still in the paper, kiddo; you're in big letters out
front, and you look like seven or eight million dollars.
Eight. I know a few young ladies with less to point to."

"You were always nice, Marcus. But you know I still
miss Jack. Miss him. After all these years."

Would the maudlin time never end?

"You're keeping him alive," I said. "Look at it that way.
He's on the signs out front, too."

"He wouldn't like his name there."

"Sure he would, as long as you were tied to it."

"No, not Jack. He liked it respectable, the two-faced son
of a bitch. He left me that night to go home to bed so Alice
wouldn't come find him, so he could be there in bed ahead
of her. Imagine a man like him thinking like that?"

"Who said he did that?"

"Frankie Teller told me. Jack mumbled it in the cab
when they left my place."

She let the old memories run by in silence, then she said,
"But I was the last one to see him," and she meant, to
make love to him. "He always left Old Lady Prune to come
to me. I don't think she had a crotch." And then Kiki
laughed and laughed, as triumphantly as Alice had in the
Coney speakeasy.

I bought her a sandwich between shows, then took her
back to the theater. I kissed her good-bye on the cheek, but
she turned and gave me her mouth as I was leaving, a gift.
But she didn't linger over it.

"Thanks for coming," she said, and I didn't know whether to leave or not. Then she said, "I could've made it with you, Marcus. I think I could've. But he spoiled me, you know."

"Sometimes friends should just stay friends."

"He spoiled me for so many men. I never thought any man could do that to me."

"You'll never be spoiled for me."

"Come and see me again, Marcus. Next time you see me on a marquee someplace."

"You can bank on that," I said.

But I never did. Her name turned up in the papers when she married a couple of times, never with success. About 1941 a patient treated in Bellevue's alcoholic ward gave the name of Kiki Roberts, but the story that it was the real Kiki was denied in the press the next day. She was hurt in a theater fire in Newark somewhere around that time, and a friend of mine from Albany saw her back in Boston in a small club during the middle years of the war, still known professionally as Jack's sweetheart, not stripping any longer, just singing torch songs, like "Broken Hearted," a tune from '27, the year they killed Little Augie and shot Jack full of holes, the year he became famous for the first time for not dying. You can't kill Legs Diamond. I've heard Kiki died in Detroit, Jersey, and Boston, that she went crazy, broke her back and had a metal backbone put in, got fat, grew old beautifully, turned lesbian, and that she still turns up in Troy and Catskill and Albany bars whose owners remember Jack. I don't believe any of it. I don't know what happened to her.

That isn't the end of the story, of course. Didn't I, like everybody else who knew him, end up on a barstool telling Jack's tale again, forty-three years later, telling it my own way? And weren't Tipper and The Pack and Flossie there with me, ready, as always with the ear, ready too to dredge up yet another story of their own? The magazines never stopped retelling Jack's story either, and somebody put it out in book form once, a silly work, and somebody else made a bum movie of it. But nobody ever came anywhere near getting it right, and I mean right, not straight, for accuracy about Jack wasn't possible. His history was as crooked as the line between his brain and his heart. I stand on this: that Packy's dog story was closer to the truth about Jack and his world than any other word ever written or spoken about him.

We were all there in the dingy old Kenmore when Packy told it, old folks together, wearying of talk of any kind by now, all of us deep into the drink, anxious to move along to something else, and yet not quite able to let go. I remember I was winding up, telling what happened to The Goose, who at age sixty-eight homosexually assaulted a young boy in a prison shower and was stabbed in his good eye for his efforts. And Oxie, who did seven long ones and then dropped dead of a heart attack on a Bronx street corner after a month of freedom. And Fogarty, who was let out of jail because of his sickness and wasted away with TB in the isolation ward of the Ann Lee Home in Albany, and who called me at the end to handle his legacy, which consisted of Big Frenchy DeMange's diamond wristwatch. Jack gave it to him as a souvenir after the Big Frenchy snatch, and Fogarty kept it in a safe-deposit box and never sold it, even when he didn't have a dime.

My three old friends didn't know either that Jack never paid me for the second trial, nor had he ever paid Doc Madison a nickel for all the doc's attention to his wounds.

"He stole from us all, to the very end," I said.

"Yes, Marcus," said Flossie, the loyal crone, misty-eyed over her wine, profoundly in love with all that was and would never be again, "but he had a right to. He was magic. He had power. Power over people. Power over animals. He had a tan collie could count to fifty-two and do subtraction."

"I wrote a story about his dog," said the Tipper. "It was a black and white bull terrier named Clancy. I went and fed him when they all left Acra and forgot he was there. Smartest dog I ever saw. Jack taught him how to toe dance."

"It was a white poodle," said Packy. "He brought it with him right here where we're sitting one night in the middle of '31. There was a bunch of us and Jack decides he'll take a walk, and we all say, okay, we'll all take a walk. But Jack says he needs his sweater because the night air gets chilly, and we all say, you're right, Jack, it sure gets chilly."

"Jack could turn on the electric light sometimes, just by snapping his fingers," Flossie said.

"So Jack says to the white poodle, 'Listen here, dog, go up and get my black sweater,' and that damn dog got up and went out to the lobby and pushed the elevator button and went up to Jack's suite and barked, and Hubert Maloy let him in."

"Jack could run right up the wall and halfway across the ceiling when he got a good running start," Flossie said.

"We all waited, but the poodle didn't come back, and Jack finally says, 'Where the hell is that dog of mine?' And somebody says maybe he went to the show to see the new Rin-Tin-Tin, and Jack says, 'No, he already saw it.' Jack got so fidgety he finally goes upstairs himself and we all follow, and Jack is sayin' when he walks into his room, 'Come on, you son of a bitch, where's my goddamn sweater?' "

"Jack could outrun a rabbit," Flossie said.

"Well, let me tell you, it took the wind right out of Jack when he saw that damn dog sitting on the sofa with the sweater, sewin' on a button that was missin' off the pocket."

"Jack could tie both his shoes at once," Flossie said.

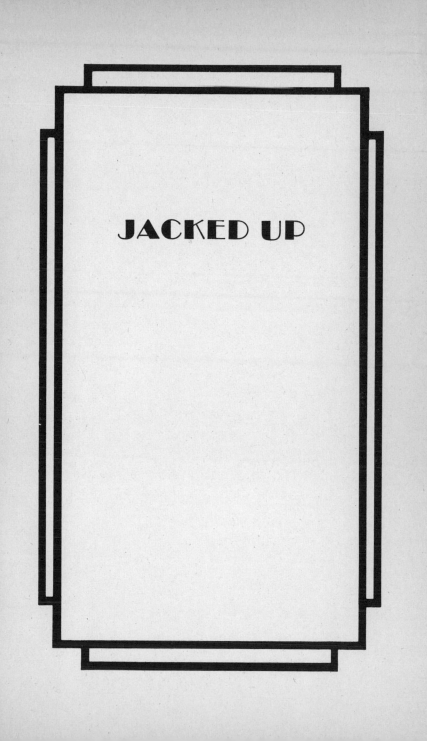

# JACKED UP

Jack (Legs) Diamond, aged thirty-four years, five months, seven days, and several hours, sat up in bed in his underwear and stared into the mirror at his new condition: incipiently dead.

"Those simple bastards," he said, "they finally did it right."

He moved without being able to move, thought out of his dead brain, smiled with an immobile mouth, his face intact but the back of his head blown away. Already aware he was moving outside time, he saw the yellow fluid coming to his eyes, trickling out his nose, his ears, down the corners of his mouth. He felt tricklings from his rectum, his penis, old friend, and knew those too were the yellow. He turned his head and saw the yellow coming out his wounds, on top of his congealing blood. He had known the yellow would come, for he had been at the edge before. But he always failed to understand the why of it. The wisdom of equality, the Book of the Dead said, but that made no sense. Death did make sense. It was a gift. The dead thanked you with stupid eyes.

"Do you think I worry because I'm dead?" Jack asked aloud.

The yellow oozed its curious answer.

The press of death was deranging. He was fully aware of the pressure, like earth sinking into water. Yet there was time left for certain visitors who were crowding into the room. Rothstein stepped out of the crowd and inspected the crown of Jack's head. He fingered that bloody skull like a father fondling the fontanel of his infant son—and who

with a better right? He pulled out two hairs from the center
of the scalp.

"What odds that I find the answer, big dad?" Jack said.

Rothstein mulled the question, turned for an estimate to
Runyon, who spoke out of a cancerously doomed larynx.

"I've said it before," said Damon. "All life is nine to five
against."

"You hear that?" A. R. asked.

"I hear it."

"I must call against."

"Then up yours," said Jack. "I'll make it my way."

"Always headstrong," said A. R.

I took Jack by the arm, guided him back from the mirror
to lie on his right side, the lying posture of a lion. I pressed
my fingers against the arteries on both sides of his throat.

"It's time, Jack," I said. "It's coming."

"I'm not sure I'll know it when it comes."

"I'll tell you this. It looks like a thought, like a cloudless
sky. It looks like nothing at all."

"Like nothing?"

"Like nothing."

"I'll recognize it," Jack said. "I know what that looks
like."

"Say a prayer," I suggested.

"I did."

"Say another."

"I knew a guy once had trouble cheating because his wife
was always praying for him."

"Try to be serious. It's your last chance."

Jack concentrated, whispered, "Dear God, turn me onto
the Great White Way." He felt the onset of clammy
coldness then, as if this body were fully immersed in water.
He remembered Rothstein's prayer and said that too, "O
Lord, God of Abraham, keep me alive and smart. The rest
I'll figure out for myself."

"Perfect," said A. R.

"Dummy," I said, "you're dead. What kind of a thing is
it, asking to stay alive?"

I eased the pressure on Jack's arteries and pressed his

nerve of eternal sleep. Then I knelt beside him, seeing the water of his life sinking into fire, waiting for his final exit from that useless body. But if Jack left his body through the ear instead of the top of the head where Rothstein had pulled out the hairs, he might come back in the next life as a fairy musician.

"Jesus," Jack said when I told him, "imagine that?"

"Easy, now," I said, "easy. Out through the top."

Then he was out, just fine, standing in front of the mirror, seeing no more blood, no more yellow.

"Am I completely dead?" he asked, and knew then his last human feeling: his body being blown to atoms, the feeling of fire sinking into air. He looked around the room, but could see no one any longer, though we were all there, watching. He felt his absent pupils dilate to receive the light, which was his own light as well as everyone else's. When the light came, it was not the brilliant whiteness Jack expected, but a yellowish, grayish light that made no one blink. The motion of the light was perceptible. It swirled around Jack's neck like a muffler, rose up past his eyes and hairline like a tornado in crescendo, spun round his entire head with what was obviously a potentially dazzling ferocity, reduced in effect now by the horrendous life-tone of Jack Diamond. It was obvious to everyone that given propitious conditions it could centripetally slurp the entire spirit of Jack into the vortex and make off with it forever; but now it moved only like a bit of fog on a sunny morning, coiled by a frolicsome breeze, then gone, with not enough force to slurp up a toupee.

As Jack's awareness of the light peaked, he was already falling backward. Though he had no arms, he waved them frantically to right himself, and as he fell, twisting and flailing against this ignominious new development, he delivered up one, final, well-modulated sentence before he disappeared into the void, into the darkness where the white was still elusive.

"Honest to God, Marcus," he said going away, "I really don't think I'm dead."